D1095185

NEW YORK 22

BOOKS BY **ILKA CHASE** NEW YORK 22

FREE ADMISSION

I LOVE MISS TILLI BEAN

IN BED WE CRY

PAST IMPERFECT

New York 22:

that district of the City

which lies between Fiftieth

and Sixtieth streets,

Fifth Avenue,

and the East River

NEW YORK 22

BY ILKA CHASE

DOUBLEDAY & COMPANY, INC., GARDEN CITY, N.Y., 1951

NEW YORK 22

1

The woman on the telephone spoke with an urgency not shared by the colored maid at the other end of the wire. "You say Mr. Asher went to Washington?"

"Yes'm, about ten-thirty this morning."

"Wasn't the trip very unexpected?"

"I couldn't say. He didn't tell me if it come as a surprise or not."

"Well, do you know who he's going to see down there?"

"All he say to me, Mrs. Goodyear, is it's somebody in a state about sumpin."

"You mean somebody in the State Department?"

"That's it. Somebody in that apartment."

"I see." But the urgent lady found the news depressing. "He didn't say anything to you about whether or not he's signed a . . . No, I suppose you wouldn't know."

"All I know, ma'am, he said not to leave nothin' for his dinner cause he's gonna fly back tonight in time for some party. He ought to be in pretty soon."

The woman's expression lightened. "A party at Mr. Oppen-heimer's?"

1

"Yes'm, I think that's who."

"All right; thank you, Nelly."

"Good-by now."

Georgiana Goodyear hung up the phone and walked thoughtfully to her bedroom window where she stood gazing down on the East River, black as India ink, flowing beneath her. The water was pierced by quivering shafts of gold, the reflected lights of the Queens shore, and opposite her, suspended in air, the scarlet letters of Pepsi-Cola and Sunshine Biscuits eclipsed the stars. Georgiana noted the scene subconsciously, her thought on Reams Asher and the maid's information. If she had guessed right and he was paying a visit to the State Department, it must mean he had gone about his passport. His trip to Europe was more imminent than she had realized.

Her heart felt heavy with that special heaviness she had not known since she was a young girl when some loved young man ignored her or she learned that one whom she regarded as her property had become engaged to another. The last time she had the feeling she and Allen had had a row and he had stamped out of her tiny apartment and all was over between them. Forever. Forever had got curtailed to half an hour when he was back asking her to marry him, and they had been married now for twenty-three years and this was the first time, almost, that she had known the old pain.

In twenty-three years of matrimony there had been pain of other types located, usually, in the vicinity of the neck, but this time it had slipped down to the heart and was caused by a man much younger than herself who, in the last year, had given new purpose to her life, fresh incentive to her daily routine. Though the vagaries of the writers with whom her husband worked in his capacity of editor-in-chief at Carroway's were normally of no more than casual interest to her, tonight she waited impatiently for him to get home with news of the office doings. The deal had been hanging fire for some time, but today Carroway was supposed to have settled for the publication of Reams Asher's new book. As he had been out of town, there could have been no signing of contracts, but possibly Allen had got his O.K. in the morning before he left. If Reams had agreed to Carroways' terms it would be a triumph for Georgiana and a reinforcing strand in the web of professional and social interests holding them together.

2

On a purely personal basis the ties between them, though disturbingly potent as far as she was concerned, were, she feared, for Reams pleasant but tenuous. This Washington junket was an example. She felt rebuffed that he should have left town, even for a day, without telling her. She expected no detailed account of local activities, but Washington was a cleavage. One announced it, made preparations, telephoned to say good-by, and telephoned again to report a safe arrival home. Still, she would be seeing him shortly at the Oppenheimers', where they both had been invited to dine. That was something.

She went back to her dressing table to finish the make-up she had interrupted to call him. She picked up her mascara brush and then lowered it despondently, thinking of his possible trip to Europe and the separation it would entail. She was staring pensively into the mirror when her daughter came into the room. "Hi, Mum."

"Oh, Karen. Come in, darling. Story all done?" The girl nodded. Home from college for the week end, she had been catching up on a class assignment. Now she went over to her mother and kissed her. "Anything the matter? You seem a little low."

"Do I? There's no reason to be."

"Everything all right at *Tang*?"

"So far, yes. Although the rumors do persist that they may close out the fiction department."

Karen looked shocked. "Mother! How could they? It's the best feature the magazine has."

"Thank you, dear; you're a loyal child, but just because I edit it doesn't mean it's invulnerable. The writers we publish come high and the boss would like to save money."

She returned to her eyelashes, her daughter watching her with somewhat more rapt attention than she accorded her teachers at Vassar. When Georgiana had finished with the mascara she adjusted her horn-rimmed spectacles and gave a searching appraisal to her reflected image. She had a narrow face liberally powdered with freckles, a rather long nose blunt at the end, golden cat's eyes, and a mouth thin and mobile as a scarlet thread. She had reached the age where, if she was a little depressed by what her spectacles revealed, she still circulated enough to make profitable the salvaging of the non-devastated areas which remained. There was little of the coquette in her temperament; she considered it merely intelligent for a woman to package as attractively as she could the raw material with which she had been endowed. Glancing obliquely at her daughter, she sighed inwardly.

To herself, built on a slight scale, Karen seemed heroic. When the child was fourteen Georgiana had been appalled by her feet, moaning in despair to her husband, "My God, Allen, she was born with skis on!" but now she had to concede that though large their daughter was all of a piece. Her feet actually seemed to shrink as the rest of her caught up with them. At nineteen the girl had the awkward, feline grace of a lion cub. She was colored rather like a lion cub, too, with tawny skin and hair and green-brown eyes. Her lips were soft and full and her big body was beautifully proportioned. With maturity she would develop into a breath-takingly lovely female, but it was a future foreseen better by men than by the youthful wolves of her acquaintance. To most of them she seemed something fashioned by Gutzon Borglum, and Georgiana and Allen worried over their daughter's matrimonial chances, sensing that for all their modernity males still cottoned to Dresden. Karen's nature did nothing to help matters either.

She had a good mind and a generous heart, and what they were likely to get her in this world, other than trouble, her mother sometimes wondered. A warm, honest creature, she was ready to tussle for what she believed right, but her candor usually frightened away such tentative beaux as she attracted. How to nurture this courage and honesty and at the same time instill a little guile was a maternal problem.

That episode of a couple of summers ago was typical. Georgiana had come upon her daughter in a swimming pool discussing, of all topics, God, with two slim-hipped baffled mermen, aged seventeen and eighteen. She yanked her evangelist from the pool, practically by the straightened hairs of her capless head, and treated her to a bit of heart-to-heart girls' talk on "How To Attract Men."

"It's all right to *like* God, Karen," she concluded, "but don't *talk* about Him." Karen, aflame with adolescent fervor, was shocked, and felt like a christian martyr in the arena declaiming her faith to the lion's last gobble, but she had sadly to admit that her mother's

4

advice seemed justified when neither of the hoped-for converts showed up again throughout the rest of the summer.

What they both regarded as her lack of femininity worried mother and daughter alike, but while Georgiana's worry was the direct result of Karen's appearance and behavior, Karen's disquiet stemmed from her mother's concern rather than from her own. Not that she was complacent. On the contrary, she was of a passionate nature but unassuming. Falling in love with most of the young men she met she was accustomed to their impersonal reactions. Shy, friendly as a puppy, she accepted a little sadly those rebuffs which she did not understand. Maybe Mother was right when she said that the best part of her life would come later on. She hoped so. It was nice to have something to look forward to. If only their money things didn't go wrong. If her mother should lose her job on *Tang* it might make a difference.

"Mum?"

"Yes, dear?"

"If there *was* any change, I mean if *Tang should* cut out the fiction —they probably won't at all, but just in case—could we afford to go on living as we do, in this apartment and me going to college and all on just what Daddy makes?"

The same query had been sniping at Georgiana's consciousness since she first heard the rumor casually dropped at a cocktail party, but Karen's question was an unpleasant pinning down. Besides, in the last couple of weeks the office grapevine had been twanging less vigorously its tune of disintegration and economy. "I wouldn't worry if I were you," she said, "it's probably no more than rumor, and if not, well, it isn't inconceivable that I might get another job. I've done it before, after all. Besides, your father makes a good salary—for the book business even impressive—and what we got from Grandma's estate is a help. The trouble is that with taxes and death duties and the cost of living these days it's impossible to save anything."

It was true that financially they were sailing close to the wind. Aside from Allen's life insurance and their small place on Long Island they had few resources; yet, pressing as their financial concerns might be, were Georgiana to lose her job she would miss it for another equally cogent reason. It made her feel important. It was a

5

relief to be too busy for daytime engagements with women which were merely social. A purely social life she found asphyxiating; she liked having an office to go to and a secretary, whom she didn't have to pay, to work for her. She enjoyed lunching with authors and discussing ideas and stories. She was pleased to be frequently in correspondence with Hollywood studios about the sale of material, and she liked having her opinion asked on young writers. Not to be a personality in her own right, merely the wife of a successful man and the mother of a daughter away at college depressed her, for although hers was perhaps not a sustained career—over the years her jobs had been varied, sporadic, and sometimes non-existent—Georgiana might still be counted a professional woman. Her present position at *Tang* she had held for more than five years, and the possibility of losing it and the man she cared about at the same time caused her deep concern.

Without him nothing of her external life would be gone perhaps; Allen, the apartment, Karen home for week ends, all these would continue, yet her days would be empty. Her meetings with Reams— not secret exactly, Allen knew they saw a good deal of each other and that in the writing she had followed his book closely, but meetings still intimate and anticipated—would cease and with them the easy, stimulating companionship, or those moments when Reams looked at her somberly, obviously troubled by her nearness and an acquiesence of mood which he had not taken advantage of but which more and more of late she felt to have been deliciously threatened.

Without him everything would be so drab. Why, *why* was he fired with the dreary, unnecessary ambition to get to Europe again? He had been in the war since the beginning and had been wounded in August of '44 during the bitter fighting around St. Malo. Surely home should have been his normal desire, but Europe still fascinated him. He wanted to see it now that the shooting had stopped, he said. He had ideas for a group of short stories he wanted to write. He'd travel around a lot but his headquarters would be Paris. Paris! Georgiana, coifing her expensive auburn hair, stopped short, her brush poised in mid-air, as an idea struck her. If she could get a job in Paris! *Tang* had no office in France, but there were other magazines. In the event that their own fiction department did close down, she would be free to try for work abroad. To Allen she had been planning to minimize the possibility of a change in policy, since it did seem to be fading, but perhaps it would be wiser to let him think it was going through, that way if she was able to provoke an offer from any other source he would not be too opposed to her accepting it. The idea was worth considering, anyway. Where on earth *was* he?

"Your father!" she said to Karen. "Why on a night he knows we're dining out and he has to dress it takes him forever to get home I don't know." The telephone pealed. "Get it, will you? They never pick it up in the pantry. If it's Dad, tell him . . ." But Karen was already at the phone.

"Hello? Oh, hello, Aunt Lola. . . . No, I'm fine, just home from college for the week end. How are the twins and Uncle Peter? . . . Good. . . . Wait a minute, I'll ask her." And, to her mother, "Aunt Lola wants to know what you're wearing to the Oppenheimers' party and do you think her black lace is all right?"

"Perfectly all right. Tell her my new bronze satin. I don't think she's seen it, and tell her that that brother of hers isn't home and we're going to be late and please to make our excuses to the Oppenheimers."

Karen repeated the message. "I guess Pa's in the doghouse, Aunt Lola," she added as she hung up.

"I guess he is," said Georgiana. "Why the devil he can't get here . . ." and her mouth tightened in the impatient way Karen knew so well.

"How would it be if I mixed a cocktail?" she said brightly. "If you are late you'll have to hurry through what they give you at the Oppenheimers' and I know how you hate that."

Georgiana, immersed in the folds of the bronze satin she was trying to slip over her head without mussing her hair, mumbled something unintelligible, which, on emerging from Valentina's triumph, flushed but intact, turned out to be an enthusiastic endorsement of her daughter's suggestion. "Cocktails are a wonderful idea. Martinis. My proportions, not Allen's."

Karen hurried on her mission of mercy and returned with two pale, brimming glasses to find her mother with her toilet completed and her own dinner waiting on a tray. Georgiana, an expert cook herself, was lifting the covers to peer at the contents of the dishes.

7

"I must say, darling, Ingrid hasn't cheated you, but it does seem kind of mean, your having to dine alone on one of your few evenings home. If only we hadn't had this date forever . . ."

"Oh, please, Mum, don't think about it. I don't mind a bit, really I don't." The girl spoke convincingly, but watching her sit down to her solitary meal Georgiana was touched.

"Darling, what a fool I am!" she exclaimed suddenly. "I know what I'll do! I'll phone Horace Oppenheimer and ask if you can't come in after dinner. He's having quite a few people later on and it would be fun for you to meet them."

"Oh no, Mother, please. I'd rather not." Karen paled at the idea. She didn't want to be dragged into a party of her mother's friends as an afterthought and have them kind to her and thinking to themselves, Poor child, home from college for the week end and can't get herself a date.

"Nonsense," her mother said. "You weren't asked because they had no idea you'd be home. You'll enjoy yourself. Nora Brown's going to be there—she's just back from Hollywood and they're running her new picture—and Reams Asher, and oh, I don't know, lots of others."

"Reams Asher? You mean the man who wrote *Another Country?*"

"The same."

Karen began to reconsider. A movie star and a famous author were tempting bait. In her short-story course *Another Country* was considered a modern classic. To meet the man who wrote it *and* see a new picture before it was released would lend her a distinct cachet back at college.

"Well," she said hesitantly, "if you're sure Mr. and Mrs. Oppenheimer wouldn't mind. What shall I wear?"

"Why not your green? It came back from the cleaner's a little while ago."

"All right. What's Reams Asher like, Mum? You know him, don't you?"

Georgiana looked amused. "Quite well. I've seen a good deal of him recently while he's been finishing his new book."

"What's it called?"

"*The Shadowed Path.*"

"Good?"

"Excellent. It's got force and imagination and it's honest. I only

8

hope your father's succeeded in getting him to sign a contract."

"Is Carroway going to publish it?"

"Well, he's letting Barnstable see it, too, but if Carroway has any sense he'll nab him. It can't miss." And, in a burst of annoyance, "Where on *earth* can Allen be?"

"I hope Daddy gets it," Karen said. "Surely he will if it's that good."

Georgiana, draining her cocktail, made an inarticulate sound which her daughter did not ask her to repeat, suspecting it was no endorsement of her father's infallibility. It was unusual for him to be so late though, and she began to be uneasy. "You don't suppose anything has happened to him, do you, Mother?"

"What would happen? He's just *late!*" But her irritability softened when she glanced at her daughter's face. Although so different in size and coloring, there was a family resemblance between them, and Karen's distress reminded her of herself when she and Allen were first married and in love, and of how she used to get upset if he was delayed even a few minutes in getting home. He would have been stuck between floors in a crowded elevator, suffocating. He would be lying cold and dead in some dark alley. There were no dark alleys between the bookstore where he worked and their apartment, there were no elevators either, for that matter, the store was at street level and the apartment a walk-up, but who could tell? He might have had a business appointment or wandered off to the water front in search of local color for a story and been struck down by a bootlegger. A taxi might have skidded and the hit-and-run driver have made off in terror, leaving Allen crushed and bleeding against a post of the Third Avenue El.

Georgiana sighed. How long ago those apprehensive fancies. Now he was delayed, and she was merely annoyed. It was sad, the way things changed.

Down the hall came the click of the front door and then Allen's whistle. "Hi," he called. "Where are my women?"

"We're in here and good and mad we are too," answered his wife, but her voice was more gentle than either of them had anticipated in view of his lateness.

He appeared in the bedroom doorway, still wearing his hat and overcoat and carrying a brief case and the evening paper. Allen

9

looked what he was—a hard-working, middle-aged New Yorker who was trying to earn enough to pay his taxes and meet the strain of living a bit beyond his means. His face was sensitive and his eyes kind, but there was a set expression around his mouth betraying a certain native stubbornness. His wife referred to this quality as "Allen's pigheadedness." He himself, when he thought about it at all, considered with modest pride that it indicated character.

His face lighted up when he saw Karen. "Hello, kitten; it's good to have you home." He kissed his tall daughter and crossed to his wife. "Hello, darling." Georgiana suffered his connubial peck upon her cheek.

"I suppose you know we're due at the Oppenheimers' at eight and it's a mere ten to now and you have to dress."

"I know," he said. "I'm sorry I'm late, but we had a long sales conference this afternoon, lasted till almost six-thirty, and after that I had to talk to Carroway about the Asher book."

"Allen, you did it! That's wonderful!" Georgiana's eyes were shining. "You got him to sign!"

Allen looked at her. He had deliberately walked home from the office instead of taking a cab so as to postpone the moment of her inevitable reaction. "No," he said at last, "I didn't. We aren't going to do it."

She stared at him incredulously. "You're not going to—— You mean to stand there and tell me you've let him get away from you? The best new writer to appear since before the war! Are you crazy? Why, when that book is published Reams Asher will be the most important author in the country, and you could have had him, he'd have made the firm a fortune. Why haven't you got him? My God, what happened?"

Allen headed for his own room, which adjoined his wife's, and started to undress. She followed him as he shed his overcoat and stripped off his jacket and vest. "Allen, listen to me. Both you and Chips Carroway are making the biggest mistake of your lives by not——"

He turned to her, unbuttoning his shirt. "Look, G, I know what you think of the book and I agree with you. It's first-rate. Believe me I did my damnedest, I used every argument I could think of, but you know Chips. So far and no further. He says Barnstables are

10

putting themselves out on a limb, for a first novel, he refuses to match their terms, and that's that. The rest of the board went along with him. Oh, cheer up, honey," he added, noting the stricken look on his wife's face, "I know it's a disappointment. Hell, it is to me, too, but one publishing house can't do them all. We've missed out on other good things before and survived. We'll just have to take this in our stride."

Georgiana spoke with a bitterness that startled him. "God, when I think of how I worked and cajoled and badgered him into letting you have the manuscript! It wasn't Reams, you know, who was so keen on you as publishers. He preferred Barnstable all along, but I finally convinced him, and he would have signed with you if you hadn't been so rotten stingy. It might have meant a whole new setup for all of us."

Allen glanced at her curiously. "How, new setup?"

"Well—I—I—— The book is sure to be a best seller. You could have demanded a bonus. The prestige alone would have been enormous." She fumed after him as he changed his clothes. "It's going to be a charming evening! Reams is invited to the Oppenheimers', you know. It'll be delightful when you tell him Chips Carroway thinks so little of the book he's worked two years on he's turned it down."

Allen had reached his bathroom, though it proved no sanctuary, and was mowing his face with an electric razor. Above its angry buzzing he answered her as best he could. "If I may say so, it's Asher who's turned *us* down. I told him the terms, and he wouldn't accept them. Why should he when he can get better elsewhere?"

"You spoke to him today?"

"Sure I did. He was in Washington, but he'd given me a number and I got him at lunchtime."

Georgiana began to laugh. "You knew! That's funny."

"What's funny about it?"

Karen, who had trailed after her parents, an unhappy witness to her mother's outburst, giggled nervously.

"Stop it!" Georgiana snapped; "it's not funny."

"I'm a little confused," said her father, "but I wouldn't be concerned unduly if I were you, G. If we're right, and the book does have a big sale, Chips is much more likely to listen to me the next time something good comes along."

11

"Nothing that good is going to come in a hurry. Anyhow, what if it does?"

Allen, peering at himself in the mirror, ran his hand over his cheeks and under his chin. Satisfied with the results, he clicked off the razor. He turned and looked at his wife. "My hope," he said, "is that you will continue to care what happens at the office even though we aren't publishing Reams Asher."

"What does that crack mean?"

"Nothing that isn't apparent on the face of it." He brushed past her and picked up the newspaper from the day bed where he had tossed it. He and Georgiana slept in twin beds in her room, but the day bed was for guests or for those occasions when Allen was banished because of snoring or illness or when Georgiana wanted to sleep late in the morning.

"Excuse me," he said. "I won't be long, but I have to take care of a matter I've been too busy to attend to all day," and he went back into the bathroom and closed the door.

Georgiana was angry and disappointed, furthermore, she was on her guard. When Allen had said that, about hoping she would continue to care what happened, he had spoken pleasantly enough, but he had eyed her a little strangely, she thought. Well, there was nothing for him to find out, her relationship with Asher was innocent if not wholly platonic. She wasn't guilty of anything, and if she should be Allen would never know it. She had no reason to hurt him and no intention of breaking up her home. She was trembling only because she must have been counting more than she realized on Reams being published by Carroways and on the friendly, permanent relation between them which it would have generated. The disappointment was acute but there was not necessarily any irrevocable break. All she had to do was to keep her head and calm any suspicions she might have aroused in Allen. Quite possibly Reams had no intention of going to Europe even. She turned to Karen. "Your father looks tired and we're in for a long evening. Be a good girl, and mix him a martini, he needs it."

"Do you want another?" Karen asked. She spoke coldly because she was unhappy. She was always unhappy when her father and mother rowed because mostly it was her mother's fault, and though she loved her father more, toward her mother she felt protective, she

12

wanted her to acquit herself with credit. Karen saw her as vital and gay and accomplished but also undisciplined and, perhaps because she herself was so much bigger, Georgiana seemed to her vulnerable. Daddy's an angel, the girl thought, but someday Mother will go so far that she can't come back; she'll undo everything they've built up. She has such a good sense of humor about everything but herself. Reams Asher! Who was he to cause such ructions? Writers were a dime a dozen in that household, why should her parents make such a fuss over one more? Wishing to lighten the gloom a little, she repeated her question more gently: did her mother want another cocktail? Georgiana shook her head. "No, I'll wait and have a dividend at the Oppenheimers'."

She knew that the frequent quarrels she witnessed between her parents made Karen unhappy but though it was, she supposed, to be expected, even amusing if you looked at it the right way, it was exasperating, too, the manner in which children never quite accepted their parents as human beings capable of emotions and experiences far from parental. Georgiana guessed that if Karen ever suspected her feelings toward Reams she'd be profoundly shocked or at least refuse to believe it. At nineteen, forty-seven doubtless seemed the brink of the grave and sex an interest long since moribund. Youth was subject to some rude shocks, she thought drily. Right now, of course, Karen was on her father's side. She thinks I pick on him, Georgiana mused. Women always do. It's that damn tired, gentle look of his. She would thank women to mind their own business. No woman knew a man the way his wife did.

Despite her annoyance with her child, however, her maternal instinct remained strong enough for her to go through with her plan for Karen's evening. She went to the phone and called Horace Oppenheimer. She apologized for their prospective tardiness and asked if there would be any objection to Karen's coming in later.

"But of course not," said Horace; "you shouldn't even bother to ask. I'm sorry we can't have her for dinner, but we're full up."

"You're a dear to think of it, Horace, but she couldn't come anyway. She's dining with a beau and may bring him along if that's all right."

"Certainly," said the obliging host. "Tell her we plan to run the picture at ten."

13

Georgiana hung up, pleased with her social fib. It protected Karen, made her seem popular. In the young world, as elsewhere, she reflected, nothing succeeds like success. Why, oh, *why* hadn't Allen been able to swing the deal? Aside from her attachment to Reams, objectively the book was good; to have been responsible for publishing it would have been a feather in Allen's cap, and she wanted to see him successful. They needed success. Compared to other people in their income bracket they lived extravagantly, she supposed, and Allen had always been grateful to her for shouldering a share of the responsibility. He would be concerned were she out of a job. Through the doorway she watched him adjusting his black tie. "By the way," she said, "the news isn't too good around the office." His fingers paused a moment, and he looked at her in the mirror.

"You mean they've said something about folding?"

"Nothing definite, but the rumors have started up again."

"Well, dear, I wouldn't worry too much. In the publishing business rumors fly thick and fast, you know that. I haven't heard a peep over at the shop and usually we get the dope on a thing like that. Agents spread the news, or writers, or happy rival editors, you know how it is."

Allen felt sorry for Georgiana, but she was right in thinking his concern more than connubial sympathy. He was proud of her achievement but he also was aware of the difference it could make to their mode of living if she lost her job.

She stood leaning against the doorjamb. In her bronze dress with her coppery hair and golden eyes she was distinctly decorative and, looking at her, Allen felt something a little more urgent than a seasoned husband's reaction to the sight of his wife. He didn't love Georgiana as he had loved her when they were first married, frequently he didn't even like her; young love, he supposed, never lasted for anybody, but if she had disillusioned him . . . Well, doubtless he had not turned out to be all that she had bargained for either, but she was a haunting woman and she was his wife. He'd give a good deal to know what went on behind those golden eyes and whether or not this interest she seemed to have developed in Reams Asher was anything to be taken seriously.

"I was thinking," she said. "There's no point in sitting around waiting for disaster to strike, what would you say to my sounding

14

out the Dauzats? There might very well be something I could do on *Distaff*, and what's the point of knowing editors if they can't give you a job in time of need? Lord knows, people are always coming in to see *me*, asking for positions. Turn about's fair play."

Allen laughed. "It might be a good idea but I wouldn't hop out of the frying pan until the fire's lighted. I doubt that a magazine like *Distaff* can pay a *Tang* salary, and it would be foolish to throw over what you've got on the strength of mere rumor. Besides, they've probably got a list of applicants as long as your arm. Although," he added hastily, realizing from her expression he had been wanting in tact, "they obviously haven't got any like you. If the Dauzats thought you were serious they might be very interested in having you on the staff."

Georgiana sent up a trial balloon. "There might possibly be something I could do in the Paris office."

"Paris is *out*. I have no desire to be a career widower."

"Well, take it easy," she said lightly. "I was only saying."

Karen returned with her father's cocktail. "Here, Daddy. Mother and I thought you needed this." He took it gratefully. "Thanks, I do. By the way, G, maybe you'd better call the Oppenheimers and say we're late and it's my fault."

Georgiana gave him a brief, mechanical smile. "It's done. It already occurred to me." Good old Allen, a great one for thinking up jobs for others.

"It's all right about you, too, baby," she said to Karen. "The Oppenheimers will be delighted to have you. The picture's to start at ten, so be on time. Come on, Allen, for God's sake, let's go."

Allen drained his cocktail and followed her. "See you later, kitten," he said to Karen.

2

The top-floor drawing room of the Oppenheimers' triplex apartment on Sutton Place was beginning to fill with the guests who had been invited after dinner to see Nora Brown's picture. The dinner party itself was disintegrating and spread and marbled throughout the room as the members blended with the new arrivals.

Social and professional New York were heavily represented and Dorothy Oppenheimer watched the guests with quiet interest. She enjoyed her husband's parties, but after twenty-five years of marriage she still thought of them as his and so did everybody else.

Horace Oppenheimer was one of those men who is the actual as well as the titular head of his house. He not only paid the bills, he organized their social life, supervised the meals, planned trips, and hired and fired the servants. He was devoted to his wife and consulted her wishes, but in their household the initiative was his and Dorothy was content to have it so.

Some men get their satisfaction in life from tackling outsized fish or large wild beasts. Horace left the animal kingdom pretty much alone, but his inner joy derived from the domination of enormous and complex enterprises.

The combination public-relations office, bank, theatrical agency, and law firm which he had created, and the establishments which he owned in Westchester, the Adirondacks, South Carolina, and New York, caused his friends to shake their heads, predicting an inevitable crack-up induced by such responsibilities, but at fifty-three Horace was relaxed, urbane, and comfortably pear-shaped. Very happy, and very, very rich.

This evening he had been moving about his beautiful drawing room greeting his guests, but now, seeing the party under way and rolling of its own momentum, he took his friend Peter Quick by the arm to lead him toward that bright star, Miss Nora Brown. Nora was an Oppenheimer client, and Horace regarded her as a combination race horse, gold mine, and crown of thorns. On occasions she also seemed to him a little child. One of the more backward pupils in an exclusive mental home although, as he was explaining to Peter, "She is very intelligent about money, sometimes indeed I am surprised that an artist of her caliber should have such a grasp of life's practicalities. Ah, my dear." This last was addressed to his client who floated toward them.

Nora was a lovely creature, slim and rounded, with skin the color of honey and a great deal of it on display. Unathletic, her energy found outlet in continuous cascading conversation. She adored it.

16

She talked as the brook runneth, and whatever she did and thought was reflected in the limpid waters of her conversation, a great deal of which dealt with her recent conversion to Catholicism. This had taken place because, as she said, what was this world all about if not the stimulation of man's intellect and the life of the spirit?

The life of the spirit meant much to Nora. Because of it she didn't dye her hair, which was a soft, shining chestnut with golden lights, naturally wavy, and she took a deep interest in her fellow man. She was less versed in her fellow woman although, at that, she didn't ignore her as did some members of her sex. Women, after all, had ears and could be talked to—a not inconsiderable recommendation when no males were available. Of course conversation with men, especially those interested in religion and therefore in love, for what was religion if it wasn't love, was more rewarding. If they didn't see eye to eye with one in the beginning, after a few hours of proselytizing they could usually be brought to agreement and how happy conversion made everybody. As Nora had once explained to Horace, they were dining at the Colony at the time, "You'll feel so happy, so released, darling. Religion gives you everything." Horace, glancing at her diamond-and-emerald necklace and platinum mink wrap, had to admit she had received a great deal, but he guessed she was just naturally God's child since fame, money, and excellent health had been hers for years, even before her formal entry into the Church.

"You've no idea how it enriches one's life, darling. It broadens one's scope, if you follow me." He guessed that was right, too, for when he had met her that morning at La Guardia as she stepped from the California plane he had observed that her intellectual life was as diverse as ever, merely supplemented. Along with her usual copies of *Life, Vogue,* and *Photoplay,* she carried one of *Jesus.*

Now, as she stood beside him in the drawing room, he darted in during a momentary lull in her conversation. "Nora, Mr. Quick is from the Columbia Broadcasting Company, and he's one of your great admirers, which is very nice for us and for *The Innocent.* He has an idea for publicizing the picture on radio which I think you will approve," and Horace moved away to greet two arriving guests, leaving the unfortunate Mr. Quick to brace himself against the cascade of Nora's monologue.

In a group at the other end of the room conversation was more co-operative. Georgiana stood chatting with Lola Quick, her sister-in-law, Reams Asher, and Claude and Germaine Dauzat. The Dauzats were French and published their weekly fashion magazine, *Distaff,* as a joint venture, Germaine doing the editing while Claude handled the business end. A turn in the conversation gave Georgiana a natural opening. "But Germaine dear, I should think the pressure of gathering weekly material *would* be great. Have you ever thought of enlarging your Paris staff?"

Germaine gave a little laugh. She was a vivid woman with a thin arching nose, magnificent dark eyes, and dark hair drawn on top of her head and worn in a coronet braid. She had a rounded bosom and hips and did not look as though she had stepped from the pages of her magazine, but she was one of the shrewdest reporters and prognosticators of fashion in the business. Because of her roundness and her rolling caressing *r*'s, on first meeting she evoked, inevitably, thoughts of pigeons, but there was nothing pigeonlike in her temperament nor in those flashing brilliant eyes focused now on Georgiana. "My little one, you speak of an idea Claude and I often discuss, but you know it is expensive and then, too, where to find the right person?"

"What about me?" Half seriously, half laughingly, Georgiana asked the question of Germaine but her eyes were on Reams. He gave her a quick, interested look.

Germaine spoke thoughtfully. "You in Europe?"

"Don't joke about these things," Claude said. "Perhaps one day we would ask you with our hopes all up but you would not leave *Tang* and our hopes would dash."

Georgiana smiled. "Try me. It's not such a joke as you think."

"Good! We'll bear that in mind, eh, Germaine?" Claude's ready gallantry and his inclination, unless thwarted, passively to allow pretty women to install themselves on the magazine were intensely annoying to his wife so, though fond of Georgiana and appreciative of the job she did on *Tang,* her acquiescence was restrained.

"I'm afraid, Claude, that our friend is too exalted for us. She is an editor of fiction, her imagination is accustomed to soaring. Fashion reporting is a question of fact. She would find us very dull." The discussion seemed closed, but knowing the Dauzats and conscious of the way Germaine had studied her, Georgiana felt she had planted a seed which might sprout in time.

Down the long room chairs and sofas were beginning to fill as people seated themselves for the picture. The Dauzats, with Lola, drifted away, and Reams and Georgiana found themselves momentarily isolated. She was glad. Like themselves, Reams had been invited to dine but he had arrived late, and they had not been seated near each other at the table. This was their first opportunity to talk. He turned to her eagerly. "*Is* there a chance of your coming to Europe?"

"I wouldn't say I'd received a firm offer, would you?"

"They thought you were joking. I think so, too, but it would be grand if you weren't."

"It's encouraging to know the idea pleases you," she said lightly.

"You bet it does." He grinned, and the crow's-feet deepened around his eyes. It seemed to Georgiana there was something wonderfully sweet and funny in the way he smiled. He was above average height but his heavy shoulders and muscularity made him appear stocky. He had rough, close-cropped sandy hair and blue eyes fringed with thick, short, almost white lashes. He appeared older than his thirty-four years, but it was the kind of face which in later life would change imperceptibly with advancing age. His hair might thin, his body thicken, a shifting of values, little else.

"Were you successful in Washington?" she asked.

He looked surprised, he didn't remember telling her he was going. "How did you—— Oh, of course, Allen must have told you."

"Uh—yes." No need to inform him she had been on his trail via his colored maid.

"Did you get a passport?"

"Yes."

"And you're sailing?" What am I going to do, she thought, what am I going to do if he leaves?

"Not right off the bat. As a matter of fact they didn't give me the passport but they agreed to issue it."

The constriction around her heart relaxed a little.

"You passed the loyalty test!"

"Not that fast. They went through my dossier with a fine-tooth comb but after they checked my service record and discharge papers

19

and the hospital data they seemed grudgingly convinced I wasn't going to hand over any atom secrets to the Nazis."

"I suppose they thought your Purple Heart and Silver Star with Oak Cluster were something you'd swiped off Goering's chest."

He laughed. "You can't blame them too much. The war's over only a year and junketing writers are suspicious characters."

"I'm sorry about the Carroway deal, Reams."

"So am I. It would have been nice if things had worked out differently. It would have been cozy."

"Allen doesn't blame you, you know. Nor do I. It's just that I wanted you for our side, but if Carroway is silly enough not to give you what you're asking that's their hard luck."

He put his hand on her arm. "Don't mind," he said; "my book can be a big flop and they'll be laughing last."

"It won't be; it's wonderful."

"My fan. My very dear fan." They looked at each other for a long moment. "What about this European business?" he asked.

"You'd really like me to come?"

"I would. Very much."

"But, with all this great work schedule you're planning, when would I ever see you?"

"It's when I'm working that I like you handy."

"I see. Can I take a memo for you, sir?"

"No," he said seriously, "you make me think a character or a situation through. You're stimulating."

"I sound like a gadfly."

"That's what's good for me."

"You must try spinach some time."

"You know damn well what I mean."

"Well, if I'm as healthful as all that, why don't you stick around? A change of diet might do you irreparable harm."

He looked at her steadily. "I'm not sure that staying here is any too safe." Her thin scarlet lips parted in a smile, her eyes gleamed. There was something glistening and provocative about her. More than once he had been tempted to try his luck, but he refrained. From a small sense of scruple. He liked and respected Goodyear, and from a stronger sense of caution. An affair with an older married woman was easier got into than out of. Still, if they should meet up

20

in foreign parts and both be in the mood, it might prove a pleasant interlude.

For her part Georgiana considered, with a regret not untinged with ridicule, that Reams was being foolish. Life was not so long nor so good that one should pass up the music. What was he waiting for, she wondered, and what could Europe hold so much better than a native offering? "I do think," she observed, "that if you half tried you could get ideas for stories laid right here in New York. Why must you have European backgrounds? Look at O. Henry. Or Runyon!"

He grinned. "Look at Hemingway or Maugham."

"I shall not look at them. They do not delight my eyes; you do." There was one compensation to being older. You could say humorously to a man the things you sincerely meant. "When are you likely to be leaving, do you think?"

"I don't know; my plans haven't jelled. I'm just glad to know I can get away when I want to."

"Nothing to hold you to the homeland, eh?"

He glanced down at her seated on the arm of a chair and their eyes held. "Nothing that belongs to me."

"Perhaps you should try staking a claim."

"Another prospector got there ahead of me."

She laughed softly. "Once upon a time there was a knight and he passed by a castle where there was a treasure guarded by a dragon, but the knight didn't try to pirate it away and the villagers gossiped about such signal behavior, and some said it was because he was honest and some said it was because he was high minded and indifferent, but *some* said it was because he was scared." Her eyes teased and challenged him.

"I am not scared," he said and he was silent, not because he was weighing what he should do but because he remembered something. Reams, although he did not look the part, was an anachronism. Born into a cynical and materialistic age, he was emotionally a romanticist and a great lover in that he loved greatly rather than frequently. He was no stranger to women but he had given his heart to only one. He had fallen in love with her at the age of twenty-nine and he loved her still. They had not married because she already had an English husband and an English son. The son she adored and

21

the husband she feared and depended upon. He had categorically refused her a divorce when she first asked for one and discouraged future essays on her part by assuring her that if she attempted to leave him he would instantly stop her bank account and never permit her to see her son again. Since he was not given to blustering and had never been known in the heat of the moment—heat not being his element—to threaten more than he meant to carry out, she and Reams, perforce, renounced each other.

Reams's own lack of funds at the time combined, shortly afterward, with Pearl Harbor made the renunciation inevitable, but he still loved Linda Schofield, and any love affairs since they parted had been primarily therapeutic or in the nature of distraction; light themes and grace notes superimposed on the solid base of what was apparently an enduring and hopeless love. Such slim hope as he nurtured of ever achieving Linda had become further emaciated two years ago, when she wrote to him of the birth of her second child, a little girl. Someday, perhaps shortly, if his book were a success, he might hope to challenge the implacable Englishman on financial terms, but if Linda's husband continued to deny her her children Reams feared she would never leave him.

These things he thought of, and then he looked at Georgiana, at the pliant figure, the taunting mouth, and the eyes promise-filled, and he said, "You are very beautiful and I wish to God we were away from all these people, far away, preferably in some picturesque yet de-luxe little inn in France. Failing that, would you consider taking tea with me tomorrow afternoon in my picturesque lair at Lexington Avenue and Thirty-fourth Street?"

Georgiana had been to his apartment several times alone or at cocktail parties, but this time the invitation was significant. They both knew it. She gave him a sidelong look. "Call me in the morning, Mr. Asher. I shall have to check my engagement book."

The pregnant pause ensued. "Very well, madame." So it was to happen on home heath after all! That had not been his intention but suddenly he wanted her. He, too, wondered what he had been waiting for. She was *not*, however, to interfere with his writing. He planned to go abroad soon, and he was going. He wished, though, that it could have been a matter of sex and nothing more. Unfortunately he respected her judgment and he had a feeling that when he was away he would miss her. "What *about* coming to Paris in the spring," he said suddenly, "with or without the Dauzat job? Wouldn't it be possible?"

"You forget there's a little matter of finance; however, I have been thinking about it. We've promised Karen a trip abroad and next summer it might be feasible." The trip sprang that moment full blown from her fancy but she did not intend him to know that one invitation to tea could persuade her to a trip to Europe or that, indeed, the tea was not even necessary. Nelly's information that her employer had gone to the State Department had been sufficient to set her plans afoot.

"But couldn't you come first," Reams was saying, "without the family?"

"You object to families?"

"Not at all. I think family life is very beautiful, and you know damn well the fun we could have if you and I were in Paris alone together."

"It sounds like a song cue. But it sounds good too."

He felt elated, eager. "It would be good, G. Come sooner than spring."

"But what about my job?"

"I hope it folds."

"Wretch."

Reams gave her a happy wink and reached for her empty champagne glass, but what he was about to reply was interrupted by Lola calling to her to come and sit down, Horace was asking everybody to take their places so the picture could begin. At the same moment a shrill young woman in purple hurled herself enthusiastically upon him and bore him away in the opposite direction.

At the foot of the stairs leading up to the large drawing room Karen stood gathering her courage. She hated entering a room alone, even when she knew the people, and to brave a throng of elderly strangers in surroundings of such grandeur was an ordeal. Her escortless state made her think of the ads for a current movie: "Only six out of ten girls ever marry. Are you one of 13,000,000 surplus females?" At the moment she was every mother's daughter of them. She reached the top of the stairs and stood looking hesitantly around the crowded room. At first glance she saw neither Allen nor

Georgiana, but a kind of bulky man, only a tiny bit shorter than herself, with a nice rugged face appeared beside her. "You have the hunted look of one who hunts the hostess," Reams said. Despite his year's acquaintance with the Goodyears he had never seen Karen and didn't recognize her now from the two or three childhood pictures Georgiana kept about, but his attention had been attracted by this shy-seeming young Amazon and she was, furthermore, a port of refuge. The belle who had borne down upon him as he stood talking to Georgiana was a trial he had been avoiding all season and the only way to shake her was to engage in single-purpose conversation with another and at a distance. Stranger though she was, he made a beeline for Karen the moment she loomed into his vision.

"I've never met my hostess," she said in answer to his remark, "and I'm not sure I'll recognize Mr. Oppenheimer and I know he won't know me."

Despite her height and beauty she seemed so uncertain that Reams was amused and a little touched. "Did you crash the party?" he asked.

"Oh, my goodness, no. I was really asked to come, that is to say they were rather on a spot and couldn't very well say no, but I *am* expected."

"Then I wouldn't worry. Here, have a glass of champagne." He reached for one as the ubiquitous Oppenheimer butler passed with a freshly laden tray.

Karen looked at him gratefully. "Thank you so much."

"Sit down a minute." Reams indicated a bench along the stair railing. Out of the corner of his eye he had spotted Nemesis in purple ready to pounce and did not wish to look unattached. "I think Horace is in a huddle with the projection-machine man. The picture's supposed to be quite good, I believe."

"I'm looking forward to it," Karen assured him.

"Will you have a cigarette?"

"Oh, thanks. I don't smoke an awful lot, but I always think a cigarette goes with a drink, don't you?"

"I do."

"To tell you the truth, I think some of the girls at college smoke more than they want to because it makes them feel emancipated."

So she was even more of a kid than he had thought. Her height, somehow, made you assume she was older, but looking more closely at the childish contours of her face her youth was obvious enough. She was nice. Simple and friendly and warm and rather startlingly beautiful if you liked them big. He smiled at her. Somewhere between his lighting her cigarette and the smile Karen fell in love with him. She looked at him and sank like a plummet. Who was this wonderful man with those wonderful eyes crinkling up like that and those shoulders and the wonderful kind way he was making her feel so at ease? Two inches taller and he would be sheer perfection. As it was, he practically was. He was probably somebody famous and she'd die if she knew.

"Where do you go to college?" he asked.

Karen gazed at him dreamily. "Hmmm?"

"I said, where do you go to college?"

"Oh, oh, Vassar."

"Do you like——" He stopped. Vassar! "Karen's at Vassar," Georgiana had said. "Karen's a big child," she had said. "Sort of a lion cub girl, something of my coloring, but her nose and her temperament are Allen's." What a fool he was! Of course it was she. "By the way," he said, "don't you think we ought to introduce ourselves? My name's Reams Asher. What's yours?"

"Oh, my goodness." She looked alarmed.

"Am I that bad?"

"You're Mr. Asher?"

"And you're Karen Goodyear."

She now looked blank. "However did you know?"

Reams laughed. "I know your family. Your father less well, but your mother, I hope, is a good friend of mine. She gave me a lot of helpful criticism on a book I've just been working on."

"Oh, I know. It's magnificent." Karen spoke with the reverence of an acolyte privileged to gaze upon the *Book of Kells*.

"You've read the manuscript?"

"No, but I know from what Mother and Daddy say it must be wonderful." She did not add what they had said to each other. Such unfortunate incidents were exclusively for home consumption, yet as she spoke her brain was spinning. Her heart had told her true. He was a great man. How fantastic that she should have sensed it and fallen in love with him. It was fate, that was all. A person had to accept it. How agonizing that her father should have failed to get his masterpiece for Carroway. She had misjudged her mother; her anger had probably been justified all along. "I haven't read your new book," she said, "but I loved the one that came out during the war, the long short story."

"You read *Another Country?*"

"Oh, indeed I did. It was absolute heaven. In our short-story class it's considered an American classic."

Reams was enjoying himself. What an interesting child she was, he thought. Too youthfully enthusiastic, perhaps, but obviously a good mind. Intelligent. "How about more champagne?" he asked. "My work might look better yet."

"I'd love it. I never believe champagne affects you. That all goes on in your head."

"That's *just* where."

"You think it does give you a hangover?"

"I think druggists will be crazy about you. Miss Aspirin of 1946."

He left her to fetch the drink, and Karen, looking about the room, saw Allen coming toward her. "There you are, darling," he called. "I've been keeping an eye peeled but I missed you. Come along. Have you met Mr. Oppenheimer yet?"

"No, I've been talking to Mr. Asher; he's gone to get me some champagne. Maybe I ought to wait for him."

"Nonsense, he can find you. Come on." Allen put his arm around her and was about to lead her up to their host when her uncle appeared. She smiled at him. "Ah, the distinguished Mr. Quick!" It was indeed Mr. Quick, greeting them with more than normal avuncular pleasure and introducing her to, of all people, Nora Brown. "Hi, Allen, I want to have a word with you. Karen, you two glamour queens should meet. You know Miss Brown, of course. Miss Brown, this is my niece, Karen Goodyear."

"How do you do," said Nora. Peter Quick, making a hurried escape, received the impression that Miss Brown barely noticed that she had been transferred from one auditor to another. It wasn't flattering, perhaps, but was compensated for by the blessed relief from the conversational pressure to which he had been subjected.

Nora, as she had been explaining to Peter, did not find his idea of a free broadcast feasible. "After all, my dear, working gratis for

Columbia, an organization with all that money, isn't very practical, is it?" she observed to the bewildered but game Karen, who found herself swept along in delicious intimacy with America's best publicized actress. The flood of Nora's confidence swerved from her only when Claude Dauzat came up to them with two or three other guests, one of whom was a producer, and the conversation switched to the theater.

Under the flurry of "sweeties," "darlings," and "notices" which filled the air Karen turned groggy. Her impressions made her think of those dazzling spectacles witnessed by comic-strip characters when clouted sharply upon the skull, and she saw with a mixture of reluctance and relief that her mother was coming toward her with another woman. "Germaine, this is my daughter Karen. Madame Dauzat, dear." As Georgiana made the introduction and took in the group with whom Karen was standing, a small chill swept over her. She had brought Germaine and Nora face to face! Well, it was doubtless unnecessary to feel embarrassment; down in Dorothy Oppenheimer's bedroom, just after dinner while the women were powdering their noses, they'd been speaking to each other, if not with cordiality at least with poise. If they could bear the situation Georgiana supposed she could, but why in heaven's name did Horace have to invite the Dauzats and Nora on the same evening? Everybody, including Germaine Dauzat, knew that Nora and Claude were lovers.

The situation was no doubt sophisticated, it was also highly explosive, and Georgiana felt a kinship with those courtiers of France, long dust, who had had to balance so adroitly over the abyss uniting Diane de Poitiers and Catherine de Medici or Maria Leszczynska and the Pompadour. At the moment, thank God, Nora's gleaming blue eyes seemed safe in her head; Germaine's sharp pink tongue and long pink nails were sheathed.

She greeted Karen crisply and turned her attention to a pair of newcomers whom she knew, tactfully unaware of the proximity of her husband and Nora. Georgiana breathed a sigh of relief and Karen, spotting Reams across the room, slipped from the group and went to join him though Reams at the moment was both baffled and slightly irritated by the family Goodyear.

Seeing that Karen was taken care of, or at least pinioned by Nora,

Allen had left her to talk to other guests and had come upon Reams. Reams considered that Goodyear started out pleasantly enough, telling him again how much he regretted that his firm had lost *The Shadowed Path*, and reiterating his belief in it and then, apropos of some remark or other, Reams had said, "I'm delighted to hear Georgiana's going to be in Paris this spring and that you and Karen will be coming over, too, a little later on. We must all get together."

It was a friendly enough remark certainly, downright pleasant as a matter of fact, but Allen had looked at him oddly and reacted with about as much enthusiasm as a fish on ice. He made a few desultory remarks which did not succeed in concealing his annoyance and had then turned on his heel and walked away. What had got into him Reams couldn't imagine. Georgiana had said they'd been promising Karen a trip abroad, they must have discussed it between them, or hadn't they? Or had Georgiana . . . ? About here in his cogitating Karen came up to him. "Are you going to Europe this summer?" he asked bluntly. She shook her head. "Would that I were, but not that I know of." Reams grunted. Mrs. Goodyear was certainly cooking up a little surprise for her family, and his own reactions were a bit tangled.

He handed Karen the second glass of champagne he had contracted for and suggested that they sit together to watch the picture. He indicated the sofa near which they stood. "How about it? This looks like a good place. I say this looks all right." He spoke more loudly. What on earth was the matter with the girl? Maybe she was hard of hearing. This was the second time she seemed to be in a trance. The first was when he asked her what college she went to. Karen's thoughts whirled in a happy mist. How lovely to sit beside him, what a wonderful party it was, what a piece of news to tell Poppy Slade, her best friend.

"Uh . . . yes, thank you," she murmured, not taking her eyes from his face; "it looks fine." In her present mood she would have sat gladly upon a bed of nails.

Georgiana, threading her way to a place a little farther down the room, was about to seat herself when Horace leaned over from the row behind, touching her elbow to draw her attention to his companion, an elderly woman with a strong, humorous face and a forthright manner.

It was Mrs. Barclay Hamilton. One of the wealthiest women in New York, she was simplicity personified, both in her manner and her clothes. Her pearls might confuse one's appraisal, but eliminate the pearls and Mrs. Hamilton looked like a kind, hearty woman without twenty cents to her name. A tireless worker for charitable causes, her bright blue eyes met Georgiana's with unconcealed interest. "I asked Horace to introduce me, Mrs. Goodyear, as soon as I heard who you were," she said frankly. "You're the very person we need to serve on a special committee of the Manhattan Aid Association. In your literary capacity you'd be invaluable."

The charity was the city's oldest and most effective privately organized institution of its kind, but Georgiana heard the suggestion with mixed feelings. Committee serving was not her forte; on the other hand, she was flattered by the older woman's interest and not unimpressed by her name and position. Furthermore, Mrs. Hamilton was the mother of five, three of whom were male, two of whom were eligible. Palpably it was no more than Georgiana's maternal duty to acquiesce in whatever proposition she might advance.

The gist of it, as that lady explained, was that Georgiana should serve on a committee of professional women who were organizing an auction of letters, rare books, autographs, and first editions, the proceeds to go to the Manhattan Aid Association. "Perhaps you would chair the committee?" she said eagerly. "It would entail really very little work."

The child Washington was not more truthful than Mrs. Hamilton, but when it came to benefiting one of her charities she happily ignored an occasional wee perversion of fact. There would be considerable work involved, as Georgiana surmised, but the idea of the auction was tempting.

"Well," she said hesitantly, "if you really think I'm the person . . ."

"Splendid. Of course you are. I'll be in touch with you and you can count on one of our girls from Aid headquarters who knows the ropes to lend a hand in any way you need."

By now the guests were all seated or standing in place, chatting, in front of chairs and sofas.

"All right," called Horace. "Everyone set? If you're ready, I think we ought to begin." The hum of conversation over the big room died. "All right, Roberts." Horace nodded to his butler who stood by

29

the light switch. The man was about to snap it off when Nora, from her place in the middle of the audience, rose to her feet.

"Just a minute, everyone. Horace, darling, forgive me, but I just want to say that I hope you'll all receive this picture in the spirit in which it was made. It's a simple tale of a simple child who, when she found that her earthly love was unrequited, sought refuge in a higher heavenly peace. You and I know that child was wrong. One should never take into one's own hands the disposition of— But I mustn't tell you any more. I just want to say that I hope you'll find the climax poignant. It's so real, so true. When we were shooting it my one prayer was that I might be able to portray for the public this child's simplicity and heartache. I felt dedicated somehow, we all did, to these simple peasant folk, to the youthful, unspoiled spirit of this lovely girl. Thank you, my dears, bless you."

Nora sat down amidst a slight stir and a smattering of embarrassed applause. Claude sighed. "For God's sake," muttered Reams, "is she talking about herself?" Even Karen's cloud of happiness was penetrated by a slight sense of discomfort.

"I expect the picture means a lot to her," she whispered.

Horace tried again. "All right, Rob——" Nora sprang up. "I don't think we should delay any longer, darling. Everyone seems ready for us to begin."

"That was my thought too," said Mr. Oppenheimer. He nodded to the butler, and this time they completed the play. The room sank into darkness, the music swelled, and on the screen Planet's famous trademark—the sun, the moon, and a starry sky emerging from shrouding mist glowed silvery white, the titles melted into one another, the picture was under way.

To the astonishment of an audience, slightly chilled by Nora's spiel, it was good. It *was* simple, it *was* touching, and although the child so movingly referred to by Miss Brown was perhaps not such a tot as all that, there was no doubt as to the ability of the cameraman. Nora looked like a dewy-eyed sexy angel astray in a celestial spring.

The bitch, the boring, egotistical, thieving bitch, thought Germaine. How *dare* she look like that? Claude was enjoying himself thoroughly. The attraction Nora exerted over him was strong, but even he was sometimes bowed by her loquacity. This evening was

30

so much velvet. He was close to the object of his desire, could admire her natural talent and beauty, and had to listen only to the brief speeches allotted to her by a screen writer who, apart from a belief in succinct dialogue, was taking sweet revenge upon his star.

Throughout the preparation of the script she had harried him with a continuous flow of suggestions and comment. Once before the cameras he shut her up, persuading her that eloquence lay in mute emotion, in the legato approach. Like the Life of the Spirit, Nora was crazy about it. For screen purposes. Off screen she reverted to her normal Niagara proclivities.

The guests paid the film the tribute of close attention while Karen wept happily, substituting herself for the star and Mr. Asher as her leading man.

When the lights were turned on at the fade-out there was a great deal of nose-blowing and repowdering, and the applause was spontaneous and prolonged. Karen's nose was gleaming and she ducked hastily into her vanity case. Reams, little dreaming of the experience he and she had shared, winked at her approvingly. It was nice to see a youngster who wasn't hard-boiled and sophisticated.

The end of the picture evoked general movement throughout the room as the guests started toward the bar or looked for Horace and Dorothy to say good night. Karen, enraptured, but fearful lest Reams feel stuck with her, said with a bright smile, "Excuse me, but there are my aunt and uncle, I must say hello to them," and left him to join the Quicks, though she felt the wrench from the top of her tawny head to the bottom of her number-eight shoes. Reams gravitated toward Georgiana.

"I've met Karen; she's grand. Better than you said even. I'm stuck on the whole family." It was on the tip of his tongue to ask her where he had gone awry with Allen, but a belated sense of caution, as well as Allen appearing at Georgiana's elbow, upon which he took a firm proprietary hold, prevented him. The Quicks and Karen were also converging upon them. Maybe Reams Asher will say something about wanting to see me again, Karen thought. I hope he does, oh, I *hope* he does. In the general good nights the hope was fulfilled. Reams shook hands with her and said, "I certainly trust we meet again some time."

"Oh yes," Karen said, "oh yes, so do I," and then taking the bull

31

by the horns—despite the dreadful schism caused by her father's not having obtained Reams's manuscript, it was the kind of thing that could cause a feud really, the Capulets and the Montagues, but she would surmount it—she said with praiseworthy if slightly breathless poise, "Mother, perhaps Mr. Asher would come and dine with us some time?"

"Of course. Reams is always welcome. Isn't he, Allen?"

Allen inclined his head.

"You're very kind," Reams said.

"Some time when I'm home from college," Karen continued with clarifying emphasis. "I get down quite often, Mr. Asher. It will be a thrill for our short-story class when I tell them I've met you."

"Don't count on it too heavily."

"We *will* count on seeing you though, soon."

There was a slight pause.

Allen spoke abruptly, "Come along; it's getting late. Georgiana? Karen? You Quicks ready? Let's go. Good night," and he shepherded them out.

"Well," observed his wife on the way down, "that was a little brusque, I must say."

Lola and Peter lived just around the corner from the Oppenheimers, if on a somewhat different scale, so the Goodyears walked to their door with them before going home, Karen trailing behind, the better to dwell upon Reams undisturbed.

"He seems like a nice chap, that Asher," Peter said. "He was very interesting after dinner while you gals were powdering your noses. Makes a lot of sense."

"By the way," Allen said coldly, "I would appreciate it if you'd let me in on your plans some time."

Georgiana stopped short in the middle of Fifty-seventh Street. "What on earth are you talking about?" she demanded.

"Simply that I feel a fool having to learn from Reams Asher that you've made up your mind to go abroad this spring. It seems to me that your confiding in him before you said anything to me was not only indiscreet but in poor taste."

"Oh, don't be a stuffed shirt. He said he was going to Europe and I merely remarked that I envied him and wished we were going too."

"I gather that he didn't understand it in that way. He seemed to think the plans were all set; that you were going first and would meet him there and Karen and I would come later."

Karen had caught up with them and overheard the last few words. "Daddy, how *marvelous! Is* there a possibility of Europe next summer?"

"Ask your mother; this plot is her hatching."

"For God's sake, what are you talking about?" Georgiana demanded. "I never heard such nonsense. I never said anything of the kind. Reams is all mixed up. And supposing I had! There's no reason for you to behave like Othello, with the handkerchief. Come on, let's go home; it's too cold and too late to stand here yapping." Georgiana was feeling tired, exasperated, guilty, and completely out of patience. Reams, she considered, had been a fool not to keep their conversation to himself and Allen was a dunderhead to bring it up in front of the others.

Peter and Lola stood listening, disturbed yet resigned to the family wrangle. They loved them both, but through the years they had evolved a philosophy of non-interference in the Goodyear quarrels. The rain that fell in their lives was lamentable but the puddles it formed were Goodyear puddles, and there seemed small percentage in the Quicks getting their feet wet.

"Well, good night, kids," Peter said. "Sorry there's been a mix-up." Lola pulled at his sleeve. "Come on. The twins' sitter is going to be in a tantrum and I can't blame her."

There was a general round of kisses on the sidewalk, the Quicks went into the house, and the Goodyears started home. In the clear October night their footsteps sounded sharp on the pavement as they went the few blocks down First Avenue to Fifty-second Street and their own apartment. There was a family feeling that the tension would be less on foot than cooped up in a cab.

"Do you think . . . I mean as long as you and Daddy both like Mr. Asher's book and it was only bad luck that Carroway isn't doing it, he isn't likely to be annoyed or anything, do you think he *might* come to dinner some time?"

"I don't see why not." Allen spoke with cutting affability. "He's been to dinner several times before. I would say that in spite of what's happened professionally he's a close family friend, wouldn't you, Georgiana?"

33

"I don't know what you're driving at. I like him, if that's what you mean, and he likes both of us."

"And having him for dinner would show him that in spite of Barnstable doing the book the friendship still stands," Karen put in eagerly. "It would be a good idea, don't you think? Sort of cement things."

Her mother looked at her curiously. "What is this? You seem very concerned with Mr. Asher all of a sudden. Are you smitten by our literary lion?"

Karen felt the blood mount in her cheeks and hoped that in the dark her parents couldn't see. "How silly. Of course not. I met him only this evening. I just thought he seemed nice, that's all."

Georgiana glanced at her daughter striding beside her. The girl's face glimmered in the starlight, her pale hair was blown backward by her movement. She was like the figurehead of a ship, her mother thought. There was something triumphant in her bearing, something young and invincible. A hand seemed to squeeze Georgiana's heart, and for a moment she couldn't get her breath. Then she said, "He is nice, Karen, very nice, but he's too old for you, darling. You should stick to your college boys. They're your real friends; you have the same interests. Reams is, what? Sixteen years older than you. He could be your father."

Allen grunted. "Pretty precocious."

"But I like older men," Karen insisted, "and, anyway, why the fuss? I'm not in *love*." The emotion she felt for Reams was too tremulous, too intimate to be hawked about in front of her parents.

Georgiana had an inspiration. "I'll tell you whom we'll ask for dinner! I said I'd serve on a committee for Mrs. Barclay Hamilton. There's no reason why we shouldn't have the Hamilton boys some time. I believe there are two who aren't married and are just about your age."

"I've met Floyd."

"You have?" Georgiana felt deflated. "You never told me."

"He's sixteen."

"Just right," Allen said. "If an Asher can do it why can't a Hamilton?"

"Oh, shut up. What about the other one? He's twelve, I suppose?"

"No," Karen allowed. "I think he's twenty-four or -five."

"Well, there you are! There's no reason in the world why you couldn't have a little party some week end when you're home and ask him. What's his name, I wonder?"

"Barclay, Jr. I don't think he likes me much."

"Do you know him too?" Really, the girl was exasperating.

"I met him at a party," Karen said reluctantly. It was one more story of social failure and she didn't want to discuss it.

"What happened?" her mother asked.

Oh, God, thought Karen, why do parents have to *probe* so? "We danced together, but he didn't ask me again."

Georgiana patted her arm. "That doesn't mean a thing; he probably had to go home early. You're just as attractive as any of the girls you go around with. More so. Since you know him it's easy. We must certainly give a little party and ask him."

In her present mood Mr. Barclay Hamilton, Jr., was, as far as Karen was concerned, a molecule, but if she gave a party she could ask Reams Asher without its seeming pointed. One among several, he couldn't think she was pursuing him. She began to view her mother's suggestion in a more gracious spirit. "Could I have a party, Daddy? Just at home, I mean."

"Why, of course, dear. I shouldn't think any home festivity would cost too much."

"For heaven's sake, what are we paying that rent for if Karen can't have a few friends in?" Georgiana demanded. One of the reasons she and Allen had alibied themselves into the expensive Fifty-second Street apartment was because the drawing room was large and lent itself to entertaining. Entertaining, they said, was necessary to their careers and helpful to their daughter.

As she spoke they arrived at the entrance of their building. Georgiana and Allen went in but Karen lingered a moment, leaning over the railing at the foot of the street, one of the sharp iron points cold under her chin, watching the dark water slipping by and the Pepsi-Cola sign glowing across the river. Reams Asher, Reams Asher, Reams Asher. The name went through her head with the rhythm of a slow windshield wiper. Would anything come of it, she wondered. She wasn't clever with men the way her friend Poppy was. Even when Poppy was teasing them or arguing with them she was able to make them think they were pretty wonderful, whereas when Karen

35

sincerely did think they were wonderful she still couldn't make them fall in love with her. I guess I'm too big, she thought, I frighten them. Still, I'm only a little bit taller than Reams, and he has marvelous shoulders and then there was the way he said, "I do hope we'll meet again." He seemed to mean that. She lingered by the river mooning about him until she feared her parents would dispatch the elevator man in search of her, then entered the house reluctantly, as though leaving her lover on the doorstep.

Later, when she was undressed, she went down the hall to her parents' room to say good night. Allen kissed her, but instead of responding warmly, as she usually did, she gave him a little absent pat on the shoulder and went dreamily back to her own room.

"I do wish," Georgiana said, "that Karen's emotions would light some place, poor child. Every new man she meets is the only man in the world. Until she meets another."

"Do you feel Reams Asher is a desirable lighting place?" Allen asked the question half mockingly but he watched her closely. His instinct about her feeling for the younger man might be ridiculous, of course. It ought to be, but he had the impression it was not.

"No, I don't. He's much too old for her."

"He seems to have been born at the wrong time all around, doesn't he?"

She turned on him. "Allen, what's the matter with you? You've done nothing but make cryptic remarks the entire evening, every time Reams' name has been mentioned. What are you driving at?"

Was it important enough, he wondered, to make a scene about? Did he want to cause a rift between them because of something that might be chimerical or, in any event, transitory? Were she and Reams in love with each other? Were they having an affair? Had he been younger, had he loved her differently, he could not have refrained from blurting out his suspicions, but he had been married a long time and he was tired; the propositions of the first part triumphed. Thus, he thought ruefully, we attain philosophy. "I'm sorry," he said; "forget it. If I had anything in mind it doesn't make sense." He went into his own room to undress and Georgiana, feeling frustrated, got into bed and poured a cup of hot Ovaltine from a small thermos the maid had left on the bedside table. She suspected it didn't do much other than put on weight, but Germaine Dauzat

36

swore it relaxed her and made her sleep, so Georgiana was trying it too.

She lay back on the pillow casually turning the pages of the evening paper and sipping the warm drink waiting for Allen to come in and open the windows and put out the light. It always takes him forever, she thought, after twenty-three years I still don't know what he does with himself. He's suspicious, though. I'll have to take it easy. Before dinner was the mistake. I shouldn't have lost my temper about the book.

It was curious, flattering probably, that Allen should be jealous. She couldn't imagine caring were he to take a fancy to another woman. It would be a younger woman, of course, that always happened to men of his age. To women of her age, too, apparently, but where was the harm? It gave life a fillip. The other partner should understand that and not assume it meant the end of the world. And she didn't think she was being a fool. Reams wanted her. He was not in love with her yet, perhaps, but that would come.

She smiled, thinking of his invitation to the apartment. Her challenge had been deliberate. Suddenly, after the despondency and insecurity of the early evening, she had had a feeling that the moment was ripe. She had known too many men in her life not to recognize that expression at once amused, responsive, and predatory with which a man looks at a woman he finds desirable. Reams himself was an appealing combination, youthful yet adult, with a remarkable air of vigor and masculinity. All women would find him attractive, she imagined; her competition was no doubt acute, for surely he met any number of young, pretty women who, even if he didn't take them seriously, would begin to dream about him, seek ways of seeing him again just as Karen . . . Karen! Suppose she were to fall seriously in love with Reams? She was too young, of course, a child really, but might he not be first amused, then flattered, then touched, and then . . . Georgiana quelled the small panic that began to flutter inside her. What nonsense. When were they ever likely to see each other? She would simply arrange to meet Reams at his own house or have him at the apartment while Karen was in college. She had spoken of a dinner, but when the Christmas holidays came along she would be so busy with young parties that she'd never give him a second thought. Besides, by that time

37

Georgiana's own position with him would be secure and would automatically govern his reaction to her child. Relieved, she reached for a small mirror on her bedside table and looked at herself searchingly, her head pressed into the pillows, the mirror held a little above her.

Her expertly touched hair glowed with live copper lights and curled becomingly about her ears. In her youth she had never gone to bed with hairpins and curlers and saw no reason to do so at forty-seven, when certainly one's face needed all the soft flattery it could get. Her golden eyes searched her reflection. Her lips had always been a bit thin and now laugh lines and crow's-feet were carved irrevocably, but there was little puffiness under her eyes and her teeth were beautiful. Looking up at herself, as she was, her jaw-line was cleanly drawn, the contour of her face almost girlish. A secret, amused smile gleamed in her eyes. Smart old nature, a woman certainly looked her best viewed from above.

Hearing Allen in the next room, she put the mirror aside and was occupied with her Ovaltine and the paper when he appeared in the doorway. She was relieved to see that the strained, suspicious air with which he had been regarding her all evening had disappeared, his expression was even friendly. Indeed, as he undressed he had been pondering, as Georgiana had earlier, the metamorphosis of the emotions of the married. Why could two people care so desperately for each other in the beginning and through the years come to boredom, impatience, and disillusionment? It was, he supposed, because to live was to change, and even the mature, as distinct from the old—if he and Georgiana could so consider themselves—might mature along disparate lines. Their own disagreements were clashes of temperament, for professionally and physically they were compatible. The last year or so, perhaps, there had been a subtle change in Georgiana's reaction to his love-making, but what else could be expected after years of marriage? No honeymoon lasted forever, and if he were to be guided by the confidences or unwitting self-betrayals of his friends they had done better than most.

He supposed he had behaved rather like a stuffed shirt, but he had been upset by what Reams had said about her plans for a trip to Europe. Why should not he, her husband, know her intentions first? Through the open door he saw her lying in bed, the lamplight molding her body, defining her profile in powdery gold, and suddenly she became to him, if not dear, intensely desirable.

He went into the room and started toward her, but she remained engrossed in the paper; the fundamental urge had apparently not yet reached her. He hesitated a moment, then crossed over and opened the window, carefully raising the shade a little so it wouldn't flap. He switched off the lights, leaving only the reading lamp, and went and sat on the edge of her bed. After a moment she lowered the paper. "Well?" she said. He leaned toward her and tentatively kissed her cheek. "Would you be inclined to . . . ?"

God, she thought, no seismograph he when it comes to sensing a mood. She lay looking at him, at his long head, with the receding hair lightly frosted, at his eyes which could be intense and humorous and kind. She glanced at the sensitive hand lying on his green silk dressing gown, her present to him last Christmas. As she did so the newspaper slipped to the floor. The boxer, whose photograph had caught her attention—there was something reminiscent of Reams in the set of his shoulders—smiled up at her from the carpet. She put out the light and moved over in bed with a little sigh.

3

"Wasn't it wonderful that you got sick? Now we have this opportunity to talk. Tell me all about it." Poppy Slade's blue eyes snapped with interest.

"I'm afraid," Karen said, "the story's kind of thin." The two girls sat in the brilliant December sunshine that flooded the Goodyear drawing room, lunching from trays placed on the square coffee table. They were discussing Karen's secret yearning for Reams Asher and owed the delicious opportunity to a heavy cold she had contracted while home from college over the week end.

"Never mind how thin, tell anyhow," Poppy insisted. "Maybe we can dope out a way to fatten it up."

"Well," Karen said, launching happily on her task, "when I went back to college after that party of the Oppenheimers in October I told everybody in our short-story class about meeting him, naturally."

"Naturally," Poppy agreed, her mouth full of cheese soufflé.

"And," Karen continued, "I couldn't forget him. I was haunted by him, so then I got my idea. I sent him a copy of *Another Country* with a letter asking him to autograph it. I rewrote it about eight times, but I guess it was all right because he did. Autograph it, I mean, and sent it back with a little note."

"Did you keep it?"

"Do you think I'm out of my *mind?* I'm never without it," and she fished about among the manifold furnishings of her handbag. "Where do you suppose . . . Oh, here it is," and she drew forth an envelope battered by hard service. "It must have been easier in the old days, when they kept such things down their fronts, but wouldn't you think they'd have dropped through? Here." She handed the letter to Poppy, who scanned it with an eye practiced in the detection of love's first flutter between the lines. She read it aloud with running commentary:

Dear Miss Goodyear,

By the way, I think and speak of you as Karen (Good! He thinks about you), but I don't want to seem forward after only one meeting and in our first correspondence. (He envisages more—yummy.) Thank you for all the nice things you said in your note. I, too, remember our meeting with pleasure (Pleasant souvenir, a good sign) and I am autographing *Another Country* and returning it to you under separate cover. (Executive type.) If you still want my signature on a copy of *The Shadowed Path* in February, when, I understand, the Barnstable Press plans to publish, you shall have it and welcome. Thank you for including me in your plans for a party. If I am not too tied up with work when it comes off I'll be delighted to be there.

Yours cordially,
Reams Asher

Poppy looked up. "I think the whole thing sounds very encouraging. Not overboard, maybe, still, encouraging."

"But what's so awful," Karen moaned, "is this lapse of time. I haven't seen him since that night at the Oppenheimers and his letter's already a month old. Where do we go from here? He probably doesn't remember he ever met me."

"Nonsense. He's a pal of your parents, isn't he? Still," Poppy conceded, "there's nothing like nursing the fire along. Haven't you even called him *once* since you've been home?"

The lovelorn shook her head. "I haven't had the nerve. I had this rotten cold so I couldn't invite him here or anything, and what was there to say? I love you?"

Her counselor's brows drew together in a thoughtful frown. "Of course it's always better to have some definite reason for calling them, otherwise they get scared you're after them and that's fatal."

"Anyhow," Karen said, "I think maybe he's not in town. I asked Mother, casually, if he was around, but she was kind of vague." Georgiana, surprised and a little disturbed to find her daughter still thought of Reams, had felt, under the circumstances, that vagueness was the best policy.

Poppy, who had been frowning unseeingly at a coal barge making its way up the East River, snapped her fingers softly. "I've got it," she announced. "The very thing. Aren't we dunces! All you have to do is to call him up now and invite him to the party you mentioned in your letter. What more valid excuse? Christmas holidays start on the twenty-first, don't they?"

"That's right."

"Have a party on the twenty-second."

Karen's eyes shone. "Do you think he'll come?"

"What's he got to lose? He meets nice people and he gets fed and liquored. He's normal, isn't he? He'll jump at the chance. Come on, let's try him now," and she half rose from her chair.

Karen's stomach turned a somersault. "No," she said hastily; "no, maybe we'd better not."

"Dear Lord God, *why* not?"

"Well, it's—it's lunchtime; he's probably out. Anyway, I couldn't definitely set a date without asking Mother if it's all right. Supposing she had something of her own planned for the night I picked?" This prevarication was sheer panic, and the cold gleam in Poppy's eye told her that Poppy knew it. She continued a little desperately. "Mother will be home early this afternoon, she's got a committee meeting for that auction she's doing for Mrs. Barclay Hamilton."

Poppy nodded. "I know. My ma's helping her."

"I'll talk to her about it and call him this evening. It'll be better

41

really, because I can say I'm going back to college first thing in the morning so he *can't* feel hunted, and I'll tell him I had a bad cold and that's why I didn't phone before."

Poppy closed her eyes so tightly that only a line of black lashes showed between her cheeks and eyebrows. A thin wail of pain escaped her. "No, no, *no*, honey. You should have your *head* examined. *That's* not the technique."

"Oh?" Karen said humbly.

"That you had a cold! My God, have you *no* sense? Either don't say anything at all, just make it completely casual, or say something like, 'I've been trying to get to this phone for the past week, but I literally haven't had two minutes. How you men can stand the pace you lead us poor females I wouldn't know.'"

"Would he believe that?"

"At least it would poison his mind. Make him wonder."

Karen nodded slowly. "I see what you mean. I'd seem kind of inaccessible, and that's when they want you, I guess."

Poppy got up and went around the table to her friend and hugged her. "Darling, don't be broody. This Reams guy could become booboo over you but he's got to get to know you, that's all. Men are dopes. A woman *has* to take the initiative."

Karen sighed. "Even the wonderful ones don't seem very bright sometimes."

"Honey, they need to be wet-nursed all their lives. Look at my old man! If *he* isn't a shining example."

"Oh, Pops, is he still bad?" Karen's tone was solicitous.

Miss Slade looked grim. "I'll say. You know what I think? I think men have change of life just like women. How else can you account for such a fabulous fantasy? Pa's forty-four years old with this indestructible intention of becoming an actor. I ask you!"

"What does your mother think about it?"

"That he's crazy, of course, same as Carl and I do. The only one who encourages him is Liz." Her brother Carl was sixteen, two years younger than Poppy, and Liz was nine, a string of a child with rattail hair, braces on her teeth, and a passion for her father and the theater. "Can you picture it?" Poppy went on. "At his age? With no experience? Who's going to give him a job? How will we eat? But I mean how? Who knows if he has any talent even?"

"I thought he was pretty good in that Comedy Club show I saw him do a couple of years ago," Karen said encouragingly.

"But that was amateurs. The only real experience he's had was one month in summer stock last July. That's what he did with his holiday. Joined Equity. He'd invested a little money in the theater so the manager let him play bits for four weeks. He made sixty bucks a week. We'll certainly be living in style at that rate!" And Poppy dropped a lump of sugar into her coffee with a vicious plop.

Karen extended her full lower lip in a very fair imitation of a Ubangi, a mannerism she had acquired when stumped by life's complexities. "Gosh, it sounds serious. You mean he's actually going to leave the brokerage firm?"

"If he gets a job in the theater. We had a regular second-act climax at the house the other night. Mother bawling him out and saying how could he be so irresponsible with her and us three children to support, and he said he had enough put by to finish Carl and Liz's education and that I had my choice and took a job rather than go to college so now I could begin to live off it. So then Mother said, 'The child only makes twenty-two fifty a week,' but he said, 'She's got an excellent chance for advancement. If she really needs the money, she'll work hard, and someday she'll make something of herself.'"

"Holy cat. It sounds spartan."

"You may well say. And then he went on and told us he'd wanted to act all his life but he and Mother got married and pretty soon we started coming along, so he went into Harmon, Bellsop & Peals instead because that was security, and he's been there ever since. But he says now that half his life is gone and he thinks it only fair that we should be willing to live his way for a while in view of the fact that for twenty years he's been living our way, and I must say"— here she paused for breath and to deliver her grudging verdict—"although it makes me very mad, I suppose he's got a point."

Karen cast about for such comforting crumbs as she could lay tongue to. "Well, don't worry too much, Pops. Maybe he won't find anything. Unless you're a big star like Nora Brown or Laurence Olivier or somebody I don't think jobs in the theater grow on trees."

"He'll find one," Poppy assured her gloomily. "Dad always gets

43

what he goes after. Stubborn as hell. Liz helps him too. She's his spy."

"His spy?"

Poppy nodded. "Sure. She pores over the theater news in the papers, she's only learned to read in the last year really, but she can even interpret *Variety,* and every time she reads that a play's being cast she tells him about it. If he wanted to be a producer even, it might make sense, but no, he's got to act! I bet if they offer him a butler's part he'll leap at the chance." Poppy glanced at her watch. "Golly, I've got to blow. Now that I'm John Barrymore's daughter I can't afford the sack. Good-by, duck, take care of yourself, and for goodness' sake don't forget to telephone me tonight after you've called Reams. I've got a date with a jerk, so I won't be late, and I'll be in a fever to hear."

Georgiana was tired, but she felt that, on the whole, the committee meeting had gone well. She was flattered when Mrs. Hamilton had asked if she might drop in, as she was so interested in hearing their plans for the auction, and she was more than pleased by the young secretary-aide association headquarters had placed at her disposal. For such a pretty girl, Bierne Honeywell seemed remarkably able. She was quiet and well-mannered but she was experienced in fund raising and had a professional acquaintance with New York society and a knowledge of wire pulling, which Georgiana found impressive. She judged Bierne to be in her middle twenties, and when she considered her own teetering position and what the future might hold for Karen if she didn't marry immediately upon leaving college and had to tackle a job, she could only hope her daughter might do as well as this young woman.

The working committee was composed of herself, Germaine Dauzat, Poppy's mother Nancy Slade, and Lola Quick. The "window dressing," who had graciously put in an appearance at the meeting, had already left but consisted of some of the most influential figures in the book world, including Chips Carroway for the publishers and Dr. Rosenbach for the collectors. It was hoped by the humble workers that besides names and counsel the distinguished connoisseurs might be prevailed upon to contribute a few rare manuscripts or letters, opinions varying as to whether chances were nil or merely impossible. The committee had agreed that Georgiana would hunt for a suitable place in which to hold the auction, and she turned now to Bierne Honeywell. "You've got a note of that, haven't you, that you and I will form a posse and go together?"

"I have, Mrs. Goodyear. I'll start tomorrow lining up galleries and hotel ballrooms, whatever seems the best kind of space for us. I'll report to you when I have the information and you can tell me which ones you want to see."

Nancy Slade was standing by the window looking out on the faery spectacle of New York at dusk. From the brilliant blue stain overhead the sky melted to cyclamen to pink to pearl at the horizon. The river stretched smooth as a river of steel, and to the south and east the city hung suspended in haze. As she was watching, up and down the violet towers, strung along the water, banks of light burst into flower. High in the deepening blue a star blazed, and its moving kin blinked green as a plane drummed home to La Guardia.

Nancy turned from the window reluctantly, her attention caught by the conversation in the room. "You know," she said, "one thing we've got to be awfully sure of on the night of the auction is an audience. We don't want to be standing around with the Gutenberg Bible and this committee the only customers."

Lola nodded. "It would be a help if we could count on a few celebrities attending to drum up trade."

"Getting literary lions certainly shouldn't be hard," Georgiana observed. "I think we can count on Reams Asher, for instance. His new book will be out by then, he ought to be a household word."

"What is this? 'Household word'?" asked Germaine.

"You know," Nancy said, "something common to everybody. Like Drāno."

Lola was not in complete agreement with her sister-in-law. "Authors are all right, G, but it seems to me people go more for actors and actresses, don't you think? If we could get some really big names from the theater and publicize the fact that they're going to be there, it would be swell."

Georgiana shrugged. "I can't think what they'd be doing at a *literary* auction, but we can always try."

"Did you have any particular actor or actress in mind?" Germaine

45

asked courteously. There was a moment of tension while the other three ladies bit their tongues lest the forbidden name of Nora Brown pop like a toad from their lips. "Because if it is something common to everyone," the Frenchwoman continued pleasantly, "a sort of Drāno, as you say, I think I know where we could get the very item." Germaine's features were composed but her eyes sparkled with malice.

Georgiana turned to her. "Germaine, would you be willing to——"

"But, my darling, why not? How that woman acts! As though she were your friend, as though she had talent, as though she were religious. It is the biggest act I know, just what you want."

The other women laughed, and Bierne Honeywell smiled uncertainly. "It sounds like a successful meeting." The deeper tones came unexpectedly, and they looked up to see Allen in the doorway. "Am I interrupting you?"

Lola held out an affectionate hand. "We're about finished, aren't we G?"

"Come in," his wife said. "You're among friends."

Allen scattered hellos to the familiar feminine contingent and looked questioningly at the young woman he didn't know. Georgiana spoke quickly. "Oh, I'm sorry. Miss Honeywell, this is my husband, Allen Goodyear. Miss Honeywell is from Manhattan Aid headquarters, Allen. It's she who's really doing the work."

Bierne half rose, holding her shorthand pad and papers on her lap. "That isn't so, Mr. Goodyear, I assure you. How do you do?"

"How do you do."

An attractive girl, he thought. A pretty face but with strength. Nothing namby-pamby. With very fair hair, which she wore in a soft bang, and deep blue eyes, Bierne was saved from candy-box prettiness by the squareness of her jaw and a gaze more comprehending than that usually emanating from the saccharine beauties of the chromos.

Allen turned to the others. "How are things going? Will Chips let you have any of his original manuscripts?"

"That, pet, is where you come in," his sister said. "We're counting on you to turn on the heat."

Nancy Slade had opened her purse and was applying powder and fresh lipstick. "I've got to be going," she announced; "it's late. Is it definite where we're having the next meeting?"

"Why not here again?" suggested Georgiana. "There's plenty of room and it's no bother."

Allen had seated himself in their midst and was surveying the group with approval. "And it's a pleasure for me to come home to such a charming gathering. I'm beginning to understand the Turkish point of view."

Nancy was pulling on her gloves. "Wait a minute," her hostess urged. "You don't have to run this second. Have a stirrup cup first. It's pretty cold out, isn't it, Allen?"

"And getting colder. I should say a cocktail would do us all good." But he made no move toward mixing one.

"Well, for heaven's sake, git. This is your house, you know." Georgiana spoke impatiently. "Allen always behaves as though he were a guest."

"He thinks he's that Turk," Lola said. "He expects the harem to wait on him. Go on, Effendi, brew us a martini."

Her brother rose and went toward the liquor table. Lola gave Georgiana a wink. She hated to hear the note of irritation creep into her sister-in-law's voice but she had to admit that Allen frequently gave her provocation. It probably was trying to come home tired at the end of the day and find the house full of clacking females just when you wanted to relax; on the other hand, her brother was by nature a passive host. He enjoyed having people at the house, but unless chevied by Georgiana he was perfectly content to let the guests forage for themselves. That way, he said, they felt more at home. If goaded into it, however, he was a moderately skillful bartender, and now passed out the pale frosty glasses with aplomb.

When he offered one to Bierne, she hesitated. "Don't you drink?" he asked.

"Oh yes," she said; "it's just that—well, I'm still on duty, so to speak."

Allen glanced around the room. The other women each had a cocktail, Lola had her shoes off, and she and Nancy were smoking. "I think we may say that office hours are over," he said with a smile. She took the drink, and he raised his glass to her. "Success to the auction."

"This is good, Allen," Nancy called. "Wish I could stay for another."

"Why don't you?"

She shook her head. "Can't. Cook's night out. I've got to get home and feed Liz and then guess what? Reuben and I are going to the theater. *O Mistress Mine* for the third time. Mr. Slade admires Mr. Lunt's performance." Her tone was sardonic. What was a treat for most people had become for Nancy a wearisome routine. The theater was her enemy and, where her husband was concerned, she feared it as some wives fear liquor or gambling or other women. "I've told Carl he'd better study while his father can still pay his tuition at Exeter. Once he starts a career of one-night stands it'll all be over." She put down her drink and rose. "Well, so long. See you next week. Anybody coming my way?"

"Me," said Germaine, following her to the door.

In the general good-bys Allen glanced at the young secretary to see how she was reacting to a conversation which must seem to her a sort of double-talk. She looked baffled but interested. There was something childish and appealing in the way she wore her small round hat, the way her thin neck rose from her close little collar. Why, she's a kid, he thought; can't be much older than Karen and apparently already on her own. If Karen were suddenly in like position would she be able to earn a living? he wondered. Where was she, by the way? The two girls ought to meet each other. He called to his wife. "Say, G, Karen didn't go back to Vassar today, did she?"

Georgiana looked up impatiently from a list she and Lola were checking together. "No," she said, "she goes tomorrow morning. I told you that. I think she's in her room trying to catch up on a little work. Why?"

"Oh, nothing. I won't disturb her."

Georgiana returned to her names and figures. There was quiet while she and Lola murmured together about their plans for the auction. Bierne waited uncertainly, not knowing whether or not Mrs. Goodyear was through with her. Not that she minded waiting in this lovely room, with the open fire burning cozily and Mrs. Goodyear's husband treating her so courteously. He looked very kind but as though he were tired, she thought. How wonderful it must be to have an attractive husband and live securely in a beautiful apartment, just the two of you, without Mother and Uncle Ben, who would be there only when they were asked. She looked over at Mrs. Goodyear.

She was well dressed in that simple, expensive way, and attractive looking too. She couldn't be very young, but somehow you didn't think of her age. She seemed to reserve a special tone of exasperation for her husband but she'd been very polite and nice to Bierne herself. Bierne didn't like to interrupt her, but it *was* getting late, her mother would be making an issue out of it. Allen sensed her dilemma. "Look here, you probably want to go home, don't you?"

"Oh, not if there's anything more I can do."

"Nothing like asking. How about it, G?" he called. "You aren't going to want Miss Honeywell any more this evening, are you?"

Georgiana looked up. "What? Good lord, no. Do forgive me, Miss Honeywell. Mrs. Quick and I are trying to get this list of names straightened out, that's all. Run along, and thanks a lot."

"Thank you, Mrs. Goodyear, I'll call you about the auction rooms."

"Allen, see Miss Honeywell out, will you?"

"Of course." He guided her into the hall toward the front door. "Do you live far from here?" he asked, helping her into her coat.

She laughed. "No, it couldn't be more convenient. I live on Fifty-third Street between Third and Lexington. I'll be home in no time. I just hope the store isn't crowded."

"The store?"

She nodded. "I have to do the marketing."

"Do you live alone?"

"Oh no, with my mother and uncle, but they work, too, so I'm housekeeper."

"I see," he said. "Well, good night, neighbor. I hope we meet again some time."

"Good night, Mr. Goodyear." He opened the door for her and stood waiting until the elevator came, making desultory conversation about the weather and the auction. When she had gone he walked thoughtfully back to the drawing room. He picked up his pipe and felt in his pockets for a match.

Georgiana and Lola had finished their business and Georgiana was being briefed on the latest activities of the Quick twins, aged eighteen months.

"It turns out that your nephews are in the pink and remarkably intelligent," she informed Allen.

"Of course," he said absently. "True Goodyears."

"You might give poor old Quick a little credit too," his sister remarked. "They have an I.Q. of infants of two and a half, I'll have you know. Maybe there's something to the theory that if you're a hundred when your childen are born they can beat the bibs off the rest of the Pablum set. Well, I'll be trotting. Good night."

Georgiana poked him in the ribs. "Mrs. Quick said good night to you, Mr. Goodyear. You deaf?"

"Ouch," he said, and then, having lighted his pipe to his satisfaction, "No, but I was thinking about something else. That girl who was just here. Honeywell, did you say? There's something rather touching about her."

"She's very pretty," Georgiana conceded, "and seems efficient. I don't know that I'd say she was touching."

"Maybe that's the reason. The very fact that she's able. And skinny and young. Supports her family too."

Lola looked surprised. "Did she tell you that?"

"She does the marketing."

The two women burst out laughing.

"Well, for heaven's sake," Georgiana exclaimed. "It may interest you to know that your daughter can occasionally be prevailed upon to do the marketing but you and I still pay the bills." And looking at Lola she tapped her forehead significantly.

Allen grinned. "Maybe I jumped at conclusions on that one, but she impressed me somehow. I felt there was something stanch about her."

"Good," his wife said. "We're going to need all the stamina we can get before this job's done."

"I'll look in on Karen on my way out," Lola said. "I want to say good-by to her before she goes back to college. How's the heart interest coming, by the way?"

Georgiana looked up. "What do you mean?"

"Didn't you tell me, or was it you, Allen, that she had quite a crush on Reams Asher?"

"That nonsense!" Georgiana said sharply. "It's a case of hero worship and nothing more. If he weren't the idol of her short-story class she'd never give him a thought."

Allen, pulling on his pipe, looked at his wife quizzically. "Oh, come, Georgie, if she likes him at all I doubt if it's as superficial as that. Asher's a nice guy, you think so yourself." His tone was placating, but apparently, he had touched a sore spot. Georgiana turned on him angrily. "Don't talk nonsense, and don't call me Georgie."

Lola, attuned to the distant rumble before the thunderstorm, waved her hand and beat a hasty retreat.

"I do wish you wouldn't go blabbing to Lola and Peter every time Karen fancies she's in love with someone," Georgiana said, "they just embroider the story till it's a mountain out of a molehill."

"Who's blabbing? I never even knew anything about this, that he was on her mind at all, till you got suspicious the other day because she asked you if he was in town. I'm surprised, by the way, that he still is. I thought he was so eager to get to Europe."

"It was never sure when he was going." She did not add that she had reason to believe his departure might now be postponed indefinitely. They had become lovers the day after the Oppenheimer party, and though Reams continued to speak of his book and his trip abroad often enough to be worrisome and to cause her to want to keep a loophole of escape from *Tang* should it be necessary, he was turning out sufficient work for magazines to keep afloat financially and every check, Georgiana calculated, cemented him closer to home shores. "Keep at it, Reams, build yourself a name as a magazine writer," she encouraged him. "Once your book is published you'll be a great name, believe me, but you can write an article in a matter of days. Cultivate the American market. That way you'll always be able to eat while you write." America was where the money was. Once used to it his wanderlust would dim. Georgiana felt she was arranging things very tidily. If only the situation in her own office would attain some equilibrium—at the moment she felt as though she were struggling to stand upright in a crazily rocking bark—life would be eminently satisfactory.

"Well," Allen continued, his thoughts still on his daughter, "I wouldn't get in a sweat over this Karen business. It's probably not serious, and, if it is, he's a decent enough guy, isn't he?"

51

"So we think, but if I were you I wouldn't be so ready to marry her off to someone we don't know much about."

Allen looked at her in bewilderment. "Considering all you've been seeing of him the past year you ought to have *some* idea what he's like and, anyhow, who said anything about marriage? I agree with you he's too old for her, besides, as far as we can tell, he barely knows she's alive. I merely meant it's normal for women to like him. Hell, you do, and you're as much older than he as he's older than Karen."

His wife's voice as she answered him was icy with reason. "Reams is thirty-four. I am forty-seven, a difference, if I mistake not, of thirteen years. Our daughter, as you may recall, is nineteen. Nineteen from thirty-four leaves fifteen. Fifteen is more than thirteen at any time, but in their age brackets it's enormous."

With the first icicle the error of Allen's computation had been borne in upon him. "All right," he said, "all right, let's drop it."

Karen, having bade good-by to her aunt in the hall without catching their words, heard the tone of their voices as she approached the drawing room. She hesitated in the doorway, sadly aware that a row was in the making, but to leave seemed more awkward than to stay. With a gallant attempt at unself-consciousness she crossed to an isolated chair and sat down, opening the book she carried and trying to pretend she wasn't there.

"Just like a man," Georgiana exclaimed, ignoring her daughter. "You make false statements, you pull ridiculous boners, and then you grandly don't wish to discuss it any further."

"What is there to discuss? The appeal of Mr. Asher?"

"Why take that tone? You just said yourself that he was attractive."

Hearing the magic name, Karen looked up from her book. The moment was scarcely auspicious but perhaps she could serve as a distraction from the quarrel. "Oh—uh, speaking of Mr. Asher," she began with elaborate ingenuousness, "you did say I could have a party, you know, Mother. Daddy, I thought it would be nice to have it the night after I get home for the Christmas holidays, the twenty-second, if that's all right with you, and I'd like to ask him. Mr. Asher, I mean. Maybe I could call him up this evening." Her lips parted in a hopeful smile, her eyes were like a puppy's who

52

watches its mistress approaching the sofa where the bone is buried.

"Why *don't* you ask him?" Georgiana said. "I'm sure he and your father are dying to get together. But I think it would be more to the point if you asked young Barclay Hamilton."

"As far as I'm concerned, my dear, you can have your party on the twenty-second," Allen replied. "I'll be in Washington. Which will, I trust, Georgiana, relieve you of the fear of any strain between me and the great author."

"You don't have to be so snooty. It's *your* face I'm thinking of, not his. I suppose you've heard that Barnstable is supposed to have got hold of the biggest thing in publishing since *Gone with the Wind.*"

"I've heard, and I agree, so don't throw that up to me. Direct your fire at Chips, he's the one who wouldn't do it."

Georgiana flared at him. "That's just it! If you'd had the guts years ago to strike out on your own, as I wanted you to, you wouldn't be in this ridiculous position now."

"Oh, for God's sake, why rake up that ancient score? What's ridiculous about it? When you wanted me to go on my own I didn't have the money nor any means of raising it. We've probably flubbed this particular deal, I grant you, but on the whole Carroway and I have done all right together. There's no reason to suppose I'd have been spectacular by myself and I'd have been staggering under a financial burden which so far I've escaped."

"Well," Georgiana said grudgingly, "I should think that after all these years you'd be in a position to insist on the publication of what you believe in, and as far as financial burdens are concerned don't begin to crow yet. You may suddenly find yourself with a non-contributing wife."

"What do you mean?"

"Simply that things are flaring up again at the office. Three people were fired yesterday. How do I know where the ax is going to fall next?"

Allen looked troubled. "But it couldn't fall on you without the whole department going."

"Which it well may do."

Involuntarily he glanced toward Karen.

"She might as well know," Georgiana said, "only remember, Karen, this is office business, you're not to breathe it to a soul, do you hear?"

"Of course not, Mother, I wouldn't."

"Actually," her mother continued, "it might be smarter to resign now than to hang around waiting for the cataclysm."

"No," Allen said sharply. "That's so much bravado. You've got a good job; hang on to it."

"Hang on to my salary, you mean."

"My dear, I can't work any harder than I do or, at the present time, make any more money. If you want to continue to live as we live now you *have* to keep working. I'm sorry. I wish I could do better, but those are the facts, and false pride on my part isn't going to get us any place."

"Supposing *Tang* asks me to take a salary cut?"

"Have they said anything about it?"

"No, but they might."

"Then I think you should accept it. As long as something keeps coming in from your side we won't be too badly off, but I can't swing things on this scale by myself."

What he said was true, and Georgiana supposed such honesty was praiseworthy yet she sometimes thought that it wasn't only their income limit that made him cautious. Allen tended to think that everything cost too much, whether it was meals in restaurants, theater tickets, or the presents she wanted for Christmas. Workingmen, she had observed throughout her career, were less inclined to spend their money than workingwomen, and an accumulated resentment of many years festered and broke in her rejoinder. "No, I don't think you can swing things yourself although plenty of other men seem to. It certainly must be wonderful to be supported. Careers for women is the burning issue of the day," she said, turning to her daughter, "but a husband who can shoulder the responsibility of his family is still an asset, dear, believe me. A career for a woman isn't all it's cracked up to be."

"I'm surprised your mother feels the burden of her work so keenly," Allen observed to the girl who sat miserably watching them, "in view of the fact that her own professional life has been perpetually on an amateur basis. Her philosophy has certainly never been able to slog on through snow and rain and heat and gloom of night——"

54

"Mere survival of the calendar doesn't strike me as particularly praiseworthy," his wife retorted. "I should say achievement was what counted. You, for instance, have been with Carroway some fifteen years, yet you have to depend on me and my amateur endeavors to make ends meet."

"Oh, Mother, Daddy, please." It was a little more than a whisper. Karen was accustomed to their disagreements and quarrels but sometimes her parents had a sense of decorum. Allen, especially, hated rowing with his wife in front of his daughter, but tonight they were both so angry they didn't seem to care.

There was rancor and cutting sarcasm in their voices and such venom in the way they looked at each other that Karen felt cornered. She was like an animal seeking escape from the scoring of spurs, the pricking of blades. She remembered their fights when she was younger and how she had tried to divert them. Once when she was a child she stood on her head. They had assumed she was unconscious of what was going on but the stunt was deliberate, and it had been successful too. Georgiana and Allen had laughed, and the row was over. If only she could think of something now. Maybe her book . . . "Look," she said desperately into the charged silence, "I —I brought this book in, Daddy, I wanted to ask you——"

But her father cut in harshly, his usually kind expression distorted with anger as he faced his wife. "I could have made both ends meet if you'd had the intelligence of a shopgirl. If you'd been as adult as a bricklayer's wife, who knows how to run her home and live with comfort on her husband's earnings and is too honest to put up a phony front. You know the value of nothing unless it costs a fortune. You're the same way about people. A snob. Nobody means anything to you unless he's a name. All this fine façade about a literary auction! You basically don't give a damn about the Manhattan Aid Association but because Mrs. Barclay Hamilton is the head of it you're all smiles and interest. And you're trying to twist Karen the same way. You don't want her to go out with the men *she* likes. No! That might be poaching on your preserves. It's got to be Mr. Barclay Hamilton, Jr. He might be unspeakable but never mind that, his father's got millions."

"How dare you! How dare you!" Georgiana was shaking. "This can't go on. I, I'm sick, I can't stand it any longer. These gross accu-

55

sations—these——" Her voice broke in tearing sobs. "The things you say to me—the things——"

"And you!" he shouted. "Do you think you don't goad a man till he can't stand any more?"

"Oh, God, this is horrible, horrible." Overwhelmed by shame and misery, Georgiana stumbled from the room, the tears streaming down her face.

Karen waited for her father to speak, but he had forgotten her. He sank on to the sofa, his face gray with suffering. She sat very still, attempting to read, remembering the way they had taught her in boarding school: chin in, chest out, hips braced against the back of the chair. That way, they said, one was mentally alert, physically fit, able to understand and cope with any problem. Some place she must have got the position wrong. The slow tears slipped down her face and dropped into her lap, forming dark round spots on her dress.

4

Her arms full of brown paper bags bulging with groceries, Bierne Honeywell climbed the steps of the house in Fifty-third Street where she lived with her mother and uncle. As she had told Allen, she was only a few blocks from the Goodyear apartment, but the enormous difference in rent and atmosphere, within a close ambience, so typical of New York, was here apparent.

Their house was the end one nearest Third Avenue in a row of identical houses, each with four stone steps leading up to the front door. Identical outside iron fire escapes ran down from the roofs, terminating in a short ladder directly above the stoops. In warm weather children and dogs lolled on the fire-escape landings outside the windows, and summer and winter bottles of milk, plants, or striped bed pillows were set out to air.

Bierne and her family lived in a railroad flat on the first floor. As she mounted the steps she noticed that in one of the lighted windows her mother's small sign, "Honeywell, Gowns," was still crooked. She had drawn attention to it that morning on her way to work but it was characteristic of Mrs. Honeywell to have passed her day undisturbed by such a trifle.

Bierne stood in the vestibule and groped unseeingly around her bundles to find the key in her handbag. She opened the door and passed into the narrow hallway. The staircase leading to the flats of the other tenants rose before her, and two or three steps to the right of it brought her to the entrance of the Honeywell front room. It was two rooms really but the folding doors dividing it were always pushed back, giving a deceptive effect of space. This area served Mrs. Honeywell as show-workroom, and in the evening it was the family parlor. Heavy blue curtains were drawn across one end, forming two small cubicles or fitting rooms, and near them a sewing machine rose like an island from the worn Brussels carpet, which had been purchased originally with the optimistic notion that it would not show threads.

Mrs. Honeywell was a dressmaker, specializing mostly in remodeling and copying. She didn't do it very well and was of the opinion that people were fools not to buy their clothes off racks as she did, but she had inherited the business from her sister, who had married and gone to live in California. It was a humble but a going concern, and the legatee, though something less than a Hattie Carnegie, was realist enough to appreciate a source of income when she saw it. At the time of her inheritance she had been widowed for about six months and was finding the going hard, so seizing her opportunity and her two children, Bierne and her sister Stella, by the hand she left Syracuse and moved bag and baggage to New York, where she picked up the metaphorical threads—the real ones remained on the carpet—and subduing her dislike and mitigating, to some extent, her ignorance of her new trade, took to the needle.

That had been twelve years ago. After Stella married, Mrs. Honeywell's brother had come to live with them so that with her narrow profits, his rent and board, and the generous share of her salary which Bierne contributed, they managed to bump along.

Her daughter had learned not to expect very much of Mrs. Honeywell. That gracious living so eloquently touted in the homemakers' pages of the newspapers and in smart magazines roused small response in the amply upholstered maternal bosom and, truth to tell, under her mother's roof, never having experienced it, Bierne did not miss it unduly. Her work, however, brought her into contact with a different world, and this evening, having just left an atmosphere of order and comparative luxury, she found the glory hole created by Mrs. Honeywell unaccustomedly irksome.

She stood for a moment in the doorway watching her family. Uncle Ben was in his shirt sleeves and stocking feet reading the evening paper, while her mother absorbed her favorite publication—*Detective Story* magazine—and munched contentedly from a tin of salted peanuts. The third member of the group, the radio sports analyst, uttered his penetrating pronouncements unheeded.

Mrs. Honeywell, turning a page, looked up. When she saw her daughter, the features of her plump, bland, pretty face rearranged themselves into an expression of wounded maternity. She leaned over and clicked off the radio. "There you are!" she said in her calm voice. "Uncle Ben and I were worried to death about you. I do think you might call up when you're going to be late. When are we going to get any supper, I'd like to know?"

"I'm sorry, Mother, but I couldn't very well call. I was working at somebody's house. You might have started dinner; you knew I'd be right along."

"How could I? What was I supposed to use for food till you got here?"

"But you said this morning you had everything in except bread and the pork chops."

"Is that all that's in those two big bags? Bread and pork chops?"

"Oh, Mother, of course not, but we needed a lot of supplies; everything's about used up."

Mrs. Honeywell registered amazement. "It is?"

Bierne often thought it would be a good idea if there were some kind of a gage on soaps and cereals and kitchen matches to warn the consumer when they were running low, the way the indicator on the dashboard of an automobile warns of an empty gas tank. At least Mrs. Honeywell would be prepared. As it was, the bottom of the coffee can always caught her off guard and she looked resentfully at the last grain of rice as though, guppy-like, it had devoured its companions unbeknown to her.

Uncle Ben slipped his feet back into his shoes and with the air of one who recognizes man's work when he sees it shuffled toward his niece. "Here, kid, let me take those for you." He relieved Bierne of the groceries and started down the long, narrow hall toward the kitchen. Her mother followed. "Well, now that you are here it won't take me long. What kind of soup do you want? I can open a can of vegetable or cream of celery."

Bierne sighed. The gracious-living press described in mouth-watering prose how French peasants kept a savory pot always simmering on the back of the stove into which they tossed everything—vegetable peelings, bits of bone, leftover scraps of meat, and at the end of a couple of days dished up from these humble ingredients a rich and fragrant soup. It was the thrifty, sophisticated way to eat, the magazines said. Or, if you didn't have soup, you had a succulent stew or ravioli with a tossed green salad, French bread, cheese, and red wine. Such meals must be delicious, Bierne thought, but Mrs. Honeywell did not see eye to eye with European cuisine. When her daughter suggested cooking scraps, her mother looked at her with genuine horror. "Eat garbage?" she exclaimed. "I should say not. It isn't sanitary and it isn't genteel. What kind of people do you think we are?"

Regretting this divergence of mores, Bierne went to her own room to wash up before going in to help with the all-too-familiar menu: canned soup, canned peas, pork chops, mashed potatoes, and brick ice cream. Later on, before they went to bed, her mother and Ben might have a snack of processed cheese and milk or thin, flavorless beer.

As Mrs. Honeywell handed her the food to put on the table she saw she had guessed right, except that they had canned corn instead of peas. However, she was young and hungry, and whatever her mother's shortcomings she knew how to fry a pork chop. Dinner disappeared quickly. When it was over, Uncle Ben unbuttoned his vest, poured himself another cup of coffee, spiked it richly with sugar and cream and, biting off the end of an aromatic cigar, settled back to enjoy the evening.

"Well, sis, what did you do all day? Any dirt or scandal at the office?"

Bierne smiled fleetingly. Uncle Ben's slang clichés got on her nerves sometimes, but he was good and kind and she could not doubt

59

his love for her. "No," she said, "nothing new, just routine work, although we have started on that auction I told you about."

"You said you'd been working at somebody's house," remarked her mother. "Whose?"

Bierne hesitated. By instinct she would gladly have related her daily small adventures but her mother had a sort of prying curiosity which she dreaded. It made her want to protect those people with whom she felt more closely allied than with her own family. Even those she disliked she was reluctant to discuss with an "outsider." But Mrs. Honeywell was quick to take offense. "Of course, if you don't want to tell your own mother, your own flesh and blood . . . Maybe you think it's gay sitting bent over that sewing machine all day. At least you get around, you and Ben, you have interesting lives, but I'm cooped up here alone from morning till night just waiting for you to get home and then what good does it do me? You sit there like a cigar-store Indian."

"Wasn't Stella here today?" Bierne asked. "I thought she was coming over with the baby."

"She never showed up. She never even let me know she wasn't coming until I called her. Petey has a cold, so she was afraid to bring him in the bus. Only Mrs. Gordon and Mrs. Murdock were here and they both made a fuss about their dresses. I do the best I can, but they've got funny shapes. They ought to buy off the rack. I almost told them so," and she sighed heavily.

Bierne felt a sense of compunction. Her mother was filled with self-pity, but it was true that her days for the most part were colorless or relieved only by petty bickering. "It isn't that I don't want to tell you, dear," she lied gently. "I just don't know if you'll be interested. I was at the Allen Goodyears' apartment."

Mrs. Honeywell peered at her suspiciously. "Who are they?"

"Mrs. Goodyear is an editor of *Tang*. Mr. Goodyear, I believe, is quite high up at Carroway's."

Mrs. Honeywell was a reader, but those publishing houses demanding intellectual co-operation from the customers were not her field. Uncle Ben, on the other hand, evinced considerable interest. He worked in a job printing plant: catalogues, menus, greeting cards, laundry lists, a flood of printed matter passed through his hands daily. He could acknowledge a colleague graciously. "Say, that sounds interesting. Carroway's is one of the biggest operators in the business. Did you get to meet the boss?"

"Yes, Mr. Carroway was at the committee meeting for a little while and then later Mr. Goodyear came home. He was terribly nice. So was his wife. I'm going back there next week."

"What's their place like? What did she have on? Are they rich? Who do they know?" Her mother released the flood of questions Bierne feared. With her limited knowledge, she tried to answer as interestingly as she could, yet guardedly, for it was impossible to avoid the impression that Mrs. Honeywell, like a rapacious squirrel, would sort out over and over again these small nuggets of information, fact, and fancy, which she had harvested from the conversation.

It was pathetic but somehow it was shameful, too, this insistence on a vicarious intimacy, this hashing over of other people's lives. It was an attitude, Bierne thought, at once derisive and sycophantic. The bragging of a toady fraught with innuendo. What I know about her! What I know about them!

She wanted desperately to achieve for herself another kind of life. If only Father had lived, she thought, how different everything would be. Stu Honeywell had been a good newspaperman, a man with objectivity and humor, and it was he who brought into his daughters' lives the color and fun of their childhood.

He had fallen in love with Bierne and Stella's mother and married her when he was young. By the time he died he knew her well: her conventionality, her lazy mind, her selfishness, and also her ability to muddle through. Gladys Honeywell didn't have courage exactly but she had a stabilizing calm which, despite frequent references to "my nerves," enabled her to ride life's swells and eddies without loss of equilibrium. And, in a self-centered way, she loved her children.

Mr. Honeywell, on his deathbed, had not worried that his daughters might be neglected, but almost his last words were, "For Christ's sake, Gladys, let the youngsters have a little fun. Don't bring 'em up in your atmosphere of godawful gentility. There are people in the world who are lusty and gay and vigorous, full of guts. That's the way I want my girls to be. Not a brace of God-damn ladies."

Mrs. Honeywell had put such talk down to delirium and had continued plodding along her genteel and godly way.

Stella was married now to Harry Grinitch, and they had a baby. Harry worked conscientiously in a factory where soft drinks were bottled. Bierne longed for a husband and baby, too, but somehow she wanted them in a different atmosphere. Father would have understood. She had not been quite thirteen when he died but she remembered the good talks they used to have and his appreciation of a world where the people were gay and charming and where, if there wasn't wealth, there was money enough for comfort and good taste and pleasant manners. Mr. Goodyear, she thought, had something of that air of urbanity, combined with vigor, which she remembered in her father. He was nice. As she fell asleep she couldn't help hoping he would get home next week before the meeting was over.

5

The Misses Slade and Goodyear, having bade good-by to three of Karen's dinner guests, were renovating their persons in the hostess's bedroom. "What are you worrying about, for goodness' sake?" Poppy demanded. "Everything's going slick."

It was true that the party of eight had gone well all evening but Karen was at present assailed by a qualm. "I know," she said, "but now that the others have left do you think Reams will be bored to death by us?"

Poppy looked at herself in the mirror. Seeing nothing in her small, vivid face, dark hair, and supple figure to repel a member of the opposite sex, she turned her gaze on her friend. There was one thing about Karen: she might be big but when she was in beauty, as she was tonight, it was big beauty. It was a mass of loveliness, Poppy decided, like a flowering tree or a great jewel or a magnificent animal. "I see no reason for Mr. Asher to be bored," she said.

"But he has such a good mind."

"So what? You go to college."

"Yes, I suppose I do. Still . . ."

"And you get very good marks." Poppy spoke severely. She sometimes felt as though Karen was the cowardly lion of Oz and herself a combination trainer-general urging her on to feats of derring-do. The lion, however, had a certain native cunning.

"Now listen, Pops, how are we going to manage Barky, Jr.? I don't see why he couldn't have gone with the others, but since he hasn't, how'll we get him out of here?"

Poppy glanced at her curiously. "I don't see any particular rush about giving the broom to thirty million dollars," she observed. "Besides, he's been looking at you all evening with a *very* interesting look."

An expression of naïve pleasure spread over Karen's face. "What a drip," she said light-heartedly. "So you noticed it too? It wasn't my imagination?"

"Sure I noticed it. Plain as the nose on your face."

"You know what? It's ironic. When he first saw me at that party at Jeannie Fairbanks' he wouldn't give me the time of day. Now that I've met the only guy in the world, he's giving me *looks*." Her grin of joy was like a clap of sunshine.

Poppy shrugged. "Love's magnetic. The best way to get a man is to have one. That's what I keep telling you."

"Yes, but how'll we get rid of him?"

There was a small, deliberate pause. "O.K.," Poppy said. "You asked for it. Dick Oppenheimer muttered something about going some place to dance, didn't he? Since Reams doesn't want to, Mr. O. and I will sweep Barky boy along in the mad tumult of our exit and you lovebirds can be alone."

"But if you all leave at once Reams may think he has to go too."

"Sweetie, look, you've got to take *some* chance in life. What's that thing about the omelet and the eggs? Come on. You look absolutely beautiful. The great author may have been wounded in the war but they didn't get his eyes, did they?"

The young ladies gave a final tweak to their hair, a final tug to their girdles, and, satisfied with the improvement of the scenery, returned to the drawing room, where Reams was engaged in conversation with the despised Barclay and Horace Oppenheimer's son, Dick. Both young men interested and amused him; he was indeed more at ease with them than with the girls. From the way Karen had worded her invitation he had arrived expecting something in the line of a large buffet supper which had been, actually, her original intention. A subsequent consultation with Poppy altered the plan. "Listen, dope," that strategist had remarked, "the whole point of the evening is for you two to get to know each other better. How can you do that with a quiet little dinner of fifty? Keep it cozy."

"But the family said I could have a real party."

"Have it another time. When you've got him embedded in concrete."

Accordingly, the enigmatic eight. It had worked too. Karen and Reams had got to know more about each other, but what Reams learned or strongly suspected, though it flattered and touched him, also made him uneasy. He would have had to be remarkably insensitive not to have been aware that he roused in Karen something other than a sense of sporting comradeship. She might be a shy girl, as Georgiana had assured him, but so much warmth and enthusiasm flowed from her it was like basking in sunshine. A certain amount of warmth, say the balmy days of May, was gratifying, but Reams had an uncomfortable feeling he had best proceed gingerly lest he release the grilling rays of July.

His situation would require nice balance with a contemporary; with the infant of his mistress it was alarming, but apparently it was his destiny to be liked by Goodyear women, and they had for him, even the youthful Karen, a potent magnetism.

He was waiting now for Georgiana to come home. Allen was in Washington, Karen had said, and her mother was dining with the Quicks and going to the movies with them. When Georgiana had left Reams's apartment the evening before she had said gravely, "I shall be out when you come to the house tomorrow night, it's a children's party," and he had asked in alarm, "Good God, what are you letting me in for?" Secure in his desire for her, Georgiana had been gaily magnanimous. "Karen wanted a party and she wanted to invite you. My daughter is very attractive; I thought you would enjoy it."

Well, he had, even though he felt a bit deoriented and certainly the two young men were pleasant companions. Due to a bad football knee, Dick had been unable to get into either service during the war but he had toured the European and Pacific theaters with a USO camp show, and his account of their adventures was both hilarious and grim. Barclay Hamilton, Jr., had served three years in the Navy and they were comparing their experiences.

64

The heir to one of America's great fortunes, this tall, thin, shy young chap impressed Reams as a distinctly responsible and intelligent citizen. It was difficult for him to believe that any two girls could be as indifferent to the Hamilton advantages as the two Graces, who had temporarily withdrawn, seemed to be. Karen, perhaps. If her interest lay elsewhere. Apparently she was the straight line made flesh, the shortest distance between two points, one of which at the moment was herself, the other, Reams. But Poppy! She was a different story. Pretty as they come, and funny, too, but a sly minx if ever he saw one. The longer they stayed out of the room the better off a man was. Besides, Dick Oppenheimer was a good conversationalist.

Alas, no masculine paradise lasts forever. Glancing up, he saw them in the doorway. Karen, the royal young lioness, Poppy, the sleek little vixen.

Considering that with her remarks in the bedroom her friend had relinquished any priority she might have held, Poppy seated herself, with intention, beside the unsuspecting Barclay.

With their advent the conversation veered gradually from the theaters of war to those of Broadway. Dick Oppenheimer, averse to taking a position in his father's organization yet as keen about the entertainment business as Horace was, had got himself a job as casting director for a prominent producer. Full of the new play they were about to do, he was talking enthusiastically of the plot and the actors they were engaging to appear in it. "The damnedest thing has happened," he said. "I think we've got a find, a real find, in a fellow who's never acted in his life, or so little as makes no matter. He's not young, either, middle-aged guy, but stage-struck. He read the part like a million bucks. I think Miles'll give it to him. The fellow's been a broker or something all his life. Hell of a publicity story."

Poppy and Karen looked at each other. Poppy turned quite pale.

"A middle-aged broker?" she croaked.

Dick nodded. "I think he said broker, and I know he's well in his forties."

She moistened her lips. "Did he mention a family?"

"No, but I suppose he has one. Say, that's a funny thing. By golly, he's got the same name as yours: Slade, Reuben Slade. Do you know him by any chance?"

Poppy made an effort at jauntiness but her voice cracked oddly. "Oh no, never heard of him. He's just my old man, that's all, the author of my being."

Dick looked at her in admiration. "Well, what do you know! Say, he's got a lot of guts starting out in the theater at his age."

She gave a sickly smile. "He's got a lot of family too. Do you mind telling me whether your boss is paying him a salary or is *he* paying for the opportunity?"

"Oh, he's getting a salary," Dick assured her. "Of course the part isn't big, so it doesn't pay much, but believe me it's something he can make a hit in."

"And get other jobs on the strength of it? And go *on* acting?"

"Bound to."

Poppy groaned and then, since she was already so bowed by his revelation, one last bitter drop could make no difference—"Is it—is it a butler part?" she asked faintly.

Dick laughed. "Lord no. It's a fellow who owns a small business he's trying to hold on to and one of those big chain organizations want to move in on him. Man versus machine sort of thing. Damned gripping."

Karen drew a breath of relief. "You see, Poppy, it's business. Your father will be fine."

"Why, of course," Reams said encouragingly; "probably get a big Hollywood contract."

It was obvious that her father's call to art found no echo in his daughter's breast, but the idea of money might assuage her anguish. Still Poppy shuddered. "When do rehearsals start?"

"As soon as the cast is set. We ought to be under way in a week. Ten days at the most."

"I see." She turned to her hostess. "Karen, is there any of that roast beef left from dinner? I better start stoking up. The lean, hard years are ahead, kids."

"I shouldn't think so," Mr. Hamilton said unexpectedly. "I should think a man who has the courage to do what he wants in that way would make a success of it. I envy him."

Poppy gave him a clinical look. Money was all very well, but who wanted a loony on their hands?

"Why do you say that?" Reams asked. To his own intense chagrin,

Barclay blushed. "I—I think I know how he feels. I want to paint. Professionally, I mean. My family's against it because as the oldest son they feel I ought eventually to be head of our interests. I've been brought up to it ever since I was a kid." And after a pause he added, "They may be right. I believe I have talent, but we probably have too much money for me ever to be really good and I respect painting. I wouldn't want to be a mediocrity." He spoke of the money naturally. The family name was old and the family fortune so long a part of the American scene it was affectation to ignore it.

"Oh," said Karen, "I think that's wonderful of you, I do indeed." Barky might be a drip, but those were distinguished sentiments. She respected them. Mr. Hamilton looked at her gratefully. Mr. Asher could appreciate his feeling. The warmth of her voice made him think of sunlight on golden fur. Poppy's reaction cooled the air a little. That Karen! A big, awkward, beautiful lion and treacherous, like all the cat family. Pretending she couldn't get beaux and then melting all over them like butter, which was just what the fools loved.

Dick, too, was conscious of a slight irritation but for a different reason. "I don't see what money's got to do with it," he objected.

"I do," Reams said. "Very few people are willing to subject themselves to the slogging grind, the heartaches and setbacks of a creative job if they don't have to do it to earn a living."

Reams knew whereof he spoke. To him writing was a locked battle between himself and the enemy, his theme. Heaving, sweating, grunting, lips set grimly in silent combat, he fought his way to the end of his tale. For him the enjoyable interludes were few and far between. For anyone voluntarily to subject himself to such grueling punishment without the spur of the landlord and the Income Tax Department pricking him on seemed to him masochism. He said as much.

"O.K.," Dick observed, "but if people only work for money how do you account for the ones who keep slugging long after the need has passed?" He was thinking of his father.

"Listen, boy," Reams said, "in our day the need never passes, it costs too much to live, but if there are a few—the rare ones who don't need the money—they're stuck with the habit. Their shop is the only thing they know. If they lose that they're goners. Nothing to fill their days."

"Hear! Hear! I agree with the professor." Georgiana stood laughing in the doorway. She had arrived home in good humor. She had just seen an entertaining picture with Lola and Peter and it was pleasant to come in and find the young people still there and Reams comfortably ensconced in her own home. It amused her to think of him as the father of a child or two.

Her pleasure found no counterpart in Karen, whose heart sank at the sight of her. *Why* had her mother come back so early? It was mean. Now her one wonderful chance to have Reams to herself was ruined.

Innocent of transgression, Georgiana greeted her daughter's guests. Reams came over to her with both hands outstretched. "High time you got home. Rumors are that you've been to the movies. Prove it. What picture did you see, who was in it, how does it end?"

A look of comic guilt spread over her face. "You've trapped me," she said dramatically. "I was really in a west side hotel with my lover. How did you suspect it? How did you ever guess?"

Karen hoped that her mother was tired, that she'd say hello to everybody and excuse herself and go to bed, but before the wish was half formulated Georgiana sat down, prepared to enjoy her youthful companions and the pleasure she experienced in Reams's company. There was a bloom on her these days, and Karen noted with reluctant pride the way Dick and Barclay hovered about her, asking if they couldn't mix her a drink, offering to put another log on the fire, lighting her cigarette, but she saw with swift jealousy the admiration and amusement in Reams's eyes as he watched her, and she heard his laughter at her mother's sallies with a sick heart. He likes her better than he does me, she thought. He just thinks of me as a kid, some sort of an appendage. That's *stupid*. Pioneer women were married and had babies at my age.

Georgiana was not deliberately trying to wean Reams's attention from her daughter—she felt secure in her hold over him, yet that security was not yet complete enough for her not to take joyous note of the quick interest, not to be gratefully aware of the excitement that flickered between them. Karen felt the limelight of her brief

68

popularity dimming and knew from Poppy's renewed warmth and the little hug she gave her that the feeling was justified.

Poppy herself, taking the practical view of when a game is over, in the particular game she had in mind it was definitely with the arrival of a parent in the home, decided to call it quits and turned with a dazzling smile to Mr. Hamilton. "Well," she said, "what was all this talk about dancing?"

Dick spoke up. "That was my talk. I still think it's good. How about it, Karen?"

Karen glanced at Reams. He had stated earlier and with emphasis that he was not a dancing man but possibly, now he had seen Georgiana, he would agree to go. How wonderful if he did. It would mean that he wanted to be with her, Karen, and then coming home in the taxicab they'd be alone and who could tell? Apparently no such idea occurred to him, however. Engrossed in conversation with her mother, he looked around only when the general movement of the group distracted him. Mr. Hamilton, too, seemed reluctant to leave, but Poppy had no intention of putting up with that sort of nonsense. On Dick's unfortunate disclosure of her father's theatrical activities she had groaned inwardly, considering her chances of interesting the Hamilton millions out the window, their predilection for conservative alliances being well known, but evidently this fabulous character didn't think her old man so balmy after all. Suppose he *had* been giving Karen looks all evening? Poppy had promised to remove him from the premises and she would keep her promise. The fact that the circumstances were now somewhat altered was no fault of hers.

"Darling," Georgiana said to her daughter, "since Reams doesn't dance I'm sure he won't mind if you run along with the others. Will you, Reams?"

He was about to answer, "God, no," but Karen's blatant affection shone so brightly from her eyes that he hadn't the heart to send her packing like a kid sister. "I would miss her very much," he said firmly, "only you're not to stay home on my account. I'm going soon anyhow."

That was enough for Karen. She waved vaguely behind her at her departing guests. "Good-by," she murmured happily, "it was lovely having you. See you soon."

Her mother felt some irritability. What an unnatural child! Why didn't she want to dance? It would be so pleasant to sit quietly chatting by the fire, just she and Reams. The children would be gone for hours, and with Allen out of town till morning . . . They had never been together in her own room. It would be lovely.

Barclay, Jr., was swept out against his will, but he overcame his mousehood enough to assure Karen that he would telephone her soon.

"Mmmm," she said. She barely heard the rustle of thirty million dollars leaving the room.

Alone with the two women, the one who held for him a deep attraction, the other who amused and touched him, both of whom cared for him, Reams felt the need of fortification. Since rising to say good night to the others he had been pacing restlessly. Now he paused. "Could I have a nightcap before I go?"

Karen flew to the liquor table. "Of course. What would you like? Scotch? Bourbon?"

"A little scotch, please, and plain water."

"Mother, do you want a drink?"

"A mild one."

"I think I'll have one too."

Karen so rarely availed herself of this privilege that Georgiana suspected her present highball to be an act of defiance for Reams's benefit. She watched her daughter with rueful amusement. To be young was awful, yet why, oh, why, as one's poise increased did one's skin have to sag? Georgiana had long thought God inept, and never more so than in His mismanagement of the balance between one's appearance and one's emotional stability. There was Karen looking large, able, and beautiful and being insecure as a house of cards, and here was she, definitely at her best with shaded lights but calm, capable of arousing and experiencing a mature passion and truly appreciative of the best in a talent like Reams's.

Karen seated herself on the sofa next to her idol. Alone with him she would not have dared, it would have seemed too much like inviting a pass, yet how sweet if only they had been alone. Reams winked at her and raised his glass. She watched him drink as though no one before him had ever executed so brilliant and complex a maneuver. What to say to rivet his attention on herself so that he and Georgiana wouldn't get off on some impersonal discussion of books? "Have you finished your Christmas shopping yet?" The question hit him like a pebble from a slingshot and surprised him in mid-swallow.

"Why, no," he said, with something between burp and gulp, "I haven't even started."

Karen looked at him aghast. "You haven't? But there's only two more days to go."

"My list is short," he assured her, making a mental note that it had just lengthened.

"We're counting on you Christmas night, you know, Reams," Georgiana reminded him, "for our buffet supper."

"Oh, are you coming?" Karen's hopes soared. How wonderful of Mother! They said propinquity was the thing. If she and Reams could be together often enough, casually enough, he'd come to feel that he was her friend just as much as Georgiana's. She could get to be part of his life, a part he wouldn't want to be without.

"I'll be here," Reams said. "I'm looking forward to it." Since becoming Georgiana's lover he had had some hesitancy about frequenting the apartment, he felt uncomfortable when Allen was home, but he supposed Georgiana was right when she said that he had been a reasonably frequent visitor, it would look odd if he suddenly stopped calling on them. "Either Allen will grow suspicious," she said, "or he'll think you're miffed because Carroway isn't doing your book."

Delicacy, Reams decided, was a selective emotion; a lover felt too delicate to go to the husband's house but not too delicate to take the husband's wife. He sighed and went. And now he was face to face with his problem, the news which, ever since he had made his decision, he hadn't had the courage to break to Georgiana when alone with her. Karen's presence strengthened him. She might soften the blow if her mother interpreted it as such or at least dissipate the thunderbolt which he feared might be loosed upon him.

"I'm looking forward to the party, especially," he said, "since it turns out it will be my last one."

"Entering a monastery?" Georgiana inquired.

"No." He held his breath and plunged. "I'm going to Portugal. Sailing December thirtieth."

"Portugal!" Karen's tone was incredulous. He might as well have told her he was going by rocket to the moon.

When Georgiana spoke her voice was so quiet he barely heard her. "When did you decide this?"

"There's been a deal in the offing for a couple of weeks. I haven't mentioned it because it was indefinite, but it was closed today." It had been closed three days before, but this was the day he had got up courage to tell her.

"How long will you be gone?"

"That's indefinite, too, though it's bound to be some months."

"Will you be in Paris at all?" Karen quavered. "Mother's said that *maybe* there's a chance of our going to Paris next spring, didn't you, Mum? It would be *dreamy*."

"Well, I—I did think that just possibly—after college closes, of course." Georgiana spoke distractedly. "Be a good child and go fetch another bottle of whisky from the liquor closet, that one's a dead soldier."

Karen turned to Reams. "Try to persuade her, will you? I'm working on her, too, and my roommate's working on *her* parents. If Mother can't get away maybe we could still come, maybe we could meet up."

"Don't worry," Reams assured her, "in my own interests I want her over there."

"Please. Get the whisky," Georgiana said.

When they were alone Reams crossed to her swiftly. "Darling, I'm sorry it came about this way, believe me, but I wanted you to know."

"You might have told me when we were alone." And after a moment, "What is the deal you speak of?"

"A series of articles for the *Saturday Evening Post*. I mentioned it to you once, but at that time it was just an idea tossed around over a couple of drinks. Now they've come through with a solid offer, a postwar comparison between the neutral countries and the belligerents. It's good money and an interesting assignment. I don't feel I can afford to turn it down."

"No, I—I can see that you wouldn't want to do that," she said, and her voice was strained, "but must you go immediately? Wouldn't early summer do as well? We've talked so much about being in Europe together . . ."

72

"I know, G, and I'm counting on it. For spring. It's not so far away, you know, January, February, March. April I shall begin to hope. You promised. April or May you said, ahead of the family. If anything should happen at *Tang* try to get that job in the *Distaff* Paris office. Try your damnedest."

"I will, of course, but that's nothing to count on. Oh, Reams, don't go now. If you wait till your book comes out you could demand double the money, you could——" They heard the telephone ring in the library down the hall. Georgiana drew away from him. It rang again, and then Karen called out, "It's for me. I'll bring the scotch in a minute. Don't parch till I get back." The library door closed. They turned to each other, and Reams drew her close. "Don't think this isn't hard for me, sweetie, it is, but we knew I was going, this just happens to push things ahead a bit, also I get to Europe at the expense of the magazine. But I couldn't have held off much longer in any event. I've got to get started on my book. A couple of the stories are blocked out, but I haven't actually begun work and time's awasting. You do understand, don't you?"

His need to work she did understand, albeit reflecting that her idea that he should write for magazines had boomeranged with a vengeance. What was harder to comprehend was his unwillingness to compromise with that work in order to be with her, she who would have been flexible as a Tammany politician in finagling her job so that it should dovetail with his plans and her desires. It was that attitude which Allen had in mind when he had accused her of being a perpetual amateur in business. There were tears in her eyes as she murmured, "What am I to do without you? How shall I manage when you're away?"

"But, darling, it's not forever. Three, four months, that part depends on you. I'm surprised at you." He gently kissed away a tear that slipped down her cheek. She, too, was surprised. When she had become his mistress no latent sense of self-preservation had signaled to her to protect herself; she had thought triumphantly that at forty-seven with the goal achieved one had done with heartache. How strange to find that she cared with the intensity of a girl caught up in her first love affair.

Reams also was discovering that the separation was going to be a little tougher than he bargained for, but since his attachment for her, though genuine, was warm rather than profound he knew that missing her would pass. At the moment he very much wanted her to join him in Europe, but if she were delayed would his concern be as poignant three months from now? His objectivity irritated him, but he had trained himself to stand aside and analyze emotion, and it made no difference to the analysis that the emotion was his own. What they shared together was delightful, it was pleasant to think that after an interlude they might resume; if not, they had the memory, so much more comforting than regret over a missed opportunity. He drew her close to him and kissed her hard. When they broke away she gasped a little for breath. "Is that supposed to last me until spring?"

"No. That's supposed to last you till tomorrow. Between now and my sailing date I thought we might store up quite a few memories."

"You mean I should have enough inventory on hand to last me till we meet? Oh, dear, oh, dear, if only it worked that way." He kissed her again, but this time she pushed him away.

"Don't. You didn't have to go now. You're just using this job as a plausible excuse."

"An excuse for what?"

"To get away."

"That's unfair," he said angrily. My God, why did she have to wrangle? The note of rueful sadness had been charming, but with a woman there always had to be accusations. Thinking to hear a move down the hall, his hand went hastily to his mouth. "How's the lipstick situation?"

"Wait a minute." She touched his lips with her handkerchief. "There. You look like the great unloved."

The library door was thrown open and a moment later, when Karen appeared, bottle in hand, Reams was lighting a cigarette and Georgiana was straightening one of the candles in the sconces above the mantelpiece. "Who was your call from, darling?" she asked. Karen blushed. Sometimes it annoyed her, her mother's curiosity about who had phoned but now, if Poppy was right and the way to get a beau was to have one, it worked out very well.

"What do you know?" she said. "It was Barky."

As a vent to his annoyance Reams spoke with unexpected sharpness. "At this time of night? I should say he was importunate."

74

Karen's heart bounded. He was jealous! What heaven. *Why* was he going away? There must be some plea, some attachment that would hold him. "What about your book?" she urged. "Don't you want to be here when it's published? An event like that! The Barnstable people will be in despair." The grief of the Barnstables shielded her own.

Reams's mood changed. She was a sweet kid. At least you knew where you stood with her. Not like her mother, thank God, who, just as you thought you had struck the rhythm of her moods, passionate desire or autumnal melancholy, suddenly swerved into shrewishness and suspicion and there you were, made to appear an old-fashioned cad when you had intended nothing but warmth and honesty of intention. Benjamin Franklin was a jackass, the sugar-coated lie was obviously with women, the only *modus operandi*. As a change of pace he turned his attention to Karen. With children you could at least make truthful jokes. "The fact is," he said, "I want the Barnstable people to bear the brunt. I'm glad this opportunity has come up because I'm an arrant coward. If my book gets terrible reviews, I won't have the guts to read them."

"But they'll be wonderful."

He smiled. "If they are, will you send them to me?"

"Oh, I will," she said fervently. "I'll clip everything."

"Thanks. I'm your fan, Karen, your grateful fan. You're a grand girl."

"And you won't forget about us? Mother and me, till we get to Paris in June?"

"I'll not forget, but June seems a little distant. Can't you shave it a bit?"

Karen, opening the bottle of scotch, felt almost happy. "I'm afraid not. I've got to stick around till the grind finishes. Mother might get over a little sooner, of course." He had spoken so sweetly, he had looked at her with such honest affection, she could afford to give her mother a little leeway.

Reams glanced at her obliquely. "I don't know that your mother would care to come."

Georgiana's lips curved in a thin scarlet smile. "I would care to very much. I shall be curious to see you turning out stories and articles like a little factory. American assembly-line methods backed by European inspiration should send you far."

Karen, having got the bottle open, took up his glass to refill it. She did it gravely, as befitted the last rites rendered a loved one. "It's plain water, isn't it?"

Reams watched her pour the whisky till the glass was nearly half full. "When," he said, "and if you don't mind I'll take it straight." He picked it up, clicked his heels, and bowed to Karen and to Georgiana. "To the feminine mind."

6

The January rain fell in long, icy splinters, pricking their skin and chilling their bones, as Georgiana and Bierne Honeywell stood on the curb huddled under an umbrella waiting for Allen to pick them up in the car.

They had been looking at the old Murray Hill Hotel as a possible site for the literary auction, feeling that that relic of another era, regarded with affection and nostalgia by so many New Yorkers and soon to be destroyed, might be an added attraction in bringing in the public.

Knowing that Allen would be unable to park, the two women stood their wet, dark ground at Park Avenue and Fortieth Street until Georgiana at last spotted the car. They waved frantically and, after a bout of aggressive tooting and an exchange of loaded looks with a blocking taxi driver, Allen swerved to the curb.

Georgiana gave Bierne a little shove. "Go on, go on, get in," she said, and, as the girl demurred out of politeness, "Don't be foolish, Bierne, we're getting drenched." Bierne slid into the seat next to Allen and Georgiana followed her, slamming the car door and tossing a pointed critique of his ancestry at a madly honking driver behind them.

"You remember Miss Honeywell," she said a little breathlessly, attempting, with no marked success, to toss the soaking umbrella into the back seat without wetting them.

Allen, intent on traffic, gave Bierne a quick sidelong glance and a cursory nod. "Of course. How are you?"

"I'm fine, thank you, Mr. Goodyear. Hope I'm not crowding you."

He grunted. "Where to, G?" he asked when, after a minute or two, he had turned east and was headed uptown again. They were all three wearing bulky coats, and the front seat was a tight fit. Georgiana extricated her arm with difficulty and looked at her wrist watch. "It's past six. I expect we might as well go straight to the Dauzats'. They want us to come in for cocktails, and it's hopeless trying to get home first in this traffic."

"Right," he said. "What about you, Miss Honeywell? Can we drop you off at your house?"

"Oh no, please don't; it's way out of your way. If you could just let me off at the corner of Fifty-third, that'll be fine."

"Nonsense," put in Georgiana. "You can't walk on a night like this. Allen, suppose you drop me at Germaine's and then take Miss Honeywell home and come on back."

Familiar with the Gordian knot which was New York traffic on a rainy night, Allen's every chivalrous instinct did not leap in his breast at his wife's suggestion, yet she was right. The girl couldn't very well walk in the storm and she'd never get a cab. The idea of asking her to come into the Dauzats' with them crossed his mind, but though it would have simplified matters he suppressed the impulse. Women were funny about things like that. You never knew when they'd consider another guest a good idea and when they'd freeze at the thought. Being wife-broken he understood that extra men were practically always permissible. With an extra woman you watched your step.

Georgiana was fiddling with the heater. "Doesn't this damned thing work yet? The car's like an icebox."

"The garage hasn't got around to it." Allen spoke with resigned disgust. "I told them to take care of it when it first broke down."

"About a month ago! I bet you haven't said a word since."

"Well, there's no use nagging them. Unfortunately they don't need our trade and the result is bum service."

"Then why don't we go to another garage?"

"Because it's the same story all over town. They all have more cars than they can handle, they charge outrageous rentals, and nothing gets done."

"Unless you keep at them. Isn't that so, Bierne? You've got to follow through, but try to get a man to understand it!"

77

Bierne made a small non-committal sound. It was undeniably cold in the car, and probably Mr. Goodyear should have been more demanding of the garage, but she did wish they wouldn't wrangle. If only they understood the automobile they drove doubtless it was something quite easy to fix.

Bierne had noticed that mechanical objects were often bones of contention among the married though they seemed to her an unnecessary hazard. She herself was an excellent mechanic. She had a small but highly efficient tool box at the office and saved the Manhattan Aid Association more money than they knew in minor repairs. She was just a little scornful of people who were helpless before inanimate objects and could herself conquer a jammed bureau drawer or put up bathroom shelves with ease.

The Goodyears drove up Park Avenue in a kind of armed truce, and at the door of the Dauzats' apartment house Georgiana got out and bade Bierne good night. "I'll be back as soon as I can," Allen called after her, and swung the car over to Madison and headed south again.

"Now, then, Fifty-third and where?" he asked.

"Just this side of Third Avenue. But I do feel it's the most awful imposition. I'm keeping you from your party." She seemed genuinely distressed about it.

"You mean that cocktail brawl? Forget it."

"You don't mind?"

Allen winked at her. The small act surprised him. It was years since he had winked at a pretty girl, and he was not, he considered, fundamentally a winking man. "I'll tell you a secret," he said. "Like everybody else in New York I hate cocktail parties and like everybody else I go whenever I'm asked. I have no will power, but an honest alibi is a godsend."

Bierne laughed. "I should think they'd be fun, but since you don't like them I wish I lived in Greenwich Village. Then you could be really good and late."

Stopped by a red light, Allen turned and looked at her. "I call that true friendship," he said. Her profile was charming and so was her laughter, frank and full-throated. Charming and somehow unexpected. She had seemed so reserved that first day he met her at the house.

"Do you like cocktail parties?" he asked.

"Yes, I do rather, but, of course, I don't go to many."

"Why, I should think——" he began, and then stopped. "Well no, perhaps not."

"Perhaps not what?"

"Well—uh—uh——" Oh, hell, he thought, why not out with it? "You're an extraordinarily pretty girl," he said. "I was going to say I should think you'd be invited to all kinds of shindigs, and then it occurred to me that it's mostly women who plan them, and I've noticed they often don't invite the pretty unattached ones."

"Thank you," she said. "That's very complimentary even if it isn't so, but there are other reasons too."

"May one ask what they are?"

"Well, you see, I'm quite busy, and if a person wants to go to parties he should be able to give them in return."

She spoke with a dignity which amused Allen and touched him at the same time. It wasn't only the press of business, he suspected, which prevented her from founding a salon. Her salary as secretary in a charity organization couldn't be princely, and then there was that family she had spoken of. Conceivably the Café Society touch was not their forte.

He was right about her income, but there was a more subtle reason too. As Bierne saw it it had to do with the class one belonged to. Her family and their friends weren't the drinking element. Their morals and capacity weren't involved; it was a question of custom, just as their food was.

In her mind the cocktail-party people were the same ones who owned extensive cookbook collections and ate the meals described in the elegant magazines. Bierne's people ate Mrs. Honeywell's kind of food and either went their whole lives without a drink, unless they happened to catch a chill or there was a wedding in the family, or else they were inclined to sporadic and violent binges. The custom of pleasant social drinking was foreign to them. Mr. Goodyear, leading the kind of life he did, probably couldn't understand that. "In a way," she said, only half aware that her conclusion might prove unintelligible, "it's rather like the people who bathe just on Saturday night."

Allen proceeded cautiously, but from the pleased way she reacted he flattered himself he had caught her implication. "You mean some people only drink for a special occasion? Weddings, christenings, and so forth."

"Exactly! That's just what I mean." The eager, admiring glance she turned on him was distinctly pleasant. "Of course," she went on, "I imagine cocktail parties are more fun if you have someone to go with. Stella, she's my sister, used to say that when she got married she and her husband would go to lots of them, but do you know I've been to more than they have."

Allen laughed. "Perhaps her husband doesn't like them either and has stronger will power than I."

"I think it's Harry's business that affects him."

"Oh?"

"Yes. He's with a bottling firm for soft drinks."

"Harry sounds like a man of integrity."

"He isn't a teetotaler exactly, he's just conscientious. All wool and a yard wide. That's what Uncle Ben says."

Allen swerved suddenly to avoid colliding with a skidding truck and Bierne swayed against him. He was aware of the merest whiff of a delicate pungent fragrance. It was—— What were those flowers, he thought—carnations? That was it, carnations crisp and fragile. The girl drew away. "I'm sorry," she said; "that was kind of sudden."

Allen muttered an imprecation against the driver of the truck and turned back to her. "Tell me something else about Harry." He felt a desire to know more of her life. At the moment it was as though she were an isolated figure in a jigsaw puzzle. He wanted to fill in the background.

"Oh, Harry couldn't be nicer. Uncle Ben also says he's dull as ditch water but that isn't so, really. It's—well, with Stella and the baby and all I expect he's just content."

Allen looked at her with interest. "Are you against contentment, as such?"

"Not as such, oh no, but Stella and I remembered that our life used to be different when Father was alive, more fun somehow, and we were determined that one day we'd get back to the fun place, but then Stella met Harry and they got married and—— Oh, I don't know, everything changed."

"You've never been married, have you?"

"No. No, I haven't." There was a silence. Two years ago there had been a boy, but nothing had come of it. Or rather something had: in the shape of another girl whom he had gone off with.

"What do you think of marriage?" Allen asked.

"As such?"

"As such."

"If you love a person, I think it must be the most wonderful way to live that there is."

A stop light turned green. Allen shifted gears and the car rolled forward. They were halfway down the block before he spoke.

"Well," he said, "it's orthodox."

In the gloom she couldn't see whether he was smiling or not. The raw night air penetrated through the closed windows and the windshield wipers whipped furiously from side to side trying to keep up with their housework as the rain teemed down. Beside him Bierne shivered and huddled deeper into her coat. The action made him feel sheepish about the heater. Georgiana had been right, of course. She often was. Rightness was a strange trait, he decided, reliable but not endearing. "Saturday night or no," he said to Bierne, "you'd better have a good stiff drink and a hot bath when you get home."

"Yes, I think I will." She was ashamed to tell him that her chances of finding any liquor in the house were slim.

Mrs. Honeywell's normal dissipation was limited to an occasional beer but she did keep a pint flask of rye handy in case of illness. Her daughter devotedly hoped that Uncle Ben had not been pilfering.

A particularly vicious gust of wind and rain buffeted the car. "Goodness, what a night," Bierne murmured. " 'Tain't fit for man nor beast." The observation of the late Mr. Fields came from her so unexpectedly that Allen burst out laughing. "Where did you ever pick that up?"

"What? Man or beast?" He nodded.

"Oh, my father used to say it. W. C. Fields was his favorite comedian. I thought of Father last month when Fields died. He'd have felt badly about it."

"Has your father been dead long?"

"Since I was thirteen." She turned and looked at Allen attentively. "Do you mind if I tell you something?" she asked. Her eyes were blue and her voice was soft. It had been a long time since Allen had experienced such a pleasurable glow in a young woman's company. In the dank confinement of the car he felt strangely buoyant, as though they were bound lightly together in a shining iridescent bubble.

"Tell me anything you like," he said.

"You remind me of my father. There's something in the expression of your eyes and in the way you walk. I noticed it that day in your apartment."

"Oh. Oh, you did. Like your father, eh?" Curiously the bubble seemed to have burst.

"I hope you don't mind."

"Oh no. Not at all. You, uh, you liked your father, I hope?"

"He was the most wonderful man I ever knew."

"Well," Allen said cheerfully, but a sensitive ear might have detected a slight note of strain, "I'm flattered. That's very sweet of you. By the way, I don't believe you've met my daughter, have you? Karen? She must be very nearly your age. Nineteen."

"Oh, I'm way older than that."

"You are?"

"I'm twenty-five."

"Are you really!" Thank God, he thought, that's better. Not good, of course, but better. At least she was out of the cradle.

They had reached the lower Fifties. He circled the block and turned into Fifty-third Street going west. "Here we are," she said. "This first house."

He jammed on the brake abruptly. "So soon?"

For a moment Bierne hesitated. The natural thing would have been to ask him to come in for a drink but she didn't dare. There was probably no liquor in the house anyway, and even if there had been she could foresee her mother's embarrassment at having to receive a stranger. Undoubtedly the sitting room was in disorder, Mrs. Honeywell would burst into a spate of apologies and alibis, Uncle Ben, trying to help things along, would be overly effusive, and Mr. Goodyear would be forced into making strained conversation for a decent interval before he could leave. She decided against the ordeal and held out her hand. "Good night, Mr. Goodyear. I do appreciate your bringing me home; you've been more than kind. I hope you haven't missed the cocktail party entirely."

"Don't worry about that," he said, "but be sure to change into something dry. If you catch cold I'll feel worse than ever about the heater. I'll feel badly about you too."

She smiled. "I'll take care." There was a slight pause. "Well, good-by, thanks again," and she started to open the door.

"Wait," he said; "stay where you are." He reached over into the back seat for the umbrella. "I'll come around and get you up the steps."

"Oh, please don't bother."

"You stay."

Allen climbed out, opened the umbrella with difficulty against the wind, and came around to Bierne's side of the car. "Here, take my arm." Pressed close together, they crossed the pavement and mounted the three or four steps to the low stoop. "Do you have much of a climb?"

"No, we're on the first floor. See, that's my mother's sign in the window."

Allen glanced at the perennially crooked "Honeywell, Gowns." "Oh, your mother's in business also? What an industrious family." He smiled down at the damp, rosy face at his shoulder.

"Uncle Ben works too," she said gravely. "Everybody has to these days." There was something quaint in the way she said it, rather like an old-fashioned child, yet for all her appeal she had an air of self-reliance. He remembered that Georgiana had remarked more than once on her ability.

Standing on the wet, windy doorstep was unpleasant, yet he was reluctant to leave her. "Are you going to be at our house soon again?" he asked.

"Well, I—I really don't know. It depends if Mrs. Goodyear needs me. I hope I may come though, it's such a beautiful house."

"Thank you. I hope you may too."

She smiled. "On a sunny day." How *nice* he is, she thought. How attractive and kind. I don't want him to go, but if he doesn't I'll have to ask him in and it won't work at all, I know it won't. Regretfully she bade him good night again. "Thank you so very, very much but please don't wait any longer; it's you who'll catch your death."

"Good night, Miss Honeywell."

"Good night, Mr. Goodyear."

"Good night."

Bierne went into the vestibule and Allen fought his way down the steps against the wind. She turned to watch him go and waved to him, but the rain streaked past the car window as he drove away and she didn't know whether or not he had seen her or whether he waved back.

7

Georgiana sat in her office at *Tang*, her desk spread with manuscripts and correspondence waiting her attention, but she ignored them. She was engrossed in reading the first reviews of Reams's book, *The Shadowed Path*. Reams had sailed according to schedule, but Barnstable had published it that week and Georgiana read the clippings with a sense of triumph and a sinking heart. As she had suspected, Reams was accepted into high company. Thomas Wolfe, Hemingway, Faulkner, in reference and comparison—the great names dotted the columns. The Barnstable Press was congratulated on bringing to the public a work of originality and power, and a new star blazed in the literary sky.

It was gratifying to have her judgment vindicated, but as she dropped the reviews on her desk and gazed out the window at the milky February clouds she was overwhelmed by a feeling of frustration. Why, why, *why* hadn't Allen been able to publish it? Thinking about him she was beset by an exasperation which softened gradually to sympathy when it was borne in upon her what his own feelings must be. True, Carroway was a successful publishing house with Allen largely responsible for that success; shepherding, encouraging, and belaboring as many writers as he could handle. Still, to muff a good one was never pleasant. He had left the house so early that morning she had barely had time to speak to him.

She called now to her secretary, who sat at a desk behind a glass partition, "Dora, get me Mr. Goodyear, will you? I want to talk to him."

In a few moments Allen's voice came at the other end of the line, "Hello?"

"I've just been reading Reams' reviews," she said.

"Princely, what? You'll be pleased to hear that both the *Times* and *Tribune* are giving it page one of next Sunday's book section."

"I'm sorry, Allen. That you lost it, I mean."

"Thanks, dear. I am, too, but at least it's nice to know our judgment's sound. Think we ought to run up to the net and shake hands? You know, send a cable or something?"

"I think it would be friendly, but make Mr. Carroway pay for it. Him and his sure judgment. Send it from the office."

"That's my plan. I'll suggest he write one too."

Georgiana laughed. "You haven't got a snowball's chance, my friend, of getting him to do it."

"Do you know where Reams is at the moment?" Allen asked.

"No. Don't you?"

"No." He sounded surprised, and his surprise spoiled for her the intimate, relaxed mood of the conversation. It had been pleasant, a congenial tête-à-tête which occurred all too rarely these days. If Allen assumed she knew where Reams was, he assumed she was in communication with him. Well, she was, but not so much as she would have liked. His letters, sent to her office, were infrequent, and it was frustrating to be credited with a game played so meagerly. Her enforced virtue was galling enough without Allen bringing it to her attention and breaking their own small spell at the same time. Really, the man had no tact.

"You have no tact," she informed him.

"I beg your pardon," he said. The frost touched the bloom he, too, was appreciating and withered it. He had meant his inquiry about Reams's whereabouts casually enough, but if she chilled so quickly perhaps his old suspicions were right, and again he was torn between wanting to know and a sense of weariness signaling him to sheer away from a course where he might be confronted with facts a husband would be expected to act upon. "Well," he said, "thanks for calling anyhow. I'll see you tonight. Are we doing anything?"

"No."

"Good. I can get some reading done. I've got a batch of manuscripts to go through, I'll bring them home."

"Do that."

They hung up. The salt had lost its savor.

Georgiana reached for a key in her handbag and unlocking the shallow center drawer of her desk took out a slim packet of Reams's letters. He was not a constant correspondent but what he did send was charming and vital to her happiness. His departure had been a physical shock to which she had difficulty in adjusting herself, and she waited hungrily for his letters as a reassurance that all was well, that he still cared, that he needed her as urgently as she needed him. Her longing, coupled with the still precarious situation of *Tang*, had decided her on a definite course of action, and she glanced now at her watch, waiting impatiently for the time of her appointment with Carter Dunlap. Dunlap was the editor of *Tang* and Georgiana had asked to see him, in the hope of finding out the fate of the department which she edited. The office grapevine was strong in the view that a revolutionary change of policy would eliminate fiction on the grounds, not of quality, but of cost since it was not directly responsible for advertising revenue in the sense that the travel, beauty, fashion, or hostess departments were. If the grapevine was right and her department was to be abolished, she would be lacking in elementary precaution, she told herself, not to go to Germaine Dauzat and ask her outright for a job on the Paris edition of *Distaff*.

An hour later, in Carter Dunlap's office, she essayed a little tactful pumping. Carter was a giant of a man with a shock of white hair, a white mustache, and a burry Scotch manner. He was not uncooperative, but battling as he was with the board of directors in an effort to obtain a hands'-off policy which would permit him to edit the magazine as he saw fit, he avoided frontal attacks from members of his staff anxious for categoric statements on their own departments. He was walking a tight rope himself and any sudden shove or pulling at that rope was disconcerting.

With Georgiana he was concerned both with saving his own face and saving his fiction editor. She was not the most disciplined journalist he had ever met but she had a real flair for her job and her non-professional appeal was considerable. Why the devil couldn't she let well enough alone? "Look here, Georgiana," he said brusquely in answer to her question, "I'm ashamed of you. You're far too experienced a woman to be taken in by all this grapevine stuff. You ought to know me by now. That's not the way I do business. If we were going to close out fiction *you'd* be the one who'd know it, not the mail clerk. What gave you the idea anyhow?"

"Well, Carter, it's nothing new; this office has been on a seesaw for the past six months. It's something of a strain, you must realize that, especially for our department; we have to work so far in advance."

"So what? You've still got a green light. Get your writers, buy any stories you like. In the end, whether they get published or not is my responsibility. If we're stuck with the bill, that's my responsibility too."

"I know that, of course, but—well, my position's difficult. I thought if you *were* contemplating any change of policy and wanted to tell me—you could trust me, you know."

"Sweet God, you sound as though you wanted the department to fold. Do you?"

"Oh, Carter, of course not! What an absurd idea. Why should I want to be out of a job?" She felt uncomfortably hot and hoped to heaven she wasn't blushing.

"Hell," he said, "I don't know why, I don't know what's in the back of your head, but you're a devious female. I don't trust you but I hope you're not up to any shenanigans. You'd be a fool to quit now regardless of what may happen. I have my differences with the board but nobody can say they don't pay well. You won't find a salary like yours on every street corner, my lass, and don't you think it. What's Allen say about this restless fit?"

"I'm not restless. It has nothing to do with me personally. I was merely trying to find out where I stood. If I can work on a long-range basis there are a lot of features I want to get under way. Reams Asher, for instance. His new book is just out to rave reviews. I think possibly we could get him to do a short story now, maybe get him to commit himself to a novel."

"Where is he?"

"Europe."

Carter grunted. "I read one of those notices. If the others are the same, he'll have a head the size of a pumpkin. What makes you think you could get him?"

"I think I might. One way or another."

"If business methods don't work there's always sex, eh?"

"Carter!"

He chuckled. "Don't get the wind up. Besides, you say the fella's in Europe. I don't suppose even your charm can reach across the Atlantic, but it's potent."

"Carter, don't talk nonsense. Asher and I are friends, that's all there is to it."

He eyed her shrewdly. "I've seen you working, lass. A lot of blarney and a tantalizing smitch of promise not exclusively professional, yet enough hard business sense thrown in to make everything appear on the up and up. It's a fine lethal brew. You'd better stick around where you're appreciated."

Georgiana laughed. "Your imagination's far too active, and I should say you're the one with the key to the blarney dispenser, but if I can get Asher to do a piece, you'd like it?"

"Sure."

She left his office a little discomfited. What she had to hope had been on Carter's part merely a shot in the dark had struck home, and regarding her department's future she was no wiser than when she went in. She would have to be careful. Apparently she couldn't yet afford to mention Reams. Ever since their affair and his departure she had tried to avoid any reference to him either with friends or with Allen, but, being in love, she found it almost impossible not to bring his name into conversations on what she believed to be a deceptively casual basis. Dunlap, unfortunately, was not easily taken in. As for herself, the last thing she wanted was to be working on a long-range basis with no hope of getting abroad. She had said it in the hope of allaying suspicion.

A few days later she received a letter from Reams written from Madrid. His publishers had sent him the reviews and his mood was jubilant. "If only you were here to help me celebrate," he wrote, "how lovely it would be. I knew I'd mind if they'd been bad, because I worked so hard, but for that very reason I didn't think I'd be elated over good ones. My job was done. Notices are always a long way after the fact, but the truth is I'm pleased as Punch, and since the story owes much to you, I should like to see your golden eyes shining with approval." He had gone on to ask her how things were at the magazine and had so eloquently expressed his hope of seeing her soon that her desire to be with him, coupled with an evening's bickering with Allen, sent her to Germaine Dauzat asking point-blank for a job on *Distaff*. On hearing her request, Germaine's warm, gurgling French manner had been instantly transformed into cool, calculating French shrewdness. She was not unkind, but Georgiana, appealing to the friend, encountered the businesswoman. Germaine showed controlled interest in the idea of *Tang's* fiction editor working for her magazine, but when she voiced her policy Georgiana found it unexpected. "In a nutshell, my dear," Germaine had said in bringing the interview to a close, "were you free, Claude and I might seriously consider you, but you are not, and in all my years in business I have never raided the staff of another magazine in order to enrich *Distaff*. We build our own people, or if we do take on names and experience, it is only when they are completely disassociated from old ties. Carter Dunlap is my colleague. Why should I work him a hardship by taking you away from him?"

"But, Germaine, I'd be leaving of my own free will, and it's not as though *Distaff* and *Tang* were rivals."

Germaine smiled. "You prove my point. Why injure an editor who is not even a rival?"

Georgiana played one last card. "Supposing I have already made up my mind to leave?"

Germaine glanced at her from under heavily mascaraed lashes. "That, of course, is your own business, but you have not left yet."

"I could do a job for you, Germaine. *If* I leave, will you say yes to Paris?"

As quickly as it had vanished the warm, feathery rolling *r*'d pigeon reappeared. "If, if, if. My pet, who are we to say what may happen? The future one nevair knows. You have experience in our business, you are yourself a chic woman, you want to go abroad, which is more than many candidates do. Possibly it might work out, but salary we have not yet discussed."

"That I'm sure we could get together on."

"Why, by the way, are you so anxious to go to Paris?" Germaine asked curiously. "You would leave Allen, you would leave Karen, you would not miss them, no?"

"Certainly I'd miss them, but 'Careers for Women,' what can you expect? That's the reverse of the coin," and Georgiana stood up. A friendly sincerity regarding the job, not over-anxiety, was the impression she wished to convey. Besides, she couldn't afford further questioning on her motives.

Germaine laughed. "Well, we shall see. You may completely change your mind and not wish to come to us, after all, but, in any event, how about dinner next week? Thursday night, eight o'clock."

"We'd love it," and the ladies parted on a social note, their business still hanging fire.

Throughout the following week Georgiana tussled with doubt and indecision. Should she give up her position on *Tang* or should she not? Should she try, possibly, for a leave of absence? On what grounds? And, besides, there was the money question. Perhaps she didn't need so large a salary as she was making, but she certainly couldn't afford to be without work for any length of time. No, a job in Paris was the perfect solution. And if at the end of the year Reams came back to New York, as he had planned before he left, what then?

The ultimate conclusion of their relationship was misty in her mind. She didn't think of it actually as concluding, it would evolve. Into what she didn't analyze. Sometimes she faced squarely the great disparity in their ages, at others it seemed unimportant. Reams was in love with her, men *had* been known to marry women years older than themselves. She ignored the fact that in the two or three cases she personally knew of the husbands were homosexuals and the wives rich. Whether she wanted a divorce from Allen she did not analyze either. True, they sometimes found each other irksome, part of their time was passed in boredom and some, the smaller part, in bitter wrangling, but he was, after all, her husband. He was an always-to-be-counted-upon escort, and in moments of candor, her sense of realism unclouded by passion and a nostalgia for romance, she acknowledged that the physical presence of a member of the opposite sex was the cement that held many marriages together, particularly from the woman's point of view. Also, of course, in most unions the husband was a vital source of supply, although in their case that didn't count so much. Come to think of it, they had more

90

than many couples. They were together, through habit perhaps, but also from choice rather than economic need.

The time was coming, however, when she would have to make up her mind one way or another. Only a couple of days ago she had seen Germaine under the drier as she was leaving their mutual hairdresser. Germaine, shouting to hear her own voice above the drier's roar, had asked whether or not she had come to any decision about "you know what." Georgiana had winked at her. "You'd be surprised," she shouted back, and passed on to the desk to pay her bill.

The question, under scarcely official circumstances, had sparked her hopes anew. It must be that the Dauzats really wanted her and were playing hard to get. Impulsively she determined to throw over the *Tang* job. It was scarcely a step she could take without consulting Allen, however, and when they did discuss it his advice was to stay where she was. "It doesn't sound to me as though you had any assurance of the *Distaff* job, G, and from what you tell me you haven't even come to terms with the Dauzats. Money's too hard to get to give up a fifteen-thousand-dollar-a-year job for the off-chance of something less good."

"But it isn't an off-chance, Allen; they want me."

"Have they made you a firm offer?"

"That isn't the way the Dauzats do business. They're Latins. They don't enjoy it unless the deal is subtle and roundabout. Offers and rejections and counterattacks. They *expect* to bargain, you know that."

"I know you sometimes make an offer you hope will be accepted, all the time suspecting you may have to raise it if you want someone badly enough, but at least you make the offer. That's what I can't pin you down to. Have they *said,* 'We'll pay you five thousand a year or ten or twenty?' Where do you *stand* is what I want to know."

Georgiana, twisting under the catechism, tried to explain to him the integrity which prevented Germaine from making an offer to one committed elsewhere, but though she spoke earnestly the words had a hollow ring. Repeated, they made her appear foolish, gullible.

"Look," Allen said at last, "it's your career and you're the one to make the decision. As a matter of fact, even at Carroway's we've heard rumors of *Tang* going on the rocks, but you were hearing that months ago. It hasn't happened yet, and it may not happen at all, and in the meantime you're getting your salary. What do you gain by leaving them?"

Here was a point she could get hold of. "If I wait till I'm out of a job to approach the Dauzats again they'll think I've *got* to have something and will take anything they offer and, believe me, it won't be princely. This way my bargaining position is much better."

"I don't see why," he said doggedly. "Whether you leave *Tang* or it leaves you, either way you're out of a job when you go to Germaine."

Georgiana saw that her honesty in repeating Madame Dauzat's remarks had been a mistake. Well, she was in for it now, but she must take care not to mention the Paris angle. So far, apparently, that had not occurred to him. If it were to come as a surprise to her, too, always supposing she landed the job, he might not be too unsympathetic, even if he didn't like the idea, but if he suspected she had planned it deliberately . . . His was a curious nature, impassive, almost, about lots of things, but sometimes aroused to unexpected action or to anger which was startling. Nevertheless, she went ahead. Driven by her desire for Reams, by an inner compulsion to take a step which would at least be in his direction, she resigned her job. Carter Dunlap pleaded with her—"My lass, this is a grrreat mistake, believe me"—but she went through with it. Carter broke the principle of a lifetime: he appealed to the family of an employee, and urged Allen to persuade her to change her mind, but Allen behaved as Carter would have. He backed up his wife, though personally, Carter felt, regretting her action.

Georgiana eagerly made known to Germaine the glad news of her freedom, which tidings Germaine received with a notable display of self-control. Feeling as though a chair had been pulled from under her, Georgiana could only wait, covering her dismay with pretended amusement at the Dauzats' childlike indecision and lack of perspicacity in not immediately pressing her into service.

Days and then weeks began slipping by, and although she and Allen occasionally saw the Dauzats at parties neither Germaine nor Claude seemed inclined to initiate a professional contact. At first Georgiana played this waiting game if not with relish at least without anxiety, but as her bank balance began to dwindle she became uneasy. Her insecurity was further aggravated by Reams, who would write a letter passionate and gay and tender, only to follow it by long stretches of silence. She might write him two and three and four times before an answer came.

Curiously enough in this period of tension and indecision she and Allen were drawn closer together than they had been in a long time. Her own career in the doldrums, she turned her interest upon him and his work. It diverted her attention and she could for a little while forget her self-induced leisure, a leisure she began bitterly to regret; all the more so that she had not love to color her days. Anxious about the future, she found sleep difficult, and at two and three and four in the morning she would lie berating herself for her folly, wishing passionately that she still had her old position and her reassuring weekly salary. Without work her life apart from Reams seemed to her nothing but a wasteful marking of time, yet she couldn't go to Europe without provoking another of Allen's catechisms and she couldn't go without money. Despite Reams's expressed longing to see her he never mentioned financing her trip, and a thin suspicion of miserliness on the part of her lover began to smolder within her.

She was very money conscious these days, for she and Allen discussed it frequently, with Karen uppermost in their thoughts. The girl was doing well in her studies and to keep her in college they were willing to make considerable sacrifice. When she learned that the home finance corporation was something less than flourishing she offered at once to leave Vassar and look for a job, but they argued her down. "No," Allen said firmly, "this business is no fault of yours. You're a hard worker, you at least deserve the break of being able to get a degree."

"Besides, my darling, with a degree it will be much easier for you to get a job which, unless you marry Barclay, you will certainly have to do, and then we expect to be supported in style." Georgiana was sitting in her big daughter's lap at the time, it never worked the other way around, and she laid her cheek against Karen's and hugged her. "My baby," she murmured tenderly.

"You mustn't count on Barky, Mother," Karen said.

"Why not? You saw him the last time you were home. And what about those three phone calls to college you told me about?"

"They don't constitute a proposal of marriage."

"Perhaps not, but mark my words, Barky is laying pipes."

"Oh, Mum." Honestly, parents were hopeless. "With all the girls in the world who are after him why would Barclay Hamilton pick on me? Besides, you don't seem to understand. I'm not in *love* with him, I don't think I could ever *learn* to love him."

Georgiana turned to Allen. "Thirty million dollars and she can't learn."

Allen was drawing on his pipe trying to light it. Over the flame he regarded his daughter quizzically. "I should think," he said between puffs, "that the lesson wouldn't be too stiff for a girl with a college education. Or is it a question of the impossibility of two bodies occupying the same space at the same time?"

Karen turned her head, a curtain of tawny hair falling over her face. Her father was right. Her heart was already furnished. Since she was separated from him by so great a distance and had heard nothing from him since he sailed, her feeling for Reams had become quiescent; at a high level, naturally, but couchant. The publication of his book and the reviews coming in from all over the country had roused it, her infatuation was once more rampant. Indeed she had overdrawn her allowance because of a long, congratulatory cable. What were Barclay Hamilton and his millions compared to this man of intellect whose spirit was laced with greatness? Heaps of girls married money. Of how many could it be said that they had espoused genius? For marriage to her idol was the difficult, rapturous, but definite goal she had in mind.

"I sent Reams a cable, you know," she said by way of reply to her father's divination, "to the American Express, and I've subscribed to a press clipping bureau. I'm sending him every review and mention of his book."

"We know," Allen said, "we got word of the overdraft."

"Wouldn't it be wonderful," she murmured, "to be with him in Europe now? Just think how happy he must be." Georgiana thought about it. "You talk of money, Mother," Karen went on. "Reams ought to be making a pile, what with his enormous sales and all the movie companies bidding for his book."

"That's my point," Georgiana said quickly. Karen's eyes were entirely too starry when she spoke of Reams. "*He* has to *make* it. The kind of money to marry is the kind that just *is*. Like Barclay's."

94

"Maybe," Karen continued dreamily, "maybe *we* should go to Europe. Even with things topsy-turvy living is still much cheaper over there than here." She suddenly sat up very straight. "How about that? We could save heaps of money."

Allen looked interested. "And tell me, John Maynard Keynes, living in Europe, how would we earn the American dollars of which we would be saving so many?"

Karen slumped again. "Oh, Daddy, you're awfully discouraging."

Allen tousled her hair. "Couldn't be more co-operative. Just get Vassar to let you take the European extension course, arrange with Chips Carroway to open a Paris office, and we're off."

About ten days after Karen had returned to college Germaine telephoned Georgiana to ask her to come to the office, she and Claude wanted to speak with her. For this vitally important consultation Georgiana selected her clothes with care. She had the knack of combining chic with femininity, a reasonably rare gift she had discovered since many women, in their desire to appear feminine, succeeded in looking merely tacky.

Arrived at *Distaff* she had to remind herself as she put her hand on the knob that she was opening the door of Germaine's office, not of Reams's room in a Paris hotel, so quickly had her imagination transported her to his side. Her prayers, however, had been answered. They were offering her a job and asking if she could be ready to sail within three weeks. Georgiana was elated. She was mentally composing the cable she would send to Reams when her exhilaration received a sharp puncture. Germaine and Claude informed her of the salary they were prepared to pay. It was half of what she had been getting at *Tang*.

"But, but you can't mean that," she stammered when she had a little recovered from the shock. "I've been earning double that amount and this is a job with a lot of responsibility. I'll be under heavy personal expense, since I have to help out with the apartment here and Karen's schooling, plus getting a place to live in Paris. I imagine you'll expect me to do some entertaining over there?"

"We'll give you an expense account," Germaine said coolly, "not unlimited, but it should suffice."

Claude spoke more cordially. "And as for the apartment, my little one, we have an idea."

"Which is?"

"That for the present you go to our place in the Place du Palais Bourbon. We will not be over until July for the openings, and you are welcome to stay there. In the meantime you can be looking around."

Georgiana relaxed a little. "Well, that would be a help, of course, but I assumed that the job was worth considerably more than your offer."

"You do not want it?" Germaine asked.

"Well, I—I——" The thoughts flashed through her mind simultaneously: Reams, Reams at all costs; Allen's, "I doubt if *Distaff* is in a position to pay you your *Tang* salary," Karen's expenses. She couldn't contribute much, but half a loaf was always better . . . The excitement of going abroad, the challenge of a new job, Reams . . . "Yes," she said, "yes, I want it. I'll take it."

That night after dinner she started summoning her courage to break the news to Allen. Telling him she was to work in Paris wasn't going to be easy. They were in the library. He was sunk in a deep chair reading a manuscript, and she sat at the desk with a checkbook and a pile of bills. In a way their pressure somewhat eased her task. Allen would have to admit they were in a spot, and if Paris was the alternative Paris it would have to be. Here they were nearing the end of April but, because of the devastating inroads made by the income tax the month before, the rent had not yet been paid. They had taken care of their two servants, the cook and the waitress, and paid the tradesmen and an insurance premium, but bills from the Fifth Avenue shops were stacked high and the balance in the checking account was low.

For nearly an hour Georgiana sat figuring and putting off the moment when she must speak. What had to be paid? What could wait over another month or two? Where could she borrow from Peter to pay Paul and not have Peter squeal at the pinch? She added, subtracted, and divided until her eyes glazed.

My God, she thought, how does *anybody* make enough money to live? One income had to irrigate so many channels. Food, furniture, and the federal government, rent, education, doctors, lawyers, clothes, automobiles, travel, charity, entertainment! Why, it was a miracle how anybody who wasn't a Rockefeller or a Hamilton or a Ford could even sustain life. If my child has the sense God gave a duck, she thought, she'll deliver Barclay Hamilton, bound and gagged, at a preacher's doorstep.

As she started once more to worry her way through the financial jungle she looked at her husband with resentment. It was all very well for Allen to turn over to her every cent he made and tell her to apportion it as she liked. That ended his responsibility and all the mistakes and extravagances became her fault and the worrying and fretting her portion. If you didn't look at the bank balance you might go along for a few days relatively carefree, but eventually you'd be obliged to face those paltry black figures, the midget digits that were so soul-destroying.

She glanced again at Allen. He was peaceably reading, the discarded pages of the typewritten manuscript growing in a neat pile at his feet as he finished one, laid it down, and started another. The room was very quiet. We could communicate with Mars, his wife reflected, and he would continue reading. Christ could reappear down the block and he wouldn't get the news till he saw it in a book. "We could be evicted for non-payment of rent," she said aloud, "and you'd look up from some goddam manuscript amazed to find your tail on the curbstone."

Allen took a count of two and glanced up. "What's that?"

"Bear with me, dear," she said through clenched teeth. "I'm trying not to scream, but the moment has come."

This time he put down the manuscript and laid aside his horn-rimmed glasses. "I'm sorry, G, what is it?"

"Allen, look. I've got something to tell you that's pretty tough. It came as a shock to me and I'm afraid it will to you, but unfortunately we're not in a position to do anything about it."

"What is it?"

"It's about my new job."

"You mean the *Distaff* thing has come through? Darling, that's grand!"

"There's a hitch. They want me to go to Paris."

"You mean for a trip? But I thought that's what you've been wanting."

She hesitated. "Well, it, it isn't a trip exactly. They've asked me to work over there. To be in the Paris office."

He looked at her, puzzled. "You mean for good? You mean you'd be living and working in Paris rather than in New York?"

"I'm afraid that's about the size of it. For a while at least."

"But that's ridiculous. You've told them you can't do it, haven't you?"

"No, I haven't. How can I? I either work where they say or I don't work at all."

"O.K. Then you don't work at all. I never heard such damn nonsense. What about Karen? What about your home? And, if you'll forgive me for bringing it up, what about your husband? Your life is *here*, in New York. Or hasn't all that occurred to you?"

"Oh, Allen, of course it's occurred to me; it's the first thing that did occur to me, but what are we going to do? We're strapped and you know it. That income-tax jam last month really got us down." They were neither of them so tactless as to remark that the jam was largely Georgiana's fault, but the unspoken thought lay between them. She hurried on. "It's going to be hard, of course, for all of us, but it's a big chance for me, Allen, and the important thing is that we'll be able to get a little ahead, get our bills paid up, and begin to save something. The Dauzats didn't want to, but I got them to agree to pay part of my salary in dollars. That I want to leave here for my share of Karen and our annuities and so on. I ought to be able to get by in Paris on the francs I draw over there."

For the first time since she had started speaking Allen smiled.

"I know you think I'm extravagant," she said quickly, "but I don't have to be. Naturally, living as we do here—entertaining, two servants all the time, and Lord knows how many extras for cleaning and parties—it mounts up, but with me gone you could cut down a terrific lot and if I make up my mind to live on a simple scale in a city where it's possible, I'm perfectly capable of doing it."

"You're hellbent on going, aren't you?"

"What choice have I got? We can't afford for me not to."

"Well," he said slowly, "I suppose it's an opportunity for you, but there are opportunities here too."

"I wouldn't say I've been swamped with offers since I left *Tang*, would you?"

"I'm afraid people thought that was an irresponsible act, but you could get something, I'm sure. Your record there was good."

"Allen, that's an off-chance we can't afford to take. Here I've got a bird in the hand."

"I know, G, but I don't like any part of it and it isn't only me. Maybe I'm feeling sorry for myself, the life of a perennial summer bachelor has always struck me as lethal, but that's not important. Karen is. How does she fit into this scheme of displaced persons?"

"She's not displaced. After all, you're here, and even though we fire the servants, which I imagine you'll certainly want to do and get by with a part-time cleaning woman, she can be home week ends. And as for the summer holidays . . ."

"Is this vie de Bohême to continue into the summer?"

"Dear, be reasonable. We're almost the end of April now. The Dauzats aren't going to pay my fare over and get me established only to bring me back in a couple of months. One reason they want me to go now is so that I'll be settled and at home by the time the openings come along. My thought was that if Karen wants to—— I mean, since you have to work anyway, if we can afford her passage, she might come and join me."

"I might come and join you too. I get a holiday, you know. In fact, I recall you'd planned a European jaunt for all of us this summer."

"Well, that's true. I had."

"At least that's what I understood last fall, the night of the Oppenheimers' party. Have you changed your mind?"

Georgiana thought it wise to ignore the dig. "Of course not. Why should I? I just didn't know whether you'd consider a trip of three or four weeks worth while."

"I'd consider it very worth while."

"Then what about the place in the country?" she asked. "We can probably get a good price for it, but if we're going to rent it it ought to be on the lists this minute. Shall I get in touch with that real-estate woman?"

"I suppose you might as well." His lack of enthusiasm was in marked contrast to her bright executive tone. "I'd like to know something about the people we rent to though."

"Naturally. So would I, but if no one turns up within the next three weeks you'll have to decide on the prospects after I'm gone."

"You're leaving in three weeks?"

"That's what the Dauzats want."

"I see."

And that's what you want, too, he thought. To get away, to be free of a routine so familiar that it has become hackneyed. To have a change, to meet Reams Asher. It was unflattering, but was it so unnatural? If it hadn't been for Asher would he find her longing for novelty, for a fresh job, unreasonable? And was he even right about Asher? He was years younger than Georgiana. Even if she had gone overboard about him, it was unlikely that a man young, vigorous, successful would respond to her desire. Certainly it was nothing that could last. In the midst of his hurt and anger he was moved to pity her. She was sincere in her wish to help out financially, he was sure of that, while sensing that their need for economy was the providential excuse upon which she fastened to give plausibility to her actions. Yet he felt she was embarking on more than a prolonged trip away from home; this seemed to him a crisis in their lives. Was it wiser to face it, to demand an accounting of her emotions, her intentions, or was it less dangerous to let her slip away, to create no scene, and to assume that the work in Europe was only temporary and that in the autumn she would come back of her own volition?

Georgiana, watching him obviously wrestling with indecision, was moved to pity, too, and to some irritation because of it. She wanted to be with Reams, she wanted to be free, and she didn't want to have to feel sorry for her husband while she was being it. But he wouldn't be lonely, men never were, there was no need. There were countless pretty women eager to make up to an unattached man. If Allen should stray a little, well, what of it? With him it would never be serious, and what, after all, were her own plans?

In his mind Allen reached his decision. The wisdom of it he couldn't vouch for but he had to speak. "Georgiana, I want to ask you something straight and I'd appreciate a straight answer. Are you considering this Paris offer only because of money?"

It was on the tip of her tongue to say "Why else?" but it wouldn't come. Infidelity was one thing, but after half a lifetime together flippancy wouldn't serve. She placed her two thumbs against the edge of the desk and stared down at them. "No, Allen," she said at last,

100

"not only. It may be a mistake to say these things, but—maybe it isn't. You and I have been married for more than twenty-three years, our relationship is a habit, a shell without much inside it. I suppose many marriages are after a time, yet perhaps frank acknowledgment of the situation is unwise. When two people are planning to go on together I can see how it might be; deliberately to say, 'Look, we're fed up with each other,' is dangerous, unkind, it can create a rift that's irremediable. Yet the fed-up feeling can be strong. That's why I think married people should take advantage of a palliative when it offers. When a break, a change of rhythm, if you like, seems perfectly natural and one can accept it without anguish or offense to either side. Suppose I *am* using this new job as an excuse? A holiday away from each other will do us both good. Maybe we'll come to see that we need each other more than we think."

"What happens if it works the other way around?"

"Well—we might as well know it."

"No," he said violently. "No, I think that's false. This idea of constantly putting marriage to the test—where's the value of it? A marriage between a man and a woman isn't a feat of strength. How high can I lift the iron bar? How far can I stretch the rubber band without snapping it? They're not analogous. You have to trust marriage, you have to work to make your relationship intensify rather than dwindle. What you propose is like a child who plants carrots and keeps pulling them up to see how they're progressing."

"Oh, Allen dear, be reasonable. In all the years of our marriage we've been away from each other very little. I assume that here and there you've been interested in other women. Why wouldn't you be? People don't become immune to the human race just because they're married. Maybe you've even had affairs. But if you have had, you've been discreet and I haven't known it. I'm not blaming you, but grant me a little leeway too. All I want is a change, and any dark suspicions you may have are of your own brewing." She smiled at him. "I can say to you in honesty that as of this evening I have no desire to uproot our carrots. It was you who suggested that we might find we didn't need each other. Do you speak against a separation out of fear that that will happen?"

"No, we do need each other. All right, we're not twenty or twenty-five any more, we don't care as we once did, what of it? We're mar-

101

ried people. Marriage isn't an eternal love affair at honeymoon pitch. It can't be."

"I'm not complaining, dear," she murmured politely. Indeed there were times when she wished to heaven he'd leave her alone. Just now, though, she found him pathetic. He was trying to persuade himself that he no longer expected, no longer even desired freshness and romance in his life. Yet probably the longing was universal and probably men and women of eighty knew it.

"What about Karen?" he asked suddenly. "She'll be lost without you."

"I told you! I want her to come to me as soon as vacation starts, but it may be that she won't want to. She's always loved you more than me, she'll probably think it's fun, camping out here with you in the apartment, taking care of you when she's home from college."

"That's complimentary," he said, "but she oughtn't to be in the city all summer anyhow, and if she has a chance to get to Europe and maybe bump into Reams Asher into the bargain she's going to take it."

That fly Georgiana decided she would not rise to. "I doubt if we'll any of us be bumping into him," she said shortly. "He's probably swept up in a whirl of success and Left Bank life and wouldn't recognize his old friends if they thumped him on the back."

There was a pause. Allen paced the book-lined room and Georgiana shuffled and restacked the bills on her desk.

"Three weeks, you say?" Allen asked.

She nodded. "I'll have to get my passport renewed but I don't think I'll have any trouble, especially as I'm going to work."

"I'll miss you, you know."

"I'll miss you, Allen. I don't want you to be lonely, dear. Go out with people. An unattached man and an attractive one! My word, you'll be dining out every night."

"Thanks, but I don't fancy myself as an escort service."

"Not even to pretty lady authors eager to take advantage of a distinguished publisher?"

"I don't know any," he said glumly.

"Nonsense. You have a skilled eye for pretty young women. What about Bierne Honeywell who worked with me on the auction? You had quite a flair for her."

102

"That's ridiculous. I barely met her. Besides, she's a child."

"Nevertheless."

"For God's sake." His tone was half laughing, half disgusted, yet as he spoke he saw Bierne as he had left her on the wet, windy doorstep, and for an instant seemed to smell again the sharp, sweet odor of carnations. She was charming, he liked her, and that ended it. He could scarcely see himself calling up a girl who had been his wife's secretary and saying he was all alone and would she come and dine with him. There was something, it was a prissy word, but there was something not fastidious about it, as an idea it was distasteful. His mind reverted to his immediate problem. "When are you going to tell Karen?"

"I'll call her tomorrow."

"It'll be a shock to her."

"I'm not so sure. At her age the idea of a little freedom from the maternal apron strings is apt to look pretty good."

"If you do bump into Reams Asher you might tell him to write to her. It's the least he can do after all this clipping-bureau service she's rendering him."

"I'll suggest it," she said.

Some three weeks later Lola and Peter Quick went with the Goodyears to see Georgiana off on the *Queen Elizabeth,* which sailed at midnight.

Peter and Lola cared for no part of the proceedings. It was a raw night, the long, covered pier was drafty, and the municipal wattage cast a pall over the jostling, embarking crowd. Added to the physical discomfort was the concern they felt over Georgiana's trip. Peter especially was convinced that once in France his sister-in-law would try to talk Allen into a Paris divorce. Lola was less pessimistic, being devoted to her brother and reasoning that Georgiana might well get lonely and come to realize that she had a good man and had better hang on to him. They tried to convince themselves that there was nothing untoward in her taking this job and, intellectually, didn't believe there was, but they confessed to each other that emotionally it didn't jell.

"We're conventional, I guess," Lola sighed.

"You bet," said Peter, and, clasping his hands around her throat, he applied a little gentle strangulation. "Never let me hear of you planning any six months' or a year's separation, Mrs. Quick. Catch?"

"Yes, sir."

They were in Georgiana's cabin now helping to stow luggage and wishing her bon voyage in scotch and soda. Allen's mood was low for, although he had perforce reconciled himself to the trip, he, too, wondered whether he and Georgiana could, in the future, find some sort of contentment together or whether his marriage was already on the rocks.

They were discussing the chances of any entertaining people being on board when Claude Dauzat appeared, a little breathlessly, in the doorway. "Hello, hello, everybody. You had given me up, I fear, no?"

"Ah! Thank heavens!" Georgiana exclaimed with relief when she saw him. "Not, you understand, dear boy, that I didn't trust you."

"With all her heart," put in Lola. "It was just her nerves that were shaky."

Claude came into the small cabin and took Georgiana's hand and kissed it. "But this is silly; you know I wouldn't let you down. Now then, here we are," and he unbuttoned his overcoat and drew from his pockets some letters and a key. "Here are the letters we talked about. Germaine has written two, I have written three, and she is sending more direct to Paris, but you will not need them; you will find you know everybody."

"Oh no, I won't." Georgiana spoke feelingly. "You forget, Claude, it's years since I've been in Paris. Since before the war."

"*I* appreciate the letters of introduction, too, Claude," Allen said; "thanks a lot. I don't want her to be lonely," though inwardly he added grimly, a little loneliness wouldn't hurt her. He himself was anticipating a large dose of it.

"By the way," Claude continued, "Germaine sends much love and bon voyage, but though her cold is better the doctor said it would be foolish for her to come to the pier. *Avec ces sacrés courants d'air il a raison, tiens.*"

Lola and Georgiana exchanged smiles. Their French was limited, but they knew enough and they knew Claude well enough to appreciate his concern with drafts.

"Now then, what—— Ah, to be sure!" He flourished the key he

104

already held. "Here is the key to the apartment. I have written the concierge about your arrival and Sylvie, the cook, she, too, is expecting you. Sylvie is all right, you understand, my dear, but she is not Cordon Bleu. *C'est une brave femme et bonne à tout faire, alors, vous comprenez . . . !*"

Georgiana comprehended, she assured him, and a good honest maid of all work was her dream.

Claude wound up his admonitions and instructions: for several hours two days a week—the hours would be at different times of the day—there would be no electricity. The elevator had not worked since before the war but the hot water was copious. If it wasn't, it was the fault of the concierge and she was to be severely spoken to. Oh yes, and Georgiana must arrange with the gas and electric people when she would be at home to receive the bill. It was cheaper for the company to deliver the bills by hand than to mail them, but the employee arrived at odd moments and one had to agree upon a mutually convenient time.

What else? Claude tapped his brow. As far as he remembered he had briefed her on the domestic routine. "Is there a telephone?" Georgiana asked, though remembering the prewar Paris service it really made little difference whether there was or not. Claude's face brightened. There was indeed a telephone, and it functioned to perfection. Until she caught the knack she might have a little difficulty with the directory. It was, perhaps, not quite so lucidly edited as its American counterpart but it was merely a question of familiarity. The numbers of the houses and the streets were in the book but not people's names. Provided one knew a person's address one could eventually deduce what the telephone number must be.

Georgiana glanced at Allen, who looked back at her in innocence. She had eagerly embraced the idea of foreign parts; if the conditions of life were primitive, well, was she a world traveler or was she not?

As Claude was revealing the idiosyncrasies of the French telephone the steward's gong sounded along the companionway. "All ashore that's going ashore, all ashore that's going ashore . . ."

Lola and Peter rose. There was a general movement toward the door. They went up to A deck together, Allen holding Georgiana's arm. Once there he drew her away a little from the crowd milling about the big double doors and flooding down the sloping covered

105

gangplank. As it was night and chilly, relatively few people lined the rail to wave to those standing below on the pier waiting to see the great ship pull away. Sheltered in the lee of the bulkhead they could snatch a moment of comparative privacy.

Allen looked at his wife. She was bareheaded and the light from a nearby window slanted on her gleaming copper hair and glinted on the collar of her fur coat held close under her chin. "Georgiana. Good-by, dearest. Have a good time. I'll be thinking about you, you know. A lot."

"I'll be thinking of you, too, my dear. But this is the best way, at least for a while. Believe me, it is. Take care of yourself now. Have fun."

"I'll do my best."

"Look out for Karen and see that she writes to me."

"You bet."

"Mrs. Yoster, the real-estate woman, said she's practically certain those people will rent the house and pay what we're asking. She's going to get in touch with you at the office."

"I'll be on the lookout for her."

"Well . . ."

"Well . . ." To Georgiana's relief the strained pause was broken by the sound of the gong and the steward's final warning, "Last call, last call, all ashore that's going ashore."

There was a flurry of farewell embraces from the Quicks and Claude. "Good-by."

"Good-by, darling, take care of yourself, write to us." Lola hugged her close. "I envy you, I wish we were all going."

"Come over with Karen in June. She needs a chaperon."

Lola laughed. "So do the twins."

"Good-by, good-by."

An officer was urging the last lingering visitors on to the gangplank. "Sorry, sir," he said to Allen, "I must ask you to be getting off." Herded along with the rest, Allen turned and waved his hat at Georgiana above the crowd. She smiled and blew him a kiss.

Although she must have gone in, they couldn't see her, he and the others waited on the pier until the gangplank was drawn away and the ship about to cast her moorings before they turned and walked toward the street.

Lola asked Claude if he wouldn't drive across town with them in their cab, but he declined, saying he had his car. He did not, however, offer to give them a lift. This seemingly unneighborly conduct was explained by Lola who, in passing near his Cadillac while Peter and Allen were hailing a taxi, glimpsed a waiting woman in the front seat. "And, my chickadees," she observed in the cab, "unless Auntie's old eyes deceive her it was that bright star of the cinema, Miss Nora Brown."

It was indeed Miss Brown, with temper somewhat frayed by the vigil she had been keeping for her loved one.

"What on earth took you so long?" she demanded as Claude slipped into the seat beside her and they started east on Fiftieth Street.

"My darling, I was as quick as was humanly possible, but I had to give Georgiana the information about the apartment."

With Nora airing her displeasure but also her relief at seeing him again they headed across town to the Waldorf where Claude went up with her to her tower suite for a little nocturnal refreshment.

Her own preference was vodka and tonic and some time later he brought her a glass to the bedside. He looked down at her lying on the tumbled pink sheets and laughed softly. She yawned. "What are you smirking about?" she asked, taking the drink he handed her.

"Lilly Rose Lestenleader of South Dakota. You made a mistake, Lilly Rose, you should never have changed your name. You have really a skin of flower petals." Having, at the moment, nothing for her beyond appreciation, he caressed her flank lightly in an objective, approving manner. "C'est gentil ça, c'est même très gentil!"

"Mmmm," Nora said. Her tone was skeptical. "That's the way you compliment a head waiter on the brandy."

Claude smiled. "I like to think I am a man of perception."

"Anyhow," she explained, "I had to change my name; my press agent told me it would never make the marquees. I happened to hit the plain-Jane cycle—Jennifer Jones, Jane Wyman, Nora Brown. I'm surprised there isn't a Helen Smith."

Claude pushed back the sleeve of his foulard dressing gown and looked at his wrist watch. "My darling, it is nearly two o'clock. What time is your rehearsal in the morning?"

"Eleven, but I have to be up early for a fitting beforehand."

"How are things coming?"

"All right." But she seemed disgruntled rather than pleased. Claude had more than once observed in his blossom a tendency to displeasure when she found herself surrounded by an able cast. Knowing her, he assumed that if he waited but a moment the difficulty would out, and he was right. Almost immediately she enlightened him. "There's one fellow, honestly he drives me crazy. You know the man who's making such a hit in that small part, a bit is all it is really, in *Donovan's Quest?* We went to the opening, remember?" Claude nodded. "His name's Reuben Slade, and I was crazy about him, so when I agreed to do this show for Delly, I suggested we get him."

"Well?"

"Well," she said with disgust, "we have."

"He is not good?"

"Oh, he's good"—she set her glass down on the bedside table with a disapproving click—"but the questions he asks! I declare that man's indecent."

A hopeful gleam shone in Claude's dark eyes, a smile of cheerful concupiscence flashed across his face. "Tell me, *chérie,*" he murmured, "what does he say to you?"

Nora gave him a little shove. "Not what you imagine. It's all *professional.*"

Claude looked disappointed. "Oh, I see."

"Things like, 'Can an actor truly lack self-consciousness in a sense of being unaware of what he does? Isn't the most spontaneous gesture or reading inevitably deliberate?' My God, how do I know?" Nora found Mr. Slade highly irritating. All those questions! It was like taking off her flesh to look at her bones. That business about how she got her laughs on the stage he could jolly well leave alone. She only hoped the critics never found out how haphazard her methods were. The laugh would be there one performance and gone the next. It was infuriating how many character people and bit players in her companies were able to hit it on the nose night after night while she fished vaguely about wondering what in heaven's name she had done at the last performance, or last week, to evoke mirth, and why she now couldn't repeat the tactic, whatever it was.

Claude chuckled and stroked her hair. "Lilly Rose, relax. This Mr. Slade is no possible competition to you. You are a famous star, darling. If he can be good in his little part it is all the better for you, since you are the play and the credit cannot fail to be yours."

"You think?"

"Of course."

Nora looked at Claude appreciatively. Whatever his shortcomings he certainly made sense. "Darling, you're very helpful, you really are." She snuggled against his arm. "You understand *true* values."

Claude patted her cheek tenderly but he rose from the edge of the bed. It was late, and he was reluctant to get involved in one of those religious discourses, but he was not to escape scot-free. With a wonderfully supple movement Nora twisted over on to her stomach and flowed down to the foot of the bed, where she lay watching him dress. Usually elusive or indifferent in their rare discussions of what the future might hold for them, to his amazement she suddenly launched a head-on attack. "Claude?" He stood in front of the mirror adjusting the gold pin he wore to hold down the tabs of his shirt collar.

"Chérie?"

"I'm worried about you, darling. I think this life is very tiring for you. Getting up, going out at these odd hours, it's not healthy. And it's so *needless*. Why don't you and Germaine get a divorce? Everything would be *much* easier."

Claude swallowed and smoothed back his hair along the temples with the palms of his hands. The roof of his mouth felt rather dry.

"But surely, my darling, you cannot urge me to that. Think of your religion."

"Yes, but you're not a Catholic; it wouldn't be wrong for you."

"But Catholics can't marry divorced people. Though perhaps you didn't mean that." He added this last hastily, fearful he might have provided her with an idea she had not considered.

Nora looked at him in stunned amazement. "Not marry divorced—— Why not?" she demanded.

"Darling, you understand the tenets of the Church better than I. It isn't considered good ecclesiastical form. Surely you learned that when you were converted?"

"I never——" She broke off in anger. His news had brought her sharply upright, and she sat back on her heels on the bed, every curve swelling with indignation. "Well," she exploded after a taut

109

silence, and he could but admire the frigid dignity of her comment, "it certainly makes it very tough. If Catholics aren't supposed to marry divorced people, who the *hell* is there left?"

"Oh, my darling, out West—I read some place a statistic—there are many male virgins."

"I'd be great on a Minnesota sheep farm, wouldn't I?"

He finished dressing while Nora assimilated this information. When he was ready to leave she slipped on a negligee and followed him to the door, twining her soft arms around his neck to bid him good-by. "Since it isn't a sin for you, darling, it would be much healthier if you were separated from Germaine. She is so suspicious, it is a great strain on you, and if you were divorced we could always be together even if we weren't married. And because we would be adhering to the laws of the Church I'm sure we would be blessed. And, anyway, look at those dispensations people are always getting. Good night, darling, think over what I've said. I couldn't bear for us to be separated, yet what choice would I have? I will not jeopardize your health and, therefore, your happiness by continuing in this way. It wouldn't be right, especially when one thinks of others in need of spiritual companionship whom it is one's duty to help if one can. Good night, my darling."

Claude, chilled by this ecclesiastical blackmail, hesitated. He wouldn't put it past her to force a rift on some such preposterous basis, and although he might marvel at her ability to juggle facts, to twist ethics to her own pretzel mold, she exerted over him an attraction he was powerless to resist until it should weaken of its own accord. He would pay a great deal for her company, though he fervently prayed that marriage was not the price.

He debated giving in to her now, going back into the bedroom, and spending the rest of the night where he was. What dissuaded him as much as his anticipation of the scene he must expect from Germaine was the realization that he would have no clean shirt to put on in the morning. He embraced his spiritual paramour and left.

8

One mild Saturday afternoon in May, when Georgiana had been gone about two weeks, Allen sat with his sister Lola in the small playground along the river at the foot of East Fifty-seventh Street. The hot sunshine had brought out the buds on the trees and phalanxes of neighborhood youth, and the little park rang with squeals and shouts, blissfully ignored by the youngest generation sleeping undisturbed in carriages watched over by nurses and young mothers.

The Quick twins tumbled in the sand pit, whacked with uncertain shovels at other infants, or occasionally tottered as far as the iron railings dividing the park from the adjoining lawn of a Sutton Place apartment house, where they forced their round pink cheeks between the bars and spit with quiet pleasure on to the costly city turf. Their propulsion was not jet, and they were working against the breeze, so that Lola, in mid-phrase, would swoop one of them to her and engage in mopping-up operations. The gesture was honorary. "I don't know why I keep doing this," she muttered; "it's like trying to bail out a battleship with a teacup."

Allen looked at his nephews appreciatively. "They certainly seem to have an inexhaustible supply," he agreed as, with triumphant squawks, they reeled from their mother back to their posts, emitting spume and spray with unquenched ardor.

Lola was seven years younger than Allen but they had been devoted to each other since their childhood and shared a strong family resemblance, though Lola's coloring was more vivid than her brother's and her manner vivacious and debonair. Her hair had been gray since she was twenty and curled crisply around her pleasant, still-youthful face. Not conventionally pretty, her abounding health and candid good humor were magnetic, and in his present mood of depression and uncertainty Allen found her easygoing ways and common sense wonderfully comforting. He was fond of his brother-in-law, too, and spent most of his spare time in their company.

Peter's salary was adequate for his family's needs but scarcely opulent, though they lived simply as much from choice as from necessity and saved their money for the twins' education. Sitting in the playground, Lola and her brother had been discussing the little boys' future until Allen was minded of his own straitened regime. "I'll be interested," he said, "when the first of June rolls around. According to Georgiana, that's when our economy drive is supposed to bear fruit." He spoke with such a lack of enthusiasm that Lola couldn't help laughing. "Cheer up, Al. It's a load off you, dear, really it is. I appreciate that you're lonely—Lord, if only we had room to turn around in we'd have you with us, it would be grand—but you *are* busy all day, and if you'd give anybody half a chance you could be bogged down with invitations."

Allen groaned. "Damn it all, you're just like G. I don't *want* a lot of invitations. Once in a while going out is all right, but a lot of the time I'm tired by evening. My idea of a good time is dinner at home in peace and quiet but all alone it's no fun, even if I had a cook, which I haven't. Georgiana fixed that. Ingrid and that loony maid, that Delia, left the day after she did."

Lola cocked an appraising eye at him. "You're sorry for yourself, my lad; you need companionship."

"I don't know what I need. I'm lower than a snake's belly, but I guess it's my own fault. I'm stale."

And, thought Lola, Georgiana's been gone only a couple of weeks. What she expects he's going to do with himself all these months I'm sure I don't know. Asking for trouble, she thought, yet she reflected a little sadly that the real trouble was that Georgiana didn't care if he did stray.

She looked at her brother. He had taken off his hat, and the warm spring sunshine fell on his long head, on his hair still brown but receding and graying rapidly, and on his thin, sensitive face saved from weakness by the intensity of his gaze and the definitely modeled mouth. He was fifty. More than half his life was gone, and how satisfactory had it been? He was one of the most successful men in his field, but it sometimes seemed to Lola that any field was a narrow part of the whole wide earth.

She admired success in a restrained way; she was anxious for Peter to achieve his ambitions, and they both hoped to bring up the twins so they might come out with integrity and reasonably on top in a tough, competitive world, but Lola frequently thought that most

112

of the people she knew, and that included her brother and Georgiana, were so busy getting ahead in life—which, in a sense, was the same as getting to the end of it—that they forgot to live. They thought living was a luxury, a state apart, with which they would concern themselves by and by, when they were rich.

Lola didn't often mention her own love of life, she supposed it made her sound naïve, but people who shut themselves in with success and cut themselves off from everyday joys seemed to her pallid, deserving of pity. A good kick in the pants might not come amiss either. She was debating which to administer to Allen, and for the time being pity won. "I'm sorry you're alone tonight, Allen, but Peter and I have to go to this dinner, it's semi-business, and I know Peter hopes the Coast deal he's working on will begin to jell a little. You wouldn't want to call up the Slades and go play with them?"

"Hell, no."

"Why not? You're all such pals."

"I know, but——" He spread his hands in an ineffectual gesture. "Anyhow, I think Reuben's out of town with that new show of Nora Brown's." Suddenly he laughed with honest pleasure. "By God, that would be a wonderful thing if old Rube should get his heart's desire. Maybe he *will* make a go of acting. I'd like to see it happen."

"I know what!" Lola exclaimed. "Suppose the night the show opens here in town we give him a little party! At your place."

He looked at her sternly. "What about my economy?"

"It wouldn't cost much! Only a few people, just sandwiches and drinks. How about it?"

Allen smiled at her. "Done. I'll send him a wire."

He was unlikely to initiate any festivities, but with someone to jog his elbow Lola had suspected that he would warm to such a scheme and her success pleased her. He would have something to look forward to.

She glanced at her watch and looked around for the twins. One was squatting under the bench on which they were sitting, the other had laboriously clambered up the steps to the little tree-shaded street above the playground and was leaning against a woman whose head was turned away from them, gazing up into her face with rapt curiosity. His mother sighed. "Look at that Rickey. Woman-crazy. What

113

did I tell you? Go fetch him, will you, Al? We've got to be wandering back."

Allen crossed the few yards to the steps, took them two at a time, rounded the baby carriage watched over by Rickey's quarry, and found himself gazing down at Bierne Honeywell.

She was bareheaded and wore something raspberry colored. Allen thought he had never looked at anyone so fresh and pretty. She smiled delightedly when she saw him. "Why—why, my goodness, if it isn't Mr. Goodyear."

"Gloo," said the gentleman at her knee.

"Is this your young man?" she asked.

Allen nodded. "In a manner of speaking, yes. Come here, you rascal," and he reached for a small grimy paw.

"Noo." The gentleman's dissenting grunt was emphatic, though he submitted resentfully to authority.

His uncle ignored the backchat and held his hand tightly. "How are you, Miss Honeywell, Miss Bierne Honeywell?"

"I'm very well, thank you. And you?"

"I'm fine." Suddenly he felt he was. He felt again that buoyant sensation he had experienced with her in the car. He peered into the carriage. "Is that your baby?"

"In a manner of speaking, yes."

"You work fast."

"That's Petey. Stella's and Harry's baby. Harry has scarlet fever. At first we were scared it might be this awful smallpox that's going around, so we've all been vaccinated. We literally had to stand in line. Fortunately Harry isn't seriously ill, but Mother and Uncle Ben and I are taking care of Petey for a while at our house. He's wonderful."

Allen watched her waste a radiant smile on the sleeping infant, who struck him as being rather suet-faced. "Well," he said, "this is a grand surprise. Where did you disappear to the night of that literary auction? We looked around to say good-by and you'd vanished." He didn't add that he had felt an odd pang of disappointment at missing her.

"I was in the back office," she said, "checking with the auctioneer and the Manhattan Aid executives on the bids and money received. I was sorry, too, that we didn't get together. Mrs. Goodyear came

114

down to Aid headquarters the next day to clean up the final details of the sale. I heard, by the way, that she's gone to Europe."

Allen nodded. "Sailed a couple of weeks ago. I imagine she's pretty well installed in Paris by this time."

Bierne looked up at the budding trees and out over the river. "It must be lovely there now."

Allen laughed light-heartedly; he felt almost giddy. "It's lovely here now."

She agreed readily enough. "Spring's good any place, I guess."

Your face is like spring. Your hair is gold as sunshine, your eyes are like spring skies. His unspoken cliché suddenly embarrassed him. Better get the hell out of tinpan alley, he thought, yet damn it all, what did you do about coloring like that? The young woman was improbable. Blue, gold, pink, white, coral—such a bright lipstick. She looked gay and soft.

Bierne turned and smiled as she saw Lola approaching with the other twin in tow. "Mrs. Quick, how very nice to see you. It's Bierne Honeywell, from the auction, remember?"

"Of course I remember you, my dear. How are you? I hope the attentions of these strange men haven't been annoying you?"

"Quite the contrary. I'm enjoying myself."

"Gloorum," crowed her enraptured swain, breaking from Allen's hand and hurling himself at her knees.

In the general laughter Lola glanced at her brother. It was extraordinary how his doldrums seemed to have vanished in the last couple of minutes. "I've got to get the boys home," she said, "but why don't you stay and chat with Miss Honeywell, Al? Bring her in for a drink in a little while."

"Oh, thank you, Mrs. Quick, that's kind of you," the girl said, "but I have to be getting back too. It's nearly time for Petey's supper and it takes me a little while to walk home."

"Try to persuade her anyway, Allen. We're only down the street, you know," and hoisting her offspring into a double gocart Lola started home, Bierne's conquest lolling over the side leering back at her like Harpo Marx.

Allen took a place on the bench next to her, at that moment vacated by a starched English nanny. "It's quite a walk from your house over here, isn't it?" he asked.

"Not really," she said, "and here it's so pretty. Besides, you can sit down."

"What have you been doing with yourself all this time?" He really wanted to know, though he had not forgotten that he reminded her of her father. Well, he would take a fatherly interest. Thank God he wasn't an old goat who went chasing after a girl young enough to be his daughter. That was fatal. The subsequent steps were taken after granddaughters and eventually after the nurse. Allen shuddered.

In answer to his query Bierne replied that it was pretty much the usual routine. "There's always plenty going on down at Aid headquarters, but I miss the excitement and fun of the auction. I miss going to the different ladies' houses too." She blushed. She did not add that beyond the charming surroundings and the good tea and cocktails she also missed the special little thrill she used to get at the possibility of seeing him. If the meeting was at the Goodyears' apartment maybe he would come home before it was over. If at somebody else's place he might come by to pick up Mrs. Goodyear. That had happened once. It had been an unexpected delight.

When she spoke of the different houses Allen smiled. "Do you mentally rearrange the furniture?" He often thought that Georgiana's real vocation must be interior decoration since they had yet to come home from a friend's house without her observing that only the veriest nincompoop would have placed the piano in the one place that cried aloud for a sofa, or that any fool could see that the lighting arrangement had been designed for moles.

Bierne was less critical. "Oh no," she said. "I think Mrs. Goodyear has done your apartment beautifully and Madame Dauzat's is lovely too. One of our meetings was there, you know, and one was at Mrs. Slade's. Mrs. Slade was upset about her bookcases, but it wasn't serious. If I had had the time I think I could have fixed them for her."

Allen looked at her, startled. "You could?"

"Oh yes. I understand things like that. My father was wonderful with his hands and he taught Stella and me a lot."

"Well, *there*," Allen said firmly, "I differ from your father. I can't change an electric-light plug without plunging our entire neighborhood into darkness."

116

Bierne thought it odd that he should sound pleased about such a failing. It wasn't very practical, but a publisher, of course, was intellectual and nobody could be everything. Uncle Ben wasn't even intellectual, and he was a dud with tools.

Bierne wondered about Allen's life. She knew so little of him. Just here and there she caught a flash, a glimpse. "Does Miss Good-year"—no, that sounded stilted—"does your daughter like doing things around the house?"

"Karen?" Allen thought about her a minute, concentrating. "Well, I should say Karen is willing but not gifted. She's none too dependable around a hammer."

"Is she at college?"

"Just gone back after the Easter holidays."

Bierne smiled. Now she knew something more about him or at least about someone who closely concerned him. It made her happy yet a little apprehensive, too; how dreadful if she were growing to be like her mother, a collector of other people's lives. No, no, she thought in revolt, I'm not like that. This is someone I know personally, someone I like enormously. It's quite different from picking over strangers' lives.

"But surely," Allen was saying, "besides your job and your carpentry work there must be other interests. What about beaux?" She looked at him quickly. "Please don't think me impertinent but I'm the father of a daughter, don't forget. I feel I should know what's in the market." His eyes twinkled. He didn't mind that he was being a fraud, he felt sure she would interpret him as such, and indeed she laughed softly but paid him the compliment of honesty, replying in that way she had, like a shy, polite child, "I do get asked out sometimes, it's very nice, but I'm not in love with anyone. Is—is your daughter in love?"

"All the time. It's a chronic condition with her, as though she had a niche in her heart which remained the same but the statues change. I'm afraid the statue of the moment isn't very responsive."

"Oh, I'm so sorry. I do hope he doesn't make her unhappy."

"So do I," Allen said. "Seems to be very attractive to women and he's a big success, too, but basically not right for her. Too old for one thing, and, for another, too far away."

The baby began to stir. Automatically Bierne's hand reached for

117

the carriage and rocked it gently. After a little pause she said, "I don't know. How can anyone say who's too old for another person? If you care for someone it isn't because of the number of years they've been on earth or because they're rich or poor, or any of those reasons. Even if they're near or far, if you love them, it doesn't matter, you love them anyway. The other things are—well, trappings, sort of."

"Do you believe that?"

"Yes, I do."

Allen stared out at the river. As the sun sank the shadows lengthened in the playground, and the air which had been unseasonably hot all day began to cool. Conscious of a slight chilliness, Allen reached for his hat on the bench beside him and set it on the back of his head. "You see, the trouble is," he said, "that little by little, unbeknownst to you for the most part, love, the body inside the trappings, can shrivel away, and there you are left with the draperies, the accouterments, but it's like a tent, hollow inside."

"Then it wasn't real to start with." Her gentle voice was firm with conviction.

"Oh yes," Allen said, "it can have been real all right, I promise you that."

"But that's sad, that's awful."

"Maybe it isn't meant to be." He was frowning in a puzzled way as though seeking a clue. "Maybe we are just slow to accept the inevitable. We manufacture drama where none is intended, I shouldn't wonder. Objectively people are often aware of that, but what we know and what we feel don't have much in common."

They sat for a time without speaking. Most of the children had gone home and the little park was nearly empty. They felt quiet. Happy because they had met, sad because the spring evening was gentle and ephemeral and because they must part, still almost strangers.

Bierne forced herself to look at her watch. "Oh, dear," she said with a little shock, "it's much later than I realized. Mother will have Petey's supper all ready. I *must* get him home; he'll be starving, poor lamb." As though to corroborate her statement, Petey's stirrings and murmurs, which had been embryonic, suddenly exploded. He opened his eyes very wide and then shut them tight, at the same

118

moment emitting an outraged blast as his stomach signaled its hunger pains to his brain. "Yes, darling, yes, love, we're going, Bierne will get you home right this minute, yes, she will, my lamb." Her attempts to soothe him met with still louder shrieks, but she kept patting him, hastily buttoning her coat, and turned the carriage facing down the street. "Good-by," she said. "I feel so rude rushing off this way but you can see I'm in a spot."

Allen fell into step beside her. "What about dropping into my sister's for a drink? She'll be awfully disappointed if you don't."

"Oh, that's so nice, I'd love it, really I would, but I don't dare keep the baby out any longer. It would be cruelty to him, poor mite."

Allen looked with disfavor on the Grinitch heir. His point won, that of breaking up his aunt's tête-à-tête, Allen was convinced, his roars had subsided, but he looked capable of letting fly again on virtually no provocation. Another few steps brought them to the door of Lola's apartment. Allen paused. If he said good-by to Bierne now, when would he see her again? The baby would undoubtedly be returning to his parents before long and it was unlikely that she would come back to sit in the playground. Deliberately to call her up to ask her to meet him . . . He remembered his feeling of distaste when he had thought about it the night Georgiana told him she wanted to go to Paris. He had to admit to himself that in Bierne's presence this nicety of sentiment seemed to pale, but he still hesitated. It might be a Step. One he would regret, one it was foreign to his temperament to take. As Lola had sensed he was long out of the habit of initiating any social life of his own, yet not to be with Bierne, not to see again her lovely bright head, nor to hear her speaking like a grave, good child . . . If he didn't bore her, if she didn't find him old and tiresome, why deny himself the pleasure?

She was holding out her hand to say good-by. "Perhaps your sister will be nice enough to ask me another time." His heart gave a little skip. Maybe it wasn't only an amenity. Maybe she really would like to see him again!

"Of course she will." He held on to her hand. To start from scratch was difficult. How much easier not to break the contact he now had. "Look here," he said. "I'm not particularly interested in a drink at this moment. Let me walk home with you, may I?"

She really did seem pleased. "Why, of course. How very nice."

As they went down the street together Bierne glanced at him surreptitiously. She was not certain of baby-carriage etiquette. Should a man take over as though the baby were a valise or an automobile, or was that woman's work? The question was settled for her automatically, since it never arose in Allen's mind. He would have been horrified to find himself wheeling a baby carriage even if the occupant had appealed to him, which the Grinitch infant definitely did not.

As they neared Fifty-third Street he thought of the empty evening which lay ahead of him. To be sure a brief case full of manuscripts awaited his attention, but the idea of them had been depressing him all day and now, having seen Bierne, depressed him still more. He was weary of paper life. What was she doing? he wondered. She doubtless had an engagement with one of the young men with whom she had assured him she was not in love, but supposing she hadn't? Supposing she was going to spend the evening in what he felt instinctively was a pretty dreary flat? Wasn't he being a fool to let that happen when they had an alternative? He stopped and laid his hand close to hers on the handle of the baby carriage. "This is so pleasant," he said, "I hate to have it end. Would you by any chance be free for dinner?" She looked at him, her eyes very blue and shining. "You'd be doing a real kindness," he went on, "if you'd dine with me. I'm alone and not enjoying it a bit."

She had never dreamed that this could happen, she had never been able to see how or why it should, and yet how wonderful that it had. Acceptance was on the tip of her tongue, but she hesitated. Mr. Goodyear was a married man. Mrs. Honeywell had brought Bierne up to regard married men as little different from the dead. As far as a genteel young girl was concerned they did not exist. In the dim past, in Syracuse, there had been a young woman who had not held this sound philosophy and she had caused Mrs. Honeywell a deal of trouble with Mr. Honeywell, and it was not the kind of business Mrs. Honeywell ever intended to see repeated in her orbit. As far as she was able she had rendered married men invisible to her daughters, and now that Stella had a husband she was doing what she could to create for him the impression that the earth had been denuded of all other females. Holy wedlock, Mrs. Honeywell considered, was no place for the free, inquiring critical spirit.

120

But Mr. Goodyear is different from just any married man, Bierne was thinking. I know Mrs. Goodyear too. In a way they're my friends. It's silly to think, that because he asks me to dine one evening when he's alone that I'm ever going to see him again except by chance. Still, if her mother found it out there was sure to be unpleasantness: chilly disapproval or, what was worse, sorrowful disappointment that a mother does all she can for her girls and it comes to this.

Allen's heart sank as Bierne hesitated. I needn't have been so damn timid, he thought scornfully; she won't have me on a bet.

"Why, I—why, yes, thank you. I'll be delighted to dine."

"You will? You're an angel! Uh—I mean, that's very nice." In his relief he had gone a bit overboard. Watch it, Mac, he thought, what about that fatherly approach? "It's nearly six," he said. "Suppose I pick you up, say, half-past seven. Will that be all right?"

"Well—yes." She sounded tentative.

"Would a quarter to eight be more convenient? Or eight o'clock? There's no rush. We might have a couple of drinks someplace and think about where we want to dine."

"I—I'll tell you what might be better," she said hurriedly. "I mean if it doesn't make any difference to you, perhaps I could meet you at the restaurant." Since it was for only this one time there was no point in getting her mother upset or making it embarrassing for Mr. Goodyear. "You see, it's because of Petey. He sleeps in the living room." In the interests of harmony she considered this small distortion of fact permissible.

Allen, having had a sample of Petey when disturbed, was easily swayed. "Just as you say. Where would you like to go?"

"Any place at all. I'm not good at things like that."

"Well, let's see. How about the Ritz Tower bar? That isn't too far from here and there are several restaurants around there we might pick from."

"All right. It sounds lovely."

"Can you make it by a quarter to eight?"

"Yes, easily."

"I'll be waiting for you."

Allen turned and walked back toward the river, heading for his own apartment. For the first time the empty, shrouded rooms did

121

not depress him. As he showered and changed into a dark suit he tried to remember how many other times since his marriage he had asked a woman to dine with him. He couldn't recall any previous occasions. It seemed incredible. Luncheon was different. He frequently lunched with women in the line of business, but the only one he could remember who might have been a dinner companion was old Miss Lebaron, who had been published by Carroway forever and who wrote novels of family life in upper New York State, and she didn't count.

Why, he wondered, this small qualm, not even a qualm, a consciousness, about Bierne? Why should he decide he would write to Georgiana at once rather than risk having someone else tell her they had seen him with an attractive young woman? Why the sense of guilt? Was he in love with the girl? He shot the question at himself so unexpectedly that he sat down abruptly on his bed, his socks in one hand, shoes in the other. After a bit of cautious nibbling around the edges of the idea he decided he was not. He had seen her perhaps half-a-dozen times at the very outside and a couple of those times had been mere glimpses.

It was all very well for that character—Juliet? Rosalind? Phebe? By George, that was the one in *As You Like It*—it was all very well for her to demand, "Who ever loved that loved not at first sight?" but Phebe was a flighty shepherdess cavorting in an enchanted forest and possessed of a gift of gab rare in her profession.

Allen Goodyear was a fifty-year-old New Yorker with a wife and a grown daughter and a long-ingrained habit of thinking of himself in relation to his family and his job rather than of himself as an individual. Love at first sight was not for him. Love was for the single and for the young. To let himself be beguiled by a pretty face exactly half his age would be a fine piece of folly which could have exactly one outcome and that one compounded of self-contempt, heartache, and an acute sense of having made a jackass of himself. As she was a charming girl and might prove a delightful friend for Karen, there was no harm in this one evening. The temptation to others would be meager. His eyes were open, and though young women were supposed to admire older men and think them "distinguished" it was hardly likely that anyone as pretty as she and as much in demand as she must surely be would think twice about a

122

man whose chief virtue, from her point of view, was that he resembled her father.

Allen finished dressing in a poised frame of mind, pleased that he had had this honest discussion with himself and knew where he stood. He was just starting out, decided, that as it was such a balmy evening, he would walk to the Ritz Tower, when the phone rang. It was Chips Carroway, who embarked on a long-winded discussion about one of their authors, which held him up for more than ten minutes. Yet if he hurried a little he could still walk and still be on time, but when he got downstairs another tenant of the building was just dismissing a cab. Allen grabbed it with a haste one might not have expected from a man on his way to meet an interesting companion for his daughter.

Although he was two or three minutes early Bierne was waiting for him. She had been there since seven-thirty, having told her mother only that she had met friends in the playground and was going out to dinner. Busy with her grandson's supper, Mrs. Honeywell didn't pay much attention other than to grumble that, when Bierne knew Ben was going to be out, too, and she'd be all alone, it was a pity her daughter couldn't give up one evening with those old office friends. Bierne hadn't implied that they were office friends, but if Mrs. Honeywell assumed they were it simplified matters not to disillusion her, yet her connivance made the girl feel a little mean. I'm a sneak, she thought, not to tell her the truth.

At twenty-five, earning her living and contributing to the family maintenance, she was placing herself in the position of a naughty child escaping the house to meet a forbidden playmate, yet to confide in her mother was to invite a flood of lecturing and platitudes, mixed with a deal of self-pity and references to their genteel background. Bierne dressed as quickly as she could so as to get away while Mrs. Honeywell was still occupied with Petey and before she had time to settle down and revert to her usual demands for explanations and family histories.

Waiting in the little bar, she had been nervous and restless, but the moment she saw Allen the glow he always invoked in her came flooding back. Mrs. Honeywell's pretty, pouting, aging face faded from her mind; there was nothing more to fret about. Allen was there, they were free and secure, and somehow he was less like her

123

father than she had at first imagined and not only because he wasn't good at mechanical things either.

They had a couple of drinks in the bar and then he took her to dinner at a restaurant called the Châteaubriand in Fifty-sixth Street. They had pâté maison, poulet en cocotte, wine, salad, and cheese, and Bierne felt that she had come home. It was a lyrical evening and immensely satisfying to them both to find that theirs was not only a surface attraction—they had much in common: Bierne's delight in her surroundings and the delicious food and Allen's delight in Bierne. By the time they reached their coffee, the black Italian kind with chicory, they had decided that their liking for each other was based on solid ground. Proof of this was the fact that their conversation did not stumble to a halt when they stopped talking about themselves. Bierne knew almost none of the people Allen referred to, except by name, but his stories about writers she thought wonderfully entertaining and, on her side, she had some funny experiences to relate in her dealings with the rich and social women who worked on the Manhattan Aid Association drives.

She was without malice, nor did she have the practiced wit Allen was accustomed to in Georgiana and her friends, but she was capable of honest appraisal and an occasional quaint commentary on manners and mores which gave fillip to her conversation and acted as tiny staples attaching Allen's interest more and more closely to her.

He found that outside of newspapers and magazines she read little. This surprised him until he realized that reading, if it isn't one's business, requires leisure, a commodity Bierne had little of. She worked in an office all day and he knew enough of her life at home to realize that her time was pretty well occupied with household chores, yet his occasional quotes, which Georgiana heard with mockery and resignation, Bierne listened to with respect and, indeed, found herself falling in love with him partly because of his knowledge of an art with which she had only a nodding acquaintance—literature. She made up her mind that she would at once read something published by Carroway so that she should not be found wanting if she ever saw him again.

It was about ten when they finished dinner, too late for the theater, too early to go some place for a nightcap. What to do? Had

Lola and Peter been at home Allen would have suggested dropping in to see them, but they were dining out. He and Bierne had spoken of Calypso music. Allen remembered that Karen had bought a new album when she was home for the spring holiday. It was at the apartment stacked with other records in the library which, since Georgiana's departure, he was using instead of the big drawing room. He thought of it but his mind shied away from asking her to come there.

Bierne was lovely and desirable and she could be his daughter. He wasn't sure whether he was in love with her, but he knew what he wanted and was determined not to put himself in a spot where its attainment might be possible. It would be no kindness in return for her companionship and gaiety to place her in the equivocal position she would be in if he asked her to come to the house, whether she refused or accepted. Besides, he reminded himself, there was a question of taste involved. The apartment was Georgiana's too. She had chosen to walk out but it was nonetheless hers. Alas, for his peace of mind, his companion was nonetheless lovely. He took a grip on himself. Since he had been having a quoting evening he silently tossed in one more. "This, too, will pass."

In the end they decided to go to a movie. Neither of them wanted to very much but neither did they wish to part, and they felt they should leave the restaurant, as the waiters were beginning to look like men who had made other plans.

They went to the Lexington Avenue Translux. In the dark theater they sat with their shoulders and arms touching. He breathed again the carnation scent she used but he did not take her hand. When the picture was over they walked up Lexington Avenue to Fifty-fifth Street and west to the St. Regis because, he said, that was on their way home and it was if you turned left on Fifth Avenue and went down to Fifty-third and then left again going east.

"It's a short cut really," Bierne said happily as he initiated her into the mahogany splendors of the King Cole Bar. To his delight she ordered a beer. Although she was so fair and slender, she had a lusty enjoyment of food and drink which amused him, the way her aptitude for mechanics amused him, and he told her that he looked forward someday to watching her change a spark plug and hammer a nail. The remark caused her heart to beat faster. It was a tendril

125

into the future. "You think I'm joking," she said; "but I can really do those things. Not spark plugs, perhaps, because we don't own a car, but I understand about screw drivers and I can fix plumbing. The traps and things like that."

Her beauty apparently made little impression on her, but she had an engaging conceit about her manly accomplishments. Allen was charmed. He thought her beautiful, entertaining, and kind. To Bierne, he was the most amusing, wise, gentle person she had ever known. They were very happy.

They left the St. Regis finally and he was about to hail a cab when she touched his arm. "Let's walk."

"All right." They walked slowly along in the spring night, their fingers linked lightly together. When the lights turned red at the crossings they waited the full time although at that hour there was little traffic.

After they had crossed Lexington Avenue and there would be no more stops until her doorway, Bierne said, "This is the loveliest evening I have ever spent in my whole life. Thank you."

"No," he said. "It is I who thank you. You were on a real rescue mission tonight. You don't know how I appreciate it."

They walked up the steps and she took out her latchkey and unlocked the front door. "Good night," she said. They were past the Mr. Goodyear and Miss Honeywell stage but they had not yet reached first names. Until he spoke. He laid his hand gently against her cheek. His eyes searched her face, the line of her brows, her nose, her soft mouth, and the little hollow at the base of her throat.

"Bierne, lovely Bierne, good night." He kissed her lightly on the tip of her nose and turned and went down the steps. She stood as he had left her, tears of happiness welling in her eyes.

9

They had dined together on Saturday night. Sunday morning Allen slept late and when he got up he prepared his own breakfast, and cleaned up the dishes afterward. He was good about that, he didn't let them accumulate until they were all used and then go out and buy new ones rather than wash them, but dry them he would not. They dried on the drainboard of the kitchen sink and he used the same ones over and over again. Georgiana had tried to train him to a revolving system on the theory that the design would wear off one cup, saucer, and plate and sets would be spoiled, but she had never succeeded.

Allen thought of Bierne and felt warm, happy, and wary. He thought of telephoning her but in the daytime, with a bulging brief case confronting him, he was able to overrule the temptation without too great difficulty and he forestalled any possibility of a nervous conscience by a long letter to Georgiana in which he gave an almost photographic account of the previous evening. That the result did not approximate the original was his fault only in that he had chosen the wrong medium.

Some objects and events may be photographed, others, if one is to render their true quality, should be painted or set to music, since their essence is more faithfully reproduced through imagination than by the journalistic report.

Allen spent Sunday afternoon and evening with the Quicks and friends of theirs who came to dinner. Monday, looking over his engagement pad at the office, he saw that his secretary had jotted down the Lord & Taylor American Design Annual Luncheon for the following Thursday at the Waldorf, with a memo that Mr. Bernard Herrmann, musical director of the Columbia Broadcasting System and a close friend of Mr. Quick, was to receive one of the awards. You have two tickets, added the memo.

Allen glanced at his other appointments. Thursday already looked pretty full and he had about decided to skip the luncheon when it occurred to him that it might be the sort of thing that would appeal to Bierne. Working as she did for the Manhattan Aid Association, she took a civic pride in New York activities. He put in a call to her. "How would you like to have luncheon with me next Thursday? It's the Lord & Taylor Awards at the Waldorf, it may be interesting."

"I think it sounds wonderful. I'd love to come."

"I'll meet you at twelve-thirty in the lobby on the Park Avenue side. Top of the stairs. All right?"

"Oh yes. I'll be there."

There was a little pause. "I remember Saturday night," he said.

"So do I. I think of it all the time."

"Good-by till Thursday."

"Good-by."

He hung up and sat for a time with his hand on the receiver. Her simplicity was disturbing. He already liked her so very, very much, if she were to like him, too, if the difference in their ages did not strike her as incongruous . . . What was it she had said in the playground? "If you care for someone it isn't because of the number of years they've been on earth . . . if you love them, it doesn't matter, you love them anyway." Love, after one dinner together. That was a little rapid, perhaps, but it would undoubtedly be more prudent to see her in the daytime at public luncheons. Something strange took place in human chemistry after sundown. He wondered if there had ever been any such thing as a single intimate little dinner for two.

In her office Bierne, too, sat with her hand on the telephone. As long as she touched the receiver there was still a connecting link between them. The sun had shone on Sunday and she had taken Petey to the river playground in the hope that Allen might be there. He had not been, and she had come back and remarked that night at family supper, somewhat to the surprise of Mrs. Honeywell and Uncle Ben who had spent the afternoon sunning on the stoop and gossiping with the neighbors, that it was too bad the day was overcast. Now her heart took wing. An invitation to dinner would have been a tiny bit more wonderful, but luncheon had its own appeal. Luncheon, being more prosaic than dinner, was, in a paradoxical way, more intimate. It was as though she were in the current of his life accepted as a part of his routine; a closer relationship, actually, than an occasional romantic evening. The more she thought about it the more splendid luncheon seemed. She would joyfully have met him at 11 A.M. for crackers and milk.

Bierne was cautious with her fifty-five-dollar-a-week salary. Fifteen dollars and seventy-five cents she contributed to the household as her share of the running expenses, the rest of it she banked. Banks, however, had been known to fail, and she felt strongly the advisability of not keeping all one's eggs in one basket. She had, accordingly, five savings accounts: one to be touched only in case of illness, one to finance her annual two weeks' vacation, one for Christmas pres-

128

ents, one for clothes, and one for insurance to pay the premiums on her tiny annuity.

The day of Allen's invitation she committed an indiscretion. That year she had had to buy a new spring suit, the clothes account was depleted, and Christmas stood at two dollars and seventy-three cents, including interest. Radiant with health and anticipation, she borrowed from the illness bank, the Bowery Savings was the one for illness, and bought a new hat.

Allen did no shopping, but Thursday morning he chose his tie with special care and left the office about twelve-fifteen, allowing himself ample time to walk to the Waldorf. Bierne was a few minutes late, arriving breathlessly and apologizing for her tardiness. "I'm so terribly sorry, but I got held up at the office and the traffic was awful."

"Don't fret; look at all these other people"—he indicated the crowded lobby—"they're all going up to the luncheon too." She smiled as he took her arm and guided her into the stream of guests moving toward the ballroom elevators.

They sat near the dais at a table for eight, and Germaine and Claude Dauzat joined them. Three of the other four people were strangers to Bierne but were apparently known to Allen and the Dauzats in the superficial way in which New Yorkers know other New Yorkers who circulate with more or less constancy in the same channels of civic life. The fourth person to arrive and join a friend already there was Mrs. Barclay Hamilton. She greeted Allen and Bierne cordially, and if she was surprised to see the girl in this particular group her manner did not betray it. When Allen asked Bierne to accompany him to the luncheon he had assumed that in all likelihood they would bump into several acquaintances, but he considered it would make no difference one way or the other.

Mrs. Barclay Hamilton, however, he had not counted on, and, though he supposed his reaction juvenile, he was a little discomfited by the meeting. It occurred to him that through her son Mrs. Hamilton was probably on more intimate terms with the Goodyear family than the Goodyears realized. His suspicion was strengthened when she inquired after Georgiana's health and remarked in friendly fashion that he must be very proud of her and wasn't her new job exciting? Such a fine magazine—here she included the Dauzats with

129

a gracious nod—but it must make it lonely for him. "I understand," she added, "that there's a possibility Karen will be joining her mother during the summer holidays." Allen acknowledged that this was so, making a mental note that Karen and Barclay must be maintaining a fairly exhaustive correspondence. He was relieved when, luncheon ended, Miss Shaver of Lord & Taylor rose to her feet in the middle of the dais and started to announce the winners of the 1947 awards for New Patterns in Artistic Expression.

Allen, remembering the theatrical discussions he had occasionally listened in on at home between Karen and Poppy, turning on Poppy's recalcitrant parent, assumed that Bierne's youthful interest would lie in Miss Agnes de Mille, who so artistically patterned the dance. To his surprise she inclined to Mr. Louis de Rochement, Documentary Approach to Films. "That's a good solid sort of thing, isn't it?" she said, her eyes shining. Allen thought of Nancy Slade's jerry-built bookshelves which Bierne had hankered to repair. She's workmanlike, he thought, a solid sort of girl in a slender sort of way, and again he was amused and touched and fell a little deeper into love.

They saw each other a good deal after that, and Allen's letters to Georgiana grew less reportorial. The following Sunday they met again in the little park, and that night he took her to a Fred Allen broadcast in Radio City's Studio 8. He could not remember such an amusing evening. But although Mr. Allen's contribution to the amusement was large, it was not entire.

Since he and Bierne were so compatible, Allen's consciousness of the difference in their ages was abating, but he still had a kind of double vision of themselves: he enjoyed being with her and he enjoyed her enjoyment. She had lived in New York for twelve years but the variety of life, not only in the city but in her own neighborhood, was an unexpected and fascinating surprise. Her enthusiasm stimulated him, aroused in him forgotten, long-moribund sensations while she, on her side, fell completely in love. Allen was the kind of man she would have loved in Timbuctoo, but to love him in New York, to have him present to her the restaurants, the amusements, the pastimes of the city was a joyful experience.

They went to the theater. She enjoyed most *The Importance of Being Earnest* and *Finian's Rainbow.* They went to an exhibition of

130

Cézanne's paintings at the Wildenstein Galleries. Bierne was awed by the splendor of the Galleries and felt right at home with the apples and lemons and civilized French forests. She decided then and there that Cézanne was her man. He was the happy medium, modern without being abstract, and a relief from those pictures which had hitherto constituted her conception of art: bulging women in plumes who looked on the verge of a belch; turbulent battle scenes in which kings, inappropriately attired in brocaded coats, rode wildly plunging horses across forty feet of canvas.

Though together much of the time, they had not yet reached that stage in their relationship where they automatically expected to spend every evening with each other, no matter how pleasant those evenings might be. Allen sometimes had business dinners, out-of-town engagements with Carroway authors, or invitations which it would have been graceless to refuse. Not wishing to cause gossip, he did not like to ask if he might bring Bierne along, and as they had few mutual friends there was little chance of their meeting in somebody else's house.

Bierne, for her part, found it difficult and foreign to her candid temperament constantly to evade her mother's probing and Uncle Ben's good-natured curiosity about her activities, yet she kept putting off that day when she would have to admit to her family that she was guilty of what Gladys Honeywell referred to as skylarking with a married man. Her mother's phrase had a rakish sound; it evoked a sentiment in no way applicable to the emotion Bierne felt when she and Allen were together. She was happy when she was with him, happier than she had ever been in her life, but even when they were laughing it was a quiet sort of happiness, like sunshine on a still day; and hovering always, just outside of acknowledgment, was the fact that Allen *was* a married man.

Bierne had not even confided in Stella. Stella would be kind enough, she felt; even if she disapproved she would be unlikely to censure her younger sister, but she would point out very definitely that married men were impractical. Wasn't it true that like herself Bierne wanted to marry and raise a family? Yes, Bierne would say, it was, whereupon Stella would explain reasonably and with a minimum of moralizing that Bierne was surely intelligent enough to realize that she was, by her conduct, defeating her own ends.

131

The Honeywells were not Catholics, but Gladys's training had told on Stella. When she married Harry she considered it was for life. He was hers and she was his, not only in this world but very likely in the next. Since God had joined them together it stood to reason they would be bound even closer once they entered into His kingdom. Satisfied with Harry, this seemed to her an admirable arrangement. Stella had never had to tussle between her heart and her common sense, between her scruples and her desires. Life's gray areas were not her bailiwick. Bierne was astonished when she found they were her own.

Occasionally she could not avoid telling her mother that Allen was her companion for the evening. She invented a little job she was doing for him, typing up some lecture notes, although from Mrs. Honeywell's expression she suspected it buttered no parsnips. Uncle Ben was more of an ally. He considered his niece an unusual young woman, certainly she was unusually pretty, and he wanted her to have a good time. She worked hard and deserved a little fun. Ben hoped she wouldn't go off the deep end and get hurt, but if she was seeing something of the world, enjoying herself, even if it was with a married man, it was all right with her uncle. Yet even he was unaware of the extent to which Allen monopolized his niece's thought. When she was with him she lived; the rest of her existence was spent in anticipation of his next phone call, of their next appointment.

For the first time she wooed Gladys into making clothes for her. Bierne had always bought her clothes in shops, both to save time and not to impose on her mother whom she felt shouldn't be asked to sew for her family after spending her days sewing for a living. Since it lightened her task, Mrs. Honeywell accepted this attitude without quibble yet harbored a little private grudge against her daughter, suspecting that she did not consider her a dressmaker of the first water. Mrs. Honeywell didn't consider herself so either, but that was for her to brood on in the silence of the night and not something to be thrown up to her by her own flesh and blood. Secretly she was flattered when Bierne asked if she would make her a dress, and after a bout of ill-fitting and ill-feeling, under her daughter's careful direction, she did turn out a very becoming frock. "It's dressy but it's refined," she said with satisfaction.

"Sets you off," said Uncle Ben.

"It isn't every girl," Mrs. Honeywell went on, "who can look so pretty and have it cost so little. Young men with marriage on their minds, who respect a girl and think about her future, appreciate a thing like that."

Bierne let the gauntlet lie. By silence she could better protect Allen and her love for him and their mutual happiness. She was aglow with happiness now because for the first time she could look forward to two engagements. The coming Sunday they were to spend together, and he had asked her if the following Tuesday she would like to dine with him at his sister and brother-in-law's.

"Look, kid," Lola had said to him over the telephone, "I have a hunch you've found yourself a little diversion. Why don't you bring it along?"

"Thanks," Allen said. "I'd like to."

"He sounded kind of thoughtful," Lola remarked to Peter in recounting the conversation. "I wish he'd been more ribald about it. A cheery, 'And how, baby, and how.' You know—more like a light-hearted lay and the hell with it."

Peter shook his head. "Allen's not the type. He's a guy who means it."

"But, my heavens," Lola protested, "here we are, what—the end of May. Georgiana hasn't been gone six weeks. He's been meaning his marriage for twenty-three years. This *can't* have developed into anything serious."

"Why not? I was pretty damned serious about you after the first meeting."

"That was different. You weren't married and, anyhow, you had a Spanish grandfather. You're the fiery Latin type. We Goodyears are reliable New England stock."

Peter tossed the twins' panda at her. "Who is the dame anyhow?"

"Bierne Honeywell, I imagine. It must be; he doesn't know anybody else."

"Do I know her?"

Lola shook her head. "She's nice, though. You'll meet her Tuesday night; Al's bringing her to dinner."

Tuesday night Bierne was keeping in a compartment by itself. Because she was to dine with Allen at his family's the evening

133

would have a special quality. She would take it out later and turn it over and think about it, but first came their whole long Sunday alone together. It was a rite to be prepared for. That morning she was up at six.

She had always been well groomed, but since falling in love with Allen her efforts had been redoubled. Like most young working-women much of her time away from the office was devoted to her person and her clothes. Today was a sort of test of her efficiency. She and Allen had planned to drive to Jones Beach, so not only did she have to wash her hair, mend a strap on her slip, shine her shoes, sew two buttons on her sweater, and supplement Mrs. Honeywell's sketchy cleaning up of the living room, she also had to fry a chicken, stuff hard-boiled eggs, and prepare sandwiches, for she had volunteered to bring the lunch and expended so much effort on planning, marketing, and preparation that Uncle Ben had been moved to ask if she was aiming to hold a clambake.

It was perhaps a bit early in the season for beach picnics, but that would be the fun. No crowds, and with spring full upon them, both she and Allen were longing to get out of the city. With every fair day he berated himself for having given in to Georgiana on the renting of their place in the country. It was true that she had arranged an excellent deal, and when the tenant's first check arrived for the first payment he banked it with gratitude, but all of Fort Knox couldn't substitute for the daffodils and the tulips and the smell of the spring earth.

Allen was not a sustained gardener, but he was not dead either. The vernal urge stirred his being, "almost" Georgiana would say, "to the mad abandon of a turtle," but she would laugh and hand him a hoe and a trowel and packages of seeds and he would go to work with a zest that lasted for at least two week ends.

He had told Bierne about the place in the country, and she had said that her dream was to make enough money someday to buy a little house. "I'd love working in it," she said, and, looking at her, Allen felt that possibly there could be more enjoyment in domesticity than he had experienced in many years.

On Sunday he picked her up at eleven o'clock. She had already done a day's work but her eyes as she greeted him shone like morning stars. She was alone in the house. Uncle Ben was off in Central

134

Park pitching horseshoes and Mrs. Honeywell had gone to church. "To call upon the Lord," she said, "in my extremity," and she had looked at her daughter and sighed, and patting her soft, still-golden hair as she arranged her churchly hat, she remarked to the mirror that it was a wonder she didn't turn white overnight.

Bierne was relieved not to have her at home. She envisaged a meeting between Allen and her family with misgiving, yet as she waved good-by to her mother from the steps and watched her walk toward Lexington Avenue she reflected that daughters were ingrates. They wanted a combination of non-interference and understanding love, which probably was inhuman, although Bierne felt that with a daughter of her own she would know exactly how to achieve the balance.

She finished tidying the living room and completed packing the picnic lunch just as Allen rang the bell.

"Hi," he said, as she opened the door. "All ready?"

"All set. Will you come in?"

He hesitated. "Mother and Uncle Ben have gone out," she said quickly. "I won't be a minute, I just have to get my coat and the luncheon. There's the *Times* and the *American* if you haven't seen the papers yet."

"Thanks," he said. "I'll be fine. Don't hurry."

She started from the room but at the door she turned.

"This is the first time you've been in my house."

"For me it's a milestone."

"That's how I feel too." He smiled, but she looked at him gravely and went out.

Allen glanced around him. He went over and cautiously pulled aside the blue curtains and peered into the tiny cubicle dressing rooms. He looked at the covered sewing machine, at the worn furniture, the old Brussels carpet, and the net curtains hanging unevenly. It was a shabby room but not uncomfortable, and the spring sunshine flooded through the windows. He thought of his own apartment. The effect was one of great charm, and he had to acknowledge that Georgiana had achieved it with a maximum of imagination and at what, she had assured him, was comparatively moderate expense.

It occurred to him that the atmosphere in which a married man passed his life was disproportionately dependent on his wife's taste.

If it was good, the man was blessed. Women never thought husbands knew anything about decoration and once the honeymoon quarters were installed were unlikely ever again to consult their wishes or preference. Life did sorry things to relationships, but one of the charming aspects of new love was the consideration two people instinctively showed to each other. The idea propelled him to considerate movement. He went down the hall and called, "Anything I can do to help?"

"No, thanks." Bierne appeared in the kitchen doorway carrying the two boxes in which she had packed their lunch. "All set. Shall we go?"

They went out to the car and Allen stowed away the boxes and checked his contributions: ice in a thermos container, the makings of cocktails, and a bottle of wine. It was, he said, a festive occasion and he intended to treat it as such. In the back of the car he had thrown a couple of rugs, a portable radio, and a camera. "I thought of folding chairs, too," he told her, "and a beach umbrella, but they're in the country."

Bierne laughed happily. "We can certainly manage without the chairs and I think we'll be glad of the sunshine."

She was right. The sky was blue and the day hot enough for them to drive with the top down, but when they got out to the beach the great expanse of sand was unprotected, and when the wind blew the sun was welcome. Dark glasses, they found, were all the shelter they wanted. Others, too, had been inspired to picnic, but the summer crowds had not yet gathered and the Jones Beach water front was so vast that by walking a little way down the shore they could find comparative isolation.

They saw the sandpipers laying their swift, delicate tracks; they listened to the crying of the gulls and watched them wheel and settle out beyond the breakers; and stared incredulously at three hardy human specimens splashing in the waves.

"I don't believe in it before July," Allen declared. "Independence Day is good enough for me."

"I don't mind the date," Bierne said, "but I like a good hot spell to heat the water for me first. I'm a sissy."

"So am I," he said.

Bierne shook her head. "Oh no. I know there are lots of men's

136

things you don't do, like sports or handling tools or boring things like heavy drinking, but I think you're tough in the way a man should be tough."

They had reached the dune they had spotted and claimed from a distance as theirs. Sand slipping under their feet, they trudged halfway up it and dropped their bundles. Allen spread one of the rugs and placed the lunchboxes and bottles on it with some optimistic notion of keeping out the sand. When everything was shipshape he turned to her.

Warm from their walk and struggling up the dune, she had taken off her coat and stood a little above him silhouetted against the sky. The breeze lifted her golden hair and flattened her skirt against her slender legs. She wore a blue angora sweater which, she had informed him on the way out, was a nuisance, as the fluff got in her nose, but he thought kindly of it for the way it sweetly revealed the curve of her breasts and molded her supple waist. Suddenly the breeze whipped her skirt above her knees and for an instant he caught a glimpse of lace-edged slip and the delicate skin above her stockings. With a swift gesture she caught the skirt against her. "Gracious," she murmured, and abruptly sat down on the sand.

Suddenly she smiled shyly, "I'm reading more, you know. It's habit forming, isn't it?"

"You're wonderful. When do you get time?"

"I manage. And you see, as you're on my mind quite a bit, I mean, because we've been seeing each other, when there's a man in the story, a nice man that is, if it's a story of adventure or heroism——I—well, it's natural for me to picture you as the hero because——" She stopped.

"Go on. Because——?"

"Well, because we're friends."

"I see. Tell me, don't you ever read romances, love stories?"

"Oh yes, of course."

"And how do you see those heroes? Clark Gable? Dana Andrews? Van Johnson?"

"No," she said quietly. "I never think of movie people at all."

"My experience," Allen said, "is that in love stories you never have to use your imagination much on the hero. He's standard. Tall, lean-bellied, gentle-eyed, two-fisted—try lugging in a three-fisted hero, see

137

what you get—an Irish grin, and a cap of unruly curls. And he is never, by any chance, over thirty-two. Over thirty-two they throw him out of the league. Not one of those bug—uh, not one of those boys is ever anything but a juvenile. I think I'll have to write a book myself."

"I don't see how you can resist," Bierne said. "You're an editor, you know much more about it than the authors who send in manuscripts."

Allen tensed a moment, waiting for the next harpoon, and then slowly relaxed as he realized it was not his wife speaking. He turned and looked at Bierne. In her beautiful face there was nothing but happiness and admiration.

"Promise me something, will you?" he said.

"Anything."

"Don't get to reading too much. And don't worry about going to cocktail parties and leading the social life. The way you are is——"

"Yes?"

There went those clichés jingling through his head again. Like a flower, like a star, you are song, you are springtime. All right, "O Lyric Love, half angel and half bird"—what's the matter with that?

He said, "The way you are is fine."

"I'll have to read *your* book, though. What will it be about?"

"My book? Oh, my book! That's going to be about my ideal man."

Bierne hugged her knees happily. "What's he like?"

"Well, when the story opens he's fifty. No, by God, he's older than that. He's fifty-five, and as the story progresses he gets to be even older. Hell, he gets to be ninety and he's still going strong."

Bierne nodded wisely. "Glands."

"Glands nothing. Or at any rate no monkey's, just his own. This fellow's an ambitious extrovert. He goes careening through life having a high old time. Big success at his job, women left and right, more and more hair on his head——"

Bierne's eyes were shining with amusement. "Does he have a great capacity for liquor?"

"Swills it by the quart. Out of pewter tankards. Never heard of a hangover. What's more, he travels all over the globe——"

"In seven-league boots."

"Begetting children by the dozen."

138

"Is he rich?"

"Rolling."

"What happens to him in the end?"

"Oh, in the end he falls in love."

"What's *she* like?"

"She? Well, now, let me see." Allen fell back on one elbow. He pulled a glittering blade of beach grass and nibbled on it as he gazed out over the sand and water. "Since this is a fairy story," he said, "she, quite properly, is a fairy princess. She has very fair hair, but as she is a modern princess she wears it short, in a golden wave on her forehead, and under the gold her eyes are bluer than the Atlantic Ocean and she has a little mole on her left cheekbone and her mouth is coral pink. She is perhaps a little thin, and this is surprising, because she has a quite startling appetite but her legs are perfect, neither too thin nor too fat. Her voice is soft, and she is a silly girl, for she wears a blue sweater that tickles her nose, but this is all right with our hero for he is able to get a more defined picture of her. Indeed, even when he is not looking at her he sees her as clearly as though she stood before him, and in the nighttime she lights up the darkness and the night is filled with dreams. Sometimes it seems to him that there is a whiff of carnation in the air and that he can stroke her golden hair and that she places her hand in his."

She placed her hand in his. She was sitting a little above him on the slope of the dune. He turned and drew himself up and buried his face against her and his arms went around her. She held him close and laid her cheek against her head and felt the hot sun on her back and heard the crash of the breakers and the crying gulls, and thought her heart would break with happiness.

"I love you, I love you." He murmured the words against her side, against her breast, against her throat.

"And I love you."

He found her mouth and kissed her. She fell back on the sand, his arm under her head. She lay in a hollow of the dune so that the grasses, bending above her striped her sunlit face with shadow; a grain of sand glittered like a diamond on her cheek. Again his mouth was on hers; they strained against each other. Presently she pushed him away. "Please, please, I—I can't——"

Slowly he took his arms from around her and leaned and kissed her hair. "My darling."

She sat up and smiled a little uncertainly. "My," she said breathlessly, "that was sudden, wasn't it?"

Allen took a deep breath. "For me, not so sudden. I've been wanting to do that for a month."

"You and your fairy princess."

"One takes a fairy princess where one finds her."

"Oh, Allen."

"Bierne." They drew close again.

He took her face in both his hands and kissed her hard, then he held her at arm's length. "That's enough; we'll get ourselves arrested. What we need, my girl, is a drink."

"Yes, I—I think it would be a good idea."

Allen opened an impressive leather traveling case and silver and crystal bottles flashed in the sun. Bierne, glancing at the cardboard boxes in which she had packed their luncheon, said in a small, awed voice, "My goodness, you must have spent all morning polishing it."

He grinned. "Bridal, isn't it? Truth to tell, this is the first time I've used the damn thing; it was a Christmas present from my boss."

Bierne opened the thermos jug with the ice and Allen mixed the cocktails. They raised their glasses, kissed, and drank. They ate their picnic luncheon, and when they were finished Bierne carefully wrapped up their rubbish and put it in one of the big wire baskets thoughtfully placed by Mr. Jones at intervals along his beach. Allen watched her. "You're a tidy girl."

"I shouldn't like people to think we were vandals," she explained gravely.

He took both her hands and pulled her down beside him. "My darling, sit here; we must talk."

"I suppose we must," she said reluctantly, "but this is so much happiness."

He kissed her softly. Her temples, her eyelids, the tip of her nose. She slipped her hand inside his jacket; he covered her hand with his and held it close against his heart. "Bierne, Bierne, Bierne."

"My dearest."

"Darling, listen. I can't not love you, it's too late not to love you, but I wouldn't hurt you for anything on earth, and yet my common sense tells me I'm doing just that. You're young, I'm old."

"You're *not* old! That's a stupid, stupid thing to say, my darling."

"God knows I don't feel it, but——"

"Then there are no buts. What people call common sense can be a vast deal of nonsense. It's so rare, dear Allen, that maybe even you don't have all you should. Don't trust that sparse thing. What does your heart tell you?"

"My heart sings. The lyrics, I suspect, are a little corny, the music is sublime. I hold you close to me like this and I could teach Beethoven a thing or two."

They kissed. "I love you," she said, "I love you."

He held both her wrists tightly. "Darling, don't. Help me. I'm trying to be honest. You're far too important to me for me not to be. I'm twenty-five years older than you, Bierne, I'm a married man, the father of a grown daughter. You're young, you've got your life before you, you have your own friends—nice boys, you said it was fun to go out with them. You've mentioned one or two. A Danny and a Todd something or other."

"Allen, what are you trying to sell me?" she said gently.

"The idea that I'm bad for you. That you should go away from me."

"Do you want me to?"

"I never want you out of arm's reach. I long for you, but what can I offer you? Georgiana and I are going our own ways, God knows, but that's not the kind of life for you; you deserve better than that. If and when I can get a divorce I don't know. You should have a man who can marry you and is your own age; you should have your own home and children. Financially, even, I'm not in the clear."

"Do you love me?"

"I adore you."

Bierne threw back her head and laughed softly to the spring sky. "Mr. Goodyear, Mr. Goodyear, you are the worst salesman I ever heard. You tell me all these awful things; apparently they are supposed to be so awful that if you had even a little teeny, weeny sales talent you would scare me to death, but you haven't and you don't. We love each other. What is there to fear? What is there that can't work out?"

He saw the love and trust in her eyes and his own eyes filled with tears. He drew her head on to his shoulder and stroked her hair and

141

held her as gently as though she had been an ill child. They sat quietly for a long time, occasionally exchanging a soft kiss, murmuring broken phrases of love and tenderness.

As the afternoon wore on the sky clouded over, and although it was not cold a dampness began to envelop them. Bierne gave a little sneeze, the impetus that started them on their way home.

Driving back to town, Allen was silent much of the way. He was trying to think what to do, where to take her. They had tacitly accepted that they would become lovers that night, but Allen reflected wryly that the hotel and apartment shortage must be driving many New Yorkers to a life of unaccustomed continence they little relished. In the end he settled for the place he had known from the beginning he would decide upon, but he had hesitated for Bierne's sake and for Georgiana's, but Georgiana was far away and his longing for Bierne overwhelmed any reservations he made an effort to cling to. Besides, there was no alternative.

They had almost reached the Queensboro Bridge leading into the city before he broached his suggestion. "Darling, let's go to my house, shall we? We can freshen up and either go out for supper, if you want to, or get ourselves something there. There are plenty of eggs and tins of stuff. We'll see how we feel."

She looked at him steadily. "All right," she said, and turned her head and looked out the window.

Oh God, he thought, what hell! This is everything that is tender and vital and real and yet it's like a cheap seduction. Married man lures virgin to apartment while wife's in Europe. "My wife's gone to the country, hurray, hurray." He felt a surge of self-disgust, followed by the determination that she must not know it too. He took her hand and squeezed it hard. "I love you."

"I love you."

"Turn about is fair play, you know. I went to your house this morning, you return the call this evening. That's the social life."

She nodded, her eyes very bright, her smile a little set.

They came down the ramp from the upper roadway of the bridge and turned into Fifty-eighth Street and down First Avenue. In three or four minutes they were at Allen's apartment. He said good evening to the elevator man who recognized Bierne from the times she had been there for the auction committee meetings and who nodded

142

to her and said "Good evening, miss." Oh, great, Allen thought. Does one bribe them handsomely or does one not, in such a situation?

As he put his key in the lock he observed that he was afraid she would find the place depressing. "It looked quite different when— uh, when you were here before."

"I shan't mind."

He took her into the library, which was in order, and turned and held out his arms. She came to him, and they stood for a minute in close embrace. He released her. "Now, madam, I'm going to tidy things up a bit. Which would you rather do? Sit here and relax and have a drink, or powder your nose in Karen's room? If that Jane who comes in to clean has been doing her job it oughtn't to be too much of a shambles."

A subtle expression of relief flitted across her face. "I'd rather clean up, too, and wait and have a drink with you."

"Good." He led her down the hall and threw open the door. "There you are. I know Karen won't mind if you make yourself at home."

"Oh, I have everything, thanks, powder, comb, all I need." She seemed to hesitate. He smiled at her and closed the door and went to his own room.

Poor kid, he thought, she looked scared. Why not? asked the inescapable voice. No, damn it, no, this is love. For both of us. Uh huh, but you're the one who must shoulder the responsibility. She's a virgin and young enough to be your daughter. A light sweat broke out on his forehead. My God, he thought, how do rakes manage it? Here's a girl I not only want but love; my feeling for her amounts almost to reverence. Why should I be guilty, apprehensive, furtive? Where's the sweeping power of passion? He wiped his brow and wondered a little grimly if women ever realized the soul-searching and plain panic a man could go through on these occasions.

While cogitating, however, he had been practically engaged. The cleaning woman didn't come on Sundays so his bed had been unmade since morning and his bathroom littered. He closed the door leading into the room he and Georgiana shared when she was home and went to work putting out fresh linen, making up the bed, and tidying the bathroom. When he had finished he looked around, rea-

143

sonably satisfied. It was a manly room with books, a desk, and tailored hangings, nothing connubial about it, nothing to remind her of his wife. He drew the curtains and turned out all the lights except the desk lamp. The room looked discreet and welcoming. He left the door open and went to the kitchen to get ice. When he came back to the library she was waiting for him. She looked lovely. Fresh and rested and shining clean.

They decided it would be more fun to get supper themselves than to go out to a restaurant, and went to work with cans and a few fortuitously discovered mushrooms and Bierne did something inventive and delicious with tomatoes. Supper was soon ready. Allen carried the tray into the library and Bierne plugged in the toaster. "There, my darling, fall to," he said, pulling out her chair and kissing the top of her head as she sat down.

She noticed two highball glasses filled with ice. "I don't think I care for any whisky, thanks."

"You're not getting any whisky, you're getting champagne. It's considered sacrilege to ice it direct, but there wasn't any cold and personally I like it on the rocks. How about you?"

"I like it any way. I've had it only twice before in my life. Once at Stella and Harry's wedding and once at a dinner Mrs. Hamilton gave for the Manhattan Aid workers."

Allen reached for the bottle beside his chair, uncorked it with a pop, and let the champagne foam into their glasses. Bierne drank eagerly. "It's delicious. So dry. The ice is a good idea, isn't it?"

Allen touched her glass with his own. " 'Drink, yea, drink abundantly, oh, beloved.' Sound advice."

"Whose is it?"

"King Solomon's to his bride."

"Oh," she said. She looked down and in a moment a tear fell on her sweater.

"My dearest, what is it? Bierne, what is it?" He got up and came and sat on the arm of her chair and drew her to him.

"Forgive me," she sobbed. "I'm so stupid. I don't mean to do this, it was just when you said about a bride and I love you so much and I oughtn't even to be here. It's another woman's house; it's awful of me."

He stroked her hair. "Dearest, I know how you feel, but the walls

144

and ceilings aren't what matter. What matters is that we love each other and are together."

"Yes, but every place you look, you must see—I mean, why wouldn't you? I—I know how I'd feel if the situation were reversed, if this were my house and another woman——"

"If the situation were reversed," he said, "the problem would never arise. Here, take a little of this." He reached for the champagne and held her glass as she drank. He took up a forkful of food but she shook her head. "Thanks, I'm not hungry."

"You don't like it? My best effort? Not even one little mushroom?"

"Darling, it's delicious, but I—it's hard to concentrate on food, isn't it?"

"Yes, it is." He kissed her mouth, cool and moist with champagne. He rose from the arm of the chair and drew her up against him. "Come," he said, and his voice was husky, "come into my room. It *is* mine, I promise you."

Arms around each other, they went down the hall to his bedroom and went in and closed the door. He went to the bed and folded back the spread. He turned around to see her staring at a picture of Georgiana which had stood so long on his desk he had ceased to see it. He cursed himself for having forgotten it, and was about to go to her when she quietly slid a pile of books in front of it.

She turned and pulled the blue sweater over her head and her skirt slipped down, and then in another moment she was coming toward him as she had come in his dreams, her body rose and gold in the lamplight. She came toward him smiling. He buried his face between her breasts and gathered her in his arms and dumped her unceremoniously on to the bed, where she lay laughing up at him.

"Wait for me," he said; "don't go away."

"I have no plans."

"*I* have." He undressed swiftly and lay down beside her. "My dearest, my love."

A long time later Bierne wakened suddenly, her eyes very wide. Allen still lay sleeping with one arm flung across her. In the dim light she couldn't see the hands of the bedside clock—I must save up, she thought and get him one with a luminous dial—and her wrist watch lay on the table out of reach. Her heart beat quickly. Suppose

145

it's terribly late? Suppose it's three or four o'clock and for some reason Mother should still be awake? Wherever shall I say I've been? Sunday night there are no night clubs open. Whatever *can* I say?

She touched Allen's forehead with her lips and tried cautiously to work her way out from under his arm. He murmured and twisted away from her but still slept. She got out of bed quietly and picked up her watch. As she crossed to the desk the thin shaft of light slitting the drawn curtains seemed to her pale as dawn. She shivered a little, but when she held the watch under the lamp she saw with relief that it was not quite one o'clock.

She was thirsty, and thought of the champagne, and remembering they had left it on the supper table she found she was also ravenously hungry. She went and sat on the edge of the bed and leaned over Allen and kissed him. This time he wakened and put his arms around her and drew her down, and for a little time quite took her mind off her appetite for food. At last she pushed him away with a breathless laugh. "Darling, darling, it's late. I have to be getting home. This has been a miracle, hasn't it?"

"It has," he said fervently.

"Do you know what I want now?"

"What, dear?" There was a shade less fervor in his tone.

"Something to eat."

"Oh, food! My blessing, you shall have it." He swung his legs over the edge of the bed and got up. They dressed with yawns and laughs and kisses and went back into the library. Allen poured fresh champagne and this time they finished the bottle, but he saw that she glanced frequently at her watch and was beginning to get restless.

"Come," he said. "There's an all-night beanery over on Second Avenue that isn't too bad. We can at least get a fried-egg sandwich and some milk or coffee."

"I suppose . . ."

"What?"

"Well, I suppose the elevator man isn't likely to believe I've just been taking dictation all this time, but I don't care," and she giggled.

Allen blessed the champagne and her empty stomach. Her marigold head was light as thistledown. "It goes to show what a guilty

146

conscience does," she said happily. "These things don't show at all."

He looked at her. "I'm not so sure. You're a pretty ravishing sight, Miss Honeywell; you seem illumined from within. There's a telltale glow, deeply flattering to your lover."

On the way down they watched the elevator man covertly, but Bierne decided he was too old to notice and Allen didn't care if he did.

They stopped for a bite at the beanery and afterward he took her home. "Now remember," he said, "if your mother should be awake, which I strongly doubt, we've been out on Long Island having dinner and dancing. One of those restaurant-roadhouses on the Jericho Turnpike."

She squeezed his arm. "Darling, you're wonderful. How do you think up such convincing stories?"

"I'm experienced. You'd be surprised some of the alibis our authors dream up when the copy's late."

They kissed on the stoop. "I'll call you at your office in the morning," he said. "We'll arrange about tomorrow night."

"Allen, darling Allen. My love, good night." She went into the house and he stood in the shadows waiting for her signal. In a few moments she was at the window. She scratched on the pane with her fingernail and blew him a kiss. Mrs. Honeywell, he gathered, was deep in slumber.

He walked home, the sense of guilt which had weighed upon him earlier in the evening dissipated in a delicious pervading languor and happiness.

10

Bierne and Allen had decided that the moment was at hand when he must face Mrs. Honeywell. The meeting would come about quite naturally, since Saturday was Bierne's birthday. It was also the opening night of Nora Brown's play and Allen had tickets. As Poppy's father, Reuben Slade, was also in it, Karen was coming down from college for the event and she and her father, Barclay, and Bierne were all dining together before the performance. Allen

147

would pick Bierne up at home, he said, and she could introduce him to her family.

She had been a little apprehensive, but Uncle Ben, who normally sat around in his stocking feet and shirt sleeves with his vest unbuttoned, appreciated that this was an occasion and of his own initiative put on his coat and shoes.

Gladys was more difficult, feeling that etiquette did not require her to prink for a man she considered to be a seducer presumptive, although Bierne felt sure that whatever her expectations she did not suspect the Worst had already happened.

In reply to her daughter's question as to what dress she would be wearing when Allen arrived she answered resentfully, "I suppose my brown's good enough? I got it off the rack, you know, I didn't make it myself."

"Your brown couldn't be nicer, Mother, I'm just asking." Despite Bierne's approval Mrs. Honeywell's small mouth sagged at the corners and she sought solace in a tin of salted peanuts.

Bierne herself was wearing black chiffon and Allen's white orchid. Her purse was thinner and her sense of style less sure than many of the women he knew yet her instinct for self-effacing clothes which framed her brightness was a sound one.

He had cautioned her, needlessly, to be ready on time. She was at the door before his hand reached the bell and brought him into the sitting room and introduced him to her mother and Uncle Ben, observing that she would get her coat and they could leave in just a minute, all in one breath.

"How do you do, I'm sure," said Mrs. Honeywell. It was not the remark she had intended, but Bierne, being in such a rush like that, rattled her. Also, she was surprised by the way in which Mr. Goodyear shook hands and said with sincerity that he was delighted to meet Bierne's mother at last. "You have a very beautiful and charming daughter, Mrs. Honeywell, I've wanted to meet the source of those qualities," and to Bierne, "You're a fraud, my girl. You never told me your coloring wasn't original with you."

Gladys sniffed ever so slightly. "Neither of my girls are bad-looking, Mr. Goodyear, but handsome is as handsome does, we always say in our family."

"And a very good saying too."

The darling, Bierne thought, the dear darling. I've been a fool to have kept them apart. He's the most understanding man in the world. How could Mother *not* fall for him? The meeting was passing off better than she had dared hope.

"Can you sit down a minute, Allen? Or do you think we should go right away?"

Mrs. Honeywell looked at her daughter obliquely. First names were a little intimate, she always thought. Maybe that meant—— Still, maybe not. She glanced at Mr. Goodyear. The horns, hoofs, and tail were well concealed.

"Why, sure he can sit down," Uncle Ben said cordially. "Over here, Mr. Goodyear, take the weight off your feet."

"That's very kind of you," Allen murmured, but Bierne was relieved to see that, though he sat, he held his hat on his knee. "I'm afraid we can stay only a moment; we're meeting my daughter and a friend of hers for dinner—they're going to the theater with us and we mustn't be late."

Mrs. Honeywell relaxed. Bierne had said that his daughter was going to be along, maybe it was true, after all. If it was, things were all right with her little girl, since a man didn't have his daughter meet his—— Well, such things didn't happen, that was all.

"It sure is a treat for Bierne to be going to the first night of a play on her birthday," Uncle Ben said. "It's mighty nice of you, Mr. Goodyear, to take her."

Allen smiled. "I'm as nervous as though I were the producer. An old friend of mine is in it. I'm anxious to have it a success for his sake."

Ben concurred heartily. "I can see how you would be all het up."

There was a slight pause. "Perhaps I'd better get my things on," Bierne said, and started for the door. "I'll only be a minute, Allen."

"From what she tells us I guess our young lady owes a lot of pleasure to you, Mr. Goodyear," Ben observed as she left the room; "we're glad to see her having such a good time, aren't we, Gladys? Especially tonight."

"It's very nice, I'm sure," his sister replied, "though we're accustomed to having our girls home on their birthdays. Bierne's sister Stella and Mr. Grinitch, he's Stella's husband, were here just a little while ago and they were surprised to hear Bierne was going out on her birthday. When Mr. Honeywell was alive we always celebrated in our home. We felt it was more genteel for a young girl to be home with her family on her birthday."

"Now, Gladys, that wasn't all of it," Ben said. "When Stu was alive the girls were just kids. They're grown up now; it's different. Wouldn't you say so, Mr. Goodyear?"

"Yes, yes, I would indeed," Allen answered cordially, "though I believe I can understand Mrs. Honeywell's feeling. To a mother her children are always babies." God forgive me for that one, he thought.

But apparently he'd hit the right note. A ray of near animation came into Mrs. Honeywell's placid countenance. "That's what Mrs. Lockfenner always said. Eloise, Ben, you remember. Mrs. Lockfenner was my friend in Syracuse, Mr. Goodyear, my *choicest* friend; we were closer than sisters and she always used to say to me, 'Gladys,' she'd say, 'mark my words, no matter how much those girls of yours grow up they'll always be babies to you.'"

"It's hard for me to realize that my daughter Karen is a woman actually," Allen said. "I'm afraid I, too, still think of her as a child."

"Bierne tells me Karen's mother's in Europe," Mrs. Honeywell remarked sociably.

Ah, thought Allen, here it comes. "Yes," he said, "yes, my wife's away on a little trip." His tone was polite, but there was something in his expression which reminded Ben of a door sharply closed.

"Are you expecting her home soon?"

"I'm afraid not immediately, Mrs. Honeywell. She has a job over there which will keep her in Europe most of the summer."

Gladys sighed. "It's very hard to be separated from our loved ones, Mr. Goodyear. Mothers and daughters especially are meant to be together, although any loss is hard. I learned that when the late Mr. Honeywell passed on. It's been a real cross to bear. I had to bring up my girls all alone, but they're good girls, Mr. Goodyear. Stella has her own home and a wonderful husband and baby. Mr. Grinitch is a fine man, no other woman exists for Harry Grinitch but his wife, and I know my Bierne will pick a fine young man too."

Coming into the room, Bierne heard her mother's last remarks and stood frozen in the doorway, her face white as paper. Gladys glanced at her and went on rocking. "I was just telling your friend, dear, that when Mr. Right comes along you'll be marrying and settling down

150

and having babies just like Stella. She already has two steady suitors, Mr. Goodyear, both choice, eligible young men, but she can't seem to make up her——"

"Mother!" Bierne's voice cut sharply across her mother's steaminess.

"Why, what is it, dear?"

"I don't think family history's very interesting to Mr. Goodyear, Gladys," Ben said, rising in relief at the sight of his niece. Gladys was a good woman, he supposed, but she certainly could go on.

"All that business about suitors is nonsense and you know it," Bierne said. "Any boys I used to go out with were simply casual friends. I do wish, Mother, you wouldn't give the wrong impression about something that's of absolutely no importance."

Quivering like an abused jelly, Mrs. Honeywell reached into the tin that was her ever-present help in time of need. "Well, my goodness, you don't have to get mad at me, especially if it's so unimportant. Mr. Goodyear has a daughter of his own, he knows it's perfectly natural for young folks to pair off together. *You* act as though having a young man interested in you was something disgraceful." She thrust two or three salted peanuts into her mouth and swallowed nervously.

Bierne's annoyance melted. "Well, never mind, let's not talk any more about it. We have to run along anyhow. Good night, Mother, good night, Uncle Ben."

"Good night," Gladys said, and sighed heavily. "Times have changed since our day, Mr. Goodyear. Home doesn't count with these young people the way it used to. I guess you have to be an old-timer to care. My, that was sweet of President Truman; I was reading in the evening paper how he's just flown back to Missouri to see his mother since her relapse. He's a loving son, say what you like about his politics."

"He is indeed," Allen said. "Good night, Mrs. Honeywell. I *quite* understand what you mean, but I hope you'll forgive me if we keep Bierne out a bit late tonight. My sister's arranged a little party after the theater and we want very much to have her there."

"Why not, why not?" Uncle Ben said cheerfully. "Saturday night, after all! Anybody's entitled to a little binge on Saturday, aren't they, Mr. Goodyear?" and he gave Allen a worldly wink.

"And it won't be any different from any other night this past week," Gladys observed. "Well, pleased to have met you, Mr. Goodyear." She extended a plump, limp hand for Allen to shake and returned to her peanuts before they were out of the room.

As they stood on the curb waiting for a taxi Allen saw that Bierne was laughing but her eyes were full of tears. "Darling, do you think she suspects?" she asked. "She can be awful, I know. Please forgive me for putting you through it. For a moment there at first I thought everything was going to go all right."

Allen squeezed her arm. "Don't fret, buglet, it *was* all right. Your mother doesn't know anything about the way I love you so she's barking up the wrong tree, but she's not a fool. You can't blame her for wanting to protect her ewe lamb."

"But it's so ridiculous! All that talk about some infantile Mr. Right. I think she thinks of you as a city slicker twirling his mustache."

"How do you think I'd look in a mustache?"

"Idiot." This time the tears vanished and the laughter triumphed.

As Bierne and Allen stepped into a cab Ben turned from the window where he had been watching them. "You were kind of tough on sis, weren't you, Gladys? She's sweet on the guy, and from what I understand he might be good for her. He's Mr. Big in his own business. Why did you have to harp on those two kids she doesn't give the time of day to? It only embarrassed her."

"That's just it!" his sister replied with unaccustomed vigor. "Either one of those two boys would be willing to marry her. You don't think this *Mr. Big* is going to get a divorce, do you? Unless—— Well, if anything should happen that Bierne *needed* to marry him one way she *might* get him to leave his wife would be to make him think another man was ready to snatch her from under his nose. That's why I want her to hang on to that Daniels boy and Todd What's-his-name, the other one."

Ben stared at his sister and shook his head. "For a good woman who doesn't believe in divorce you've cooked up a real little stinker."

"Ben, that's not nice talk, but you know as well as I do that any man's more interested in something someone else wants. Bierne's real coony about her *money,* having it in those different banks and all, wish she wasn't such a fool about putting all her eggs in one basket when it comes to this Goodyear!" And Gladys sucked up a

152

palmful of peanuts and munched belligerently. Ben shook his head again and went off down the hall to the kitchen to get himself a beer.

They dined at a corner table at the Baroque, a small rococo restaurant in the East Fifties: Bierne, Allen, Karen, and Barclay Hamilton, Jr.

The meal had started with small, polite sorties from first one member of the group then another, rather, Allen thought, like the tentative opening steps of a quadrille. In a remarkably short time, however, the four diners had fallen into rhythm and the conversation was animated and easy. Karen and Bierne, he saw with gratitude, seemed genuinely drawn to each other, and though Barclay was attentive to his big, beautiful daughter it was obvious that when his eyes rested on Bierne the message they conveyed to his brain was pleasurable. Allen felt a little pang, a combination of jealousy and the realization that they were young and he was—well, he was older. If one were older and richer than one's young companions there was a certain compensation, an air of patronage might even be permissible, but to be older and poorer than some callow youth was trying.

As if sensing his mood, Bierne reached toward him under cover of the table. He held her hand hard and gratefully and when she looked at him with her happy, confident smile his apprehensions vanished. Karen, too, was smiling at him with affection not unmixed with curiosity. He was a dear, she thought to herself, and considerate, too, inviting that nice young Miss Honeywell to make a fourth instead of some woman his own age, although from the way they looked at each other she was beginning to feel that Miss Honeywell might not have been selected solely as a companion for herself and Barclay. Daddy had good taste, though, for she seemed gentle and kind and certainly she was as interested as any of them in Poppy's father and his success. Daddy must have briefed her on the way over in the taxi. "You didn't see Mr. Slade in his last play, did you, Miss Honeywell?" Karen asked.

Bierne said she had not, and Barclay laughed. "Poppy hates the idea of her father acting, but I think she's wrong. I saw the play, it was his first part, the one Dick Oppenheimer was talking about that night at your house, Karen, and he seemed to me awfully good. He didn't have a lot to do but you believed him."

Karen giggled. "Poor Pops, she must have been terribly depressed," and added, "I've never been to an opening night when I knew *two* people in the cast. We mustn't be late," and she gave a happy little bounce, at the same time indicating to the waiter that she would have a second helping of mousse with raspberry sauce. Allen ordered coffee and finally, after considerable urging, he was able to extricate them from the restaurant twenty minutes before curtain time.

Reuben had reserved their seats, but since he was a humble tyro ranking well below producer, author, director, and star, they were not good. Their advantage, however, was that being far back the occupants had a splendid view of the first-night celebrities sweeping to their elegant places down front. The Quicks, no grander than themselves, were across the aisle, and in the row ahead the Slade family sat like steps: Mrs. Slade, Carl, Poppy, and their sister Liz, the muscles in the child's skinny little neck tense with excitement. Her brace had been removed for the occasion and she licked her teeth nervously. Her nerves, however, were professional. She was keyed up out front as her father was backstage, but nothing would have persuaded either of them to cancel the ordeal confronting him. Reuben was pretty sure he could do the job and his youngest child knew he could. She had cued him with religious fervor throughout rehearsals, listening to his lines over and over again till both of them knew the part by heart and backward. Liz was no desultory partner mumbling indifferently the last words of speeches of other players. Her dramatic fire was constant.

In the big fight scene Reuben had a stanch, enthusiastic foe and no excuse for slackening his own tension and tempo. Indeed, during their professional rehearsals he had on occasion been hard put to it to remember his station and not correct Nora Brown's reading in stirring passages where Liz's thin but vigorous pipe rang in his ears. "And for this, for *this* I left Rinaldo Corsi! The very gods must be bursting their sides with laughter." Liz had been fine in that. It was the play within the play scene, a melodrama. Reuben considered her more convincing than Miss Brown, though Miss Brown did have a certain appeal, notably in the line of physique, lacking in his younger daughter.

In the front of the house Allen watched with interest as Germaine

154

and Claude Dauzat moved down the aisle together to their seats in row D. It wasn't a situation he would have cared to find himself in, but he admired their aplomb. Two or three of the critics Allen knew by sight and pointed out to his companions; the rest were as anonymous to him as they were to most actors. He remembered his surprise and Reuben's own surprise when after his first play he told him that the majority of actors wouldn't recognize a critic if they bumped into him in broad daylight. "Critics must *have* friends," Reuben had added dubiously, "but it doesn't seem to be anybody in the theater."

The curtain was about to go up. Bierne had never seen the friend they rooted for, but such was the family contagion that she was murmuring in a breathless little whisper that she just *knew* he would be wonderful.

Backstage they were calling "First act; places, please," and Nora's maid was exhorting the doorman to "Hold 'em, Harry! I can't take another thing in here till Miss Brown gets on," and refusing further delivery of flowers and telegrams at the dressing-room door. The supporting cast in turn knocked to wish their star success, and Nora in her simple first-act dinner dress, which so discreetly revealed Claude Dauzat's interests to the paying customers, welcomed them sweetly. "Bless you, my darling, bless you. Oh! There *you* are, Reuben. Well—you come in, too, darling, bless you. I've been praying for all of us," and she indicated a little shrine she had constructed in the corner of her dressing shelf: a small statue of Mary and the Infant embowered in flowers, a light bulb wrapped in pink gelatin glowing at its feet. She had wanted to use a candle, but the fireman had made quite an unpleasant scene. The fact that she was the star of the production hadn't seemed to percolate at all, and she had been forced back on the commercial-looking bulb.

"Still, it's the spirit that counts, isn't it?" The cast agreed.

The stage manager appeared at her door. "It's eight thirty-five, Miss Brown; may we go? Critics' deadline, you know."

"Them!" said Miss Brown. Her reading of the simple word was eloquent. She threw one last challenging look at her shrine and swept toward the stage. "I'm ready; take it up."

The stage manager signaled the electrician; the house lights dimmed. Through the heavy curtain the cast subconsciously registered the effect on the audience. As the lights went down their voices rose in pitch for an instant—they're afraid of the dark, Reuben thought, they're reassuring themselves—and then the wave of sound receded and died. The curtain whispered up. Time: seven o'clock on a June evening. Place: The Chenley drawing room in Gramercy Park.

At eleven-twelve the curtain fell on a play assured of a run throughout the summer and well into the following season. The applause was for Nora, the management had seen to that. They believed in the star system for bows, and none of this entire-company-on-stage-for-all-curtain-calls business, but in the auditorium the conversation was about a hitherto-unknown actor, Reuben Slade, who had apparently played only one other part on Broadway and a small one at that. "My dear, he's *terrific!*" "Who *is* that divine man?" "He's always been a banker or a cloak and suiter or something, can you *imagine!*" "What *heaven,* I mean . . ."

The Slade family, catching the comments, shook their heads. Reuben, Nancy thought, it's only Reuben, don't they *know* that, the idiots. Poppy and Carl looked at each other. "They're talking about Dad," he croaked.

Poppy closed a vise-like grip on his wrist. "Shut up," she muttered. "Don't let on we're the family. God knows what we're in for now."

But Liz was ecstatic. She hung on to her mother, her eyes sparkling, her face like a shout in the morning. "Daddy *did* it! Daddy *did* it! I knew all along he would. He's the greatest actor in the world."

Carl and Poppy tried to hush her. "Take it easy. He's got no Hollywood contract yet, you know."

The child turned on them with dignity. "He's a *real* actor. That's better than movies, but you'll see! Any time he wants to go to that old Hollywood he'll be the biggest star there is."

As the audience rose Allen leaned over and patted Nancy's shoulder. "I understand there's a very interesting radio program called *Backstage Wife.* You might be able to pick up a few pointers."

Nancy looked at him, pride, bewilderment, irritation fighting for predominance. "Do you think he's *really* good?"

"*Really* good! We'll go on over to the house, Nancy. Bring Reuben along as soon as you can. You might tell him, by the way, that the

156

star will be present too. Claude called me this afternoon. From what he said I gather he thinks it would be nice to bring Germaine *and* Nora along."

Nancy grunted. "That's good. I was afraid we might be in for a little relaxation."

Thanks to their inglorious seats, the Quicks and Allen with his brood were out of the theater, had made their way through the Broadway traffic, and arrived at the apartment in time to greet the first guests, among them the Oppenheimers who, in Horace's capacity of angel and agent, had gone backstage to congratulate Nora and the cast. Horace had been planning a party of his own, but when Allen's invitation arrived Dorothy urged him to accept. "It'll be a wonderful experience, dear, just imagine! Somebody else's house. We can leave and go to bed any time we want to." The novelty of it had piqued Horace's curiosity so he had agreed to one of his rare appearances as a guest.

Dick Oppenheimer was with his parents and immediately cornered Poppy and Carl.

"Mother and Liz are waiting at the theater till Father gets his make-up off," Poppy said. Her parent's run in the other play had still not conditioned her to a father with paint on his face. Her expression was half incredulous, half that of a duchess importuned by drains.

Carl's face was blank, but he emitted a subdued howl of pain. "Dad, for Pete's sake. With that muck all over him!"

Dick was amused by them but impatient also. "Listen, you kids, you don't seem to realize that your old man's an extraordinary guy. He's got courage and a hell of a lot of talent. Someday he's going to be a big name in the theater. He'll be making more dough than he ever did in Wall Street," and Dick went off to say hello to Barclay and to be introduced to the excellent blond number who seemed to be sticking so close to Mr. Goodyear.

Carl turned to his sister. "Is that Oppenheimer screwy?"

As she had been out with Dick several times since meeting him at Karen's dinner party the previous December, Poppy resented this impugning of her taste. "No," she said, "he's not. He's *very* theater wise. If he says Dad's good I guess he is."

Carl shook his head. "Boy, I can hear 'em at school. They think

157

I'm down here this week end for my teeth. Wait'll they get a load of this. Everybody else's pa is in business or an architect or something; my old man's a ham actor. Holy cow!"

"Well, it's a little *odd*, I grant you, but there's nothing *disgraceful* about it." Poppy was beginning to find her brother slightly irritating. She, too, had been opposed to their father's switch in careers, she didn't yet quite accept it, but he seemed determined on it and apparently a sophisticated first-night audience had found him good.

What if he was an actor? Barclay Hamilton had seen nothing wrong in it, and money made by actors was, after all, perfectly legal tender. Besides, she didn't care for that suspicion of a brush off in Dick's manner, as if he found her distaste for her theater-minded parent naïve and herself not worth bothering about because of it. Glancing around the room, she realized suddenly that Barclay was in earnest conversation with Karen and that Dick was concentrating on an unknown and menacing blond while she stood chatting animatedly with her *brother!* "I think your attitude about Dad is silly and grossly disloyal," she said sharply, and walked away, leaving Carl as startled as though a trapdoor had dropped from under him.

In getting herself a drink and a sandwich she maneuvered so that she came into the circle of Karen's and Barclay's attention. Mr. Hamilton was naturally the number-one choice of any girl, but only a fool would let a desirable alternative get away. Poppy felt she must check on Mr. Oppenheimer's activities. She inquired casually about one or two guests she didn't know and then lighted. "Who's that attractive girl Dick's talking to?"

Karen spoke warmly. "She's lovely, isn't she? Bierne Honeywell. She's a friend of Daddy's and Mother's. I guess your mother knows her, too, she helped them on that literary auction in March."

"Oh, I see." Poppy's heart rose like a balloon. The creature could be Dick's mother! Considering she was an older woman, Miss Honeywell wasn't so bad, Poppy conceded charitably, especially when she saw what Karen, who had turned back to Barclay, did not. The room was filling with people, and Mr. Goodyear, doubtless unaware that anyone was watching him, slipped a proprietary arm around Bierne and led her away from Dick. Well, well, thought Poppy, I wonder! And then, abhorring a vacuum as vehemently as

158

does nature, she made her way across the room and just happened to be at Mr. Oppenheimer's elbow when he turned from mixing himself a drink.

"Come," Allen murmured to Bierne, "this is my hour of need." They crossed the room together to welcome the Slades, the Dauzats, and a little dark monkey man, the author of the evening's success, upon whose arm hung Miss Brown, rather, Allen considered, like an outsize jewel in the ear of a small, defenseless Ethiop.

"Darlings, darlings, bless you!" cried Nora, rested and refreshed after an evening of uninterrupted appearance from curtain rise to curtain fall in one of the longest parts written for the modern stage.

Allen greeted her. "How nice of you to come, Miss Brown; we're delighted to have you. May I add my compliments to those of all your other admirers?"

"Oh, Mr. Goodyear, did you *really* like me? If I *was* good it was because I was buoyed up, *buoyed* up by belief. What happened poured from me as though I were a vessel. I believe that's what we all are, *vessels* through which goodness and spirit flows." And with a liquid movement of its own the vessel turned from Allen to Claude, who was talking, with unwonted concentration, to his wife. "Claude, my friend, you haven't said whether you thought I did justice to Mr. Crandall's beautiful, beautiful play. Oh, this is Mr. Crandall, everybody, our author." There were murmurs, and Mr. Crandall bowed but was eclipsed as speedily as a pea by a pitchman's shell. "Germaine dear," Nora's voice, lush but compelling, riveted the attention of the group near the door, "darling, as a wife of so many years you must know well Claude's thoughts even when unspoken. Do you think he liked me?"

Germaine's tone was silky. "Why don't you ask him later, darling? Between two old friends such thoughts as Claude may be having are better spoken in private, do you not think?"

The rapiers, having flashed, were temporarily sheathed, and general conversation resumed. Reuben was warmly congratulated on his performance and Allen introduced Bierne to those guests whom she had not already met. Germaine's luminous dark eyes glanced curiously from him to Bierne. Yes, she was right, it was the same one who had been at the Lord & Taylor luncheon with him. The girl, she was amused to see, had the blooming look of a woman loved and in love, while Allen seemed a little tired perhaps but serene.

"Tell me, Allen," she said, "what do you hear from Georgiana? Is she liking her job as much as she thought she would?" Bierne, standing close to Allen, was very still, her only expression a smile of polite interest. She is contained, Germaine thought; that is good.

"The last letter I had from her she seemed keen about it," Allen said, "although her letters are a bit on the skimpy side. I gather she's busy; you people must be slave drivers."

Germaine laughed. "Not at all, but a weekly fashion magazine, that requires work."

Allen would have liked to ask how Claude and Germaine really thought Georgiana was getting on, what she said in her letters to them, and if they were satisfied with the job she was doing. He hoped so. He wanted her to be good at it, he wanted it so to command her interest and fill her time that she would not be lonely, that she would not want to come home. Not yet. Not yet. How selfish he had become, he thought, how fickle-hearted. When she had left him after so many years of marriage he was fearful of his own loneliness, and now, a few brief weeks later, he was clinging more and more avidly to his new-found happiness.

With Germaine's mention of Georgiana, Bierne was reminded again of the shadow that lay always beyond the periphery of her happiness. She was grateful when Liz came up to her and said, a little tensely, "Excuse me, but my family are all talking to people, and I haven't been in this house before. Do you happen to know where the bathroom is? You see, my father is Mr. Slade, he had that big success tonight. It's quite exciting."

Bierne smiled at the child. She was a distraction, and with her Bierne did not have to maintain the delicately balanced pretense of a guest who knew the house but not too well. "I do. Come along," she said, and led her down the hall to Karen's room.

As they were coming out Karen herself came in. She had a highball in her hand and from her manner Bierne suspected she was a little tight. "Don't go," she said to Bierne who, explaining their intrusion, was about to follow Liz back to the drawing room; "they won't miss us for a bit and I do want to tell you how much I'm enjoying this evening. Dad wrote that he'd met someone he thought I'd like. I'm awfully glad we've been able to get together."

"So am I," Bierne said. "Your father's been very kind to me and he's told me a lot about you. He loves you very much, you know."

Karen laughed. "He's a sweetie. I'm afraid I worry him, though. He and Mother both worry."

"Why?"

"Well—well, why not tell you? Daddy may have told you about it anyhow. You see they want me to marry somebody very nice and rich but he hasn't asked me, and anyway I'm not in love with him. I'm in love with somebody else."

"You should marry the one you love," Bierne said.

"It's not always easy."

"I know that."

"Besides, he's three thousand miles away and *he* hasn't asked me either."

Bierne smiled. "How could he if he's three thousand miles away?"

"He could write. He writes very well. It's the thing he does best, in fact," and, thinking of the literate non-corresponding Mr. Asher, Karen made her Ubangi lip and brooded. Presently she said, "I think Daddy's more for the guy I want than Mother is. Daddy thinks he's old for me, of course, and so does Mother, but I think Daddy believes if he loved me it could work out. With Mother, I don't know, she's sort of funny about it." Suddenly she laughed. "What a bore I am. Why should you care? You do know my mother though, don't you?"

Bierne nodded. "I was her assistant when she did a job for the Manhattan Aid people. I work there."

"She's in Europe now," Karen told her. "She has a good job there and it's cheaper to live in Paris. Right now our finances are what's known as straitened." She giggled a little. "Maybe Pa told you?"

Bierne shook her head. Karen's candor was beguiling, but it made her feel very old and full of secrets. She replied that Allen hadn't spoken of money matters.

There was a little silence between them, and then Karen said, "You like my father, don't you?"

"Well, I—I imagine everybody who knows him must like him. He's so good and kind and intelligent and well—likable, that's all."

"It doesn't matter that he's older than you, does it?"

"I never think of it. Between friends such things aren't important."

161

"He likes you too."

"I hope he does."

"He does."

Did she suspect anything? Bierne wondered. But that was silly. How could she guess? Where would she have heard? Karen took a long swallow of highball. "He wrote me in college and said he'd met you and that you were very nice and he was sure I'd like you too. He was right. I do."

"That's nice to hear."

"What's more," Karen continued with a little lilt in her voice, "I suspect he more'n likes you."

"What do you mean?"

"Well—the way he looks at you, the way you look at him. I can tell."

"Don't you think you're imagining things?" Bierne said gently. "It's just that—that——"

"Don't mind. I'm in love with someone, too, so I know the signs. That's why I want to be nice to Barclay. He likes me better than I like him and it's hard to be in that position. I know. When you love each other the same amount it must be wonderful."

Karen had sat down on a chest under the window. She leaned her forehead against the glass and stared out at the river. The great glowing signs on the opposite shore were blurred by fog and the hoarse, lonely tone of a tugboat horn called through the darkness.

So that was it, Bierne thought. In love herself she was susceptible to the love of others, and apparently, at least in this mood, willing to accept what Allen and Bierne felt for each other. Yet would her mood last? A revulsion, a sense of outrage if she felt her mother was betrayed would be only natural. A romantic attachment she might condone, an actual love affair was a different story.

Bierne said, "Supposing your father and I should like each other a lot, would you feel upset about it?"

Karen turned from the window and looked at her. "I don't know. I never thought of such a thing happening."

Feeling it was wiser to say nothing, Bierne yet felt impelled to statement. Karen was the only one who had guessed, the only one she could be honest with. "I am in love with Allen," she said at last, "and right now he perhaps thinks he's in love with me, but I know

162

very well he's a married man and the big important thing in his life is his family, his home."

"Has he told you that?"

"No. He wouldn't want to hurt me, but he doesn't have to say it."

Karen frowned thoughtfully. "Did he imply it?"

"Don't you *believe* that it's so?"

"I don't know," the girl said. "It's very strange. I've never questioned the relationship between my mother and father. I've just assumed, I suppose the way most children do, that they were married since the beginning of time and would be married forever, but now I meet you and I think of their life together, and in one evening the whole structure of my ideas of my family is whirled about. Not destroyed exactly, but it's as though a house had been facing one way for years and a hurricane came and blew it completely around."

"I'm sorry, Karen."

"Don't be. I don't resent you."

"But you must. You love your mother."

"Yes, I do, very much, but I can see that Mother and Daddy aren't always good for each other even though they *are* married. If you and he *are* in love, it's possible that you'd be much better for him."

Bierne said, "If you'll be my friend, I'll be terribly grateful and happy, but even if you should change your mind and be angry with me some time, please don't ever be angry with your father. Don't ever be disillusioned about him. He's a wonderful person. A wonderful person."

"Who's so wonderful?" It was Allen in the doorway. "I resent women praising other men while I'm around, and how about coming back to the party? There's a rumor afoot that you've joined the Foreign Legion." He held out his hand to Bierne. "Who is this sniveling varmint pussyfooting around in your affections?"

"Don't tell him," Karen said, "keep him on tenterhooks. I never could, but I'm told it's the only way with a man."

Allen glanced quickly from Bierne to his daughter. "What is this?"

"Daddy, Bierne would never have said a word. I guessed it. I knew from the way you wrote she must be someone you liked very much, and I can quite understand why. I give you my blessing, children." She spoke a little hysterically.

Allen took her by both shoulders. "Just what do you think you know, Karen; what are you talking about?"

"I think maybe you and Bierne are in love, and I'm glad. I'm glad that *some* time in this house *somebody's* love is requited."

Bierne broke in, "Allen, I told her it's true that we're very fond of each other and that we're friends, but she knows that I understand quite well about Mrs. Goodyear and your home, the family life you have together being important. That's unchallenged."

Why, oh, why, Karen was thinking desperately, did Mother have to leave? I do like Bierne, and I love Daddy, and if they're in love, well, something like this was bound to happen, Mother should have known that. She's rough on him sometimes, but she's sweet, too, and he *is* hers. Georgiana's image was suddenly poignantly clear: the shining coppery hair, the hazel eyes, the thin laughing red mouth that could be cruel or curve in quick, wholehearted merriment. Oh yes, they were better off as a family, even a troubled family. This warm, gentle Bierne was an intruder, no matter how charming, but perhaps she was right when she said that they, as a family, were the big thing, a solid unit unchallenged. Of course she was right! This thought and Allen's hands, strong and steady on her shoulders, calmed her. "I'm being a nuisance," she said. "Please forgive me. Please don't think I'm a prober, Daddy, I couldn't bear to be. I just think it's nice when people are happy."

"So do I, darling, and I can promise you there's no need for worry. Neither of us will ever have a better friend than Bierne."

Karen impulsively took Bierne's hand and squeezed it. "I know that. Gee," she added, "what about poor Aunt Lola holding the fort out there alone? I'll go help. See you in a minute," and she ran out of the room.

Allen turned to Bierne. "Why did you lie to her?"

"Allen, what could I do? It's too sudden for her to know about us, really. That would have been brutal."

"I don't mean that, I think you're right about that, though only for the time being. But why did you say that my family life was important and in no way challenged?"

"Well, I—because I think it's true."

He went to her and took her chin in his hand and tilted up her face. "Are you being coy?" he asked, and his voice was cold.

164

"Oh no, Allen, no. I believe you, darling, when you say you love me, but you've been married many years, you have an established home. No matter how close we are I can't expect that overnight what has been important to you for half your life will cease to matter."

Allen frowned the way Karen had frowned when Bierne was assuring her also that his marriage was the big thing in her father's life. "It isn't a question of its ceasing to matter," he said, "but the emphasis has shifted. It matters now more than it ever did, because my marriage or my state of matrimony is an obstacle in the way of my being with you and I have to be with you, I have to." He put his arms around her and held her hurtingly close.

"My dearest," she murmured, "don't. We mustn't. Someone is sure to come in. Besides, I want you too much."

He covered her face with kisses. "I know. Lola's idea of a party was hell. I had hoped that in some way my blessed child might be getting back to college tonight, but she doesn't go till late tomorrow afternoon."

"I think it's better, Allen, if we don't see each other tomorrow while Karen's here. She's wonderful, she's truly gallant; let's not push her too far."

"My love, I consider you overly cautious."

"Please."

"All right, we'll do as you say. Her train goes around five. I'll take her to the station but—you have your key?"

"Oh yes."

"See that you're here when I get back."

11

The Ritz Bar was jammed with the usual afternoon cocktail crowd among whom, in the heart of Paris, not a Frenchman was to be found. This corner of some foreign land was forever America. Even Americans who might have depatriated themselves to the point where they contentedly handed over their ration cards for sautéed kidneys in bistros as yet unpolluted by their fellow countrymen, who drank wine with luncheon, or who were so indoctrinated with *la vie Parisienne* as to ride the metro instead of taxicabs, around six o'clock still felt an urge for the native martini. As the most ardent novice embracing holy orders may experience one final flare of revolt before forever renouncing the world, so the American convert to France, though wrapped in the mystical union, still jibed at the mystical French *apéritif*.

Georgiana and Dorothy and Horace Oppenheimer shared a tiny table which would have to be still further partitioned when the Oppenheimers' friend, who was joining them for dinner, should put in an appearance. Georgiana had been in Paris a little more than a month when she bumped into Dorothy, newly arrived, in the Rue de la Paix and eagerly accepted her invitation for the following evening. They had just exchanged greetings and ordered their drinks. Allen, the Oppenheimers were able to assure her, was looking well. A few nights before sailing they had given one of their big parties and he had dropped in for a little while.

"Was he alone?" she asked. Dorothy and Horace had decided not to volunteer any information but pinned by her query the casual response seemed best. "When I invited him, I think he did say he was taking someone to the theater and might he bring her along afterward. Do you remember whether he did or not, dear?" and Horace turned to his wife who, to punish him for having so blandly passed the buck, next day ordered two dresses more than she had planned on at Dior's.

"Yes," she said, "I believe he did, a young woman, a Miss Honey something, I didn't get the name. She seemed pleasant, not much personality, I thought."

Georgiana laughed a little and shook her head as at some childish escapade. "Poor Allen. I know that girl. She's a nice little thing but more in Karen's bracket. I can't think he's finding much entertainment."

"How about you?" Horace inquired. "How are things going? Are you having fun?" In reporting her meeting with Georgiana, Dorothy had observed to him that their friend didn't strike her as looking any too gay.

Georgiana answered quickly. "I love it," she said. "I adore this city and I'm up to my ears in work. My problem is to get a little rest.

There's always so much doing." It was true that she managed to have few empty evenings, but it was less because she was enjoying herself than because she was afraid of loneliness. She went to entertainments which bored her with people she cared little about rather than face the Dauzats' empty flat. The flat was cozy and pretty but it had been many years since she had had to depend on her own company, and unless she was exhausted the thought of an evening alone sent her spirits plunging. She was determined, however, that Allen and New York were not the answer. On her arrival in Paris she had suffered bitter disappointment in learning that Reams was not there. A day or two later came a telegram from Portugal saying he would be arriving in June but they were now in June's second week and there had been no further word from him.

"Who've you been seeing?" Dorothy asked pleasantly. "Anybody we know?"

Georgiana hesitated. She had met two or three people, members of a small clique, who had introduced her to their friends and who seemed to enjoy entertaining her. They obviously had money and they spent it generously, but there was something about them which made her uneasy: a violent and unexpectedly stumbled upon anti-Semitism, their attitude toward the war, remarks they had made about the Vichy Government—she was beginning to believe that though they might not have been out-and-out collaborationists any lack of co-operation with the Germans must have been of degree rather than of inclination. She suspected that if the Oppenheimers knew or had heard of her new friends they would disapprove; indeed she disapproved herself, but she glossed over her disquiet since they were amusing and kind to her personally. At their houses one met the sort of people and led the sort of life that made good copy for *Distaff* and they were an insurance against loneliness. She answered Dorothy's question by another, put a little tentatively.

"Do you know the De Longvilles? Or Nellie Baranguanya?"

"Yes," said Horace, "I do," and then he stopped, and his expression was exactly what Georgiana had feared it might be.

"I—I don't know them well," she went on, "but they've been very pleasant, and their houses, Nellie's especially, are beautiful."

"It's your business, my dear," Horace said, "but I'd watch my step with those babies if I were you. During the war their reputation was pretty smelly. Ask Dorothy what she thinks of them."

"They were bad," Dorothy said, and there was a hardening in her usually gentle manner. "Believe me, Georgiana, that isn't just hearsay. When the Germans came into France and things got bad for the Jews my aunt Miriam, my mother's sister, was put into prison. They kept her there for eight months, until she died. She knew the De Longvilles, and we have reason to think that they made trouble, that in some way they informed against her."

Georgiana turned pale. "I'm sorry," she murmured. "I had no idea . . ."

Horace patted her hand. "There is no reason why you should know," he said, "and it is true they have great taste. Marc de Longville has one of the finest collections of porcelain in the world, but they're a motley crew. Don't mix them up with Karen when she comes over. Two of the boys are fairies and there's a cousin or someone who's a notorious chaser."

"Didn't you know about Karen?" Georgiana asked.

Horace and Dorothy looked at each other. "What about her?" Horace inquired. "Isn't she joining you as soon as college is out?"

Georgiana shook her head. "I'm sunk. I only got Allen's cable yesterday. The poor blessed young idiot has gone and broken her ankle. The doctor says it'll be almost six weeks before she can travel. The whole summer's in the soup."

"Oh no!" Dorothy's face reflected her distress. "What a disappointment. What will you do?"

"What can I do? Wait around and miss her." She did not add that genuinely as she longed to see Karen the missing would be less acute had Reams been there to console her. She had occasionally wondered how she would manage matters when they were all three of them in Paris together. Now her worry was that she would have no worry. Karen and Allen were very close, and although her daughter was undoubtedly disappointed by the enforced idleness, since she was with her father she would probably find the delay in her trip not too frustrating. Reassured by Allen's cable that it was a clean break and should mend without complications, Georgiana focused her attention on Reams. His silence, his absence were disconcerting.

She asked the Oppenheimers about two or three mutual friends and then inquired casually if they had heard anything from him.

"We had one postcard from North Africa," Dorothy replied, "but the rest has been silence. We thought he'd be in Paris, but nobody seems to have seen him."

"I thought so too," Georgiana said, and felt, bitterly, that she had been a great fool, and then she looked up and saw Reams coming through the doorway. Involuntarily she called his name and half rose from her chair. It was doubtful that he could have heard her above the racket of conversation, but he saw her almost as soon as she saw him and, after an instant's hesitation, forced his way through the small, noisy bar to the Oppenheimers' table.

Horace stood up, an achievement in that congested space, and shook his hand. "We conjured you out of a bottle, my boy. That's what we're doing here, finding old friends in bottles." He indicated the other customers many of whom he knew. "We've got quite a bag. Sit down. What'll you have?"

"Thanks, nothing. I'm meeting someone. It's great to see you." He shook hands with them and took Georgiana's hand and held it hard. "How are you?"

"I'm well. It's a surprise to see you. I—we had no idea you were in Paris."

"I got in at noon. I've just been on the phone trying to reach you at *Distaff*."

"Really?" She looked suddenly so happy and eager that Reams wished he were telling the truth. For a wistful moment he wished he were back on their old basis. It would be a relief to recapture the mood of their brief affair in New York where novelty, desire, and freedom had been so happily blended and where heartache and portentous fate were not involved. From the tone of Georgiana's voice, from the way she looked at him he felt perhaps she was ready to resume, but in the meantime something had happened to him, and unfortunately it had happened only recently, after he had written her many fervent letters. He was a man in a dilemma and neither his heart nor his conscience was clear.

His trouble was that in Portugal fate had caught up with him, for in Portugal he had come upon Linda Schofield. Linda, who was eternally his love. They said you got over things. The world's full of girls, they said, and many of them he had met and some he had been beguiled by and some he had desired, but Linda he loved, and he had never got over her. The instant he saw her it was as though he

169

had never been away from her, and there was nothing and nobody else he wanted and nothing had changed for them. She was still married to the implacable British husband, she still adored her children, and the husband was still not consenting to a divorce.

They had met incredulously in Lisbon where, his imagination fertilized by his first visit when he had been writing his articles for the *Saturday Evening Post,* he had gone to do research for a story. Linda had been there on a holiday staying with an ancient cousin in a vast, ramshackle old palace, and they had passed ten enchanted days and nights before they had to part. She said she would talk again to her husband, she would try to bring him to reason. With Reams's book a success his financial hold over them was less potent, but there were the children.

Herbert Schofield was in Paris. She would go there ahead of Reams, and when he arrived would tell him how the interview had gone. The decision to meet at the Ritz Bar was hers. They had planned at first to go to the Luxembourg Gardens, but a pelting rain which started in the early afternoon made that impossible. An out-of-the-way place, she felt, would be unwise since she suspected her husband was having her followed, and over the phone she observed to Reams, a gleam of relish piercing her gray mood, that there would be no room in the bar for a detective and if he stood in the doorway peering after her and saw her meet Reams, who was to say it was not a casual, unexpected encounter?

Against his better judgment Reams agreed to her choice, half fearful that what did happen would happen. His reaction as he spotted Georgiana had something of the elements of a baked Alaska: hot delight, chilling apprehension as he thought of the two women meeting.

It was true that he had arrived in Paris only that noon, and intent on business engagements and his appointment with Linda he had not phoned Georgiana, but aware that she could reasonably consider his behavior callous he invented his telephone call to her, justifying the lie by the certainty that he would have called her the next day. His pleasure in seeing her was genuine; if only it had been under other circumstances!

"Reams, where are you stopping? Whatever took you so long to get here? Dorothy and Horace and I were speaking ill of you this

170

very moment, saying what a bad correspondent you are. You *must* have a drink with us, mustn't he, Horace? Do you realize how long it's been? Five months!" In her excitement at seeing him Georgiana was bubbling over.

Sensing her pleasure, Horace urged Reams to dine with them. "A fellow from my office is meeting us. Why don't you join us?"

"Thanks a lot. I'd like to, but I'm tied up." He was not at all sure that he was, but he wanted to leave himself free for Linda. "We'll meet for a drink," she had said. She had added nothing about dinner.

Georgiana looked at him with a little shock. "You made a date?" It had never occurred to her that when he did arrive they would not spend his first evening together.

"I have to dine late," he explained; "it's a business thing. I promised this guy weeks ago I'd see him the first night I got to Paris. You see, I—I didn't know when it would be or just how things stood." He looked at her pleadingly. He was a poor liar, and even to tell her the painful truth would have been a relief, but with the Oppenheimers there it was impossible. But when Georgiana knew the truth could she believe that he ever had cared for her? Or after the things they had said and done together would Linda ever be able to accept the fact, even the past fact of Georgiana?

For a moment he understood the urge that drives a man to a monastery. Because his position was both delicate and equivocal he began to smolder inwardly, to resent both women and to blame them for the encounter. It somehow placed one of the climactic moments of his life in a slightly farcical light. His whole future hung upon the news that Linda would bring him, but instead of a noble, a dedicated rendezvous—he rather fancied something in the style of nineteenth-century steel engravings, lovers meeting in flowing draperies and a denuded wood—instead, he and Linda were meeting in a chatter-cluttered bar importuned by the presence of a former still-admired mistress.

He thought of leaving the Oppenheimers and Georgiana, of intercepting Linda before she could arrive, though whether she would enter the Ritz from the Vendôme or the Cambon side he didn't know. His deliberations were interrupted by her appearance in the doorway. She wore navy blue, and her small white hat and white veil, her white-gloved hand as she caught sight of him and waved, were sharp accents in the dim, smoky atmosphere.

"Excuse me," Reams said. He got up and made his way to her through tables, chairs, and jutting elbows.

"Reams." When she spoke his irritation, his embarrassment, and his sense of guilt melted away.

"Darling." He murmured the word so softly she read his lips rather than heard him. "They're holding a table for us by brute strength, but come over here a moment, there are some old New York friends I want you to meet. Only for a minute, but I think we should."

"Of course." She smiled at him as though they were embarked on an intimate and charming adventure.

Back at the table he performed the introductions. "Georgiana, I'd like you to meet Linda Schofield. Mrs. Goodyear, Mr. and Mrs. Oppenheimer, Lady Schofield."

They murmured how-do-you-do's. Georgiana, scrutinizing the newcomer, felt a little chill around her heart as she saw a slender woman in her early thirties who, while not beautiful, had an appealing and feminine charm made more piquant by the severely tailored suit she was wearing. One fragile wrist was encircled by heavy gold bracelets, and the crisp white veiling of her small hat served to accentuate her dark hair and lashes and gray-blue eyes.

How and where had Reams met her? Georgiana wondered. Why, his first evening in Paris, was he having cocktails with her? If he had time to telephone Lady Schofield, why had he not had time to telephone her? Her mind churned with questions. Was he spending the evening with this pretty stranger, or was it true that he had a business appointment?

His hand was on Georgiana's shoulder. "We'll lose our table," he said; "we've got to worm our way over there. I'd like to call you in the morning, Georgiana; I've got to talk to you."

"Or call me when you finish your business dinner. It shouldn't be too late."

"I'll try, but if I miss you, what time do you leave home in the morning?"

"A few minutes past nine."

172

He drew a small dark blue leather notebook from his pocket. "What's the number?"

She told him. Her lips felt numb, as though she had been given Novocain.

"Sorry you can't join us," Horace said, and, with a slight bow, "You, too, Lady Schofield. We're going to try a new restaurant where the food is supposed to be fabulous."

Linda smiled. "Thank you, I wish I might. I should like so much to stay with friends of Reams, but I have an engagement."

They turned and left the table, Reams with his arm half around her as he shepherded her through the small crowded room to a place farther along the banquette.

Georgiana watched them, his broad silhouette like a protecting shadow behind Linda's slender figure. The line of his shoulders, the curve of his arm brought tears to her eyes. Sick, humiliated, angry, she bent her head so that her hatbrim half hid her face, and fumbled in her bag for her handkerchief, but before she could blow her nose a tear dropped into her empty cocktail glass.

Under the table Dorothy gave Horace a wifely kick. He at once turned and waved to an acquaintance two tables away, and when he turned back he exclaimed in surprise, "Good heavens, we've entered the desert wastes around here. *Garçon!*" His hand described a circle over their three glasses. "*Encore et vite.*"

Dorothy laughed. "He speaks better English than you do, for heaven's sake."

"And better French too," Horace replied, "but it is we who are thirsty."

The Oppenheimers were puzzled by Georgiana's obvious emotion yet in a sense it was self-revelatory. She had been elated at seeing Reams, but the appearance of Lady Schofield had thrown this elation sharply into reverse; mentally their eyebrows rose. Though too tactful to question her unless she volunteered some information, they were human. The time before she and Horace could be alone to discuss their speculations began to seem very long to Dorothy.

On her part Georgiana hesitated. The desire to pour out her story was urgent, yet, until she had spoken to Reams, what was there to say? A palpitating, successful love affair was one thing, one could be regarded as a glamorous and enviable, even if sinning, heroine, but the pity extended to a bypassed mistress was galling. At the moment, involved and miserable, she was incapable of the suggestive smile, the casual comment she had seen women achieve when they wished it inferred that they had known some particular man very well indeed.

Besides, possibly, just possibly, she was imagining something which didn't exist. Reams had tried to telephone her, he said. Maybe this meeting with Lady Schofield was necessary, unavoidable, tomorrow the whole thing would be easily explained. She had been badly jarred, but instantly to leap from the cliff was foolish. She blew her nose vigorously as the waiter set a fresh round of drinks before them. "The smoke in here is really awful," she said, "and in spite of being warm it's drafty too. I must be catching cold."

Horace pointed to her cocktail. "Drink your grog; wards off the plague."

"And the blue devils," Dorothy whispered softly.

Georgiana began sipping her cocktail and made a determined effort not to let her eyes rest on the back of a sandy head and the corner of a gray flannel shoulder which was Reams.

At their own tiny table Reams sat with Linda's knees locked between his own, one hand clasping hers. She had asked him who his friends were. The Oppenheimers he disposed of quickly. "And Mrs. Goodyear, who hopes you will call her tonight?"

He hesitated. He supposed he would have to tell her eventually, but the time and place seemed inauspicious. After a moment he said gently, "Mrs. Goodyear, my wily little monkey, is an old friend to whom I owe a great deal and whom I'm fond of. You'll get to know her some time and like her."

"Will I now? I shouldn't be surprised if I didn't."

"You are a goop. I love you." The waiter set their cocktails before them. They touched glasses and drank.

"Well," Reams said. "Let's have it. Since you haven't blurted out the glorious news of your freedom I gather you didn't get it."

Linda spoke with an obvious effort. "We had a long talk. I had to tell Herbert, of course, that I'd seen you in Lisbon and that I wanted a divorce."

"What did he say?"

"He said he wouldn't dream of it, that he had no intention of

174

divorcing me now or ever. I know Americans think that British divorce laws are stuffy, I think they are myself, but they're all on Herbert's side. There's never been a divorce in his family and he's very family-conscious. The title, the estate, they mean a great deal to him. And then, too, he's ambitious. He's been in and out of the diplomatic service all his life, and I believe now he's trying to intensify his activities. He was in our embassy in Turkey, you know, and he's always wanted to be top dog. That's why he's been spending so much time in Paris. He's never told me in so many words, but I think he's aiming for Paris or even Washington. Naturally any scandal would be very bad for him."

After a moment Reams said, "Did you tell him that you're no longer dependent on his money?" and he added, "By the way, has he heard of me? Does he know what a ripsnorting success I am?"

Linda laughed ruefully. "Oh yes, I rubbed it in, isn't that what you say? I told him you were extremely distinguished and had a great deal of money. I made you sound like the richest American author, and I think for a moment the idea of your having money disconcerted him. He's always suspected I've never got over you from before the war when we first knew each other, and the fact that you were poor and he was rich made him feel safe, but after a bit he said, 'Asher may have the money, as you say, but I have the children.'"

"Ah, the hostages."

Two quick tears slipped down Linda's face but they were not followed. "I tried to impress on him that they were my children too," she said huskily, "and he replied that he was aware of that, and as I loved them he was sure I would not be so unwise as to take a step which would cut me off from them irrevocably, and my solicitor tells me that as a matter of fact that isn't an idle threat. If I leave Herbert to live with you, even if I get a divorce and we're married, under English law, I'm the guilty party. He could have me declared an unfit mother, and the courts would never let me see the children even."

Reams's eyes narrowed till they were no more than cold, gleaming slits. "The sanctimonious son of a bitch. The hell with him! You could fight him on the children. Even the British courts must have *some* humanity. Ronny's twelve, isn't he? He's old enough to know what's

175

what, and as for the baby, the noble lord would be in a fine fix trying to bring up a little girl without her mother."

But Linda shook her head. "You don't know him, Reams, he can be ruthless. He'd turn Ronny against me, he'd give Linda to his own mother to bring up."

"But, darling, you could still see them, and we'd have children of our own."

She gave a little cry. "Don't say that! Don't talk as though the children were old clothes I could discard and get others to take their place."

He took her hands quickly. "Please, please," he urged. "I didn't mean that, I didn't mean it the way it sounds. Oh, Christ! Darling, get hold of yourself. We don't want everybody listening in." It was true that people at adjacent tables were beginning to glance at them curiously. Even when their conversation was inaudible, the tension apparent in their manner and gestures was unusual in the Ritz Bar.

"I'm sorry," she said. "I'm sorry."

"If only we could go some place where I could have you in my arms. This is hell. Let's get out of here. I'm just up the street at the Vendôme. I think you imagine the detective, anyway. Schofield can't be having you followed."

"Yes, he can, I'm sure of it. This morning when I went out shopping I had a funny feeling, and I walked here deliberately through the rain, taking a roundabout way. I noticed a small man in a brown suit taking the same route, and he came in from the Rue Cambon right after me." She looked around the bar. "I don't see him now, but when I leave he'll be out by the door, you'll see." Reams considered that she was overwrought but she was apparently convinced. "I'm not sure that there wasn't a man in Lisbon too. There was something in Herbert's manner when I told him I'd seen you there. I can't describe it, but the information seemed to come as no surprise."

Reams gave a dry laugh. "If the detective regaled him with all that went on in Lisbon he got his money's worth. And a good job too! If he's got something on us anyhow, why aren't we perfectly free to do as we like?"

She kept her voice low, but she spoke a little hysterically. "Don't you see that's where he's so diabolically clever. If he has documented proof that you and I are seeing each other, alone, I'm com-

176

pletely in his power. If he wants to bring action, he could get the children away from me even without a divorce."

"O.K.," Reams said. "He's won this round and it's his last, I promise you. I tell you what, let's have another drink and then we'll go some place and dine and plot our next move. We'll be as public as you like, the Café de la Paix if you want. Let old Private Eye make something out of *that*, but I won't let you go, I won't not see you."

"Darling, I—I can't."

"Can't what?"

"Dine. Lord Schofield has arranged a dinner party at our hotel." She gave a dreary little laugh. "To give the devil his due I don't think he suspected I was meeting you this afternoon; he arranged it while I was in Lisbon. Some of the embassy people are coming. They know I'm back, I can't very well not be there."

"I see. What about tomorrow?"

"No, Reams."

"The next day."

"The next day—— Forgive me, don't look at me that way. The next day we're going home. Back to England." She had once seen a bullfight in Spain. When the matador's barb had gone home between the animal's shoulders, piercing down into its heart, the great beast raised its head and in its eyes was a look of dumb surprise. Reams's heavy shoulders seemed to sag, his eyes had the expression of the bull's eyes.

After a moment or two he said very quietly, "Then this is good-by." Mutely she nodded. After a while he asked for the check and they sat in silence while he paid. He put his wallet into his pocket and pushed back his chair. "Ready?"

"Oh, darling, please. Just a moment. Say something, tell me what you're thinking."

He was about to rise, one hand on the back of his chair, the other on the table. He paused. "I was thinking that the meek shall inherit the earth, that's all. I gambled against two children and the children won. Very biblical."

The tears slipped unchecked down her face. "I love my children."

"You should."

"I love you."

"And I love you. We're surrounded by love. Like the Ancient

177

Mariner and the water. Our love seems to be just as ineffectual. Come."

The crowd in the bar was thinning out. When they passed the table at which Georgiana and the Oppenheimers had been sitting he noticed that they were gone and that a man in a brown suit had replaced them. They walked down the long corridor leading to the Place Vendôme lobby.

Linda asked painfully, "What are your plans?"

"I haven't any."

"Will you be in England at all this summer?"

"I doubt it. I've got to finish a book of short stories, then I'll probably go back to America."

She was staring straight ahead of her. "We *can* live without each other, I suppose. We separated once before and somehow the years went by. We didn't kill ourselves."

"That's right. You even had a baby."

"You might have spared me that. I shall love you until I die, Reams."

They passed the concierge's desk; they were at the glass doors.

"Perhaps someday, when your family is all grown up and married," he said, "we shall meet again."

She cried, "I don't want to wait till I'm old!"

"You will always be beautiful, you have lovely bone structure. I shall be the disillusion. Bald and fat."

"How can you joke at a moment like this."

"A bad joke for a bad moment."

A taxi drew up under the porte-cochere from the rank in the Place Vendôme. He helped her in. "I'll telephone you late tonight," she said, "when I'm alone." As he closed the door and stepped back, the small man who had been sitting at the table in the bar brushed past him, hailed a second cab, spoke rapidly to the chauffeur, and drove off after Linda.

That night the Oppenheimers dropped Georgiana at her apartment shortly after midnight. She climbed the four flights hurriedly, the elevator was in its chronic state of non-levitation, and inserted her key in the door with a trembling hand. As she switched on the electric light the phone rang. She flew to answer it. It was a *Distaff* photographer announcing triumphantly that he had finished a fashion sitting and that the picture was this instant being transferred to New York by radio. "Just think," he gloated, "it will be at the engraver's in the morning."

"That's fine, Mac," she said; "that's a good scoop." She lowered the receiver into the cradle as though it were stone. At two o'clock she took a sleeping pill so that when Reams phoned in the morning she would have had a few hours' rest. If she was still sleepy, so much the better, she would be more relaxed, not tense and demanding. The pill was slow to work and was effective only three or four hours. She got up very early, dressed, breakfasted, and waited until half-past nine before leaving for the office. Just before she went out she telephoned her secretary to say that if a Mr. Asher called to tell him she was on her way and would call him as soon as she got in, but when she arrived there was no message.

The next two weeks passed in an anguish of uncertainty. Every time the phone rang at home or at the office a sharp, stabbing question punctuated her thought, her activity, but it was never Reams. She called his hotel unnumbered times; sometimes she left messages, sometimes she didn't, sometimes she asked to speak to him and gave an assumed name. Finally, distracted, she took the Oppenheimers into her confidence and three times persuaded Horace to call for her —even though Reams might be evading her it was unlikely he would refuse to speak to a man who was his friend. At last she had no alternative but to believe what the hotel operator had told her from the first: Reams was not there, he had not been seen for many days. Certain, then, that something must have happened to him, she wanted to notify the police but was dissuaded by Horace. "Reams," he argued, "is a strong and resourceful man and he is also a pretty well-known one. It seems to me highly unlikely that he could have got into trouble without our having heard of it, but none of the *Herald Tribune* crowd, nor any of the rest of the American press, has got wind of anything."

Dorothy, too, sought to comfort her. "Horace is right, dear. No American as well known as Reams is since his book's been published could vanish into thin air here in Paris without its being shouted from the housetops."

"But he *has* vanished," Georgiana insisted, "and nobody seems to

179

know where. He said he only got in that day at noon, remember? Most of his friends wouldn't even know he was *in* Paris."

They were in Georgiana's apartment. Dorothy sat on the couch with her hat on, surrounded by packages, the result of the day's shopping tour, while Georgiana, looking, the Oppenheimers thought, exhausted, paced the floor restlessly, and Horace sat like a plump presiding judge meticulously arranging the tips of his fingers against each other, drawing his hands apart and bringing them gently together again in precise rearrangement. When he next spoke it was with a certain diffidence. "Uh—there is one thing, Georgiana, we must remember. Reams is a man of quality. While it is true he has no, shall we say orthodox, domestic responsibilities he is not a philanderer. If you had reasons to believe in his devotion he cannot have forgot those reasons, but the fact is, why we do not know, when we last saw him he was with a very pretty woman."

"I don't agree," his wife said tartly.

"But yes, my dear," he remonstrated, "don't you remember? In the Ritz Bar. A Lady Schofield, I believe he said."

"I remember Lady Schofield. I just wasn't struck by any dazzling beauty." When her husband mentioned Linda, Dorothy had seen Georgiana's pale face turn paler still. He was showing, she considered, a marked lack of the diplomatic tact he flattered himself he always brought to bear in dealing, not only with movie-star clients, but with females in general.

Sensing a switch in the accustomed wifely acquiescence, Horace cleared his throat and continued mildly, "You are right, of course; that is merely a habit of speech. Unfortunate. What I am driving at is that I think we should refrain from bringing the police into this. We would not want to involve a perfectly innocent lady."

Georgiana gave a twisted laugh. "You are more charitable than I, Horace. I cannot assume the innocence."

This time Horace did exert diplomacy, the best kind, since it had a straightforward, prosaic ring. "I assume it, my dear friend, because I do not think Reams is a fool. If he has been able to gain your respect and affection, he also has the wits to hang on to them. Be patient for a little longer, I beg of you. When you see him he can doubtless explain everything. We are fond of Reams, too, you know. If he doesn't turn up in the next day or so we'll act. I'll call his pub-

180

lisher in New York, we'll make discreet inquiries about Lady Schofield. All I beg is that you not worry yourself sick."

But Georgiana was ungrateful. "If he's lying in the bottom of the
Seine a lot of help that will be," she said.

Had he not spied the lady whom, despite his wife, he considered
uncommonly attractive, Horace himself would have been more concerned, but it was his creed, evolved from long experience and
deeply ingrained, that when two members of opposite sexes were as
engrossed in each other as Reams and Lady Schofield had appeared
to be it was doing them scant favor to involve the constabulary.

12

Bierne knelt on the library floor concentrated on her task of mend-
ing the gallery of a small occasional table which had broken off.
She worked deftly with sandpaper, glue, and very fine nails, and
Karen and Allen watched her in awed admiration. It was early in
July and Karen, home from college for the summer vacation, sat
with her leg extended, resting her broken ankle in its cast on a low
chair. She was the master's apprentice, holding out to Bierne equip-
ment as required. "I wish to goodness you could fix my hoof too,"
she observed; "after two weeks this plaster still gives me an eerie
feeling, as though it would creep on up my leg and cover me entirely," and she added with ghoulish relish, "I'll get numb and die
like Socrates and the hemlock." How charming they were, Allen
thought, young and compatible and lighthearted.

Matters had turned out better than he had dared hope. His misgivings about Bierne's youth had undergone a metamorphosis; the
difference in their years now struck him not as incongruous but
providential. Had he fallen in love with an older woman, Karen
might have found a readjustment of her affections almost impossible,
but Bierne seemed more like a friend of her own than a rival of her
mother's and had slipped easily into the pattern of their lives, although on objective reflection Allen found it difficult to understand
how this kind, beautiful, gentle young woman, who was also a gifted
carpenter, should have taken him for her lover and have become

181

in a few brief weeks his vital need, but since it was his fate—he had, he supposed, given fate a slight nudge—he accepted it with a mixture of humility and delight, a premonition of trouble ahead, and a dawning wonder as to whether all this happiness could just possibly be his due. Maybe, he thought, it could be, since, if he was going to keep it, and his heart gave him no choice, the purchase price would be high. He quailed a little thinking of Georgiana. If only they hated each other how easy the solution would be.

Bierne looked over at him and smiled. "You're very quiet. What are you brooding about?" Because he loved her so intensely and Karen's firm, gay presence made an adequate declaration impossible, he attempted a little mock severity. "How can I say a word with you two chatterboxes holding the floor? Really fine craftsmen concentrate on the job. I don't see how you two can tell nails from sandpaper."

Karen giggled. "You forget, Daddy, we're the new generation. Two things at once is our specialty. Do all our studying to radio, helps our mental powers."

"God knows they need assistance," said her father, "but I'm dubious about radio."

"Ouch." Karen's ejaculation was less in reply to the barb than because she had strained a muscle trying to lower her leg to the floor.

Bierne sprang up. "Here, let me help you." She put Karen's arm over her shoulder and heaved her up from her chair. "Lean on me, Grandpa. Where do you want to go?"

"The couch, I guess, but don't bother. I can use my crutches just as well."

"Nonsense. They're a nuisance. Why should you?"

The two girls made their way awkwardly to the couch. "I'll certainly be glad when this damn thing is off," Karen muttered with a baleful glance at her cast.

"What did the doctor say the last time you saw him?" Bierne asked.

"I saw him yesterday. He said another three weeks almost."

"Golly." Bierne's sympathy was genuine but her question was a feeler into the future as well as a request for information. Karen's arrival home from college posed a real problem for her and Allen

182

in that now they had no place where they could be alone together. When they might hope to be, when Karen would be able to sail to join her mother, was uppermost in their thoughts.

Daily Allen's intention of asking Georgiana for a divorce grew stronger, yet daily he hesitated. His marriage was an old habit, his feeling for his wife, while not love perhaps, was rooted in affection, a compatibility of sorts, and he found, a little to his shame, that despite his great love for Bierne, he was reluctant to initiate an action which would inevitably open up vistas of pain, anger, and recrimination. Also, the age question occasionally recurred to him. She was twenty-five and he was fifty. When she was thirty-five he would be sixty. When she was sixty he would be—doubtless dead. At 3 A.M. in the morning he used to worry about leaving her widowed at sixty. Most women were still vigorous and able to enjoy life at that age, but they could rarely hope to marry again. The thought of her lonely senescence made him sad until struck by the slightly lunatic aspect of his putations he would laugh and roll over and go back to sleep. Still, action was becoming imperative. The present situation was unfair to Bierne and the routine of daily living too complex.

Karen, since her powers of observation were normal, had by now guessed they were lovers, but how, tactfully, to remove herself from their presence, or where to go, especially with the handicap of her broken ankle, was beyond her. It was her old problem in reverse. When her father and mother quarreled she had found it difficult to leave the room; it seemed ostentatious or superior. Now that her father and Bierne were so happy, to absent herself, she felt, would imply that she knew they were lovers, and perhaps before her they preferred to keep up the pose that they were not. Since they were so charming about trying to save her feelings, she connived in their deception. Besides, she wanted to be with them, to belong to them. In some respects, when the three of them were together, there was a warmer family feeling than she had ever known when Georgiana was home.

The shock of discovering that one's own father was still a functioning male had somewhat abated, but torn by her loyalties she rotated in a turmoil of indecision as to what her reaction should be. In accepting Bierne was she betraying her mother? Yet hadn't her mother behaved selfishly and with little foresight in leaving her father? And had she done it—a suspicion that more than once flared and died in Karen's mind—because she cared for Reams in a way that she shouldn't? Yet if a love affair was all right for Allen, why was it shocking and wrong for her mother?

Her loyal young heart felt sadly buffeted, and once she broke down helplessly with Lola and Peter. Uncertain as to how much she knew or suspected, Lola tried to comfort her. "There, there, darling," she said as her niece sat sobbing on her sofa, "I know it's hard for you, but often a man of Allen's age who's been married forever takes a fancy to a young girl. That doesn't mean it's anything serious." As Lola spoke the words they rang like tin on her own ears and Peter, with a look of disgust, turned away and poured himself a stiff highball.

"If it d-d-doesn't mean anything s-s-serious," Karen sobbed, "Why do they look so p-p-pleased any time I say I've been invited out some p-p-place? And when I c-c-come home they've either gone and the house is all empty or else they're sitting a mile away hardly t-talking to each other, looking like c-cats full of canaries," and she wailed with woe and self-pity.

"Oh, darling." Lola leaned her head against Karen's shoulder laughing and trying to comfort her at the same time.

The moment had come, Peter decided, for masculine intervention. He drew up a chair and sat facing them. "Now, Karen, listen to me. Stop acting like a baby."

"She's not," Lola said stanchly. "It's a tough situation and I don't blame her."

"I don't say it's not tough, but these things happen in life and she's got to face it. How much do you really know, Karen?"

Karen blew her nose. "Well, if you mean do I know that B-Bierne and Daddy are having an affair, yes, I do."

The Quicks looked at each other and drew a sigh of relief. "O.K.," Peter said, "at least we know where we're at. Do your father and Bierne know that you know?"

She shook her head. "I don't think so. I don't mind it really, I don't feel embarrassed or upset about it, but I can't bring myself to tell them. Uncle Peter, if you and Aunt Lola maybe would say something. They must know that you know, don't they?"

"Yes," Lola said, "us they accept, I think."

"They're terribly sweet and polite to me, but they can't want me around. When I told them last night at dinner that I was going to spend this evening with you they looked at each other and you'd have thought that every flower in a garden had suddenly bloomed. I feel so mean being in their way because deep inside when I'm with them I feel I've won something for Mother. They can't be making love then, and that's a point for Mother's side." She flushed painfully and hung her head till her tawny hair fell forward mercifully hiding her face. "Sometimes"—her voice was muffled—"sometimes I feel just the other way. I say to myself, this is nonsense. Since we all know it and it's so frightfully hard these days to find any place to live, why shouldn't Bierne just come and stay at the house with us, and then I realize that it's still Mother's apartment, too, and I could die."

Peter and Lola looked at each other. He stood up and put his hand on her bent head, gently rumpling her hair. "Poor kid, you're in a tough spot, but it needn't be so bad if you can look at it a little objectively. What do you think of Bierne?"

"That's what's so terrible," Karen wailed. "I like her. How *can* I like her when I love Mother? How can I *do* this to my own mother?" and the tears splashed down again.

Peter spoke slowly. "Karen, listen. Your own mother is a remarkable woman in many respects, Lola and I are devoted to her, you know that, but she's no rose to live with, your father has a lot of provocation. On the other hand——" Here he hesitated, he was on ticklish territory.

Lola was deeply devoted to her brother; however, she was generous. "Go ahead," she said with a grin. "I won't bite."

Peter raised his glass in grateful toast. "Well, it's only fair to say that your pa has a lot of habits and mannerisms that drive Georgiana crazy. Furthermore, she's never thought he was aggressive enough in business, and being ambitious and energetic herself that galls her so she up and declares a marital moratorium."

"Mother went to Paris because of a job over there, isn't that true, Aunt Lola?"

"Well, she did get a job, yes."

"But that's what she *went* for. At least——" Karen's voice trailed off. There came that persistent drumming suspicion again like a dark, evil gnome tapping in her consciousness.

"Look, Karen," Peter said, "you'll get on a lot better, not only now but all your life, if you don't try to make other people's behavior your personal problem. This one is pretty close, I grant you, but you've got to realize that even though Georgiana and Allen are your parents they were human beings long before they had you and they still are. Yet the comforting thing is you *are* their child and whatever they may do to each other or with anybody else their love for you is steady and enduring and nothing can diminish it. Here, have a little snort and cheer up," and he handed his niece his highball glass.

Karen took a deep swallow and in a moment bestowed upon them her slow, wide smile. " 'Malt does more than Milton can to justify God's ways to man,' " she murmured.

Peter burst out laughing. "By God, a chip off the old block. Quotes yet."

Lola smiled, too, a smile of affection and relief. "If you have any sense, my girl, you'll emulate the old folks. What about your own beaux? What gives? Any sign of life from the wealthy Mr. Hamilton?"

Karen nodded. "He sent me a forest of flowers when I got home from college and he's been to the house three times. We've been out twice."

"Good," said her aunt.

"Well, yes, I suppose it is."

"You sound doubtful."

"He's been seeing quite a bit of Poppy."

"Oh." Though she knew the girl only slightly, Lola's private conviction was that she wouldn't trust Poppy as far as she could spit against the wind. She didn't care for the idea of her weasling in on what she had come to regard as Karen's private territory, although she did remember the alternate in her niece's affection. "What about that other fellow, what's his name? Reams Asher?"

"Oh, him," Karen said; "he's in Europe. I'll probably see him when I get to Paris." She tried to speak casually but her tongue was dry. "I wonder if I might have a drink of my own, Uncle Peter?"

Her uncle mixed one. "Do you care anything about young Hamilton?" he asked.

"I like him a lot, I just don't consider he belongs to me, that's all. If Poppy or anybody else wants him they're welcome to him. Anyhow, anyone as eligible as Barky, it's silly to behave as though all I had to do was crook my little finger and he'd ask me to marry him."

"Well," her aunt remarked, "quite possibly he won't, but I certainly wouldn't let Poppy beat me to the draw." Her tone implied that Miss Slade was a new low in womanhood.

"Besides, I think it's disgusting," Karen went on, "everybody running after him because he's rich. He's nice and he deserves better than that. I don't intend to make myself one of the crowd."

"I'm for that," Lola agreed. "Make yourself stand out," and because the stakes were too great not to fight for, "Of course if you don't want to encourage him because you don't love him, that's one thing, but I'd hate to see you put yourself out of the running because you're afraid you couldn't lick Poppy."

Peter groaned. "Good Lord, what is this? A slug fest? I thought it was up to the fellow to pick the girl he likes."

The two women ignored him.

"I'm not afraid of Poppy," Karen said. "It isn't a question of competition at all. I'm just not—not very interested."

Her aunt regarded her quizzically. "Interested enough to remember every time you've seen him, though."

"That's my nature," her niece explained. "I'm an elephant for my men. I remember every time I saw Reams before he went away and now I haven't seen him in months." She smiled, but her eyes were sad. Lola was troubled. It was really too bad if this trip to Europe were to revive what might have been a moribund infatuation on Karen's part just when young Mr. Hamilton's interest could perhaps be nurtured to the point of fruition.

"When do you sail?" Lola asked.

"I just got definite word. I have a cabin on the *Indo-Chinois* for the twenty-seventh. I'm certain to have the cast off by then and Dr. Steele says I can go."

"You're all set on it, aren't you?"

"Oh yes." Karen's eyes shone. "Even though I won't have the wonderful long time we'd planned on it'll still be marvelous."

Peter, unaware of Lola's misgivings, spoke his thoughts. "I wish

187

we could travel, it's a good thing, the best. A three-way pleasurable stretch: the anticipation, the trip itself, and the memory."

"You *must* travel," Karen exclaimed generously, "both you and Lola would enjoy it so enormously. Why don't you? It's romantic."

Lola chuckled. "Pete and I did take a trip nine months before the twins were born. It's the results of romance that are keeping us home now."

About a week later the event so devoutly wished for by Georgiana and the Quicks took place. Barclay had asked Karen to spend a week end at his family's house in Oyster Bay and she accepted gratefully. She liked him so much, it would be a relief to get away from the hot, dirty city, the Hamilton country seat was opulent, and from Friday to Monday Bierne and her father would be free of her chaperonage.

They drove out in Barclay's Cadillac with the top down, arriving with their skin stretched hot and tight across their faces, but to keep the top up on a bright, sunny day was to offend every tenet of their age group.

The week-end gathering was small and, with the exception of Karen, consisted of members of the immediate family—the senior Hamiltons, Barclay's younger brother Floyd, and a married sister and her husband and child. Karen had assumed there would be at least one large dinner party and had packed accordingly. She was right, but the dinner was given by older friends of the Hamiltons in a house three miles away and she and Barclay were not invited. The younger members of the household dined together, Floyd then went off to pick up the girl he was taking to a dance, the married sister and her husband retired early, and Karen and Barclay were alone. They sat on the terrace in the moonlight overlooking the water. Barclay gazed at the lovely young goddess beside him and his heart melted. How beautiful she was and how serene and honest. He thought of the other girls he knew. They were amusing and attractive, fun to play tennis with or to take to night clubs. When he danced with them their hair smelled good and their supple young bodies molded themselves to his seductively, but the invitation in their eyes never quite concealed the calculation as they looked not at but through him. His flesh and bones and blood were transparent,

188

the eyes pierced them easily. They pierced through the brick and concrete of banks, through the underground vaults of steel to the hard core of paper: stocks and bonds and currency.

The conventional offerings he tendered—flowers, books, perfume, a charm for a bracelet—these they accepted, but they looked beyond them, too, expectantly, anticipating the diamonds, the motorcars, and the minks. Barclay knew them well, the pretty, voracious girls, the delicately bred voluptuaries, and his own realization of their covetousness worried him. Supposing they did want the money, was it unnatural? What had he ever done to earn it? Was he becoming a prig, a tightwad? Would he in time develop into that most lamentable of figures, a man whose wealth served only to make him suspicious of everyone, even the loving and disinterested?

Humor was not Barclay's strongest point, but he was not devoid of a gift for self-appraisal, and though pathetically sincere in his desire to be loved for what he was he was also aware that a man murmuring the rich girl's plaint, "I want to be loved for myself alone," could be construed as faintly comic. Yet that was what he did want, and because he did, his feeling for Karen was paradoxical. He was not sure that she cared about him and he was equally sure that his money would not weigh her decision. Much as he wished to be accepted as a person without the bolster of his wealth, to stand trial without its benefits frightened him. If Karen cared about the money, even if she didn't love him, she would be likely to say yes, and he wanted her so much he was willing to accept her even on these terms. He had made up his mind to ask her to marry him but he had talked it over with his mother and father, for the Hamilton family did these things with a certain protocol. Had he chosen someone of whom he knew his parents would disapprove he would have married her despite them, but the protocol would have been observed. The Hamiltons did not rush to Greenwich or to Easton, Maryland; they did not fly to Las Vegas at 2 A.M. to be wed. Like the framers of the Declaration of Independence they considered they owed a decent respect to the opinions of mankind. They sent out announcements and were married like Christian folk in St. Thomas's at half-past four in the afternoon and they went to Europe on their honeymoons.

Fortunately the Hamilton seniors liked Karen, though Barclay's father had seen her only once when he and his wife and the young people having gone to different theaters met afterward for a drink in the Oak Room of the Plaza. Mr. Hamilton had found her big but bonny, and when he sensed his son might be serious about her thanked God the lad stood six feet three in his stocking feet. Both Barclay's parents were willing to accept her though they had hoped he might be drawn to someone in, not comparative financial brackets —that was almost impossible, but say to a daughter of one of the twenty wealthiest families in the country. Mr. Hamilton liked the idea of consolidation. "Let the rich young people marry each other," he would chortle with malicious pleasure, "that gets the government roiled. They can tax your heads off but they can't sue for monopoly." However, Karen's father seemed to be in a reasonably reputable business, and from what his wife told him about the girl's mother, though he could form only a vague opinion of her character, if she was all right with his Annie she was all right with him. "By God, they'll breed a race of Titans, won't they?" he observed, and his mind turned to amiably lewd thoughts.

The small week-end gathering had been arranged deliberately that Barclay might have a clear field for operations, and for two days before Karen's arrival Annie Hamilton and her husband had been planning the little speeches of welcome and congratulation they would make when the young couple should appear before them, the glad tidings written on their faces. As they drove off to dinner Saturday evening they were pretty sure that upon their return the moment would be propitious.

Meanwhile, at home, Barclay and Karen dreamed in the moonlight. She lay on a wicker chaise longue, the ugly plaster cast on her foot concealed by a cashmere blanket he had tenderly laid over her. His eyes dwelt on the youthful, voluptuous curves of her body and on her soft, full mouth. Her hair was a pale aureole in the shimmering gloom. She reminded him of figures he had seen in Greece the summer his father chartered a yacht and the family cruised through the islands. They were statuesque and vital yet there was amazing subtlety in their modeling. They were deeply female if not feminine in the modern sense. Barclay thought delicately modeled women attractive but he mistrusted them. They were feline and vicious. For all that Karen was colored like a tawny cat she had a canine

190

forthrightness of manner and the wonderful ability to be companionable without suggesting a Girl Scout.

A boy's best friend may be his mother, but a man's best friend is his mistress, or so Barclay hoped, and though he wanted to marry Karen because he wanted to be with her always, it was the mistress angle which struck him as being of more current interest than the respect and compatibility upon which, his parents had explained to him, successful marriages were built. Respect, compatibility, and the family unit, that's what counted, his parents said. When he was adolescent it had a dark brown sound, and he had been greatly relieved when he discovered in extracurricular activities that at least one aspect of the male-female relationship could be absolutely delightful. The unit-founding process had turned out to be all right, and feeling as he did about Karen he didn't care if the unit itself didn't start materializing until after many, many attempts.

As he sat beside her in the starlit summer night his projection of what their future together could be like if only she would say yes hit a small snag when he remembered that she was sailing for Europe in what amounted virtually to no time at all. She had told him about it as they drove out from town. She would be gone for only a little while, but in another country, in another climate, what might not happen to her and to his chances? She had mentioned Reams Asher. Barclay remembered him from the party at her house. It had occurred to him that night that she liked Reams just about the same time it occurred to him that he had overlooked something pretty important when he first met her at the house of their mutual friend, Jeannie Fairbanks. The party was months ago. What about Asher? Did he mean anything to her now? He was years older, but you could never tell about girls. That lovely-looking Bierne Honeywell, for example, seemed to feel Mr. Goodyear was Christmas. A man who could be her father! Barclay cared nothing at all for the European trip and he cared less when he heard about the *Indo-Chinois*. A boat that could accommodate twelve passengers! What kind of tub was that? Suppose there was a storm? Karen might be drowned! Could he dissuade her from going? It sounded embarrassingly smug and conceited, but was it possible she was going because she cared for him a little and thought maybe he didn't care for her at all? She couldn't think that. A girl knew, after all, whether

191

or not you liked her, and they had written long letters to each other whenever she was at college, but it was true that he had never committed himself.

He wasn't quite sure now how it had happened, but he imagined that it was probably Karen's broken ankle which had finally crystallized his feeling about her. The first time he had gone to her house and seen her encumbered by the cast, joking and laughing about it but helpless, he thought of a lion cub with one foot in a trap, and he had been moved. How dear and kind and sweet she was. And when he had helped her about the room or in and out of the car, she turned those luminous eyes on him and murmured, "Thanks, Barky, that's grand," and he suddenly felt that he, Barclay Hamilton, *was* grand, and helping her in that way was something he could do as a man and the money had no part of it. He could help her and take care of her always. They could be together always and she would bless him with that radiant smile and he would be reassured and made whole.

He was about to speak, to pour out his heart, arguments to persuade her came thronging to his mind, he was thinking exultantly that he would make a splendid lawyer swaying judge and jury to his will, when she turned to him and said wistfully, "Bark, if two people are separated, don't see each other for quite a long time but like each other, or—or, anyway, one of them does, do you think it's possible for them to scramble back together over all the people and adventures and memories they may have experienced during their separation?"

Young Mr. Hamilton's cardiogram would have been of interest to specialists. His heart missed a beat, plunged like an elevator, and rebounded like a bucking horse. His thoughts seethed. She doesn't want to go to Europe, she's afraid the separation may spoil things between us, but she has to go because her mother's expecting her. "I think," he said huskily, once he had regained the power of speech, "that if people care for each other they shouldn't be separated, but if they have to be because of a trip or something, what possible difference can it make, except that meeting again will be that much more wonderful?" He reached out and covered her hand with his.

"Oh, Barky, do you think so?"

"Oh, Karen, yes."

Barclay's eyes were brown, but as Karen looked into them she suddenly seemed to see two bright red lights flash on, stopping her dead in her tracks. My God, she thought, he's going to ask me to marry him. He mustn't! I must spare him; it will be so desperately hard for him if I say no, and if I'm tempted because of the money and say yes, I'll never be able to go through with it because of loving Reams. I've got to stop it, I've got to prevent it. Suddenly she knew how. She could say it but she couldn't look at him. "Barclay, do you mind if I tell you something?"

"No, Karen, of course not." The dear darling, what could she be wanting to say to him? "You're such a good friend, Barclay, it's why I'm telling you. I'm terribly in love with someone. It's silly, I suppose, I hardly know him really, and maybe he won't even give me the time of day, but that's what I've got to find out. I'm afraid he may think of me as just a kid because he's famous now and all kinds of women must be after him, but that's one reason I'm dying to get to Paris, I have to know. It's better to know, don't you think?"

After a long time Barclay said, "Yes. Yes, I guess it is." His hand lay heavily on hers like a dead weight. He stared down at it for a minute and then drew it away as an afterthought. The look in his eyes made her feel sick. "Is it Reams Asher?" he asked.

"You remember him from the party that night?"

He nodded. "I hope . . ." After a bit he tried again. "I hope you find everything you want."

She looked at his young face white and drawn in the moonlight. How changed he was, how changed they both were. A soft, lovely bird had hovered between them. She had killed it.

13

The day after the Oppenheimers had been in her apartment Georgiana worked late at the office signing letters and getting off a long business cable to the Dauzats in New York. She had no dinner engagement and walked slowly home through the warm summer evening watching the Paris twilight bathe the gray stone of the old houses in pink and lilac radiance. Her youth that night seemed far

193

away, but the delicate light on the most civilized of cities reminded her, oddly, of the barren Colorado mountains of her childhood when violet and rose and dusty gold they mirrored the evening sky.

She went in through the great arched entrance to the building and was surprised not to see the concierge taking the air. Usually on mild evenings she sat in a straight chair on the sidewalk making derogatory comments on the passers-by to her dirty white poodle.

Climbing the stairs to the apartment, Georgiana thought once or twice to hear footsteps behind her. It was a normal enough sound—other residents of the building might well be coming home, too—but tonight there was an eerie quality about it because it was their neighborhood's turn to be without light, and the stairway mounted into blackness. Coal was still severely rationed, and Paris electricity was more than normally an off-again, on-again quantity. Georgiana carried an electric flash but its feeble beam did little to illumine the stairwell, though on the landings the windows opening on the courtyard glimmered with a pale, aqueous light.

Before attacking the last flight she stood for a moment, tensed and listening. There were the footsteps again climbing upward. She counted two, three, four steps. The tread was fumbling but inevitable, and she rushed up the last flight in unreasoning panic. She fitted her key in the lock, hurled herself through the door and slammed and bolted it behind her. She stood panting a minute, trying to get her breath, and with trembling hands reached for the candle and matches on the small table in the foyer. The flame dispelled her dread a little, and when she got into the salon and found the familiar room shadowy but still visible in the lingering twilight, smelt the fragrance of the great bunches of lilacs she had bought the day before, and heard the reassuring toot of taxi horns borne on the evening air, she recovered enough to laugh at herself and to blow out the candle. Economy of candlepower had by now become as much second nature to her as to true Parisians, since the shops were frequently sold out and even the churches—at one time a rich source of supply—were now, in a most unchristian spirit, tending to treasure their tapers to burn before the saints on high feast days.

She unlocked her precious small stock of hard liquor—the thought of a highball was tempting—and went to the kitchen for ice. For

194

once she blessed the old-fashioned box with old-fashioned ice cakes since, in these rationed days, an electric refrigerator would have been of little use.

On the way back to the living room she listened at the door. All was quiet. Whoever had been on the stairs behind her had apparently found the apartment he was looking for. She mixed her drink and lighted a cigarette, wondering what on earth the French did when they were tired. Those apéritifs and *vin du pays* were all very well, but they didn't pick you up the way a martini or a shot of scotch did. She thought she would put a record on the phonograph and sit by the window and sip her highball. There were two or three friends whom she supposed she might call, but the intricacies of the telephone were discouraging and, besides, those who had plans for the evening would be already embarked on them. Those who were quietly at home would doubtless prefer not to be disturbed. She tried to cheat her loneliness by assuring herself that an early night was what she needed and reminded herself proudly that this was the first solitary evening she had passed in two weeks and that the immediate future was well taken care of. Even through her unhappiness and worry over Reams she worked at keeping her free time occupied and was aided to a considerable extent by the requirements of her job. Germaine wanted a weekly letter on Paris life: theaters, night clubs, exhibitions, a smattering of politics, as well as the goings-on in the *haute couture*. Georgiana was given an expense account for these activities but it was French, and she was frequently obliged to augment it out of her own pocket. The available escorts whose way she paid, were, for the most part, since they, too, worked in the world of fashion and the arts, ambiguous members of their sex, and though their company made it possible for her to cover a good deal of night life, they left her inviolate at her own front door. She mounted the stairs alone, went alone to bed, and lay alone with memories of Reams or Allen through the wakeful night.

She was beginning to feel hungry and was trying to remember what the larder might provide by way of supper when she was conscious of a slight noise at the hall door. She went quickly and silently, relighted her candle, and laid her ear against the panel. Her heart was pounding so hard she couldn't be sure, but it seemed to her a

195

sound of breathing came from the other side. For a moment she was stiff with fear. What friend would come at this hour or stand so silently? If it was somebody else, what should she do, how could she call for help? There was no house phone to reach the concierge, and it would take time for any friends she might appeal to by the regular telephone to get to her, nor were they likely to take the trouble simply because she imagined she heard something. Their practical advice would be to open the door and see who was there, but to throw it open with only the candlelight behind her and the blackness of the echoing stairs on the other side required more courage than she could muster. There it was again! The sound of *something*. She stood back a little from the door and in the gleam of the candle saw beneath her terrified gaze the handle of the old-fashioned lock slowly turning. She stifled a little cry and the lock held; the handle went slowly back to position. She was thinking desperately of knives, of scissors, of screaming at the window when the thick, beating silence was shattered by a loud knocking. The suddenness of it startled her so that without meaning to she cried out, "Who's there?"

"Georgiana?"

"Who is it?"

The voice came thickly. "It's me. Reams. Can I come in?"

"Reams!"

"I can't find the damn doorbell."

She threw open the door. He stood on the threshold, a looming shadow in the obscurity. "Reams, come in."

"Thanks," he said, but he didn't move.

"Are you all right?"

"Yes. Yes, I'm fine. I'm a little drunk."

"Never mind. Come in, for God's sake." She led him into the drawing room. There, where the light was better, she looked at him, and was shocked by what she saw. He had lost pounds and seemed to have aged ten years. His eyes were haggard and he badly needed a shave.

He looked slowly around the room and back to her. "Mad at me?" There was no slurring of his speech but his voice was unwontedly low, heavy.

She had heard the tone before in men who were drunk. "You

196

frightened me to death just now. Was that you coming up the stairs after me?"

"I guess so. The concierge said you'd just come in."

"I didn't see her."

"She was in the rear of the courtyard."

"Why didn't you call out, for heaven's sake?"

"I—uh—I felt a little shy." He smiled faintly and walked over to an open window. He rested his hand on the sill, hunching one shoulder, and stared down into the street. "Pretty city, Paris. Trees. Ever noticed? At home just the leaves move in the breeze, here the trunks sway too."

Georgiana, watching him, felt puzzled and insecure, but the joy of seeing him was physical, like the relief from a tight hatband. She sparred, waiting. "Did you come here to deliver a Burton Holmes travelogue?"

"I wanted to see you."

"From the way you spoke that day at the Ritz I'd—I'd thought to see you before this."

His back was to her, something outside seemed to command his attention. "Can I have a drink?" he asked.

"You don't think you've had enough?"

He glanced at her own half-empty glass. "You haven't become a lone tippler, have you?"

She mixed a highball and handed it to him. It was on the tip of her tongue to say, "Does it interest you at all what I've become?" but he looked so ill, the hollows in his cheeks and temples accentuated by the candlelight, that her heart ached. "Come and sit down." He followed her docilely to the sofa. For one terrible moment he seemed like someone vacant of mind. Gentle, obedient, empty. They sat down next to each other and sipped their drinks in silence. When she had finished she set her glass carefully on the coffee table and leaned back into the corner of the sofa. "Reams, you look bad. Have you been ill?" He nodded. "Do you want to tell me about it?" He didn't answer, so after a bit she said, "We've been desperately worried about you, you know. I was afraid something had happened to you. Even the Oppenheimers were beginning to get uneasy. Another day or so and Horace would have gone to the police."

He looked startled. "To the—— Sweet God."

197

"Does that surprise you? You were going to call me early the next morning, you said. When I didn't hear I—I didn't know what to think." Another silence. "What is it, Reams? What's happened?"

Suddenly he stood up. He seemed to have got hold of himself. When he spoke it was with something of his old vigor and he didn't seem drunk at all. "You want to know about Linda Schofield, don't you? You've got a right to know."

"Well, I admit to a certain curiosity. Is she an old friend? A new friend? Are you in love with her?"

"I don't know."

"Haven't you been able to find out in these past three weeks?"

"I haven't seen her. I haven't seen her since that day in the Ritz Bar."

"Then, good God, Reams, where have you been?"

He stood with his hands in his pockets and stared down at his feet for a long time. Finally he said, "Mine is a commonplace story, though parts of it will probably sound unlikely. Would you care to hear it?" She looked at him silently. "I met Linda Schofield a long time ago and fell in love with her. We never got married because she was married and had a child she wouldn't leave and I had no money. The war came and she went back to England and I went into the Army. Then I was wounded and I got out of the Army and I wrote a book and I met you. I liked you and I wanted you and I think you felt the same, and I hope for that time in New York you were as happy as I was. When I left New York I missed you and I wrote to you, and what I said in the letters I meant. And then I went to Lisbon and I was walking along the street one day and I saw Linda. She was there visiting some daft old relative. We went back to my hotel and we went to bed and for ten days and ten nights we were never separated.

"I went and lived in the palace with her. It's a huge barracks of a place. You could quarter a regiment in it and nobody would ever know. Finally she left me to try to talk her husband into a divorce. When I told you in the Ritz that I'd only got here that morning it was true, but it wasn't true that I'd telephoned you. My mind was on Linda. She came in and I introduced her to all of you and then we went to our table and she told me that a divorce was impossible and she wouldn't leave her husband because of the chil-
198

dren. Now she has two. Then we went out and I put her in a taxi and that was the last time I saw her. She said she'd telephone me that night, but I don't know whether she did or not because I didn't go back to my hotel. Instead, I got drunk. I met up with some newspaper guys I know and we got very drunk, and a couple of nights later, I think it was, although through here my chronology is not sure, I got pneumonia. They finally wangled some penicillin out of the Army in Berlin and I got better, but they tell me that for a while I was as good as dead, which is why I look like this. It sounds romantic, as though I'd got ill from love, but I got ill from being drunk and getting drenched in a rainstorm and not having been sober enough to get my clothes off."

There was a long pause. The twilight had expired completely and the room was dark except for the remote gleam of the candle in the foyer and for the reflected glow from the night sky through the windows. Reams paced slowly up and down, his hands in his pockets.

Curiously enough the thing that hurt her most in his story, even more than his candid revelation of the love affair, was his not having telephoned her when he got to Paris. At last she said, though she found a little difficulty in pronouncing the name, "Where is—where is Linda now?"

" 'Willow,' I expect, that's their country place. Or maybe she's in London. It doesn't matter. I shall never see her again."

"Where were you all the time you were ill?"

"With Jeep Harrigan, one of the fellows I got drunk with. He's a good guy, I knew him in the Army."

"But Horace said none of the American press, at least none of the ones he knows, had heard anything about you."

Reams chuckled softly. "He may not know Jeep." But Georgiana suspected it was not only that. There was a freemasonry among men of a kind: the press, writers, medicine, the law; they were apt to stick together. If, for any reason, reprehensible or innocent, one of their members wished to lie low for a while, they were capable of presenting a surface as impervious to probing as that of underworld characters questioned by the police. "Jeep has an apartment in the Rue du Bac," Reams continued; "he took me there."

"Oh, my dear. Didn't it occur to you to have him get in touch with me? After all, we were friends before we were . . . It was so un-friendly, what you did. I was sick with anxiety."

His voice was kind in the darkness. "I'm sorry, Georgiana, truly I am, but for several days I was out of my head, and then when I was better—well, I didn't want any emissaries or disembodied voices coming to you over the phone, I wanted to come myself. When I could." He sat down suddenly, as though the strength had all drained out of him.

"You shouldn't overdo it, Reams. *You* could have telephoned me and I would have come to you."

"No, this is better." It was a curious conversation, he at one end of the long room and she on the sofa at the other, but the darkness gave them an intimacy which offset their physical separation.

"Are you still very much in love with Linda, Reams?"

After a while he said, "I'll try to tell you how it is. I don't know if I can, but I'll try. Loving Linda seems to be part of me, there's nothing I can do about it any more than I can help the color of my eyes or being the height I am. But by the same token it doesn't demand any ceremony either. It's queer. In the old days, when people loved hopelessly, they went to the Crusades or into the Foreign Legion or rushed into monasteries. Nowadays we just go on living. Having children by other people, working with other people, making love to other people. Nothing to it. The way we know we love is that we function without joy in an inescapable element. From your point of view, though, there should be no change in me since I was this way when we met. Granted, something has hap-pened to me, and when something happens it can't be as though it hadn't happened, since everything you experience is what consti-tutes *you* as a human being, but the experience passes away and the person's left. The person is the residue."

Georgiana listened, wondering. She had been deeply humiliated, she had been hurt, and she had had moments of frantic anxiety for this man. The fact that he informed her, without self-conscious-ness, of his affair with another woman when she might reasonably assume that she held his affection and loyalty indicated, she sup-posed, that he apprehended, with neither malice nor regret, the difference in their ages. He spoke in candor. Probably, when one had been recently as near death as he had, anything else was a waste

200

of time. His candor, to Georgiana, was bitter medicine, the sequel to his behavior, but that behavior had had in it nothing of calculated cruelty. In a sense it was she, Georgiana, who had taken him from Linda, for he had known Linda first. She thought of that face, seen so briefly in the crowded bar, she remembered the blue-gray eyes and the dark hair and the way Reams had held her in the curve of his arm, and she felt a searing pang of jealousy, and yet against her will, stupidly, supinely—my God, what pranks age could play upon a woman—she felt for Reams a maternal pity. Possibly he had relied on that, she couldn't tell, but she was responding. She wanted to comfort him. He was alone now and had come to her voluntarily. He needed her as much as she needed him. Pride was a luxury she couldn't afford, nor did she desire it. Let us be mutually grateful, she thought, for the mutual comfort we can offer each other. What had he said? "From your point of view there should be no change in me . . ." Was that a request to be taken back, to continue where they had left off? If it was, she knew quite well that she would acquiesce, and gratefully. This was the wry advantage the advancing years brought in their wake: you knew what you wanted, you appreciated your luck, you were realistic.

"What are you planning to do?" she asked.

"I thought I'd try to get a little starch back into me. Jeep knows a house he thinks we can rent, it's about an hour from Fontainebleau. Americans have had it before and there's a swimming pool. We want to try to get it and live there for the rest of the summer. Dunk in the pool and lie in the sun and sip tall, cold ones."

"Sounds all right. I'd go easy on the tall colds." They lapsed into another of the silences which seemed to be so much a part of this nocturnal dialogue.

"I was wondering," he said at last, "whether you'd like to come too."

"You mean me share the house?"

"Would you like to? It wouldn't cost you anything, and you and Jeep would get on. He'll probably be there only week ends, as he's got to work in town most of the summer."

"Do you want me?"

"I'm very fond of you, Georgiana. I think you're fond of me, or has what's happened changed that? It could, I suppose."

She thought he spoke wistfully and she found his naïveté faintly irritating. "I have to work, too, you know."

"But surely that dragon—what's her name?"

"Germaine Dauzat?"

"Won't she give you a holiday?"

"I don't see why she should. I've been on the job only about six weeks and the openings will be along the end of this month. She and Claude will both be over here. It's the big season for a fashion magazine."

"But you'll have week ends, maybe you can even commute a bit? It's only a little over an hour by car."

"Where will I get the gas? Besides, Karen will be here before long."

"Good. I like Karen. The house is big enough for all of us."

"It might be a bit difficult, don't you think?"

"I don't see why." For the first time since he had got up from the sofa to talk about Linda Schofield his voice held again that low note of a man who has drunk too much, and this time his tongue was thick.

You don't see why! Georgiana thought with exasperation. On what basis, my friend, are you offering me this invitation? Indeed, on what basis do I want to accept it? There should be only one, she knew that, but it was not the one she wanted.

The silence prolonged itself. She was about to suggest getting some supper when against the window the dark shadow that was Reams slumped forward in the chair. She rose and crossed swiftly to his side. She raised his head, cradling him gently against her shoulder. His eyes were closed. His breathing came deep and regular. He was sound asleep.

She giggled a little hysterically. The erring, the truant lover returned, the scene of reconciliation mounting to a climax, and practically in the middle of a sentence he had fallen asleep. Georgiana was torn between tenderness and exasperation. She was physically and emotionally hungry, here in her arms was the object of her desire, and the evening obviously was to end in frustration. She propped Reams in his chair as best she could and pulled forward another one to make a kind of chaise longue for his legs. Then she went into the kitchen and cooked some supper. She tried halfheartedly to wake

202

him that they might share it together, but his weakness and fatigue and the liquor he had consumed proved too much for her. She washed the dishes, covered him with a blanket, and went to bed. In the darkness she lay straining for some sound from the drawing room, hoping he might come to her, half fearful lest he wake and go away, till her own nerves, unable to stand the tension any longer, relaxed in a spasm of tears and laughter and exhausted she fell asleep.

14

Within a week Reams secured the house in the country he had told her about. If not exactly "a true jewel, comfort modern, set in a garden of all beauty"—a description the renting agent had originally given Jeep—it still proved very adequate. The garden, Reams said, on return from his tour of inspection, had the ravaged charm of an aging, well-used beauty and the "piscine" was the nuts. "That piscine always sounds lewd as hell," he added, laughing, "but the boy who built it must have been a bug on 'la natation.' He was an American, rented the place for years before the war. It's a swell break for us."

The following Sunday, on hoarded gasoline, Reams and Jeep drove Georgiana out to view the premises over which she had agreed to preside as chatelaine. She was beginning to look forward to the week ends and to the thought of occasional mid-week trips to the country as well, since once the Dauzats arrived she would be obliged to move out of their apartment and the thought of hotel life was unappealing.

She had met Jeep with curiosity. He turned out to be a lean brown young man with a crew haircut and an intense interest in everything and everybody. How much Reams had told him about their relationship or how much he took for granted Georgiana didn't know, but his manner toward her was easygoing and impersonal. He specialized in the newspaper business, girls, and liquor in that order, and his capacity for the last two was impressive. From time to time Georgiana wondered how he and Karen might react to each other but anticipated little moth-and-candle interplay since Jeep, though well built, was small in scale. She remembered Karen's interest in Reams but assured herself that after all these months it must be moribund. Still, remembering it, a few days after his return she got Reams to write to her child, feeling that a letter from him would help offset any change of plans Karen might be contemplating because of the injury to her ankle. Georgiana was longing to see her and feared, jealously, that Allen's affection might outweigh herself and Paris. Also, she was looking forward to some information on the status of his relationship with Bierne. He had written of her in two or three of his early letters and a couple of times since the Oppenheimers had mentioned that she had been at their house with him Georgiana had gleaned a stray phrase from touring friends, leading her to wonder if they were not fairly constant companions. From the Quicks' letters she gathered little though they did tend to harp on the desirability of her return to New York. They stated no reason other than that they missed her, but this, combined with the sudden dearth of any reference in Allen's occasional correspondence to whom he was seeing, led her to suspect that his time must be pretty well occupied.

She wondered idly whether he was in love with Bierne and whether or not he was having an affair with her, but if he was she could not, in all honesty, pretend to be miserable. She thought little of the future. The present, if not joyous, was enjoyable, and for the first time in a long while she felt she was living.

One morning about ten days before Karen was due to arrive Reams handed her the mail on his way out. He was often at the apartment and spent several nights a week there, although now, the relief of his return having a little abated, she was subject to constantly vacillating moods: compassion for what he had suffered alternated with flaring anger, bitter resentment at what he had done. In the latter frame of mind pride would stiffen her determination to resist him, she would behave in friendly fashion but with dignity. It was essential that he understand that after what had happened there could be no question of resuming their love affair. As time passed and he made no move to do so it showed nicety of feeling; she should have been pleased. She was heartsick. She was also disgusted with herself considering she was behaving like one of those females in French popular songs delineated with such feeling by the artists of the Paris night clubs—creatures helpless to resist the sound of their man's voice, the touch of his hands. His very glance could reduce them to unthinking, quivering pulps of passion. The songs had always struck Georgiana as slightly repellent nonsense. They still made her laugh, but uneasily.

One evening when Reams was dining at the apartment she went to fetch a book from the drawing-room bookcase she wanted to show him. She was standing on tiptoe, reaching for an upper shelf, when he came up behind her. "Wait," he said, "let me." He took down the book and she turned against him and his arms went round her. He rubbed his cheek against her hair and laughed very softly. "Back at the old stand," he said.

If, since then, the times they were lovers tended a little toward an old married sparseness, they were at least on a loverlike basis. She could find comfort and stimulation in his companionship as well as moments of racking indecision and uncertainty.

He was thoughtful of her, however. They never referred to Linda, and as he regained his health he seemed, she thought, if not exactly happy, contented and philosophical. From the point of view of holding him this even keel was perhaps lucky. If his life flowed peaceably, he would be less apt to seek a change, and who could tell? He might become so accustomed to it that possibly marriage . . . But that was a sleeveless fantasy. She wasn't at all sure she even desired it.

This morning she took the letters and kissed him good-by. He was lunching with a couple of men, he said, at La Cigone, but he wished she would join them. She promised to if she didn't get tied up at the office, and took the mail back to read while she finished her breakfast. She glanced at the envelopes and laid aside the red-white-and-blue airmail one from Allen. She opened the bills, read through the three or four announcements and invitations, and digested a newsy letter from Nancy Slade regaling her with latest bulletins on Nora Brown and Claude Dauzat and recounting a bit incredulously the Hollywood offers Reuben was receiving since his success in Nora's play. She folded the pages and slipped them back in the envelope. She would answer the letter in a day or two. She took up her knife and slit open the one from Allen.

Reading it, she felt curiously drained of emotion yet interested, as though it concerned a friend.

Dear Georgiana,

I send you this letter with an odd feeling that when you left home you somehow anticipated, without grief, that you would one day be receiving it or maybe sending one of the same kind yourself. If you are shocked at all it is probably because it has come more quickly than either of us would have believed possible. I write to ask if you will agree to a divorce.

I am pretty certain that in the past year or two, if not before, you have weighed the idea, and my belief is that when you left for Paris, although money was one factor influencing you, another may well have been the thought, even if vague, that a prolonged separation might eventually evolve into a friendly divorce. I suspected then, and I still think, although believe me, without rancor, that Reams Asher meant a lot to you and that you wanted to be near him. Whether or not you are seeing him I do not know, and I am aware that under the circumstances I have no right to inquire, but I want you to be happy. My hope is that your private life is going as successfully as your work seems to be. I gather from the Dauzats that you are doing a bang-up job. I never doubted that you would.

My reason for asking for a divorce is, I am afraid, banal. I have fallen in love. After twenty-four years of marriage I do not have to tell you that I am no self-sacrificing hero, yet I think I am being honest when I say that if you loved me or depended on me, if you were deeply content in our life together, then I would sacrifice my own desire and the desire of the girl I love to preserve our marriage. However, since we both know that this is not the case, I see no point in creating heartache and misery simply to maintain a pose.

You know how I feel about Karen, so you must know that I have devoted some long, hard thought to what is best for her. My opinion is that she is grown up enough so that a divorce can cause no real harm to her emotional life—certainly some of our family rows can't have been very edifying or given her any sense of security—and the fact is that she and Bierne are great friends. Don't feel bitter about this, Georgiana, and don't, I beg you, blame the child. She has suffered deeply from a feeling of divided loyalty because she loves and admires you more even than I think you realize, and I believe she loves me, too, but we might as well accept the fact that she and Bierne are the same generation, their interests are similar and their temperaments compatible. They have fun together as friends rather than as child and parent, but that has nothing to do with her feeling for you or her pathetic eagerness to see you. She will be on her way to you in another day or so, which is one reason why I write now. I don't want her to be under the strain of having to conceal something. If only the travel situation and business were on a different footing at the moment I would be coming over myself to have this out with you rather than setting it down on paper, but since I can't manage the trip this is the only alternative I have.

I don't know whether the fact that the girl is Bierne Honeywell will surprise or amuse you or what. I imagine some rumors about us must have drifted over to you. In any event, I doubt if you will be shocked, though you may consider me a fool. Yes, my dear, the gap in our ages and backgrounds has occurred to me, too, but these things make no difference. She and I are in love. We want to be married.

I am asking you for a decision which no one makes offhand. I expect no overnight cable saying divorce under way nor, I hope, divorce impossible. All I ask is that you will think objectively and honestly about what I have written. Talk to Karen, who comes not as an ambassador to plead my cause, indeed, though I do not think so, she may be opposed to the idea, but I am anxious for you to talk to her. My belief is that she can help us both because she loves us both and she is our child whom we love.

If you agree you know that financially I will do all that is fair and all that I possibly can and will discuss it with any lawyer you name.

Allen

Georgiana laid the letter down, her golden eyes very wide. Suddenly she burst out laughing. "The nerve!" she exclaimed, "the cool nerve. Oh!" She paced nervously around the breakfast table. She lifted the letter, riffled through the pages, and tossed it down again. She was shocked, yet it induced in her a sense of wild amusement. That Allen should be asking *her* for a divorce! Allen, who, only three months before, felt so strongly the sanctity of their marriage, the necessity for its enduring. He now wished to toss it overboard for someone who had been her secretary! A child he had just met! It was fantastic. Her first instinct was to turn to Reams, to try to get him on the telephone, but reaching for it she changed her mind. Better think it over, better plan the manner of her revelation. She did not doubt his affection for her but she was realistic enough to suspect that he might originally have started and then resumed their love affair, as distinct from their friendship, because she was safely anchored to another man and not in any position to become too demanding.

She wanted to talk to someone, but the Oppenheimers had gone to London and no one else was close enough to her.

She looked at the time and saw she was already late for her first appointment in the office. Deciding she wouldn't meet Reams for luncheon, as she wanted time to think, she scribbled a note in pidgin French to the cook-cleaning woman who came in by the day telling her to prepare a salad, she would be home around one, and hurried out. Miraculously the elevator was functioning. Once downstairs she hailed a taxi and was almost at the office before she realized that her first reaction to Allen's letter had not been a categoric no. She was flabbergasted, incredulous, but she was not outraged. Why should she be? she asked herself. In this case what was sauce for the gander had turned out to be sauce for the goose. It was unfortunate, it was somehow comic, but it was not without a certain ironic logic.

She expected to find a cable at the office saying that Karen had sailed. She would wait, she decided, until her child got to Paris and they had had an opportunity to talk before replying to Allen's letter. She would wait, too, before saying anything to Reams. Their situation was ameliorating, but was still too precarious to risk any sort of upheaval.

That, during the next few days, she was able to conduct herself without betraying her secret by moodiness or change of manner pleased her. She had herself well under control. She had seen too many women of her age lose out in their relationship with men through being nervous, exacting, and undisciplined. Middle age, she decided, could be a distinctly pleasant period if a woman understood what luxuries she could not afford. Of course it worked that way for a man, too, especially when he was in love with someone far younger than himself, and thinking of Allen she found to her surprise a certain anxiety and compassion for him, mixed with the amusement his dilemma afforded her and with the unhappiness which, despite her, was creeping insidiously into her heart. The breakup of a marriage

208

was a sorry business except that as long as she had Reams her concern over her personal problem remained objective.

The *Indo-Chinois* was to arrive at Le Havre early on a Saturday morning. Friday, as soon as the *Distaff* office closed, Georgiana and Reams left Paris in his car and drove down. They registered at a hotel as Monsieur and Madame Asher and shared the big double bed which, even in July, abounded in down quilts and the bolsters which Georgiana said always made her think of dead ancestors.

She and Reams had debated the wisdom of going together to meet Karen, but Reams had said, "Why shouldn't we both go? In the few weeks she's here I can't see any reason for her finding out about us at all."

"I don't know how she'll accept the house."

"Why shouldn't she accept it? You're helping out two grateful bachelors. Besides, she's always known we're close friends, why shouldn't we be seeing a lot of each other over here? Especially as you haven't got Allen to take you around?" Silently she thought, especially as I haven't got Allen, period. "I'll drive," he continued, "and you two can admire the scenery. It'll be fun for her, seeing the French countryside for the first time. Besides, we'll be able to pick up some milk and eggs." These were luxuries still hard come by in Paris and week-ends city dwellers swarmed over villages and farms trying to replenish their depleted stocks, and an invitation to a country house was more eagerly angled for than seats to the opening of the opera.

"What about gas?" Georgiana asked.

"I got sources."

"Nubian?"

He grinned. "Sort of. I wouldn't do it normally, but this is an event, kid's first trip abroad."

As she thought it would be fun herself, Georgiana was not hard to persuade, but she hoped everything would go smoothly. She didn't want to antagonize Karen on her arrival. Not only did she want her daughter's love, she needed her as an ally. Karen might have accepted Bierne as Allen had said in his letter, but if things came to a showdown she must consider her father the one at fault. It was he, after all, who had asked for the divorce.

As they drove out of Paris early Friday evening and along the white roads toward Le Havre Georgiana said, "Karen used to have a crush on you, you know. Even Allen likes you. What is this fatal charm you have for the Goodyear family, Mr. Asher?"

"I should say it was mutual, wouldn't you? I go for Goodyears."

"One at a time, if you please."

"Relax. The cradle has never tempted me."

She hoped that through association he did not consider her the grave. She gave a little sigh. "I'm so happy I'm going to see Karen," she said. "But I'll be missing you. With her in the house . . ."

"I'll be around."

"It won't be quite the same." She wanted him to say that they could meet frequently in the Hôtel Vendôme in Paris, where he kept a room, but he didn't. It doesn't mean anything, she assured herself, he's just not in the mood.

Karen, a few hundred yards off the coast of France, wondered fleetingly whether Reams would be there to meet her along with Georgiana, but decided that that was too wild a hope. Anyway, the thought of her mother and France was thrilling enough. Then, as the boat was made fast alongside the pier and she spotted them both, she started waving madly. "Mother, Mother!" she called. "Here I am. Reams! Hello, Reams!"

"Hi!"

"Darling, darling. Hello, hurry up." In another moment she swarmed ashore in a maelstrom of luggage, porters, and the other passengers. Karen threw her arms around Georgiana and they embraced for a long moment. She turned to Reams with shining eyes. "Hullo, this is wonderful."

"Don't I rate a kiss? An old friend on a foreign shore?" He kissed her on both cheeks. "You're looking grand. How's the ankle?"

"Mother told you about it? Such nonsense. Look, Mummy, I can wiggle it and everything," and she proudly rotated her large but shapely foot. "And I have the most wonderful thing for it, Bier—I mean a friend of mine who's good at carpentry made me a cute little folding footrest in case my ankle got tired. I only used it once on the whole trip."

"He sounds ingenious," Reams remarked. "Anybody we know?"

210

Karen looked at him vaguely. "Oh, *here's* my luggage," she cried as her trunk was catapulted on to the pier beside them.

They finally got through the customs, got the trunk checked on the boat train and the suitcases packed in the luggage compartment of the car. Two large cartons, each containing fifty kilos of food which she was allowed to bring in duty free, one for herself and one for Georgiana, constituted more of a problem. In the end they decided that the only way they could manage was to unpack them on the dock and stow the contents in the back of the car.

"Hop to it," Reams commanded, "and don't spread the stuff around. It'll be snatched before you can say knife." They believed he knew whereof he spoke as a curious crowd began to gather and jostle while they tried quickly and a little shamefacedly to transfer cans of soup, packages of rice and chocolate, powdered milk and tinned butter, soap and toilet paper into the rear compartment. With a carton of cigarettes apiece and two pounds of butter they enlisted the help of a couple of porters and at last, their storage completed, closed and locked the rear doors and crowded, all three, into the front seat.

Karen was dizzy with happiness and excitement, drinking in the French countryside and babbling to her mother and Reams. Her mother, she thought, looked wonderful, Reams seemed thinner, and, for all the warm welcome he had given her, different or, maybe over the long months, she had forgotten him a little although that was impossible. It was funny, on the boat coming over she had got her thinking of him mixed up with thoughts of Barclay. Barky's staying power in her memory was surprising. Apparently it was in Georgiana's, too, for she said, "Darling, tell us all about everything. Have you seen the Slades? Have you seen Barclay Hamilton? How are Lola and Peter and the twins?"

"Yes, they're all fine. It's wonderful about Mr. Slade. The day I left, Poppy called me and told me there's some talk of his doing a movie that was meant for Spencer Tracy. Imagine! Spencer Tracy's got some other commitments or something and *maybe* Mr. Slade will get the part. He'll be a big movie star."

Reams laughed. "What does Poppy think of her father now? As I remember she was very low in her mind over the prospect of his becoming an actor."

211

"Oh, she's much happier about it," Karen assured him. "She's already picked out the mink coat she wants." She turned to her mother. "Have you got Aunt Lola's letter yet with their big news?"

"No, what? Not another baby?"

"Lord, no. Not that I know of, but they may be going to the Coast for the rest of the summer. Peter's working on a big deal for a radio program and if it goes through they may be out there for some time, the whole family."

"Oh." Georgiana couldn't say why, but the thought of the Quicks in California gave her a small sinking feeling. She felt orphaned. California was a long way from Paris. Without the Quicks, without Allen. . . . She shivered a little.

"Why, Mum, what's the matter? You aren't cold, are you?"

Reams, too, was quickly solicitous. "Is this window too much for you?"

"Heavens, no," she said lightly, "it was just one of those goose-flesh things. Someone walking on my grave." That was the second time in twenty-four hours she had been thinking of the grave. How could she when she was so happy? "What about Barclay?" she asked. "You say you've been seeing him too?"

Karen smiled. "I spent the week end before I left with him. At his family's," she added hastily. She said nothing of the strained, sad moment between them.

"He's a nice young man," Reams said. "I approve of him." He was suddenly amused. He was Georgiana's lover and it gave him a fatherly feeling toward her child—a feeling unfamiliar but not unpleasant.

For the first time Georgiana mentioned Allen. "How's your father?" she asked.

"Oh, he's fine. He's working hard—wants to know if you're well and not overdoing it on your job." Karen spoke with the heartiness of one who hopes good fellowship will pad out the meagerness of the message he bears. They drove in silence for a few minutes while she gazed wide-eyed down the long, straight road between its rows of poplars and at the neat fields and at the old walled farms the color of the earth. "I'm hungry," she said suddenly. "I was so excited on the boat I couldn't eat any breakfast."

Reams and Georgiana laughed. "Sweetie," Georgiana said, "we'll be feeding you soon. Why, we haven't even told her the plan yet!"

"What is it?" Karen asked.

"Well, a Paris week end in July is just as dull as in any other city so we thought it would be more fun to stay overnight at the house in the country and get into town late tomorrow afternoon. How about that?"

"It sounds like heaven." She spoke with such sincerity that Reams and Georgiana were touched.

"Your mother was a little worried," Reams said; "she thought maybe you'd want to get to Paris swift as an arrow, but then we decided to gamble on the delay. Anyhow, we want to see what you think of the house. Parts of it are kind of weird."

"I'll love it," she breathed. "It sounded wonderful in Mother's letter. You were angels to plan things this way." Maybe her mother would go to bed early tonight and she and Reams could stroll hand in hand in the tangled garden under the French stars. For a moment the American stars and Barclay rose to the surface of her consciousness but were submerged again and faded under the French sunshine.

Karen was thrilled when they arrived before the house and had to honk loudly for the gardener to open the heavy wooden gate in the wall. "It's just like medieval times," she exclaimed happily.

"Pierre dates from the same period," Reams informed her as the gate swung slowly back revealing the dour face of the gardener who came with the place. "Pity the moat's dried up, he'd be ideal fodder for carp." The dislike between the French gardener and the American tenants of his employers was mutual, but Georgiana tossed him a cheery *bon jour* and smiled cordially as Reams nosed the car through the gate. Since Pierre might reasonably consider her position in the household ambiguous, let him at least find her amiable.

They drove around to the side entrance they always used and, as he saw the car, Jeep, who had been basking on the edge of the swimming pool, rose and came forward to meet them. He gazed with appreciation at Karen's wide-set green-brown eyes and her wide and friendly smile, but started just a little as she unfolded out of the car and he saw what a splendid amazon she was. Puts a man on his mettle, by God, he thought, extending a hard brown hand in welcome. Georgiana, watching them together, felt firmly that they

213

should be cronies. Cronies and have fun, and sex no part of it. Besides, as she well knew, Jeep had interests in three or four Paris precincts—in fact she was surprised that none of his projects had been invited for the week end. Also, she wanted to protect Barclay's franchise. That visit Karen had mentioned sounded promising.

Throughout the day Georgiana observed her daughter watching Reams with admiration in which was occasionally mingled an expression of questioning concern. Her own interest, as after dinner the two of them discussed his articles which were running in the *Saturday Evening Post* back home, was tinged with uneasiness. It was obvious that Karen's feelings about Reams and his work were more than casual. Apparently the passage of time had not dimmed her preoccupation with him. Yet behind her enthusiasm, exalted a little perhaps by her first evening in France and the excellent wine they had drunk at dinner, Georgiana thought she sensed a kind of puzzlement also. Had Karen guessed anything? Had she and Reams in some way betrayed themselves? She couldn't believe that they had. Reams, even to her alert and nervous eye, was behaving admirably; he was cordial, friendly, non-committal, and observing that they must have countless things they wanted to talk over, and that he was tired, retired to bed around ten o'clock, to Karen's keen disappointment and somewhat to Georgiana's relief. She accepted philosophically his obvious determination that the mother and child motif should not be marred on their first evening together, and even fell in with it to the extent of suggesting that they leave Jeep to his own devices and go and unpack Karen's luggage, sorting out the things she would want to leave in the house and those she would be taking to Paris. "The hotel closets aren't any too hot, darling," she said; "leave as much stuff out here as you can."

The bedroom allocated to Karen was large, hung with *toile de Jouy* and furnished with the barest necessities, but it did include a vast oak wardrobe and on the mantelpiece a marble bust of an eagle-beaked dame from the Court of Louis the Fifteenth. Karen stared at it incredulously. "My gosh," she said, "she looks just like Miss Parsons in Physical Ed," and she clapped a beanie upon the classic brow.

Georgiana laughed. "What do you think of our installation here?"

"Dreamy, but doesn't it cost an awful lot?"

214

Her mother hesitated. She hoped Karen wouldn't feel they were heavily obligated to Reams if she learned they were his guests for several weeks; on the other hand she didn't want the girl to think that after all her talk in New York about economy she was now foolishly extravagant. Reflecting that she would have enough dissembling to do, she decided that truth in the simple things was the best policy. "It isn't costing a penny, duck. Reams and Jeep have rented the place together though it's mostly Reams', I imagine, and they begged me to run it for them. It's a fair give and take, I think, as I save them a lot of trouble by looking after the servants and planning meals and all."

"Oh, well, in that case I think it's fine," Karen said happily. "What can I do? Help with the gardening or dishes or something?"

"No. You're to rest and have a holiday."

"Maybe I could type manuscripts for Reams. How's his book coming, by the way? I was going to ask him this evening, and then I had a funny feeling I shouldn't. You know," she added after a troubled pause, "I got the impression from that letter he wrote me that he'd been a little peaked maybe, but something terrible must have happened to him."

Her mother glanced at her sharply. "Why do you say that?"

"Well, he's awfully sweet, he couldn't have been nicer to me, but I got the queerest feeling—that he's dead, sort of. Haven't you noticed?"

Georgiana's heart contracted. To her he was philosophical, passive perhaps in the acceptance of his life, passive rather than enterprising but content, yet here was her daughter looking with fresh young eyes upon a man she remembered being in love with, perhaps thought she still was, and he seemed to her an automaton. Georgiana drew a deep breath. "I—I think you're a little overdramatic, aren't you? I'd say he was very much alive but he *was* more than 'peaked.' He was desperately ill, in fact."

"Oh, Mum, how awful! I *am* sorry. Gee, it was lucky for him you were here."

"Yes, well, he—he was ill in Paris, of course, it was before we got the house."

"What did he have?"

"Pneumonia. It's very debilitating, it can take a long time to get

215

over it, but Jeep and I are very pleased with the way he's coming along."

Karen laid a pile of sweaters and some underwear in one of the only two drawers the room boasted. Fitted into an old-fashioned commode, they were deep and impractical, but they made up in cubic footage for what they lacked in convenience. She closed the drawer with difficulty. "I'll soap it tomorrow," she said, and then added thoughtfully, "He's drinking quite a lot, isn't he?"

"Well, I—I think he does take more than he used to in New York, but I've never seen him actually show it."

It was true that since the night he had come back to her in the Dauzats' apartment Georgiana had never seen him drunk, but he seemed to feel the need of a glass constantly at hand. She did not tell Karen of the small subterfuges she resorted to in order to lengthen the time between drinks. She would ask him to drive into the village to pick up a Brie cheese she had deliberately forgotten to bring home, or Pierre, she would say, was worse than useless, wouldn't Reams weed the herbs in the kitchen garden? An English family from the British embassy living a couple of miles away had a tennis court, so thinking also of Karen's pleasure, should her ankle be strong enough, she had gone to considerable trouble to get an introduction to them hoping that the household would be asked to play. Anything to occupy Reams so he wouldn't be bored. She worried a good deal about his morale during the week when she and Jeep and Karen would be in Paris and he would be alone. "It'll be an ideal time for you to work, though, dear," she had assured him, but he only smiled and said, "Why work? Got a lot of money; don't have to work."

"But the money won't last forever, and what about this book of short stories? You need only three or four more, and the ones you have are *good*, Reams."

He winked. "Anthology stuff," he said mockingly.

"Don't disparage yourself; this is your big period; don't break the flow."

"Hot as a pistol Asher, that's me. Don't you be a policeman." He had hugged her and gone off to freshen his drink. She had turned away in distress. The good, strong thing they had in common was the way she was able to stimulate him to his best efforts. When he had

216

been working on his novel he responded quickly to her criticism and suggestions and the book had profited, and now here he was letting himself go to seed for love. Her resentment was double-edged: that it should be for another woman, and that a fine talent should be dissipated. Also there was a deep inner conviction, unexpressed but potent, that those who disintegrated because of love were the lesser beings. Thinking of this, she said in answer to Karen's comment, "If he'd work more he'd stop drinking. Help me in a campaign to get him started again." Heaven help me also, she thought, to hold his interest. In idleness he will inevitably become restless and want to be off again to the far corners of the earth. And then what?

She turned to her daughter. Karen, by an adroit balancing act, had managed to stow two suitcases away on top of the big oak cupboard and, a little flushed, was plunking down on the bed to revive herself with a cigarette. "Oh, excuse me, Ma, you want one?" She extended her case to her mother. "I brought lots; we don't have to stint."

But Georgiana shook her head. "No, thanks. And you shouldn't smoke too many either, you bad egg. At your age what have you got to be nervous about?"

"Adolescence is the most nervous time; we're insecure. All the psychologists say so," her daughter announced gravely. "I'm a bundle of jangling wires, you can hear me all over the house." Her mouth opened unexpectedly in a cavernous yawn.

Her mother patted her cheek. "We'll be hearing you snore all over the house."

"Daddy sometimes snores quite loudly, doesn't he? I heard him a couple of times; gave me a real shock."

"Your father gave *me* a real shock too." Georgiana said it before she realized and was touched by the sudden apprehension in the girl's face. "You don't have to pretend anything, Karen. Allen wrote me a long letter. I understand you know what it's about."

The cool, high room was very quiet. Karen meticulously broke the ash of her cigarette into a saucer she held in her hand. "I'm so sorry, Mum." Why did she feel guilty, as though it were her fault? Why, oh, why had it had to happen?

"Do you like Bierne?" her mother asked.

"Yes, I do. She's nice." The truth was painful to them both.

"Your father didn't say so specifically, but I imagine they must be having an affair, aren't they?"

Karen felt, inside her, a contraction. She loved her mother, she felt her loyalty should lie with her mother, but her reluctance to answer sprang less from her feeling about either parent than from the way she felt about Bierne. Bierne was her contemporary and her friend. Her mother and Allen, even though Allen was Bierne's lover, were grownups. She and Bierne were one team; adults were the enemies. For all that Allen loved her Bierne was alone, outside, her youth and unfamiliarity her great handicaps. Allen and Georgiana had the experience, the long habit of their established life together, and their common memories. As they were older they were, their daughter assumed, less vulnerable.

Her mother's voice broke in upon her musings. "You must have seen them together. How serious do you think your father and Bierne Honeywell are about each other?"

Karen rose abruptly and walked around the foot of the bed. She went to the window and stood looking out over the garden and the deserted swimming pool. "They're in love, Mother. I guess a lot." And then, a little desperately, because she couldn't bear the situation she was in, "I thought Daddy had written you all about it?"

"So he has, but it's possible for people to think something's more important than it actually is or at least to think it's going to last forever when maybe it's only transitory."

Karen hesitated because she, too, wondered why, if he was so sure of his love for Bierne, her father never mentioned divorce. That he could love Bierne without hating Georgiana, that he could long to be free and still dread to break old ties was baffling to her, seemed indeed impossible. It was baffling to her father as well, except that he knew it could happen.

The night before she sailed Allen told her about his letter to her mother. "She knows now about Bierne and me, dear, you don't have to hide anything for our sakes. I don't want you to, and God knows it isn't fair for you to have to break the news." That was true, and he meant it, but also it was important to him to appear thoughtful, to stand well in his daughter's eyes. For that reason he didn't tell her he had asked outright for a divorce. Georgiana would be quick to do that, no doubt! Well, let her. If she agreed, it would be time

218

enough for Karen to know; if she didn't, and they were in for a long period of waiting and attrition, well—that was time enough too.

As Karen still didn't speak, Georgiana said, "What do Peter and Lola think?" adding with a glint of amusement in her eyes, "Who's side are *they* on?"

The girl turned from the window. "It isn't a question of sides, Mother," she said earnestly; "they know something about it, of course, but it's not a gossiped-about thing. They just wish you'd come home. If only you hadn't ever gone away!"

But her mother veered her quickly from that line. "You seem to forget I had to go away. It was a question of cash, remember?"

"I *said* that!" Karen's unconscious air of vindication was not lost on Georgiana. "I told Aunt Lola and Uncle Peter that you came here to France because of *Distaff* and everybody says you're doing a marvelous job. I just mean—well, if you'd stayed home, if you'd been able to—I mean—all this might never have come up." Suddenly she felt limp, exhausted by the excitement and strain of her first day in France. She sat down again on the bed, resting her head wearily against the high walnut footboard. "Oh dear, if only we could see where it's going to end." She blinked two or three times and her voice was husky.

"Your father's suggestion is the divorce court."

"What?"

"Didn't you know that? That he's asked me for a divorce? I thought he told you about the letter."

"He did, but I—I didn't realize—I didn't understand——" Georgiana noted her child's reaction with mixed emotion: a sense of triumph that in not taking his daughter completely into his confidence from whatever motives, Allen had, temporarily at least, shocked her and forfeited her trust, and a rising hope that just possibly, regardless of his request for a divorce, this Bierne business was a passing fancy which, if she waited long enough, might blow over. Had he and Bierne and Karen been as cosy as he implied surely the future would have been discussed and solidly plotted. His letter had sounded sober and considered in all conscience, but possibly it was Bierne-inspired, possibly he would be grateful not to receive a reply. Since Georgiana had been separated from him, relieved of the friction so quick to spark in their daily lives, the knowledge that she had a husband was reassuring. "I think," she said to Karen, "that I'll write your father telling him I've received his letter and that I'm thinking it over." She chuckled. "If I had any feeling of wanting to get even I'd *give* him the divorce, worst disservice I could do him. It's nonsense to believe his feeling for that girl can last—she could be his daughter."

Karen, thinking of the strange pangs she felt for Reams, said, "I guess the years don't matter."

15

For Karen the next three weeks were magical. All her customary activities—eating, sleeping, walking, shopping, were heightened and enhanced because they took place in France. Georgiana was amused to see that her child, frequently shy in her dealings with the world, spattered about in the French language completely uninhibited, her college French used as a springboard from which she plunged into happy, garbled discussions with whomever crossed her path: taxi drivers, shopkeepers, or her mother's Paris friends, the ones the Oppenheimers had advised Georgiana to steer clear of. When she saw Karen and that particular group together she wished she had followed their counsel. Her daughter might be naïve but she had a disconcertingly clear gaze; compared to her the De Longvilles and Nellie Baranguanya and their cohorts seemed, not so much sophisticated, as mincing and corrupt. Karen appeared as a kind of Gulliver in the land of the Lilliputians, and when Georgiana asked her what she thought of the De Longvilles she replied affably that she found them drippy, kind of, but was sure they must be nice if her mother enjoyed their companionship. When in their company the girl was invariably polite, but from the letters she wrote home, though they implied no criticism of her mother, Bierne and Allen gathered that Georgiana tolerated gnomes around the premises. "They're not lethal, you understand," Karen said, "but occasionally you wish there was some DDT handy."

Everybody else she considered "summa super," including Germaine and Claude Dauzat, who had arrived, and of whom, since

Georgiana kept her with her pretty constantly, she saw a good deal.

Americans were the ones who vaunted themselves on being hard-working businessmen, but Karen noticed that in his insouciant Gallic fashion Claude managed to pile up an impressive record of accomplishment. She did not know that one reason for his concentration was that he wished to be free before the end of August to join Nora Brown in Venice.

Nora had cannily inserted a clause in her contract whereby she was to have a three-week holiday in the month of August regardless of how successful the play might be, and she was planning to fly to Italy to spend those weeks with Claude. Germaine was not blind to this arrangement but was more angered by the fact that her husband was taking a vacation during the press of the Paris openings than that he was taking it with another woman. She called him a species of dirty one and thriftily arranged for a larger share of the magazine's profits to accrue to her personal account.

One day when she and Georgiana were discussing men and marriage Georgiana told her about Allen's letter and his request for a divorce. It was the first time she had mentioned it to anyone since the night of Karen's arrival. "I'm thinking," she said, "that I may go ahead and give it to him. Though it's ridiculous he's apparently in love with this girl and I—well, I have other interests."

Germaine looked at her a long time. "I live in America," she said, "yet it is still very hard for me to understand the American point of view, this persistence in confusing sex with marriage. Marriage is a partnership, a business like any other. Though they are immature, on the whole Americans do not get sexually involved in their offices. Oh, once a year maybe at the Christmas party—everyone gets tight, the president makes a pass at the art director's secretary—but nobody breaks up the organization because of it. Is marriage, which is also an organization, an association, to be dissolved by every little sex adventure? That is impractical. Even when there are only two, it is impractical. When there is a family, it is weakening."

"But you see, Germaine, in America, theoretically, we marry for love."

Germaine eyed her quizzically. "You should seek a more enduring reason. American love is an ephemeral emotion."

"Oh, come, that's not fair."

"Look at your divorce rate."

Georgiana laughed. "Then we remarry for love. We are incurable optimists."

"No. You are incurable children."

When Germaine spoke in that manner Georgiana did feel, and not for the first time, childlike. The Frenchwoman was poised, impregnable. Georgiana wondered if she had ever felt an undisciplined emotion in her life. "I think," she said, "you do not allow for the human heart."

Above her lustrous eyes Germaine's strong brows rose in surprise. "*I* do not? Would I put up with what I do if I did *not* allow for the human heart? When I embraced Claude in marriage I embraced his frailties too. I knew there was a side of his character which was not serious, but I also knew that we could build a business and a life." She paused, then added in a flat tone, "I did not know there would be no children."

After a moment Georgiana said, "This business with Nora, you have learned not to mind that?"

Germaine shrugged. "I mind, I suppose, but I understand. I do not feel either humiliated or ridiculous. That is for Claude. It is he who behaves without dignity. Do you feel defrauded because Allen goes with this young Miss Honeywell?"

Without intending to, Georgiana found herself taking up the cudgels in her husband's defense. "That's different. I think Allen believes himself genuinely in love."

Germaine's eyes twinkled. "And Claude is not?"

"Well, Claude is—Claude, I should imagine, is more objective in the matter."

"You mean, though going to bed with her, he sees Miss Brown for what she is?"

"Well, something of the sort, yes." Georgiana wished that through logical French legerdemain Allen had not been put in the position of seeming naïve, a man of fifty beset by blind puppy love as opposed to the worldly Claude, who had too much *savoir-faire* to break up his marriage for a passing fancy.

Germaine, her thoughts diverted for the moment from her husband and his iniquities, suddenly seemed quite human. She murmured mischievously, with much rolling of her pigeon *r*'s, "Tell me,

222

chérie, what are our other interests, mmm? *You* wish to *re*marry for love, maybe?"

Georgiana hesitated. Not out of reluctance to talk about Reams but because she couldn't quite define either their current status or their future. They were lovers, of course, but she couldn't get over the impression that Reams's love-making was something hooked on to their relationship as an afterthought. He was absent-minded about it, while to her it was a vital, cherished part of their life together. At last she said, "You know Reams Asher slightly. Do you think I'd be crazy to get a divorce and marry him?"

If Germaine was surprised, she didn't show it. "Has he asked you to?"

"Not in so many words, no."

"If he asked you, I think you would be unwise to do it. Since he has not asked you, I think to give up your husband and your home would be the wildest folly."

"You forget," Georgiana said drily, "that, Allen has asked me to do."

"You laid yourself open. When you left New York."

"Aren't you at all glad that I'm working for you?"

"Very glad. You are doing better than I anticipated, but I hope you are not going to find it too high—the price of a glamour job in Paris. You are an attractive woman, Georgiana, but you are no longer a young one. There are fewer men than there are women in the world. If this love affair makes you happy, well and good, and you have no grounds for interfering with Allen's, but I would try to hang on to him as a husband if I were you."

The two women were sitting at tea in Georgiana's small salon in the Hôtel Vendôme. They had come there after viewing the Schiaparelli opening and now, somewhat refreshed, Germaine slipped her cigarette case into its suède envelope, put it into her handbag, and took out her vanity case to freshen her make-up before leaving.

"What's Karen's position in all this?" she asked as she powdered her nose.

"Well, she doesn't know anything about Reams and me, but, unfortunately, we have a slight complication."

"Ah?"

"I'm afraid she's in love with him herself." Georgiana spoke lightly

223

but there was no responsive smile from Germaine, who asked soberly, "And Reams? Where does he stand, besides in the middle?"

"If he's aware of it, and I'm not even sure he is, he thinks it's nonsense. He's years older than she is."

Germaine gave her friend a penetrating look but refrained from comment. Her face arranged to her satisfaction, she closed her vanity case with a little snap and stood up. She was drawing on her gloves when the sitting-room door opened and Karen burst in.

"Oh, hello, Madame Dauzat. Hi'ya, Mum?"

"Darling, where have you been?" asked her mother. "She's an honest-to-God tourist, Germaine. She's already been through the Louvre twice to my certain knowledge."

Karen plunked herself down in an armchair and pushed her hat back on her head. "I gave one of the galleries a quick whirl this morning too. But guess where I've just come from? The Musée Carnavalet."

Germaine laughed. "And are the serious students still studying the star attraction?"

"There was quite a little group around it, if that's the one you mean."

"Excuse me," Georgiana said, "but as one who hasn't these cultural advantages, do you mind telling me what you're talking about?"

"You know, Mum. That famous chastity belt they have there."

"Oh, for heaven's sake!"

"Don't they, Madame Dauzat?"

"But of course. When men went on the Crusades they had those contraptions of leather and metal locked around their wives in the naïve hope it would keep them faithful during the years they were absent."

"It was revolting," Karen said with enthusiasm, "and, anyway, it didn't work because *that's* where the old saying, 'Love laughs at locksmiths,' comes from."

Georgiana shook her head. "Nothing like getting to the source of a classic. For these precious nuggets your father and I are paying out perfectly good money for your trip abroad."

"And it's wonderful! I'm learning heaps more than I do at college."

"If in a different field!"

224

Germaine chuckled. "You want her well rounded, no? *Au revoir, mes petits, à demain.*" With her hand on the knob, she turned back. "Think over what I have said, Georgiana; they do not grow on trees." She went out, closing the door behind her.

Karen was making her Ubangi lip and blowing a wisp of hair from her forehead. "What doesn't grow on trees?" she asked, and without waiting for an answer, "Say, Ma, can I go with you to whatever opening it is tomorrow?"

"Dior. If we can manage an extra place for you, you can. Maybe Claude Dauzat won't be using his. Why? Are museums beginning to pall?"

"Well, I'm beginning to run out of them. I've done the Louvre, Jeu de Paume, Cluny, Luxembourg, Carnavalet . . . I think I'll take a breather."

"That seems fair enough." Georgiana lighted a cigarette. She lifted Karen's hat from the back of her head and set it on the table. "You asked me just now what doesn't grow on trees." The girl nodded. "Germaine meant men, specifically husbands. She strongly advises me against divorcing your father."

"Oh." Since coming to Paris, Karen had had three or four letters from Allen, one of them with a brief postscript from Bierne. Suspecting that his wife might not be above the common temptation to read another's mail, Allen's correspondence was non-committal, but there was a kind of assumption in what he wrote that matters would work out as he and Bierne desired. Georgiana's reply to his request for a divorce had been of a temporizing nature and was, Allen considered, a to-be-expected delaying tactic rather than a categoric refusal.

"I must say," Georgiana observed, her golden eyes glinting with a malice which if unpraiseworthy was not unbecoming, "your father strikes me as a remarkably cool customer. After twenty-four years of marriage he proposes to toss me off like—— What's that old thing people are always being tossed off like? Oh yes, a glove. I see no reason for submitting to it. I don't say that a desire for change isn't understandable, but it's common to both sexes. He should have the grace to supply me with a new husband."

"Oh, Mother."

"This shocks you?"

"N-no."

"You think perhaps I would be hard to dispose of? No one else would want me?"

"Oh no, Mother. That isn't so. You're one of the most attractive women there is. I guess Daddy thinks so too. I guess he thinks that if you wanted to remarry you could take your pick."

"Though he himself prefers a girl half his age he guesses that other men have better sense and want mature women, is that it?" her mother asked drily.

"I can't see that age matters," Karen said; "attraction is what counts." She was beginning to get her miserable lion-cub look and Georgiana relented.

"Don't worry, darling," she said, and added, hoping she didn't sound like a coy soubrette, "as a matter of fact there is someone whom I like very much and I think he likes me too."

"Oh, Mum, how exciting! Then you *will* agree to the divorce?" The eager question was an unrealized betrayal of where her sympathy lay.

Georgiana felt a little shock. So Karen, too, wanted her out of the way. Hurt, her first reaction was one of anger, but to rail against her daughter was futile. She might, out of courtesy or remorse, change her outward attitude but the inner feeling would remain. Georgiana acknowledged a little bitterly that Allen was right: he had said that Karen was devoted to Bierne and obviously she was. The pull of one's contemporaries was a powerful force. She didn't rail, but she couldn't help saying in a tone a little edged, "You sound rather anxious to break up the home. Your father wrote me that you and Bierne Honeywell are good friends and you yourself tell me you like her, but don't you think your loyalty might lie with us as a family rather than with the 'other woman,' so to speak?"

Karen flushed painfully. "I—I don't mean to be disloyal to you, Mother, but often you and Daddy don't get on, and you just said there's someone you like. I thought maybe——" Her voice trailed away.

Georgiana studied her daughter. "How would you feel," she asked after a time, "if I *were* to marry again?"

"If he was nice and you loved each other I think it would be fine. Darling Mother, I *do* want you to be happy. Is it anyone I know?"

226

Naïveté was all very well, but Georgiana reflected that she and Reams must be playing their role of friendship with unnecessary emphasis. It was disconcerting to think that her child considered an alliance between them so preposterous that it never occurred to her. It was on the tip of Georgiana's tongue to enlighten her, but she changed her mind. Better wait till she had told Reams that Allen was asking for a divorce and see how he reacted.

"*Is* it anyone I know?" Karen asked again.

Her mother bent and rubbed the tip of her nose with her own. "Curiosity killed the cat," she said.

Karen's dormant suspicion about Georgiana and Reams had not been reawakened simply because she herself had been so caught up in the old glamour he held for her that she thought of nothing else. Barclay, to be sure, had captured her interest, but Barclay she considered callow. Not that she wasn't looking forward to reading the letter from him which she had just now found at the desk when she came back to the hotel, but Reams was older, he was a man of achievement and fame, and he had for her the same virility and magnetism that drew her mother. At the moment Karen was anticipating with delight a trip he had promised her. They would all be spending the week end at the house in the country, but Georgiana had to be back in Paris by Monday morning. The plan was that Reams, Karen, and Jeep would set out very early Monday and motor to Rouen—Karen was reading up on Joan of Arc that she might re-create the burning in the market place—absorb a bit of history, and then drive on to lunch at the Inn of William the Conqueror at Cabourg. The food, the gleaming copper cooking utensils, and the ancient brilliant fuchsia festooning the courtyard had been described to her by Jeep so enthusiastically that the inn had become for her the promised land. They would leave there in the afternoon, returning to Paris in time for a late dinner.

It was at supper the following Sunday that Jeep announced that he had to work the next day and would be unable to accompany them. Karen's heart bounded at the thought of a long, lovely day alone with Reams.

Georgiana's reaction was more restrained. She knew her child's imagination, knew, too, a sharp pang of jealousy. She trusted Reams, of course, but he was a man, and Karen aglow with happiness and excitement these days was very beautiful. "Darling," she said kindly, "what a pity, but never mind. We'll just postpone the trip a little, make it another day when we can all go."

Karen looked at her blankly. "But why? I'm sorry about Jeep, of course, but why shouldn't Reams and I go as we planned?"

"Karen, use your common sense. You can't go off all day alone together, just the two of you."

"But why not?"

"Well, really! If you can't understand there's no use my trying to explain it."

Reams, studiously masticating his *blanquette de veau*, groaned inwardly. There goes the ball game, he thought. Wait till I get my hands on that Jeep, I'll lacerate him. His work, my eye! More likely the fourteenth blonde of the season, and a fine lurch he's left me in.

Karen was angry. Her mother, she considered, was being idiotic. What was the idea, anyhow, of this Victorian thing about a chaperon which must obviously be on her mind? In this day and age! As though she couldn't take care of herself! It was humiliating. Her mother's sentiments were more nearly akin to hers than she imagined. Georgiana was experiencing a sense of embarrassment and humiliation herself. Her protestations made her seem an old fogy separated by many years from Karen and Reams, and the fact that she suddenly realized how insecure she was—she was afraid of her own daughter—was deeply distressing.

"Reams, what do *you* think?" Karen insisted, her tone a blend of exasperation and pleading.

Reams was habitually blunt, but he had heard of diplomacy, and having a normal instinct for self-preservation employed it forthwith. "I'm game for whatever you and Georgiana want, my dear. I'm afraid my venerable age will make me a very safe companion, but I am indebted to your mother for her flattering assumption," and he winked at Georgiana with warmth and good humor.

The atmosphere suddenly cleared. He was shrewd and amusing and dear, she thought, and his whole attitude about Karen had been correctly paternal from the start. Whatever was she worrying about? She said with a grudging little laugh, "Well, I don't think Emily Post would approve, nor do I, but if your uncle Reams is willing, I don't want to spoil your fun."

228

Uncle Reams. That, Karen decided, was a dastardly foul blow, but what could she do? The important thing was that the trip was authorized.

Jeep suddenly tipped back his chair and broke into full-bellied laughter. Reams eyed him coldly. "What's the matter with you?"

The exquisite joy of his comrade in arms abated slowly. "First goddam time I've ever been considered a chaperon," he said. "Hell of a note."

The following morning, with reiterated assurances that they would be back in Paris in time for a late dinner, Karen and Reams saw Georgiana board the train to the city and set off with their hoarded gasoline.

It was a radiant day: warm, dry, sunny, with a little breeze, and at Reams's side sat a beautiful and pliable companion, but Reams felt discouraged. And why shouldn't he, poor darling, thought Karen, sensitive to his mood of depression, with no one to love or to love him? If only he had eyes in his head, if only he would realize . . . ! She set about cheering him up, a little fun and gaiety but not too much chatter, men didn't like that. An occasional silence could be very restful. She required one herself, every year or so.

Reams was fond of the girl. Who would not be? he asked himself, but he was concerned about Georgiana. Something, he was sure, was troubling her, something she hadn't spoken of. One reason he wanted time alone with Karen was to engage in a bit of detective work. It struck him that she was speaking very little of her father to whom she was devoted, nor had Georgiana so much as mentioned him in the last few weeks. Not, all things considered, that he was likely to be much on her mind, but the behavior of the two women wasn't natural. Allen might have dropped off the edge of the earth.

Reflecting that it was amazing how often a straight question elicited a straight answer, about halfway along the road to Rouen he turned to Karen and said, "Something's been puzzling me. You've talked very little about your father since you've been here. I thought you and he were such pals. Anything the matter?"

Karen looked at him oddly. "Why, my goodness—why, no, what would be the matter?" It was her turn to be puzzled. Reams and her mother were old friends; she had taken for granted that Georgiana had confided in him.

229

"I don't know," Reams said, "it's just that he's quite a guy. I'd like to hear news of him. I've been missing shop talk recently. I thought maybe he'd have written some of the latest book dope to you or Georgiana."

"Oh." Karen looked thoughtful. Again she was beset by divided loyalty. She cared for Reams so much, he was so intelligent and wise, to confide in him, to ask his advice would be an enormous help, but if Georgiana had not felt it necessary to do so it would hardly be proper for her to take it upon herself. On the other hand, elderly people, like her mother, frequently needed the help of someone younger, more vigorous. At last she said, "I doubt if Daddy and Mother are corresponding very much. I—I think there's a rift."

"I'm sorry to hear that. What kind of a rift?" Reams put his question casually, his attention ostensibly focused on a flock of geese crossing the road in slow majesty, but his interest was alerted. If there was trouble, why had Georgiana not told him?

Two tears slid down Karen's cheeks. "I wish it had never begun, then there wouldn't have been this awful decision to make."

"What decision?" He spoke so gently that her tears came flooding. Reams pulled up to the side of the road and stopped the car. "Now then, what's all this? You know how I feel about your mother and about you. Do you want to tell me? Maybe I can help."

"Oh yes, I want to. Maybe I shouldn't, but I can't help it. I don't know what to do, I don't know whose side to be on. I'm on both sides and it's awful." She blew her nose and continued more calmly, "You see, Daddy's asked Mother for a divorce because he's in love with Bierne Honeywell and wants to marry her."

Reams put his arm around her shoulder. "You poor kid," he said, "what a rough break for you." His solace was so sweet, his touch so overwhelming that Karen relaxed against him, tears, this time of pure joy, slipping down her face.

Reams bent and kissed her hair, lightly he kissed her eyelids, and might have succumbed to the delicious temptation of her mouth had she not at that instant buried her face in his neck, murmuring, "Oh, Reams, I love you so."

The words numbed him. He remained bent over her, but now it was as though they were playing the children's game of "Statues" where, when the command comes, one remains riveted in position.

230

He thawed only gradually, putting her gently from him and sliding back behind the steering wheel.

"I'm sorry," she said humbly. "I didn't mean to scare you."

"Karen, little Karen."

"I'm big Karen, remember?"

"You're *young* Karen. You're my darling young Karen."

"But you don't love me."

"I love you, but I am not *in* love with you, and, believe me, you'll realize soon that you're not in love with me."

"But I am, Reams, I can't help it. I've always been. From the first moment I saw you—that time at the Oppenheimers' party. I don't know why, really, we've been so little together, but I seem to care a lot. Unrequited love is quite painful, isn't it?"

"You make me feel like a heel."

"Darling, darling," she said quickly, her eyes very bright, "how stupid you are. As though you could help whether you love a person or not. It's just that I thought—well, even though you don't love me, if you don't *mind* me, I love you enough for two, and you seem so lonely, Reams. I thought maybe I could be a help; you could forget about being lonely with me. It's hard to live alone, you know."

"Where did you learn that, oh, sage?"

"Don't laugh; it is hard. When Mother left Daddy and went away he started going out with Bierne at *first* because he was lonely, and now Mother—— Well, she told me she has someone she likes too. I guess she's thinking maybe she will give Daddy the divorce and get married herself, and I hope she does; I couldn't bear for her to be alone."

"Did she mention who the man is?" Reams asked.

Karen shook her head. "The only friends of hers I really know are you and the Dauzats and some of the pansy boys around the office. I do hope she wouldn't go for anybody in that De Longville crowd. Sometimes people do things even when they know better, but they do them out of loneliness."

"That's right. And I know better than to do what you suggest even though I also know that never in my life will I ever again be offered anything so generous and so lovely." He took her two hands and kissed them. "I should like to make a pact with you," he said.

"Of course. Anything."

"When one offers love and asks for love, friendship is a cold substitute, I know. But for what it's worth you can count on my friendship and affection as long as I live, and I should be very grateful for yours."

"Oh, Reams. Until I die."

He looked at her searchingly. "If the time ever comes, I hope you'll remember that."

"What a funny thing to say. Of course I'll remember."

He took her head between his hands and kissed the tip of her nose. "That's the way you seal a friendship pact."

Half laughing, half crying, she said, "I thought it had to be in gore."

"Just wait! The gore comes later. Now then, all set?"

"All set."

He released the brake and the car slowly moved forward.

"Joan of Arc, here we come!"

He watched Karen out of the corner of his eye. When she had powdered her nose and seemed more composed he said, "By the way, my dearest and most lasting friend, what about that scion of the millions? Has Mr. Barclay Hamilton ceased to play any role in your life?"

"Mr. Hamilton and I are very good friends too. I have a knack for inspiring platonic friendship in men. Oh, dear." Her voice broke on a quavering little squeak, and again the tears splashed down.

Reams burst into wholehearted laughter. "I never saw such arrant self-pity! I doubt that any face and figure have ever been less calculated to rouse the brotherly instinct!"

She made a noise between a grunt and a sob. "Except in you. Oh, Reams, *why* can't you love me? Is there something about me? An unpleasant mannerism? A trying family trait?"

"Good God, no! Your family traits—I mean—I'm sold on your whole damn family. I respect your father, I have the warmest feelings for your mother, and I'm fond of you."

"What more do I want?" She asked it in such a comical way they both laughed.

"Karen, my love, it wouldn't work, I promise you."

"What wouldn't work?"

232

"Look, let's be honest. Right now you think you'd like to be married to me, don't you?"

She looked down, carefully outlining the handbag in her lap with her two index fingers. "I think it would be heaven. If you wanted me."

"It wouldn't be heaven. There are things that—— There are reasons why you'd hate it. And, besides, I'm fourteen years older than you. It makes a difference."

"Daddy's twenty-five years older than Bierne and they're wonderfully happy."

"Now, yes."

"They always will be."

"At luncheon," he said, "we'll drink a toast to them."

They rolled along the straight white road through the apple orchards and came at last to Rouen, where Karen saw with a shock the results of war. It was her first experience with a bombing target, and although the damage had not been of major proportions the barbarism implicit in that kind of destruction was striking.

They wandered through the narrow, crooked streets and gazed upon the lovely façade of the Hôtel de Ville and remembered all the pictures they had ever seen of the martyred Joan. "It wouldn't have seemed so bad," Karen said, "if the British had just come right out and said they hated her without all that slimy hypocrisy about how they were burning her for the good of her immortal soul."

"They weren't necessarily hypocritical," Reams observed. "The Bishop of Beauvais may have been sincerely convinced that the only way to save the heretic was to burn her, but I have noticed that the zeal of the just usually results in the most acute discomfort to others. Beauvais himself, I believe, died in his bed full of honors and very well heeled."

"And cool as a cucumber, no doubt."

From Rouen they motored to the Inn of William the Conqueror, a secular retreat festooned in the churchly splendor of its purple-and-scarlet fuchsia. While the menu was perhaps not at its prewar flood it was still festive fare, and the cellars had survived admirably the onslaught of the Hun. It was over a little *eau de vie de framboise* after coffee that Karen extracted from Reams a promise that he would say nothing to Georgiana about the divorce. "It was wrong of me to mention it," she confessed. "If Mother had wanted you to know she'd have told you, though I can't imagine why she hasn't." Reams had wondered the same thing, although on analysis Georgiana's reasoning was becoming clearer.

Karen's misery over her unrequited love was somewhat alleviated by their superb luncheon and the delicious golden wine they had drunk, and she listened docilely to Reams's championing of Barclay. "He's the fellow for you, my girl. Big guy, young, puts Croesus in the shade, and is nuts about you. Grab him."

"If he was as nuts as you seem to imagine, I should have thought he'd have asked me to marry him, and he never has."

"Has he ever had a chance?"

"Heaps of times. As a matter of fact, that week end I spent at his house just before I left home—I had an awful feeling he was on the brink."

"But he didn't say it?"

"I didn't dare *let* him say it. I told him I was terribly in love with *you*. At least I said it was somebody, but I didn't tell the name."

Reams looked alarmed. "Look here, miss, you've put me in a hell of a spot. You'd better beat it home and revive Barky's interest. I can't go through life feeling I've done you out of a fortune."

"Don't be crazy. I was probably wrong anyhow, maybe he didn't have that in mind at all. And, anyhow, whoever I might marry, Barclay or anybody else, all my life I'd have a secret sorrow in my soul."

"Me?"

"You."

"You think that's romantic?" Karen giggled. "Well, yes, rather."

"It isn't. It's like a growth that's relentless and can't be cut out." He spoke with a sudden harshness that shocked her into silence, but the mood, she decided, was only momentary, for after a bit he said, and his voice was once again friendly and teasing, "Come on, let's get going. Your ma will be in a state if we're not back as promised in time for dinner."

They reached Paris shortly after eight to find Georgiana waiting with cocktails, wearing a new and highly becoming frock. She had made up her mind that in the event Reams's attention had wandered from her during the day he should find on his return that there was a great deal to be said for a poised, easy companion who was attractive yet made no demands upon him. As a matter of fact, although flattered, Reams was also somewhat exhausted by Karen's emotional escalator and the mature approach worked. He looked at Georgiana appreciatively and suggested that they dine at La Rue's near by and come back to the hotel right afterward. "I don't want to drive back to the country tonight," he said. "I expect this joint's full of tourists, but La Salle can dig me up a cubbyhole somehow and I'll go back in the morning."

They were in the middle of dinner when an Indian war whoop shattered the reverent atmosphere in which the true gourmet dines and which suffused the great Paris restaurant. "Karen! This is terrific! Hello." The greetings burst from the flower of Vassar and Princeton as a group of young Americans came surging through the doorway.

Karen leaped up. "Kids, how are you? When did you get here?"

Georgiana and Reams exchanged a paternal glance at such youthful exuberance, and Reams thought, wincing just a little, of how right he had been when he spoke of the difference in age between him and the young goddess who was to carry his image eternally in her heart.

When the geyserlike burst of enthusiasm had somewhat abated it developed that this was the twenty-first birthday of one of the Princetonians. His family was backing him in style for the occasion and he and his companions were giving the *ville lumière* a whirl, dining at La Rue and going on later to do the night spots from the Left Bank to the Bois. Why didn't Karen join them? They were a girl short, it would be summa super. This Georgiana agreed to while Reams, feeling like a venerable oak festooned with beards of Spanish moss, gave his blessing to the expedition. Karen hurried back to the hotel to change. She was to return to finish her dinner with her friends who, in the meantime, impressed upon her mother that she was not to worry if dawn was lighting the chimney pots and her child was not yet home.

When Georgiana and Reams reached the hotel Karen was just leaving to go back to the restaurant. Georgiana went into the bedroom to take off her hat and Reams saw Karen to the door. "Have fun."

She looked at him a minute, her green-brown eyes very wide. "I'll try. I might as well get used to living without hope. I suppose I'm not the only one buffeted by fate."

"You're not. Keep my memory green until you get back to La Rue's."

"You are cynical, *Uncle* Reams."

"My dearest niece, good night."

When Georgiana came back into the sitting room she found Reams moodily lighting a cigar. "What's the matter?" she asked.

"Do you suppose I'm getting old?"

She glanced at him sideways. "I hadn't noticed. Why?"

"Because Karen got up before seven this morning, had a hell of a long, tiring day, and now, fresh as a daisy, is starting out on an all-night tear. I got up before seven, had a hell of a long, tiring day, and I'll be damned glad to get to bed. With you," he added, noting her expression of questioning innocence.

"Well," she said, lightly brushing his cheek with her lips, "senility doesn't seem to have set in yet, does it?"

He put an arm around her. "Come, Karen won't be home for hours." They went into the bedroom and closed the door.

It occurred to him after a while that he should be getting back to his own hole in the wall which was all the hotel management had been able to produce for the night, but, relaxed and satisfied, the effort of getting up and dressing seemed unduly arduous. Besides, there was ample time. Judging from the number of *boîtes* the young people had been planning to visit, Karen would be lucky to make breakfast. Also, Georgiana was charming. Seductive and languorous, she had the quality rare in women of still appealing to the spent desire. Lazily caressing her arm with the back of his hand, the events of the day began to come back to him, and he remembered what Karen had said about her parents. His hand ceased its gentle hypnotic motion. "Tell me about Allen," he said.

He knows, Georgiana thought. How? Where? Could Karen . . . ? But she was not surprised. Suddenly secrecy seemed pointless. She told him: how Allen had felt when she left for Europe, his suspicions of Reams, and now how he felt about Bierne. "He wants a divorce," she ended. "I don't know what to do." In the silence she waited for Reams to speak. There were silk pleated shields on the wall brack-

236

ets. Gold color. Just one bulb of one bracket was lighted. From where she lay she could dimly discern the number of pleats—six, seven, eight. She counted them over again.

At last he said, "Do you still love Allen?" and she answered, "I don't know that either. After twenty-four years the man, or woman, I suppose, to whom you're married acquires a shape and color which have little to do with him as an individual. If the relationship has been on the whole successful, you say you love them; if you've been unhappy——" Her voice expired.

"Were you and Allen unhappy?"

"I—I think we lost respect for each other and often we were bored. I don't know what I feel really. In a way I'm not unfond of him, but what I feel for him is a million miles from what you and I have together. It's the palest carbon copy of what we have that you ever saw. It's even in another language." She was lying on her stomach, propped on her elbows.

He drew her head down and kissed her, his hand rumpling her hair in a lazy caress. "You and I are lucky," he said.

"Do you think I should give him the divorce?"

Reams thought, If I say no, she will take it that I don't love her, but if I say yes? Will she then assume that I do love her, which in a way I do, but for now, not for all time. He said, "I think, darling, that is something only you can decide. I am close to you, but even I don't know all that you two have woven together, all that you think and feel. Hell, I couldn't even explain *our* relationship to anybody else, but it's right for us." And then, because he knew she wanted to hear it and because it was partly true, "I need you. Don't leave me yet, Georgiana, don't leave me." I can't be alone yet, he thought, I still have to have someone to concentrate on, someone who can blot out Linda.

He held her close against him so that her face was half buried in his neck and in the pillow. After a moment she raised her head and laid her cheek against his. "My dear," she murmured, "I won't leave you." She knew that she would stay with Reams as long as he wanted her and that it would be he who would terminate their relationship, and whether she and Allen were married or divorced would not affect him. Unless, with time. . . . But with time she would grow older. Time was both her enemy and her ally.

Unintentionally they fell asleep. When Reams wakened with a little start and glanced at his watch it was nearly three o'clock. He got up and dressed quickly, fearful that for all the youngsters' talk about rollicking till dawn just possibly something might have happened to bring Karen home ahead of time. Georgiana stirred and wakened. As Reams bent to kiss her she thought she heard a sound in the next room. "Sh!" They waited tense and silent for a moment, but nothing disturbed the stillness. "This door's locked," she whispered with an alarmed but suppressed giggle. "If it's Karen, I'll pretend I locked it by mistake. You'll have to crawl under the bed and wait till she's asleep. Or stand behind the screen. My God, it's like a bad play."

"Nonsense," he whispered back, "I'll just say you weren't feeling well and phoned my room and asked me to come over."

"With the door locked? Don't be a jackass." They listened again. Still silence. "Wait," Georgiana murmured; "I'll reconnoiter." She slipped on a dressing gown and carefully opened the door into the salon. It was very dark, and nothing stirred. "Come on, the coast's clear." The one light switch was by the door leading into the hall. Using his cigarette lighter as a beacon, Reams picked his way across the room, opened the door a crack, and peered down the dimly illumined corridor. It was empty. He turned, blew a kiss to Georgiana, and slipped out, closing the door behind him, and stepping jauntily along so that should he meet anybody it would seem perfectly correct to be cruising the corridors at 3 A.M. Georgiana went back to bed leaving the door half ajar. In about fifteen minutes she was sound asleep.

Presently, in the dark salon, a darker shadow stirred. From the deep angle formed by a large cupboard and an alcove in which she had been caught when the bedroom door opened Karen stepped forward. She moved slowly, as though she were old and very tired, and stood for a moment in the middle of the room staring into the blackness. Her knees began to tremble and she slumped into a chair. She sat there for a long time before she started slowly to undress, and then the effort of picking up her clothes seemed beyond her. She left them where they fell, and after a time went into the bedroom and got into the other bed and pulled the covers over her. About six o'clock she fell into a stuporlike sleep. Georgiana, on awakening, seeing how deeply asleep she was, assumed her child had only just got home from her gay night and dressed and breakfasted without disturbing her. She went off, leaving a little note telling Karen to call her at the office.

Around noon Karen opened her eyes. She lay for a moment trying to recall through a fog of sleep what had happened to induce in her this heavy aching feeling, as though she had been beaten. Then she remembered: the two figures in the doorway silhouetted against the dim light from the bedroom. Her mother in a half-open dressing gown—her mother and Reams, the lovers, the two conspirators. A scalding wave of shame swept over her so that alone in the darkened room she blushed scarlet. Her mother's lover, and she had proposed to him. He had been honest, though, you had to hand him that. He was Honest Jack. "There are reasons why you'd hate it," he had said, "being married to me." He had a point there, she thought bitterly. Going to bed with both mother and daughter would be a little involved. "I'm sold on your whole damn family," he had said. With a vengeance! He was fond of her, he had said. What more natural? She might someday be his dear little stepdaughter, for it was Reams her mother cared about, Reams she might marry. How could she? But Karen knew all too well, for she remembered his hard male body and his eyes smiling and sad, and the way his arm had gone around her shoulder in the car, and she turned into her pillow and sobbed as though her heart would break.

After a while, when her tears were spent, she tried to organize her thoughts. She rang for café au lait and *croissants* and took a bath, hoping that some course of action would be revealed to her. She had read once that a sect, maybe it was the Hindus, believed in emptying themselves of all personal will and desire; they made themselves empty channels into which divine guidance, filling the vacuum, flowed. Either she didn't make a clean enough sweep or divine guidance was occupied elsewhere, for she received no inkling as to how she was to face her mother and Reams.

She found her mother's note, but to call her up, to chat perfectly naturally about the party the night before, where they should lunch, where dine, when they would go out to the country again, was beyond her powers. She was debating how best to avoid speaking to Georgiana when the phone rang. It was her mother, quite normal

239

apparently, inquiring affectionately as to what kind of evening she had had. "You looked as though you'd been knocked out with a shillelagh, you were so sound asleep when I got up," she observed. "What time did you get home anyhow?" She waited, suspended, for the answer. Not that it mattered really; the noise she thought she had heard in the living room had obviously been her imagination or that loose shutter she'd spoken to the concierge about a dozen times, still, it was a natural maternal question.

"I don't know exactly," Karen said. "Pretty late, I guess. You seemed to be asleep when I got into bed."

"Oh, I was. I'd been asleep a long time, and you were very good and quiet. How about picking me up here at the office? I'll take you to lunch at a new little bistro Claude Dauzat has discovered. It's way over in the Rue du Cherche-Midi and he says we must go at once before it's ruined. He says by the end of this week all the French will know about it and by the end of next the Americans will have invaded and that will finish it. How about it?"

How could her mother! Babbling on as though everything were clean and honest and hunky-dory. The affair must have been going on for ages or she wouldn't be so hardened to it. And Reams! Reams to act this way behind her father's back. Maybe it had happened right in New York, too, right at home. "I say," came her mother's voice in light mimicry of the English expression, "I say, old girl, are you there?"

"Yes, I—I'm sorry. I won't be able to lunch. I told Pauline and the others last night that I'd meet them today. The boys are leaving Paris this afternoon."

"Oh." Georgiana sounded disappointed. "Well, all right, dear, just as you like. I'll see you later back at the hotel. Are you feeling well? You sound a bit down."

"I don't mean to."

"Try to get a nap this afternoon."

"Good-by, Mother."

"Good-by, dear." Georgiana hung up slowly. Her hands were quite cold and she felt a little sick. That noise she had heard, had it been Karen? Could she have been in the dark sitting room? Did she know?

240

"What is it?" asked Germaine, who had stopped at her desk for a moment before going on to her own luncheon appointment.

"Karen sounded funny," Georgiana said. "Awfully sunk somehow."

Germaine's eyes gleamed with amusement. "One does not think of it with one's own treasure, but quite possibly she has a hangover from last night's party, no?"

"Do you think so? That never occurred to me."

Germaine chuckled. "It is only the childless who appreciate the depravity of the young. We look upon them as people, not ewe lambs."

Georgiana smiled, but her smile struck her friend as a little forced. "I'll read the riot act to her," she said. "I hope to heaven that's all it is."

The tension between Georgiana and Karen mounted steadily throughout the week. The girl's behavior, Georgiana considered, was intolerable. She, of all people, was by turns pompous, sarcastic, touchy, and had on two or three occasions fabricated obviously transparent excuses as to why she couldn't stay home when her mother was there or accompany her when she was going out. The suspicion that Karen knew about her and Reams waxed and waned in Georgiana's mind, but she kept dismissing it as improbable. In the country house Karen was on a floor above them and she and Reams were circumspect. That one night in the hotel had been indiscreet, but they had gotten away with it, she was sure they had, and there had been no repetition. Considering knowledge the only possible excuse for her daughter's conduct once that reason was ruled out Georgiana was at a loss to account for it.

Karen had seen nothing of Reams all week because the day after their trip he returned to the country and she had stayed in Paris with her mother. Every time she looked at Georgiana she thought wildly of scarlet A's and experienced a burning embarrassment that deepened to shame whenever her own longing for Reams swept over her. For the awful thing was that he still seemed to her desirable, and she felt she must, in some dreadful way, be incestuous.

Matters came to a head Saturday night after dinner. Jeep and the girl he had invited for the week end departed on bicycles to call on the English neighbors, and Reams, Karen, and Georgiana were spending the evening playing records Karen had brought from New York. Reams was pacing back and forth as he listened, and when the repertory was exhausted he declared suddenly that an idea for a story which had been incubating in his brain was ready to hatch and that he was going upstairs to make notes. To Georgiana this first revival of interest in his work was like blood which came flooding back softly and gradually without pain into a numbed arm. As he was leaving the room she called after him, "Oh, Reams, just a second; there's something I meant to tell you." She followed him hastily before he could turn back. Out in the hall she took his arm and drew him a few steps from the doorway.

"What is it?" he asked.

"I love you. I could do with a small parting kiss."

He kissed her and rubbed his cheek against her hair. "It's strange," he said. "I feel a surge of industry. I thought you'd want me to take advantage of it."

"I do. It makes me very happy. Go up there and dig in."

He gave her a small pat on the behind and went on upstairs.

Georgiana returned to the drawing room smiling. As she was picking up the needlepoint slippers she was working on Karen spoke. "You didn't have to go outside to kiss him."

Georgiana's heart missed a beat, but she replied easily, "What on earth . . . ?"

"You don't have to pretend, either. You were reflected in the mirror," and she pointed to a tall, dim looking glass hanging over a console table. "I know about you and Reams, Mother. I saw you that night coming out of the bedroom in the hotel." Georgiana stared at her. "I wasn't spying, but Pauline felt bad, so the party broke up earlier than we expected and I came home."

Her mother's continuing silence shattered her attempt at calm statement of fact. She began to speak with tremulous sarcasm. "I'm sorry I'm in the way, I don't mean to inconvenience you. If having me here is too much nuisance I can—I can——" She was going to say, I can always go home, but at home Bierne and Allen were doubtless grateful for the respite from her presence. She broke into hysterical laughter.

"Karen, stop that!" Georgiana's tone was deliberately stern and had a momentarily restraining effect upon her daughter.

"I'm sorry," Karen said in a strangled voice, "but to find that your own mother——"

Georgiana pitied her, but the pity was objective: sympathy with the abstract poignancy of youth unseated, its infallibility betrayed, its security shattered, rather than with her daughter's personal sense of shock. This was so partly because the implied censure in Karen's attitude made her impatient and partly because her child's statement of her knowledge had come as a shock to Georgiana herself. Yet in a way she was also relieved; the chips were down, they knew where they stood. "All right," she said, and her tone, if matter of fact, was not unkind; "you've learned the truth. Reams and I are lovers. I'm sorry if that hurts you, but I don't think it should. He is taking nothing from you, my feeling for him in no way affects my love for you as my child, and, after all, though I do not consider it the ideal situation in any family, a love affair can't come to you as a novelty. Reams and I are no different from your father and Bierne Honeywell. You don't seem to think badly of them."

"But you *are* different," Karen cried silently, "you are." How could she say aloud, You tell me Reams is taking nothing from me, but the truth is if he were to take some of your love from me I could bear it. What I cannot bear is that you should be taking *his* love which, without you, I might have a chance of winning. Though she did not speak, the atmosphere was charged with her inner struggle and her mother sensed it. Knowing that Karen cared for Reams, her fear of her daughter as a rival was unacknowledged rather than subconscious, but she also knew what Karen did not know. She knew about Linda. If Karen did not even show in the Reams Asher sweepstakes, so to speak, she herself did little better than place. She was above gloating over the meager edge she held on her daughter, but her gallantry and candor stopped short of revealing Lady Schofield. Karen had discovered enough. The Asher-Schofield parlay was none of her business and too painfully Georgiana's. Yet her child's choked silence touched her. She crossed the room to where Karen sat with her head turned away, her mouth working, her eyes brimming with tears. She drew up a small straight chair and sat down beside her. Tentatively she laid a hand on Karen's arm and was grateful when she did not twist away, although the outburst which did greet her was unexpected, pathetic, and a little comic.

"No wonder it's all right for us to live in this grand house," Karen exclaimed. "I suppose we're being kept, aren't we? I tag along and Reams has no choice but to accept me." She flung it out bitterly, and her mother's amused reaction, though short-lived, was disconcerting. "You are being insulting, my dear," Georgiana said after a moment, "and a little ridiculous. I think Reams would be the first to agree that the arrangement we have together, he and Jeep and I, is perfectly equitable and you are here as a very welcome guest as far as they are concerned and as far as you are concerned, until you're married or earning your own living where your mother is is your home."

"I'm sorry," Karen murmured. She wanted to say more but the ache in her throat prevented her.

Georgiana studied her. "My child," she began, "listen to me. There's no use my telling you I'm sorry Reams and I are living together or that I think there's anything immoral in it because I'm not and I don't. I'm sorry that you found it out because it seems to be causing you so much distress. I know it's hard for you to have your parents separated, each one in love with someone else, but tell me, did you feel this bad when you learned about Allen and Bierne?"

Karen shook her head. "Mother, you don't understand. It isn't that I feel so shocked, it's just—it's just that I can't believe it. You and Reams!"

"Why is it any more incredible than Bierne and your father? Or any less acceptable?"

"Well, it's—— He's much younger than you are—I shouldn't think——"

"That he would want me?"

"That you'd want him."

"Your father wants Bierne, doesn't he, and there's twenty-five years' difference in their ages."

"Yes, but that's different."

"No, Karen, it's only different because you've persuaded yourself you're in love with Reams and finding out about him and me seems terrible, but you haven't lost anything; Reams would never have cared for you."

244

For the first time since she had seen her reflected in the mirror Karen faced her mother directly, and her gaze was level. "Did you know in the beginning that I'd fallen in love with him?"

"I, I suspected it, yes. You didn't confide in me, you know."

That was true, but Karen had a feeling that her mother's reason for advancing it was not the true reason. She couldn't prove it, but she was sure of it. "You didn't give us a chance!" she cried. "Reams always seemed to like me when we were alone, but I think you were afraid I might get him."

"Karen!"

"You'd come and take him away. You're fascinating and it was easy, but why should you have wanted him, Mother? Why? You had Daddy."

"Yes, I had your father and we were miserable together. You witnessed enough scenes to realize that. But as for your ridiculous accusations—— I knew Reams before you did, remember, and there was never any question of my coming between you. The first time you met him we were not lovers, he and I." She did not add that the situation had changed the next day. That had been coincidence, in any event. "There was nothing on earth to keep him from falling in love with you if he was going to, and you had all the advantage on your side—youth, which, as you point out, I have not—and beauty and intelligence. I did nothing to keep you apart, but I didn't think in New York, and I don't think here, that he's the man for you. If you have any sense, my dear, you won't go mooning over Reams Asher, especially when you might have somebody like Barclay— rich, fond of you, and your own age. My God, what more do you want?" She rose abruptly and paced nervously about the room. "Reams is a lost cause, Karen; leave him alone." It was said with such bitter sadness that, jarred from her own sorrow, Karen looked at her in dismay. "Oh, Mother."

"Well?"

"You're not happy with him, are you? It *is* different from what Daddy and Bierne have. Oh, Mummy, why are you going to marry him if he doesn't make you happy?"

"What makes you so sure I'm going to marry him?"

"But you said—— I thought—— What other reason *is* there for this if you don't love each other, if you don't want to be together always?"

"Karen," Georgiana said, and stopped. She stroked her daughter's tawny mane and tucked a strand of hair back of her ear. "My big girl, what a baby you are. Life isn't always so simple. Reams and I aren't sure we *want* to be married. There—there is some difference in our ages, of course, and he's not an easy man to live with. He's moody, he—— Well, sometimes he goes away and I don't see him. I haven't always known where he is."

"Something happened to him after he left New York, something changed him, didn't it?" Karen said.

"Well, a little while before you got here he was very ill, I told you that."

"Yes, but I mean something else."

"What kind of thing?"

"I don't know." Karen looked thoughtful. "His book was such a success and his articles in the *Post*—everybody's talking about how wonderful they are—it can't be anything about his work. Maybe . . ."

Georgiana, against her intention, was held by her daughter's tentative yet surely aimed probing. "Maybe what?" she asked.

"He said something the other day when we were at luncheon at that inn, William the Conqueror, we were talking about love and secret sorrow, I mean just as a topic of conversation, and I said I guessed that such a thing would be romantic, and then Reams said, and I remember he said it in a hard way, out of key with the whole rest of the day, he said, 'It isn't romantic, it's like a growth that's relentless and can't be cut out.' *Has* he asked you to marry him, Mother, and you said you wouldn't?"

"I told you, we haven't decided about that yet."

"But is that what's making him unhappy?"

"No," her mother said, and to her reluctance, her eyes filled with tears, "that isn't it."

"Then——" But suddenly Karen knew, she knew the truth incontrovertibly. "He's in love with someone else! He wants somebody else. Oh, how could he! How *could* he do this to you?"

Georgiana, her heart warmed by her child's indignation, laughed a little shakily. "Darling, don't all of a sudden think too badly of him. He didn't do it deliberately. It's a woman he's known for a long time and she's married and they can never be together."

246

"But how could *you*, Mother? Why should you be second fiddle to anyone?"

"Well, I—I don't quite see it in that light. Reams and I have a very deep feeling of friendship, I think I've been of some help to him in his work, and you will find, Karen, that often in this world you take what you can get. Second fiddle is better than no music at all."

But Karen was on her feet, indignation animating her every move. That Reams was her mother's lover had been a blow, that he should be a lover without love was an outrage. "Why don't we get out of here," she cried. "Why should you stay as a convenience for this selfish man? Why, he—he's insulting."

Georgiana, fearful lest her child rescue her from her life of sin through sheer animal spirits, tried hastily to placate her. "Darling, hush; he'll hear you. For heaven's sake don't let's drag him into this. I'm very grateful to Reams. He's kind and generous and a good companion. Companionship, Karen, is important to a woman. I don't consider that I owe any excuses or explanation for what we've done, but I think you should appreciate why things like this happen. Passion and pride are an intense but narrow segment of the over-all pattern. Other qualities are far more vital."

"You mean you think it's all right for Reams to treat you this way?"

"I mean I understand him and I'm willing to accept him as he is." She did not add, And for as long as he will have me. The thin wind that whistles around borrowed time sounded faint in her ears, but with Karen on her side, with Reams apparently ready to take up his work again—work in which he came to her for advice and co-operation—she felt secured against the winter and spring was far behind.

16

While telling Reams that Karen knew about them Georgiana tried to make light of their equivocal status and tactfully glossed over her daughter's indignation at the reasons for that equivocality, but Reams was still up against the realization that however contented or resigned two people may be in an irregular relationship others, see-

247

ing them factually, without the subtleties, color, and texture which infuse that relationship for the lovers, are apt to pass flat-footed judgment upon them.

It was not to be divined from her behavior, for Karen treated Reams with grave courtesy, yet he had an acutely uncomfortable suspicion that she regarded him as a heel. He knew well that the more exalted the regard in which an idol is held the more bitter the disillusionment when it tumbles, and he could not doubt that his pedestal had been knocked from under him. Poor kid, he thought, she's received one of the bad jolts in the process of growing up, but being the jolt was not enjoyable.

They did not see much of each other, as Karen spent the week-days in Paris with Georgiana, coming to the country only late Friday night or Saturday morning, but on her last Saturday afternoon—she was sailing for New York the following Wednesday—Reams asked her to walk with him through the park which formed part of the house property. It was a lovely day, warm with the still, golden warmth of autumn, and the leaves were already turning. They walked through the woods to a place where the trees thinned and sat down on a log overlooking the stubble of a wheat-field recently harvested. Off to their left squatted the red-brown farmhouse with the gray-brown stones of the barnyard wall encrusted with lichen. Beyond it stretched a twin line of golden poplars bordering the road. The woods had been hot, and they sat resting a minute, welcoming the airiness of the open field. Karen was wearing a wheat-colored dress and a russet sweater. Reams thought she looked like an autumn goddess with the golden quality and lushness of autumn and some of its sadness too.

"I'm sorry to have been the one to hurt you, Karen," he said, "but I knew that if you ever found out about your mother and me I'd forfeit your love. That's why I asked you for a pledge of friendship. I needed it. You've been very nice to me ever since—well, ever since you discovered. I guess it hasn't been easy, and if the friendship part seems too hard I release you."

She shook her head. "My being hurt isn't important, Reams. It's my own fault, really. I invented something and fell in love with it but it was never there. It's my own stupidity that makes me ashamed. I don't like to be stupid."

248

She was trying to see it that way, he knew, trying to spare him from what she must consider his perfidy, but she hurt him the more. "I let you down," he said.

"There was no reason for you to buoy me up. You don't owe me anything, you never did, and you never pretended. That was right of you. But I don't think you should pretend with Mother either."

"I don't pretend anything with your mother, Karen. My feeling for her is true affection. I think I respect her more than anybody I know, but——"

"You don't want to marry her."

"The way things are in my life it wouldn't be right for me to marry her, but we haven't made any decision one way or the other. Because something may not last forever doesn't mean it hasn't got value." After a pause he added, "Matter of fact, I have no proof that your mother's so hell-bent on marrying me. Your feelings about me, my lovely friend, are, or rather were, very complimentary, but there are circles where I'm considered a mixed blessing." She smiled a little sadly, and they sat in silence gazing out over the quiet scene watching the color drain slowly from the sky, feeling the evening dampness rise from the earth. Presently he asked, "What are you thinking about?"

"Myself," she said. "I'm thinking that although love is sad maybe it's better to have it than never to have it because then you aren't empty inside. You and Mother, well, you sort of have each other, I guess, and Bierne and Daddy, they care with all their hearts. They have the wonderful thing."

"Darling Karen, you'll have someone of your own someday. I've always thought you could have that good Barclay Hamilton if you wanted him."

"I was thinking of Barky too. He always seemed uninteresting compared to you, colorless in a way, and I thought of him as too young, but maybe that was because I hadn't grown up. Now he seems to me important and strong."

"Tell him so when you get home."

"I will. Even if it's too late I'll tell him. I wish I could get back to the place where we were that night at his house. I wish I wouldn't be too late." She said it earnestly. Molded by the thin cashmere, he could see her hands clenched in her sweater pockets.

"Why should you be too late?" he asked.

She turned her green-brown eyes upon him. In her gaze there was surprise followed by the dogged resignation of one whose lot it is to break the news of the income tax to a starry-eyed spendthrift. "Mr. Asher, Mr. Hamilton is very rich. Every girl in New York City is determined to marry him, and my friend, Miss Poppy Slade, has a determination like nobody. That, among other reasons, is why I hope I am not too late."

It was good, Reams thought, good she felt that way. Relieved of her concentration on himself he need no longer feel guilty. Well, he didn't. Come to think of it, in the long run the shock she had received would probably have therapeutic value; from it she would derive new maturity, new wisdom. For her sake he was glad. Curious, though, how the sensation of basking in sunlight he had experienced when she was in love with him had faded. These early autumn twilights carried more chill than one would have thought possible. And as for Mr. Hamilton, a worthy young man, no doubt, if perhaps not quite so flawless as Reams had at first supposed. Sounded fickle, as though he couldn't make up his mind about women.

The following Monday morning Karen said good-by to the household, to Jeep and to Reams. To say that the servants had grown fond of *la grande mademoiselle Américaine* would be excessive; she created more work in the house and to the *femme de chambre's* hint that, because of her, higher wages were indicated, Monsieur Asher had responded with a chill almost French, but even they had thawed a little before her flowering beauty and beaming good humor. The gallant and incomprehensible way she spoke their language made them laugh, and when she tipped them more than she could afford they shook her hand warmly and wished her bon voyage and a speedy return. Jeep leered at her. "You can't ever tell, Lady Agatha, the scourge of journalism may be back on native heath someday and I shall come to claim you as my own." He gave her a great hug, they were warm, affectionate friends.

Her good-by to Reams had been said as she stood that night in the dark sitting room in the hotel; shocked and heartsick, and every day since they had journeyed a little further apart, but now she went

250

to make her manners, to thank him for his hospitality. He was in the library writing a cable Georgiana had promised to send for him from Paris. She went in and stood quietly till he had finished. He half turned in the chair and looked up at her. His square face looked older, she thought, the lines in his forehead were deeper, and the blue eyes between the thick whitish lashes seemed to her to have acquired a steely gleam in place of the old twinkle. But maybe she imagined that.

They gazed at each other across the fifteen years, the experiences and desires that divided them, and they were both sad. They could hardly be said to have lost very much, since they had had very little, but each one was taking physical farewell of a memory which would last out their lives. "Good-by, Reams."

"Good-by, Karen. Be happy."

"You too. Thank you for having me here in this strange nice old house. And thank you for the kind things you did to give me good times. I'll never forget them."

And thank you, you rotter, for all the rest, he thought. I shall never forget that either. "It is you who are kind," he said; "it is you who have behaved like a friend."

"Well . . ." There was no more for them to say.

"Is Georgiana ready?"

Karen nodded. "She's on the terrace waiting for Jeep to bring the car around."

"We better go." He picked up the cablegram from the desk and they went out. He and Jeep were driving Georgiana and Karen to the station. He had suggested going to Paris with them and on to Le Havre on Wednesday to see Karen off, but both she and Georgiana had felt that the parting would be much easier if they went alone on the boat train.

Georgiana would return to the country for the week end and then she, too, was off for a couple of weeks to cover the Biarritz season with one of the *Distaff* photographers. Shortly after her return their lease on the country house would be up. Their plans after that were uncertain although, with Georgiana's belief in Reams's stability re-affirmed, any idea of returning to New York to live with Allen grew more and more remote. Gradually the possibility even of marriage to Reams began to sharpen in her mind the way an image comes into focus in a lens. Sitting in the train on the way to Le Havre, she said to Karen, "I don't know, but I doubt very much if I could ever live with your father again. I think he's making a fatal mistake with this Honeywell girl, but"—she shrugged—"I suppose there's no use being a dog in the manger all your life. How would you feel about our being divorced if I continued to live over here?"

"It would seem awfully far away, but I've loved it here. I suppose I could always be with you in the summer holidays." She sounded a little wistful.

Her mother smiled brightly. "Of course you could. And don't forget, darling, you're twenty; in all likelihood you'll be getting married before very long, then your own home, your own life will be the most interesting and important thing in the world to you. Poor old ma will be taking a back seat."

"Oh no, Mum."

"Oh yes, child. That's the way it goes."

"Well, even so, I don't expect I'll be married for a long time yet." She was gazing out of the window as she spoke. They were past the ugly outskirts of Paris and the train clattered through the gentle cultivated French countryside. The fair land of France, she thought. Wasn't that what Mary Queen of Scots had called it? How she must have missed it in gruff Scotland with those heavy tartans and bony hairy knees about the lochs and braes.

Georgiana's vision of the moment tended more to white satin and rose-point lace as she saw Karen floating down the aisle into the outstretched arms of Mr. Hamilton, who awaited her eagerly, up to his knees in money bags. They would make a lovely couple. "Nonsense," she said in answer to her daughter's comment. "You are large, my love, but you are beautiful, and men are beginning to like you more and more. Just give them a chance. I hope you'll try to see Barclay as soon as you get home." To her pleased surprise Karen agreed. Georgiana had been fearful that in her unhappiness over Reams the girl might retire into a shell from which she would peer mistrustfully at the whole male sex. They hadn't discussed the situation much since the night Karen had seen her mother and Reams in the hall, but Georgiana accepted gratefully and without questioning her apparent resignation to fact.

As she kissed her good-by on the dock, the last thing she said to her was, "Tell Allen not to give up hope. I'm writing him that if we can get together on finance, and I consider that in twenty-five years I've been responsible for a good bit of his finance, I'll probably go ahead with the divorce."

17

Mid-September found Reams and Jeep keeping bachelors' hall, pleasantly relaxed in a circumstance which Jeep had always considered to be dangerously fraught with strain. To his surprise he found his reflexes still functioned and he got a good deal of work done. Surveying women from a pinnacle, he stretched and preened in new independence.

"Dames," he exclaimed one evening as seated in indolent ease before the fire he sipped a gin and tonic, "try to make you believe you're pooped without 'em. Goddam lie." He glanced across at Reams, who lay on the sofa reading, his heels higher than his head. "Of course I can imagine something more decorative than your hulk adorning the couch, but what the hell, you got to take up the slack some time. Also, in the full life I would be drinking scotch instead of gin, but they tell me there was a war. Still, this ain't bad, son, 'tain't bad." Reams grunted and went on reading. "As I look back on it," Jeep continued, undeterred by his companion's less-than-fervid response, "the one thing that used to gripe my old man when his women ran out on him—he had a lot of them, you know, Ma was his second wife and there were a batch after that, some legal, some extra-curricular—his one household gripe was dishes. Beds never bothered him, we never made 'em, but dishes! As a kid I can remember big stacks in the sink. They got to be a pretty good barometer of whether the current dame was coming back. As long as we got through only about half our inventory there was still hope, but if we got to eating straight out of the cans the jig was up. It was an interesting relativity: the less the women the more the dishes. How does it happen that you and I, being womanless, are also dishless?"

Reams cocked an eye at him. "Stow it, will you? You're breaking my heart with this tale of your beat-up childhood. We pay a retinue

253

of menials to smash crockery so that we can relax in sybaritic ease. Worth every cent too."

"Yeah. And when we do have women in the house leaves 'em free for more co-operative purposes." He got up off the end of his spine. "Say, how about that? Couple of dolls for next week end maybe?"

"Suit yourself, Mac, but not for me. I've got all the complications I can take on at the moment."

Jeep considered him. "You can't tell. Always room for one more."

"Not for me; I'm hibernating. I told you I was going to work days and loaf evenings and I mean it."

"Oh, that reminds me," Jeep said—it occurred to Reams his manner was elaborately casual but he passed it off as another prank—"you've got a bid for an evening do if you want it. The Hillyers are having a dinner party. They asked me, and their eyes lit up when they heard Georgiana was away. They see you as an extra man."

"Nuts."

"What have you got to lose? It's not far, the food's pretty good for an English household, and Geoff Hillyer's a nice guy."

"And young Daphne's a real sweater queen. I've seen them, too, don't forget."

With a knowing finger Jeep traced piquant silhouettes in the air. "Not bad for the provinces, not bad. Well, how about it? Shall I say you'll come?"

"When is it?"

"Wednesday." He picked up Reams's empty glass from the floor beside the sofa and started to refill both it and his own. "As I understand it it's a little shindig for a friend of theirs over from England."

"Oh?" Reams's attention was still on his book.

"A woman friend. Titled, I believe."

He glanced up. "What did you say?"

"Snob, eh?" Jeep's eyes gleamed with amusement. "I thought the title would fetch you."

"Who is it?" Reams asked shortly.

"Who do you think?"

"Is she here now?"

Jeep handed him his drink. "I believe she only arrives the day of the party."

Reams took his drink mechanically and set it down on the floor

254

beside him. After a moment he got up. He hesitated, as if not knowing where to move, what to do, then he burst out angrily, "I don't want to see her. I don't want to look at a corpse. For me she's dead. I said all the things I knew how to say in Portugal and I said them all six years before that. It's a dead issue; it's over. The hell with it. Why should she come here?"

"As I understand it she doesn't know you're in these parts and Hermione Hillyer hasn't the foggiest notion you know each other."

"Then why in God's name does she ask me to dinner?"

"You're a celebrated author, she is a hostess ferociously trying to balance her dinner table."

"I refuse to be any part of her sniveling damned arrangements." Jeep suppressed a smile. "Good," he said. "I'll tell her we both accept with pleasure."

The following Wednesday, duly accoutered in black ties and dinner jackets, looking more civilized than they felt, Mr. Asher and Mr. Harrigan, having bicycled the two miles separating them from their neighbors, presented themselves at the Hillyers' front door. A very British maid showed them into the drawing room where the Hillyer family and two or three other guests were already gathered.

The introductions over, Jeep attached himself to Miss Daphne, the sweater queen, while Mrs. Hillyer murmured conspiratorially to Reams, "We have the most charming house guest, but we won't wait any longer for her to come down, we'll just go right ahead and *have* our cocktails. Geoffrey," she called to her husband. "Geoffrey, do start mixing, dear. Mr. Asher and Mr. Harrigan have had all that great ride on their cycles and it's *very* tiring. More so for Americans," she added solicitously. "You're so unaccustomed to your legs, aren't you? I'm sure this petrol rationing is a real trial for you. Even Daphne and I notice it, and at home we never *cease* cycling, do we, dear?"

Daphne agreed that they spent their lives on wheels. "We're the *rolling* Hillyers you know."

The martinis were not very cold, but Mr. Hillyer had the correctly light touch with the vermouth. Reams had just downed his with, his host thought abstractedly, a grimly determined air unusual at a party, when Hermione Hillyer, glancing toward the hall, called out in her clear and cordial voice, "Ah, there you are, dear. You're a naughty late girl and we're well ahead of you. Come, get your cocktail at once." Reams turned and saw Linda Schofield standing in the doorway. Immobile, they stared at each other, aware of their peril, aware of their joy. Mrs. Hillyer bustled up, breaking the spell. "Here, pet, here's your drink. Now let me see. I don't believe you know anybody, do you?" She introduced Linda to the other women and then to the men. "Mr. Harrigan, one of the best American journalists in Paris and our local lion, darling; you can't not have heard of Reams Asher."

"Of course," Linda said, "I've heard of Mr. Asher. We met once in New York."

"My dear," cried Mrs. Hillyer, "how fascinating! Fancy, Geoffrey, Linda and Mr. Asher met once in New York. They're old friends."

"We are friends of old," Reams corrected, "which is perhaps a little different from being old friends."

Mrs. Hillyer looked distressed. "Don't tell me you've had a falling out. I couldn't *bear* it. You *must* get together again," and giving Lady Schofield a little pat she moved away to welcome new arrivals. "French people, aren't we fortunate, they're always so clannish." The comment was tossed over her shoulder like a scarf.

Reams turned to Linda. "When did you get here?" he demanded. "How long are you staying? Is your husband with you?"

"This noon. A week. No. He's shooting in Scotland."

"I love you. You are the most beautiful thing in the world and day and night I have never stopped loving you."

She looked him over coolly. "Shall we sit down?"

They moved to a sofa and he seated himself beside her. "Are you well, my love?" he asked. "Are you all right?"

"Yes, I'm well. I'm quite strong, you know." And after a little pause, "Tell me about yourself and the house you've rented here and your friends who live with you."

"I see the good Hermione has wasted no time."

"What can you expect? English-speaking peoples living near each other in a foreign country, their interests are mutual."

"What has she told you?"

"What I take to be merely common gossip. She insisted that I be

256

quiet this afternoon, so while I was being it she came in and sat on my bed and chattered to me about the dinner guests."

"I gather you did not mention our acquaintance?"

"I thought there was little point. Especially in view of your new interests. Tell me about them. I'm sorry Mrs. Goodyear isn't here, I remember her from the Ritz Bar." He was about to answer when dinner was announced. They rose in the general movement toward the dining room.

"In case I don't have another chance tonight," Reams said, "I shall pick you up at ten o'clock tomorrow morning."

"Won't Hermione think it rather sudden?"

"What Hermione thinks doesn't interest me, but if you like you can say that I'm showing you the house and we are renewing our old friendship."

"I must tell you I—I feel rather shy about going into another woman's house while she's away."

"This is not another woman's house. It is a house I rent from a French family and my lease is almost up. I will be here at ten o'clock in the morning."

The next day the rain fell in curtains, and Reams broke out a bit of precious gasoline in order to fetch Linda and drive her back to the villa. "Come in here," he said, ushering her into a small, high, sparsely furnished room. "I work in here and we won't be disturbed." They went in, and he closed the door and took her in his arms and they stood in a close, fierce embrace.

"No, Reams, no," she murmured against his mouth as his hands moved over her. "Please. I don't want to. It isn't like that at all."

"It's like that and every other way too," he said, but he released her. He went over and touched a match to the already laid fire, and she came and warmed her hands over the heightening flames. "Hermione told you that Georgiana was living here with Jeep and me. What else did she say?"

Linda hesitated. "Well, the consensus seems to be that you and she are, well, living very closely together."

"I see."

"Since you and I have said farewell for always, I expect the question is academic, but—are you?"

"Yes. Sporadically."

"But you have never ceased loving *me*. Your capacity for affection must be very great."

"What I told you last night was true," he said. "I love you and I would marry you today if you'd have me and I would be faithful to you in my mind and in my body until I died. But when you told me in Paris that it was no, when I knew I had nothing, I went back to Georgiana. We had been together, briefly, in New York, and she's good to me. As she's older than I am, and my mother died when I was three, a psychoanalyst would doubtless find some filial-maternal tie-up involved. I don't know. My own theory is that I like her, and we're compatible."

"Do you love her?"

"No. That has happened to me for the only time in my life. She knows about you and she understands that."

"It can't be very gay for her."

"It isn't very gay for either of us. It's what we have."

"At least you're honest, aren't you? If that's a virtue."

He shrugged. "I believe in telling the truth when I know what it is."

Linda studied him for a moment. "You deny yourself nothing, do you, Reams? Not even the luxury of a clear conscience."

"I have gone to bed a few times with a woman I like, if that's what you mean. Also, though I think alibis stink, if I need one in your eyes I have done what I have because I thought I would never see you again, and if I am to continue to live I must do it as normally as I can." She didn't say anything, and he asked, "Are you angry? Are you unhappy? You think I am without chivalry."

"No," she said at last. "I think you are a realist. Women are supposed to be the realists, but in this case it is you. I was sentimental. I refused to accept the fact that we would never be together again and I wanted my life to be uncluttered, from the last time I saw you to the next time, then we could come instantly together. I had to go back to my husband because of the children, but we have not been lovers. I preferred it that way, and I thought you would too."

"And now that you know about me, do you feel that you've been cheated? That you've missed out on something?"

She said, "I feel I've been a fool. This time when we part I shall

258

assume a more realistic attitude, and then if we ever meet again we can *both* purge our souls and confess all and rise up shriven." Tears were in her eyes, and his arms were around her, and they were clinging desperately together. "Are you going to be married, you and she? Then you could live even *more* normally."

"No, my love, no, my life, we are not going to be married. Oh, Linda, Linda, is there *no* way?"

"I don't see how, but sometimes, even with the children, I don't see how I can bear it either. Herbert's a strange man. He's always been difficult, but recently he's become nervy, terribly irascible, and fantastic about money. He used to enjoy the grounds so much; the gardens were one thing we had in common. He was *too* extravagant about them, I always thought, now he gets in a rage if the gardener buys a flowerpot. He's obsessed by money except where the children are concerned. He talks all the time about how expensive Ronny's school is but how excellent, and he lavishes toys and presents on the baby till she's surfeited. He's started now planning her coming-out party, her wedding; he talks continually about how much he's going to be able to do for both the children. I tell you he's like a madman. It's partly the strain of that new company, I expect."

"What new company?"

"Commonwealth Futures, I believe it's called. He and some other men have formed a syndicate. He claims that even with Labor in the saddle they can make millions." She laughed a little. "I think he's going to get his ambassadorship, too. He's been very circumspect, but more than once now he's implied that an embassy will make a nice background for the children. I suppose, from a worldly point of view, I have no right to deprive them of what he can give them and after all, he is their father. His concern for them would be touching if it weren't so unbalanced, so out of proportion."

Reams looked troubled. "Listen, Linda, I don't believe that's a safe guy for you to be around. You make him sound nutty as a fruitcake."

She gave a dreary little laugh. "Don't worry about that. I'm very valuable to him. Many diplomatic posts one can't get without a wife."

They talked for a long time, seeking desperately a way out but always they came to the same impasse, her son and daughter.

259

"Look," Reams said at last, "will you agree to this then? I can write in England just as well as any place else—it's an arrangement that makes me heartsick to think about, because it falls so short of what I want for us but at least if I'm near you we can see each other, we can be together in bed sometimes. If I come to England, *will* you see me?"

"Oh, Reams, don't. How can I? If he ever found out . . ."

"He doesn't have to find out, and if he does, what of it? If he's so hell-bent on a diplomatic career, he's not going to want any scandal. He wouldn't *dare* try to take the children away from you. How could he explain *that* to the press and foreign office?"

"I don't know, but that isn't what I want either. I love you, I want to be your wife, but we're in an impossible situation, both of us. Even if the children didn't exist, what about Mrs. Goodyear? You like her, you told me so. Why shouldn't you? You can't calmly walk out closing the door behind you."

Reams said, "But there's no future for her and me, there's no question of our marriage."

"Are you sure? Are you sure she doesn't hope and plan?"

"No, it's absurd. Darling, darling."

She was sobbing in his arms. "I don't know what to do, I don't know."

To be together was all they wanted in the world and to be together was the ultimate torment.

Reams at last took her home. The following day the Hillyers had planned an excursion to the nearby cathedral, and although Linda dined with Jeep and Reams it was a family party, including her hosts. The next night was the Big Party. "Buffet, darling, twenty-four," said Mrs. Hillyer enthusiastically. "Fancy, it would have seemed nothing in the old days, but now, what with saving up and substituting, *and* the black market, it's quite an adventure. Geoffrey is so honorable I don't confide in him *all* about the black market, so unkind to make people feel guilty I always think, at least when they're hungry. One can bear guilt better on a full stomach. I do wish, though, we could be in the American embassy. All that whisky!"

Mrs. Hillyer, who was accustomed to Herbert Schofield, and considered him handsome, secretly thought it rather a shame he had chosen to go shooting in Scotland and wouldn't be at the party, but she refrained from mentioning it to Linda. Where her husband was concerned Linda, habitually so friendly and gay, became a bit stony.

Saturday evening the Hillyers' plans and preparations burst into bloom. A distinguished Anglo-French gathering, resplendent in their best bibs and tuckers, some of which removed from moth balls for the first time since the war enveloped their wearers in a delicate fragrance of camphor, moved through Hermione's double salon drinking champagne, of which there was an abundance, and nibbling hors d'oeuvres most of which seemed to be composed of herring or anchovies. Everyone participated in the universal difficulty in obtaining food, but some of the French guests did find it in their palates to wish that their hosts hailed from less insular parts; they seemed to be overdoing the fruits of their silver sea.

About sixteen people had gathered when shortly before eight-thirty Geoffrey Hillyer turned on the radio. Linda was seated near it, her lovely figure outlined like a Tanagra in a cunningly draped dress of soft gray jersey that fell in sculptured folds to the floor. She was talking to one of the young attachés from the British embassy and to a well-known Frenchman of letters who distributed his talents impartially between his publishers, the daily press, and the cinema. Across the room Reams stood watching her while ostensibly devoting himself to an elderly Frenchwoman remarkable for her heavily wrinkled eyelids and the apparently endless layers of scarves and jackets in which she was entombed.

A newscast preceded a short-waved speech of Mr. Churchill's which they wanted to hear and in the drawing room the chatter abated as the commentator's elegant diction informed the guests that among other sanguinary items a group of Sikhs had been butchered on a Pakistan train, Indian riots flared in Calcutta, and that under a Berlin date line the United States and the Soviet Union vigorously denounced the British and French policy on reparation.

There was a pause, presumably to let the glad tidings sink in, and the recitation continued. "We have just received word that the very large and recently formed investment trust, Commonwealth Futures, which, because of its audacious policies, has been of interest to financiers around the world, has foundered in bankruptcy. Further details will be made available when known although it is thought possible that many fortunes may have been lost in the collapse, including that of one of Britain's distinguished figures of international diplomacy. Paul Ramadier, the Socialist Premier of France, has demanded a . . ." "I say, what a shocking business," broke in the young man from the embassy; "my people were interested in Futures, although I do not believe my father had invested anything. I certainly hope not."

"Shut up, Peter," Daphne observed amiably; "who cares about your old company? I want to hear the figures on the Ramadier vote of confidence." The two young people turned down the volume and plastered their ears against the speaker as other guests, losing interest in the news, picked up the conversation. The French contingent paid small attention to the fate of Commonwealth Futures, but among the British there was considerable speculation as to what had happened and who was involved.

As the news came over the air Linda had risen from her chair instinctively turning toward Reams. He was already at her side and took both her hands in his. "Hold tight; it may be exaggerated."

"God forbid," she murmured swiftly; "it's our chance."

Hermione Hillyer came forward clucking sympathetically. "Linda, my poor child, isn't that the company you were telling me only this afternoon Herbert was interested in? Oh, I do hope he's all right."

Linda moistened her lips. "I don't imagine he's in very good shape; he was chairman of the board." She said it quietly, but it was overheard by one or two nearby guests and spread swiftly through Hermione's double salon. People gathered around Linda murmuring condolences or offering words of encouragement.

It lent quite a fillip to the party. Beautiful titled women didn't go bankrupt every day before one's very eyes. "Not, God knows, that there's very much difference between us," murmured one of the English guests. "Lady Schofield merely had an arm cut off all at once. Less painful, I should think, than the government's way, a finger at a time."

As the wave of curiosity and pity swept over Linda she kept saying a little breathlessly, "Thank you for your interest, you're very kind, we don't know the details, it isn't as serious perhaps as we think."

Reams close beside her felt her start to shake. He turned to Geoffrey Hillyer, "Look here, isn't there a room where Lady Schofield could be alone for a few minutes? This has been quite a shock."

"Of course it has," Hermione cried; "how thoughtless of us. This way, darling."

"Perhaps," Mr. Hillyer said to his wife, "we ought to call off the party. Under the circumstances——"

Linda laid a hand on his arm. "No, Geoffrey, you *mustn't*. It's not the fault or the concern of anybody here, why should you spoil your party? I'm quite all right, quite, quite all right." Her eyes glittered, the Hillyers thought, a little strangely. She looked almost as though she were going to burst out laughing. Hysteria, of course.

"Please," Reams said, "I think if we can be alone for a few minutes. You'd probably like to put in a call to London, wouldn't you, Linda?"

"Oh. Well, yes, if you think I should."

"Come."

He led her out of the drawing room across the hall to the small office Geoffrey used when he worked at home.

The moment the door was closed she started to laugh. "Thank God, thank God we're away from them. I thought I couldn't bear it, all that fetid sympathy. I was afraid I'd disgrace myself, laughing in their faces, shouting at them I'm free, free at last. Darling, do you realize what this means?"

He took her in his arms. "It had better mean that you're mine."

She drew back a little. "Darling, my God, you may not want me."

"Not *want* you?"

"Well, if it's true, we must put in a call by the way, I'm poor. I haven't got a bean."

"Hurray! I'll have you in my power." He kissed her hard, but in a moment she pushed him away. The excitement which had buoyed her up seemed to collapse.

"There's another side to this, you know. Are you sure you're going to want the responsibility? My first thought, you see, was that without the money Herbert can no longer have the same hold over the children. He's sincere about wanting the best education for them, every advantage, that's the card I'll have to play with him: that you can give them these things, that you're willing to. But are you? If you marry me, Reams, you'll be taking on a lot. Think about it."

"I don't have to think about that. I've been thinking about marrying you for six years. I'm sorry for your sake that things had to happen this way in order for it to be possible, but better this way, *infinitely* better this way, than not at all."

"Poor Herbert," she said sadly; "poor devil."

Suddenly he was afraid. "Linda, you're not going to think you mustn't leave him because he's in trouble, are you?"

"No. Oh no, but——"

"But what?"

"I'm not going to look very nice, am I? My husband goes bankrupt, he loses his money, the family estates, everything. And his wife walks out on him. She walks out on him and takes the children. Not an attractive picture."

"Linda, stop it! You're dramatizing this."

"Am I? Why? Isn't that what's happening? Isn't it true?"

"No, damn it, it's not. He's been impossible for a long time; he isn't suddenly noble because of adversity. To begin with, there'd never be any question of his not seeing his children, and in the second place why assume the worst? Possibly the news is a rumor, but even if it's true——"

She forgot her misery long enough to say mockingly, "*If* it's true. Dear old boy, we heard it on the B.B.C., remember? That cathedral of communication. Not like your low American competitive channels rushing into speech for the sake of a scoop."

"All right, so it's true; but why think he's lost everything? Maybe only a part of his fortune . . ."

She shook her head. "I doubt it. He must have been mortgaged to the eyes, that's what was making him so frightfully nervous, so viciously ill-tempered. Poor dear, I suppose that's why he was difficult about the gardens. He must have been afraid deep down that he could lose. If Willow had to go, too, he didn't want to spend any more on it." Suddenly she was crying. "It's a lovely place; it will break his heart."

"I realize," Reams said, "that I am a relative newcomer, but would you think about my heart too? I thought we were so in love, I thought we longed to be married?"

"Oh, darling, darling sweet, of course, but oh, dear *God*, why can't people be happy without others being miserable?"

"I don't know. I wish I did."

"Reams."

"That one I do know. Georgiana."

"What will you do? Are you willing to give her up and take the risk that Herbert won't make any difficulties now about a divorce?"

He smiled fleetingly. "You have a bad opinion of me, haven't you? You think I hedge on everything, always being sure of a cozy place."

She smiled back at him. "I think to want comfort and affection is very natural and I think we're beyond the age of hats over windmills."

He kissed her very gently.

"That was very gentle," she said.

"It was a kiss for my grandmother."

"But what *can* you do?"

"Georgiana gets back from Biarritz day after tomorrow. I'll be in Paris to meet her."

"What will you say to her? The truth once more?" There was an edge of malice in her tone but it dulled as she said a little sadly, "I'm sorry she's going to hate me. If you like her so much, maybe I would, too, and now we shall never know each other."

"I don't see why not, after a time. Oh, I think now and then Georgiana may have wondered if marrying me was such an insane idea, but that she ever seriously wanted to—no."

"At least it's more comfortable for us to think that."

"Damn it all, she has got a husband, you know," but he added doggedly—if Linda was going to laugh at his honesty let her—"I believe she *is* on the brink of divorcing him."

"Oh, God. Now maybe she won't, and if *he* wanted the divorce his whole life can be smashed. Only isolated virgin orphans should ever fall in love."

"You are neither a virgin nor an orphan and I love you."

As the train pulled into the Gare de Lyon, Georgiana saw with delighted surprise that Reams was standing on the station platform. He's glad I'm back, she thought happily; maybe he's really missed me. She lowered the window and leaned out waving. "Yoo hoo, darling, here I am. Grab a porter." So her hunch that he might, after all, come to accept the idea of permanency between them was right!

Well, why not? Stranger things than that had happened in this world. She remembered the address of a beauty specialist who had been highly recommended to her by a woman in Biarritz. "Peels the years off you, my dear. A wizard." She would make an appointment tomorrow. The train slowed to a stop. Reams opened the carriage door and helped her down the steps. "Hi, sweetie," she said. "It's wonderful to see you."

"It's good to see you, G, you look fine." The turmoil of the station, questions about Biarritz and Karen's departure carried them back to the Hôtel Vendôme, and Georgiana felt, as always, that if coming to Paris was wonderful, coming back to it was like coming back to a lover. They went up to the suite and deposited the luggage. Georgiana said she had to go to the office but would get home early and what time would Reams be there and where would they dine? "It might be more cozy to have something sent up, if you like?"

He agreed. "I'll be here between six-thirty and seven," he said.

Going up in the office's bird-cage elevator it occurred to Georgiana that, while affable, Reams had been a little less than ardent. Still, she had been in a rush, what could she expect? This evening, after dinner, things would be very different.

But at dinner she had a strange feeling, as though she were in a room charmingly and gaily furnished, Reams was charming and gay, but every time she went to open a door the door was locked. As long as she stayed in the center of the room she was all right, but to touch a door was to touch a forbidding surface. A little chill began to creep into the brightness. He had ordered brandy and now they sat over the table with their balloon glasses and cigarettes and sipped it appreciatively. Two or three times he was on the verge of telling her what had happened, but just as he opened his mouth to speak he heard Linda's voice a little mocking, a little bitter, "At least you're honest, aren't you? If that's a virtue." He was about to be honest again, but he knew now that honesty was not enough. The thing was not to get embroiled in the first place, though where he had done anything wrong or mean or unnatural . . . The hell with it, he thought. Linda is my home, and once I'm home I'll be safe and I'll be there forever. This is the last sortie. But he remembered how in the war the one more operation before leave was the toughest.

Georgiana said something about giving the house in the country a thorough cleaning before turning it back to the owners. She put forth the remark as a feeler. Possibly Reams would say, Why not try to renew the lease, it would be fun to go there winter week ends and as the months went by gas rationing would be sure to let up. Instead, he said, "That's a good idea; tell the servants whatever you want done."

Possibly he simply hadn't thought of it. "I don't suppose it would be feasible to consider renewing the lease for a few months?" she asked. "You're working so well there and I could always be down week ends."

"No," he said. "No, it wouldn't be."

"Well, perhaps you're right. A needless expense probably."

"It's not the expense." And then, here we go, he thought. "Georgiana, while you were away something happened. I don't flatter myself that it's going to cause any irreparable difference in your life but we are close, you and I, and this is hard for me to tell you and it may be hard for you to hear. At least it may be hard on you for a while." He told her about Linda's arrival at the Hillyers' and about the news of Herbert Schofield's bankruptcy and what, in all likelihood, it would mean to them. "You know how I feel about Linda," he finished, "and now that the chances are that she'll get her freedom we want to be married as soon as it can be arranged." He stopped, waiting for her to say something, but she was very still, looking at him, he thought, in a curiously detached fashion. "I've been in love with her for many years," he continued, "but believe me when I say I'm terribly fond of you, Georgiana, and I'll be grateful you're on earth till my dying day, but I've always felt that as far as you were concerned what we had was pleasant and amusing but—an adventure, that someday you would certainly go back to your husband and your normal way of life." He had anticipated every sort of response except laughter. To his discomfiture she began to laugh; she was shaken with laughter; she laughed while the tears poured down her cheeks. Alarmed, he said, "Stop it! What's the matter with you?"

She stopped, breathless and gasping. "You, you fraud! You always felt that what we had was merely 'pleasant and amusing'! I suppose I left my husband and child, gave up a good job in New York for my pleasure and amusement?"

"Then why else?"

"Because I was in love with you, you jackass! You goddamned fool! Because I was imbecile enough to hope that you could learn to appreciate what I had to give you."

"What? Your advice on my work? Your passion? Your companionship? I do appreciate them, but you tendered them of your own volition, don't forget."

"You disgust me." Her mouth was distorted with fury. "You never made love to me, I suppose, never urged me to come to you? I suppose I importuned you with my desire."

"I think we've had enough of that," he said coldly.

She was silent, trying with trembling fingers to open her vanity case, apply her lipstick. Suddenly she looked haggard, pitiable.

"Georgiana, listen, when you told me in New York you were going to try to get to Paris I said it would be fine and I meant it, and once we get by this moment I think I'll still be glad it happened, but we always knew it was bound to end. Let's not ruin everything we've had by tearing each other apart."

"All right, let's think it out then! What makes you so sure your titled friend will leave her husband? Bankruptcy may be disagreeable but I never heard that it is *ipso facto* grounds for divorce. He may not choose to give her up or she might even get a spasm of conscience and feel she should stay with him."

"Those things are possible, of course, but I think unlikely. She flew back to London yesterday and I talked to her this noon. Her husband *has* been wiped out just as the news announcement hinted, and though there's been no time to discuss anything he apparently assumes she is going to bring up the matter of divorce again, and her feeling is that he's so frightfully involved in his business affairs he doesn't give a damn any more whether she goes or stays."

"I can understand his point."

"Those things can happen, you know. Sometimes one just comes to the end of caring."

"It's handy when one gets to that end fustest with the mostest indifference, isn't it?"

"Georgiana, please."

She laughed gratingly. "You must forgive your aging mistress if she inconveniences you, but it's upsetting to see one's life come to an abrupt halt."

"What the hell kind of self-pity is that?" he demanded. "You're far too vital and important a woman to let a transitory love affair upset your life. You've got a job that interests you, a magnificent daughter, and a husband who may have strayed off the reservation but who probably will be damn glad to welcome you home."

"Or so you hope. Well, for your benefit, my friend, I wrote him from Biarritz that I would file papers for a divorce as soon as I got back to Paris. I called a lawyer today and made an appointment for tomorrow morning, so I am afraid you may have to revise your plans a bit."

"What do you mean?"

"From all you've said about her, Lady Schofield sounds like an intensely conventional suburban little woman. She may not be so eager to marry you when she learns that you and I are living together, that you come to her, so to speak, fresh from my arms."

He looked at her and shook his head. "I've done some pretty strange things myself because of love, but blackmail isn't your style. Besides, it would be a waste of effort. Linda knows about us and she thinks you're getting the dirty end of the stick and she's sorry. So am I. Desperately sorry, but not sorry enough to renounce her and go on living in a setup which would terminate now anyhow, even if she died tomorrow."

Georgiana stared down at the table, one hand nervously pleating her napkin into tiny folds. He reached out and covered her hand with his. "Don't be bitter." She drew her hand away. "After I'd seen her in Portugal I should have had the guts not to come back to you, but you were my wonderful friend, I turned to you instinctively. You gave me everything, you saved me from a real crack-up, but I know that if you ever did contemplate marrying me the idea also filled you with misgivings. It would have had to. Isn't that so? Isn't it?"

She blinked hard to hold back the tears. "Marriage to you, my dear boy, would never strike me as a sound idea for anybody. You're profoundly self-centered, Reams; you can never make a woman happy in marriage, you have to realize that. Of course, if that isn't important to you . . ."

"It is. Terribly important to me, and I'm going to try terribly hard."

She cleared her throat. "With you and me, well, I wouldn't have expected happiness. We were companionable, without you it's—— If you persist in this insane idea I must simply accustom myself to loneliness, I suppose."

"Why should you? Look how *very* well you did before I came along."

"Not so well as it pleases you to think. Besides, I had a husband. We were scarcely lovebirds, but I had him. Now I have no one."

"Would you consider going back to him? It would mean a lot to Karen to have you together."

Georgiana blew her nose and eyed him wryly. "And she and I could walk off into the sunrise in new close understanding, both jilted by the same man."

"You're exaggerating things a bit."

"And you, dear Reams, are oversimplifying. I don't know how much she confided in you, but Karen is very fond of her father's mistress and is entirely on their side and eager to see them married. You must have been weaned on B pictures. In this feature the tot does not take Daddy and Mumsy by the hand in sweet reunion."

"I don't know anything about that, but I bet you that if Allen knew he had a chance of getting you back he'd take it. You may have had your rows but you had a good life together. If you're both willing to overlook the mutual hiatus which has taken place in your marriage you and he have a hell of a lot in common. Infinitely more than he and that youngster certainly."

Georgiana laughed. "Dear Reams, how well you arrange other people's lives to suit your convenience. Your own, too, of course. You have a real knack."

"Georgiana, why don't you write Allen? Why don't you go home?"

"And leave you in peace. Well, why not? 'Dear Allen, my lover has kicked me out, so I'm coming back to your bed and board, your ever-loving wife.' Allen is a compassionate man, he *exudes* human understanding, but that might be a little too much even for him. Besides, I enjoy Paris. As you will probably be spending a good deal of time in England allow me some use of the city."

"As you like, but your welfare is important to me. I just thought you'd be less lonely in your own home with your own family."

"Reams, how many times do I have to tell you? My husband wants

270

to marry another woman. You should be able to understand that."

"Well, I don't. Karen said her father started going with this girl, Bierne whatever her name is, because *he* was lonely, but how do you know he wouldn't welcome you gladly?"

"Because he has written to me and because I can read. Because Karen has told me how things are. No, Reams, you may want to brush me off, but don't try to comfort me at the same time." Yet for a moment her belief about Allen and Bierne wavered. Could Reams be right, after all? Georgiana wasn't sure she wanted her husband but she wasn't sure she didn't. The only incontrovertible fact she had to deal with was that Reams was lost to her. He had called it an adventure. The adventure was over. "Journeys end in lovers meeting." Not always, my fine-feathered Swan, she thought, sometimes they end in a great crashing separation and this is the case in spades. She had once had a friend named Ethel who slashed her wrists when her love walked out on her, but the doctor got to her in time and she recovered. The worst damage had been to the bedroom—it had been awash with gore and Ethel said the cleaner's bill was frightful. Georgiana wondered if she was likely to slash her wrists after Reams should get up from the table and say good-by and walk out the door for the last time. Sometimes jilted women took an overdose of sleeping pills. Well, she had plenty of those. Gas ovens were effective, too, but in a hotel the process would be involved.

"What are you thinking?" Reams asked.

She came back to him with a start. "What? Oh. I was thinking that hotel kitchens are inaccessible."

He looked puzzled. "Do you want something more?"

"Thank you, no. Forget it. When may I go to the country for my clothes?"

That one hurt. "Whenever you want to, of course, whenever you were planning to go down anyway. Would you prefer to live there until the lease expires?"

"Would you be there?"

"Well, I think it would . . ."

"Oh, of course, I forgot. You'll be in England."

They sat in silence. They looked at each other; they even smiled slightly but Georgiana's smile was non-committal and Reams's uncertain. He was going on to the life he had dreamed of with the woman he loved, but the woman across the table from him was magnetic and warm and he knew quite well there would be times when he would need that curious flashing insight which made her so valuable a critic and which stimulated him to his best work. It was what made him say, quite simply, the man protecting the artist, "When the last stories are complete I'll send them to you. You'll read them, of course, and let me know what you think."

"Lady Schofield won't object?"

He looked genuinely surprised. "How could she? This is my work."

"Women have strange jealousies."

"Georgiana?"

"Yes?"

"I love you, you know."

"If neither as mistress nor wife."

"I love you as a person. It's more important. I'm not up on those things, but I guess you could say I love the essence that's you. I love your spirit."

"The way ghosts love," she said.

They talked a little longer, but the words had all been spoken and after a bit as he was leaving he said, "I—I don't know just when we can be married, it probably won't be for several months yet, but I'll be in touch with you, of course."

"I'll see it in the papers."

"I'll be in touch with you long before that. Frankly, it seems to me idiotic for the three of us not to be friends." Something in her golden eyes made him add, "After a bit of time."

"Say ten years, when I can no longer be considered the competition."

"Georgiana, my dear, dear——"

"Please," she said. "Do you mind going?"

He went out the same door he had gone out of the night Karen learned about them, and Georgiana closed it behind him. She rang for the waiter and he came and took away the table. And after a while she spoke to the concierge and asked him to call her at eight o'clock the following morning. Then she wrote on a pad beside the telephone, Cancel Lawyer's Appointment. She undressed and got into bed and turned out the light and went to sleep. She slept soundly for an hour and a half and then she woke up and sleep was over for the night and she knew that it would be a long, long time before she would ever again sleep a night through.

18

Satisfied that Mrs. McTavish at least had the cookbook open to the right recipe, Allen uttered a silent prayer for her success and carried the ice bucket from the pantry into the library. He was waiting for Bierne and her family to come to dinner, and as he poured himself a highball he quietly cursed the impulse that had made him tell her to bring them along that evening. He wanted to talk to her, and for what he had to tell her they needed privacy.

When, some three weeks before, Georgiana's letter had arrived from Biarritz saying she had decided on the divorce and would consult a lawyer in Paris, he and Bierne had been elated. "For God's sake, darling," he said to her after the first rapturous hug, "build me a little character with the home folks. Prove to them I'm an honorable guy concerned with your fair name. Tell 'em we're going to be married the minute the law allows." Bierne had done so and, while Mrs. Honeywell's sentiments against divorce were firm and frequently aired, if her daughter was going to carry on with a married man better he be married to her than to another. Allen had put off inviting them to the house longer than he decently could, since confirming his engagement in his wife's apartment seemed a step too far. I may have slipped, he thought, but on this, by God, I stand.

However, the continuous pressure exerted on Bierne by her mother's curiosity proved too much for him. The family were to come but Bierne and Allen assured each other that they were no different from any other two people who might be coming to eat a meal. It was in no sense an official thing.

With peace of mind Allen might even have looked forward to the evening for, while her family was Bierne's cross in life, Allen took a gently malicious pleasure in Gladys Honeywell and he considered Uncle Ben to be a good Joe. Scarcely a seminal intellect, but kindly and a friend. Since mid-afternoon, however, his peace of mind had fled, and the uneasy premonition which had haunted him the past few weeks had been proven all too accurate.

He was trying to think how best to cope with his unwelcome knowledge, how to break the news to Bierne, when the doorbell rang. On his way down the hall he stuck his head in the pantry door and called through to the cook, "I'll take it, Mrs. McTavish." Mrs. McTavish was the gem who came in in the afternoon, cleaned up, and prepared dinner. If completely unharassed, she was capable of some surprisingly good efforts—when pleased with a dish herself she would remark, "Glamorous, isn't it?"—but doorbells and ice cubes were disturbances among which she foundered so Allen spared her whenever possible.

The interval before dinner passed more easily than he had dared hope, being devoted almost entirely to a sightseeing tour of the apartment, with Uncle Ben politely admiring and Mrs. Honeywell casting an appraising if uncomprehending eye over the fruitwood, raw silk, and walls solid with books. Allen and Bierne walked close together, and when he had an opportunity he whispered to her, with some erroneous idea that it would encourage her, "There's bad news, darling, but keep your tail up; we'll lick it yet."

Her heart naturally sank to her boots. "What is it?" she whispered at the next opportunity.

"Georgiana."

"Oh, God. She's not here?"

"No, no."

"She's changed her mind about the divorce?"

"Not necessarily, but it's what we have to—— Oh, by the way, dear," he continued in a normal tone as having gazed in embarrassment at an African sculpture on his desk Gladys and Ben came toward them, "Mrs. Carroway *is* having that business party tonight and has asked us to drop in."

It was to Bierne's credit that hearing of the festivity for the first time she picked up her cue without missing a beat. "How nice. Does it matter that I'm not dressed?"

"Not a bit," Allen informed her; "completely informal. We'll have plenty of time after dinner before we have to get there," he added graciously to Gladys. "I only found out as I was leaving the office.

Sorry it's tonight, but one of our English authors is over here and I can't very well not show up."

Gladys accepted this affably enough. She would find out the details from Bierne later, and the Carroway house would probably be much grander than Mr. Goodyear's, though heaven knows Mrs. Goodyear must have spent plenty on those gee-gaws and fabrics in the funny washed-out looking colors she seemed to fancy. Gladys wondered what kind of settlement her daughter's intended could make with his present wife and how much of the furniture Bierne could count on.

They were blessed in that dinner turned out to be one of Mrs. McTavish's glamour efforts, even the chocolate soufflé rose to the occasion, and though Mrs. Honeywell refused to drink wine she was enough awed by the good food, candlelight, and Georgiana's china—different kinds of plates for every course, "and intended, it looked like," she observed to Ben later, "not just different because the dinner set was broken"—to watch in silence while Allen filled the glasses of the others two or three times. Disapproving of the whole situation, Gladys acknowledged to herself, not without pride, that her beautiful daughter fitted very well into one of those society backgrounds.

Throughout the meal, though she tried to do it unostentatiously, Bierne's attention was on Allen, and while she smiled a good deal her smile was strained. What could have happened? Karen had come back from Paris virtually certain that her mother would agree to the divorce and Georgiana's letter from Biarritz had seemed to be the final consent. Why, now, had she changed her mind if that's what it was?

The moment came at last when Allen said, "Well, darling, I suppose we'd better be going along." They offered to drop Mrs. Honeywell and Ben off at the house, but Ben wouldn't hear of it, it was so near they could easily walk. "Shake down some of that good grub," he said sociably.

They went down in the elevator together and as her mother and uncle departed Allen hailed a cab. "*Is* there a party?" Bierne asked. "Where are we going?"

"Around the block a couple of times and back upstairs. No, my love, there is no party, but it would have been a little bald to send the family home and say we'd be along later. Give them too accurate an idea of what we're up to. Besides, something's happened. When you're close in my arms I'll be better able to think what to do."

Back in the apartment he told her his news. "Germaine Dauzat called me up this afternoon and asked me if I'd heard from Georgiana. I told her not recently, I explained that as a matter of fact we've been expecting a letter from her lawyer for a couple of weeks and that if we don't hear in the next day or so I'm going to phone her in Paris."

"But why did Madame Dauzat call you?"

"She called me because they *have* had a letter from Georgiana. This morning. She wants to leave Paris and come back to work on *Distaff* in New York."

"Did—did the letter say anything else?"

"Yes. That she is terribly lonely, that she feels she made a great mistake, and that all she wants is Karen and her home and me."

"Oh, Allen." It was rather that the air moved than that she made any sound.

"My dearest, it makes no difference. I'm afraid one more delay, possibly, but no real difference. If she does come home, I'll move out. In the end she'll have to realize that I'm through."

"You say *if* she comes. Is there any chance she may not?"

"That's the silver lining. Germaine doesn't want her over here. She's doing a good, useful job in Paris and the Dauzats want her to stay on it, but naturally they're curious as to why all of a sudden she's changed her mind, why suddenly this craving for the U.S.A. I had to admit I didn't know."

Bierne was silent, remembering something Karen had told her when she came home.

She had babbled about her trip, talking of the house in the country and Jeep and the other people she had met and what it was like to live with everything rationed, but when it came to Reams and her mother she was not very informative. "I was silly about Reams," she said quietly in answer to a question from Allen on how she had found the great American author. "Before I went over I thought it was awfully important. It was only a delayed schoolgirl crush."

Her father stroked her hair. "Don't mind, old lady, those things happen to us all. The first thing you know you'll have a *real* beau."

"Well," Karen said, "I don't know how much of a beau of mine he is but I called Barclay to tell him I was home—funny, I would never have dared call Reams, but it seemed natural to call Bark, and I'm going out with him this evening and something very peculiar has happened."

"What?"

"*Well,* after we made our date I happened to be talking to Poppy, catching up on all the dope, and she said, casual-like, without me saying anything about *my* plans, that she had been going out with Barclay tonight but such a nuisance, he'd called her up to say he was terribly sorry but some business person of his father's was in town and he had to be with them."

"You didn't enlighten her, did you?"

"No. I was scared. I hung up fast. But what do you think it means?"

Bierne laughed. "I think it means he'd rather be with you than with Poppy."

"But, my Lord, if she ever finds out! That was awful of him. I feel like a worm."

"What about your mother, by the way?" Allen asked. "Any beaux in that neighborhood? I would be grateful for a passionate man of principle who wished to marry her. Reduce my alimony problem considerably."

Karen hesitated. "Mother goes out quite a bit," she said carefully; "there might be somebody, she didn't say."

"Funny," Allen observed, he was concentrating on lighting his pipe and his tone was offhand, "I guess I was wrong, but I used to have the notion that Georgiana had kind of a crush on Asher herself. When she went off last May I had the feeling she wasn't too sorry our finances were tight. Paris looked pretty good to her."

"Yes. Well, they're very good friends, of course. He values Mother's opinion of his work and they shared the house and all, the three of them that is, but that was just a convenience. They were lucky, as a matter of fact, that Mother was willing to go to the country week ends. She'd tell the servants what to do and order meals for the whole week and the fellas just lived in the lap of luxury."

"Your mother was always an excellent housekeeper," Allen observed dryly.

Bierne quailed, hoping she would be able to meet the standards set by the first Mrs. Goodyear.

Shortly afterward Allen had gone out. He was giving a series of talks on the publishing business to a group of postgraduate students and this was one of his evenings. The girls went into Karen's room to sort out the clothes she was taking to college. It was after she had packed the fifth sweater that she said suddenly, "Don't worry, Bierne, I'm practically certain from what she said that Mother's going through with the divorce. I hope things are going to work out for her, too, but there's somebody else Reams likes. Don't tell Daddy, will you?"

"Not if you don't want me to."

"I don't, because—well, if she's going to get the divorce it can't matter in the least." She had turned away abruptly and gone on with her packing. Bierne was puzzled but she had given her word to say nothing to Allen, and in the excitement of their plans and in waiting for the lawyer's letter it slipped her mind. This evening it came back to her.

"Darling," Allen said, "you're a long time quiet. Don't fret, chicken. I thought of keeping it from you, but that seemed too unfair. I just wish I knew——"

"Why she's coming back?" He nodded. "Maybe she *is* lonely. Maybe something she hoped for—didn't turn out."

"Oh," he said. "By God, I bet you're right. If *I've* been right about the Asher business . . ." And he added very softly under his breath, "Poor bastards," but just which characters in this drama he was referring to Bierne wasn't sure.

Georgiana's letter which Germaine had mentioned to Allen arrived at an unfortunate moment. Madame Dauzat had arisen that morning, not so much on the wrong side of the bed as on the deserted side. Theoretically, Monsieur should have been occupying the area adjacent to her but there had been only empty space. Of course she couldn't be entirely sure he was in New York, his last cable from Paris had said merely that he would fly home one day that week depending on the accommodation he could get and to

278

expect him when she saw him, but she learned the worst shortly after reaching her office. One of their Seventh Avenue advertisers called to confirm a conversation about space he had had with Claude coming over on the plane the day before. Her husband then was in the city if not in the home. He had obviously cleared customs and headed straight for Miss Nora Brown.

Germaine could visualize him doing it like a character in a strip cartoon. The arrival at the airport, customs, the taxi, going up in the tower elevator of the Waldorf, the ring of the doorbell, the opening door, the door slammed in her face. Nora's leave of absence from her play had terminated some weeks before and she was once more a fixture on Broadway.

Germaine's vision did nothing to sweeten her temper, and when Georgiana's letter was laid on her desk she received it with antipathy. The lack of professional responsibility which she considered it disclosed would have displeased her at any time, and that, coupled with its mawkish sentimentality—a woman who had deliberately left her husband, who made no bones about her affair with another man, calmly assuming that at her convenience she could return to that husband while she, Germaine, who could have represented Connubial Virtue in a pageant, had to put up with that alley-cat Claude—— No! It was too much. She turned to her secretary. "Take a letter to Mrs. Goodyear."

My dear Georgiana [she dictated],

I am in receipt of your letter retailing your personal problems and telling me of your desire to return to New York to work on American *Distaff*. You apparently assume that this is easily achieved—simply because you wish it. May I point out to you that only a few months ago you wished to be in Paris. You wished it so intensely that you accepted a salary which was half of what you formerly earned. My arranging a position for you in our Paris office required engineering but I managed it, and you are doing a good job. We need you there, but here we are sufficiently staffed and have no use for you.

I am sorry if you are disappointed, and I hope you will find your present unhappiness only temporary, but you got yourself into this job and I must insist that you abide by the terms of our contract which still has seven months to run.

By the way, the Biarritz stuff I thought was thin, but you probably had thin material to work with. The photographs and copy on the ball at the Duchesse Sèvres' were excellent.

Yours faithfully,
Germaine

The letter, when she received it in Paris, filled Georgiana with dismay. A gulf seemed to open before her. Her values, she realized, were upside down. Feeling as she did, that Germaine tolerated her in Paris because she had wanted so much to come and had accepted the job at a salary so advantageous to the Dauzats, she had nevertheless been convinced that they would prefer to have her in New York. To find that they didn't was a shock. Seven months! Reams could be married and she could have lost Allen for good. What would she have in her life? There was Karen, of course, but Karen was three thousand miles away in a world of her own. There was her job, Reams had said, and she was imprisoned in it. Alone in her small hotel suite she took stock of her life. Next week was her birthday, she would be forty-eight; a bleak milestone to face by oneself. Some women, of course, did marry again at that age, it was by no means unheard of, and she remembered having seen in a magazine statistics proving that those who had been married before were most likely to do it again, but for all that, at forty-eight, one had to acknowledge the law of diminishing returns.

Also, the Paris glamour was wearing a little thin. Not that she missed the tourists, it was refreshing again to hear French spoken in the streets of the French capital, but having the Oppenheimers and other friends available had been pleasant. Now the fall days were closing in and rationed electricity and rationed coal and rationed taxis were constricting. She had always thought that poor lighting did more to create an atmosphere of gloom than any other single factor, and on the evenings when she sat just not shivering in her little sitting room or found her way through the dirty gray blur which was the nighttime street lighting, the General Electric Company shimmered in her fancy like the pearly gates, and she longed for her apartment with its good reading lamps and crackling fire with the intensity of all three Brontë sisters yearning for their parsonage.

She had called up the friends whom Karen had looked at as she

280

had looked at unusual bugs when she was a child and whom Georgiana had deserted through the summer, and with a tolerance unmerited by her actions they welcomed her back. They were unchanged. The change was in herself. She had been a little uneasy with them before but it wasn't important, they were merely a stopgap until Reams and Karen should arrive in Paris. Now they were the people she saw and she saw them as shoddy, yet no one was coming to join her, there was nothing to bring her seeing them to an end.

If she went ahead with the divorce she would be alone, a lone woman in a country not her own with friends who were in a sense not her friends. She thought of Lola and Peter, how close they were and kind and always fun, and of the intelligent, civilized people, their wits sharpened by their work, who were so much a part of their lives, hers and Allen's, when she was home. The De Longvilles, to be sure, were intelligent and civilized but they had never worked. Georgiana began to realize that for her the disciplined minority, the professionals, were the only ones she found strong and sympathetic.

It was early October. In New York now daylight saving would be over; in the late afternoon the sunset sky glimpsed between the towering buildings would darken quickly and the great electric signs would burst like star shells in the night. The Forty-ninth and Fiftieth Street busses, so much less grand than the behemoths of Fifth and Madison, would be filled with office workers going home to her neighborhood. Often in the fall evenings the river rolled gray beneath her windows under the smoky sky, but sometimes the river would be black splashed with green and crimson lights, broadening below Fifty-second Street and sweeping in a spacious curve to the harbor. People thought of New York as a hard, indifferent town, but where else was a city rising from the sea which welcomed with careless hospitality the world's great ships at her very doorstep? Which needed no dinky tenders and little trains tootling across the country before you hit the big town? And when the fleet was in, it didn't have to be in at Brest or Hamburg or Baltimore or Boston, it was in at New York, sprawled in majesty along the Hudson. Steel ships as long as city blocks, as long as skyscrapers, observing the vertical giants to whom they were kin, soaring to the heavens. Anatomies of steel and stone, and their souls were human souls.

Georgiana, who was not much of a sailor, longed passionately for the ships, and remembered how one evening she and Allen had dined with a captain friend aboard his carrier. They had been taken out from shore in the captain's gig and the waves in the Hudson River had been as violent as the waves of Long Island Sound in a nor'easter. She had been frightened then and seasick. She was proud of them now. A river, to be so powerful. What could the Seine kick up? A puny ripple.

She was submerged by homesickness and remorse and a longing for the life she had known and for her husband. Their money troubles, Bierne, even Reams, nothing mattered if only she could have Allen back, if only she could *belong* again. "I'll phone him." She was alone, but she spoke aloud. Germaine, she thought, how *dare* she, how *can* she do this to me? There isn't any contract in the world that can ruin my whole life. I'm going home. O God, don't let it be too late, please don't let it be too late. She picked up the telephone and put in a call to Allen. It was six o'clock in Paris, it was 1 P.M. in New York. The report came back that Mr. Goodyear was not in his office. Of course, how stupid she was. He would be at lunch. Yes, she did want to keep the call in, yes, she would be at home all evening, she would accept it any time. It was about two hours later when the phone rang and she took it up to hear Allen's voice for the first time in nearly five months. How charming it was, easy, well-bred, at the moment perhaps a little restrained.

"Allen."

"Georgiana. How are you, my dear, are you all right?"

"Yes, yes, I'm all right. Allen, I'm coming home, I've got to see you."

In New York there was a pause. "Well, that's—that's good news, I'll be glad to see you, to talk to you. Have you been able to arrange it with the Dauzats?"

"They've got nothing to do with this, it's a personal thing. Why? Have you been talking to Germaine?"

"She called me, yes. I understood that she intended to stick by the contract."

"But that's another seven months. I simply can't stand it that long. I've got to see you, Allen, to explain. I've been terribly wrong about a lot of things but I know it now. We must get together, you and I.

282

If only I could talk to you. I don't give a damn about the contract, I'll break it if I have to."

"No, Georgiana, I urge you not to do that. It will only cause trouble for you and you'll regret it. Germaine says you took on the job and she expects you to see it through and she's right. Believe me, I wish you could come, it would be much simpler to iron things out, but this is not the way to go about it. Now we'll do better to rely on lawyers."

"But, Allen, that's the point, I—I don't want the divorce. I'm not going to give it to you."

"You gave me your word," he said; "you've got to go through with it. I want to do this in a friendly way and as painlessly as possible for both of us, but if you won't instigate proceedings I will. Between us, God knows, we've got grounds enough." She murmured something muffled by huskiness and three thousand miles of ocean. "What did you say?" he asked. "I can't hear you."

"I said, are you absolutely certain you want to marry Bierne?"

"Yes, I am. I'm sorry it had to happen to us, Georgiana, but it's happened, and I'll never change my mind."

"Well, look, will you do one thing for me?"

"I'll do anything I *can*. What is it?"

"I don't think that after twenty-four years of marriage it's too much to ask. After all, you've known this girl only a few months. Even the heart can be wrong. Wait till Christmas. I'm still going to try to get over sooner, I don't care *what* the Dauzats say, but I think even they will agree to my taking a week at Christmas if I do it at my own expense. I'll fly home. I want to be with Karen then anyhow, and we can talk. You'll see, Allen, once we're together, once we understand each other . . . Will you wait? Will you?"

"It won't do any good."

"I beg of you. Please, Allen, please."

"Very well," he said at last, "I'll wait until Christmas, but don't expect me to change my mind, and if you don't come then don't ask me to wait any longer."

"But you'll wait *till* then, you promise?"

After a little pause he said, "I promise."

"Well—it's just a little over two months. I'll be there."

"Right. Take care of yourself, have a good time."

"I don't have a good time without you, but I'll try."

They hung up. Allen gazed thoughtfully down on Rockefeller Plaza, his eyes focused on those segments of Prometheus visible from his window, one shoulder, the gleaming crown of his head. Georgiana, feeling as if a huge stone had been lifted from her chest, drew back the curtains, opened the windows, and taking a deep breath exhaled into the raw night air of the Place Vendôme.

19

Through dint of good work in the office and an unremitting campaign via the mails Georgiana obtained the Dauzats' consent to spend Christmas in New York. Geared to live in an emotional vacuum for the next nine or ten weeks, for the first time in her life she put her job first and found unexpected satisfaction in so doing. She even worked through a brief bout of jaundice induced, the doctor said, by an emotional distress, though who would cause distress to so charming a woman was hard to see; she felt it only because her beauty was matched by her sensitivity. Georgiana, who had called upon French medicine with misgiving, wondered when the Gaul had last visited the Blarney stone, but she recovered, and once her buttercup hue had faded was rather pleased to have been proven a woman of such heart. The doctor, whom she had unjustly suspected of voodoo practice, had had real discernment.

Her hard work paid off better than she dreamed although the letter from Germaine announcing her reward caused her to break into a clammy sweat: "I know I said you could come home for Christmas," it read, "but that is no longer practical since we have another need for you." At this point she started to tremble violently but managed to turn the page. "If the caliber of the material sent from Paris keeps up," the letter continued, "we would like you to assume more responsibility but will need you here in the New York office at least for a while. We want you to come immediately after the first of the year and stay for a few months. Claude and I have been seeing something of Allen and know of the arrangement you and he made together. I hope you will not think me interfering but

I have asked him to be patient until your arrival and he has agreed."

Georgiana started to cry. Germaine, Germaine of all people, an angel of beneficence.

On the seventh of January Georgiana flew to New York. She cabled Allen when she would arrive, asking him to meet her at La Guardia. Alighting from the plane, she looked about eagerly for the lean, familiar figure but to her great disappointment he was not there. She telephoned Carroway's to ask if he had been delayed in leaving but was puzzled by the information from the girl at the switchboard that there was no answer from his office. Apparently he and his secretary were both out. She telephoned the apartment but there was no answer. The Quicks and the Slade family were in California and Karen had gone back to college after the holidays. She at last got Germaine on the phone, who greeted her warmly but who was surprised to hear that Allen was not at the airport. "It's been several days since I have seen him," she said, "but I'm sure he knows you are arriving."

"He knows. I cabled him."

"Well, can you manage by yourself?"

"It isn't that," Georgiana assured her. "I can manage. As soon as I'm through customs I'll take a cab to the house, but I'm worried, this isn't like him." I suppose, she muttered to herself as she hung up, the person I ought to call is Miss Honeywell. She doubtless knows his whereabouts.

She cleared customs quickly and drove into town, the excitement of seeing New York again after more than eight months temporarily obliterating her uneasiness. Vital, noisy, and dirty, the city welcomed her home. Her eye, accustomed to the streets of Paris, missed the trees, but she was exhilarated by the hard, bright sunshine. Coming off the parkway, the taxi struck into that apex of confusion spanning the East River, the Queensboro Bridge.

Georgiana endured the Queensboro Bridge as one endures the dentist's drill, because he must. On sunny days the vast span was a shimmering checkerboard of light and shadow. The movement, the din, the speeding cars, the rumbling trucks bewildered and frightened her, and she wished too late that she had told the taxi to go by way of the Triborough. Without mercy the cars whizzed past you

285

on the Triborough, too, but at least you were in the open without the length of an upper roadway turning a bridge into a tunnel. She welcomed Second Avenue with relief, and as they came into Fifty-second Street and headed back toward the river and the taxi drew up at her own front door she felt a little thrill of happiness, she had a premonition that all would be well.

The driver set her bags on the sidewalk and even co-operated to the extent of calling the doorman, "Hey Mac, get it out. Help the lady." Georgiana tipped him generously. The doorman was new but the elevator man was their old Victor, who greeted her cordially. Victor wished the world well, but he couldn't help nurturing the hope that he might be in on maybe just the tail end of the fireworks which he assumed were inevitable once Mrs. Goodyear found out what had been going on in her apartment while she was away. Not that Mr. Goodyear was to blame probably, the housing shortage being what it was a man had to have his girl at home if he was to have her at all, and she was a sweet little thing, pretty as a picture and real friendly and polite, and Karen liked her too. Whenever the two young ladies were together they were always laughing and jok-ing, but you couldn't expect Mrs. Goodyear to see it quite the same.

Victor felt sorry for her. She asked him if Mr. Goodyear had come in yet and seemed upset when he told her nobody was home. He refrained from telling her that Mr. Goodyear had gone out of the house at ten o'clock last night looking kind of funny and hadn't been back since. He'd offered to let her in with the passkey but she had her own key with her, had it in Paris with her all that time and remembered to bring it back.

"The sixty-four-dollar question," the doorman observed to Victor when the elevator returned to the ground floor, "is what kind of reception the Missus is going to give the Mister."

Victor looked at him with scorn. "That ain't no sixty-four-dollar question, that's one of them little easy ones they start you off with, 'For one buck who's the President of the United States?' Come on, ask me sumpthin' I don't know."

Upstairs Georgiana was going from room to room greeting her possessions. Some were more attractive than she remembered, others were unexpectedly shabby. She knew that through the summer Allen had confined himself mostly to the library, his own room, and the

286

kitchen, but he had apparently decided that during the winter it was foolish not to be comfortable, for all the rooms were obviously in use, though here and there the dust had settled. Georgiana smiled. Economy had been the motive for drawing in his horns, but, like other natural phenomena, he expanded with the cold.

In Karen's room, with the exception of two or three evening dresses and summer things put away in bags, the closets were empty, but in her medicine chest and on her dressing table was evidence of her occasional presence at home. Georgiana quickly went through her own room and Allen's. The telltale properties she half wondered if she would find were missing. No comb and brush, no make-up, no dressing gown. She did not believe that Bierne had never stayed overnight but apparently she and Allen had been fastidious enough to remove all traces. Anyway, that was something she wanted to close her mind to.

She started to unpack but felt curiously like an interloper in her own home. Again she telephoned Allen's office, and this time she got through to his secretary. It struck her that the girl was over-effusive in her apologies for his absence from the airport; she said he had been called unexpectedly to Washington when Mrs. Goodyear's plane had already left Paris and it was too late to reach her. The secretary was sure he must be coming home that evening or he would certainly have telephoned her by now. Georgiana couldn't say why, but she was convinced that the girl was lying. However, as there was nothing more to be got out of her she perforce accepted the story.

The afternoon darkened to evening and more than once she started for the door thinking to hear the elevator but always it went past their floor. She was beginning to feel famished but didn't dare go out for fear of missing Allen. Finally she mixed herself a drink and went to the kitchen to see what she could unearth for dinner. He must be dining in a good deal, she thought, as she took from the icebox the remnants of a leg of lamb and uncovered two or three small dishes containing snippets of succotash, string beans, and beets. She peered suspiciously at a coagulated lump of caramel custard. When they dined alone she and Allen rarely ate dessert. Doubtless the sweet tooth of Miss Honeywell was being catered to. She sliced off two or three pieces of the lamb, deriving a dry pleas-

287

ure from the thought that if the cook was counting on it for a curry she had another count coming. Must be a part-time job, she decided, as she opened the doors to the two maids' rooms and saw that they were both untenanted.

She dined on the lamb, the cold vegetables tossed into a salad, and coffee. Still Allen didn't come. Possibly the secretary's story was true after all. Maybe he *was* in Washington, but if that were so surely he would telephone. She nearly considered calling Bierne but was put off as much from a sense of embarrassment as from the fact that her number was not listed. Tomorrow, she decided. If I haven't heard by morning I'll call her at the Manhattan Aid office. She did manage to reach Karen at college, and they had a fine, warm talk, but the girl was as much in the dark as she regarding Allen's whereabouts. When they had said good-by and she was once more alone she turned on the radio, but the programs were boring and she turned it off again. She tried to read—there were dozens of new titles in Allen's room and in the library all unfamiliar. How funny, she thought, I always used to know about the new Carroway books and about those from other houses as well. That was a thread of her life it would be good to take up again, but just now concentration was difficult. She tasted bits from several books and laid them down.

Maybe she should call Chips Carroway. He, if anybody, would be likely to know where Allen was, but she hesitated. It was humiliating to say, "I've just got home, yes, Allen knew I was coming, but he doesn't care enough to meet me." She waited until almost midnight when fatigue at last overcame her and she started to prepare for bed. Her bed was freshly made, evidently she had been expected, and she was nearly undressed when she heard Allen's key in the lock. She slipped on a bathrobe and hurried out to the hall. "Where on earth . . ." she began, and stopped as she saw him. He looked like a man who had been beaten, like a man who had been subjected to the most grueling pressure he could endure, and who was extinguished by the ordeal. "Allen, what is it? Come in here and sit down." He followed her into the library and sat heavily, as though he would never rise again. "Can I get you a drink?" she asked. "You look ill."

"Georgiana," he began, and stopped. Then in a moment, "I'm

sorry I wasn't at the airport, I—I should have sent somebody to meet you. I'm sorry."

"Well, I *was* a little upset. Were you in Washington?"

"Washington? No."

"That's what your secretary told me."

"Oh," he said dully, "that was stupid. She was trying to make excuses, I guess."

"Excuses for what? Never mind. The hell with it! You look awful. Has anything happened?"

He stared at her, seeking her comprehension, seeking to comprehend himself. "Bierne," he said. "She has polio."

"Oh, Allen! Oh, my God! When did this happen?"

"Last night. She was taken ill last night. She's been feeling miserable for the last couple of days, a little swelling in the gland in her throat and a little nausea, but we thought it was just a cold. I took her to dinner last night and took her home. It was barely eight o'clock. She promised to go to bed right away. I came back here to read a manuscript and around ten her mother called me. She said she seemed pretty bad. I went around to her house, she was—she was—— The pain." His knuckles were white and the sweat stood out on his forehead.

Georgiana poured him a stiff scotch. "Here," she said; "drink this." He drank it like water. "What happened? What did you do?"

"I got hold of Herb Smith. He came right away and the ambulance was there almost as soon as he was. We took her to the hospital. I've been there ever since."

Georgiana's first swift reaction was one of release. The threat was gone from her life, she would get Allen back. Her next feeling was a sense of genuine pity. She had had reason to fear and hate Bierne but she had once admired the girl, she was beautiful and young and intelligent. That she should be the victim of such tragedy was cruel. "Is she entirely paralyzed?"

"Apparently her whole nervous system is affected but the doctors don't know yet how seriously nor how permanently. It may be several days before they can tell. Her left arm and leg are the worst."

"Well," Georgiana said, "she's not my favorite person, as you may imagine, but I'm truly sorry about this, Allen. I hope you believe me."

He looked at her with gratitude. "I do, of course. It wouldn't be like you to feel any other way."

"Oh, God." Suddenly her face was white.

"What is it?"

"Karen. Were she and—were they together much? Recently?"

"I thought of that too. They saw quite a bit of each other during the Christmas holidays, and New Year's Eve we had a little party, but the doctor says there's no reason to think Karen's in danger. You know how people get frightened about swimming pools in the summer when there's an epidemic. Some kids get it, others who have been in the same places are never touched."

"I know, but what's the period of incubation or whatever it's called? This is only the seventh, and you say that New Year's Eve . . ."

"I told you. The doctor *believes* there's nothing to fear. The time varies, they can usually tell in from three to ten days. He believes she'll be all right."

"That's what he hopes, he doesn't actually know."

"It's impossible to know. Who could have known about Bierne?"

"Oh, Allen, if anything happens . . ."

"Stop it!" he said harshly. "I forbid you to say it."

They looked at each other with stricken eyes.

"What are we going to do?" she asked.

"Wait. It's all we can do."

"We must get Karen home, though, there must be tests and things. We'll have to warn the college too."

"Well, if you think so. I'll call Herb first thing in the morning."

"I phoned Karen as soon as I got in, she said she was feeling fine."

"And she probably *is* fine, dear. Don't make yourself sick over it."

There was a little silence. Finally she said, "You look all in. You'd better get some sleep."

"You must be tired too. How was the trip?"

"Very comfortable. How's the family?"

"All right. I got a letter from Lola this morning—no, yesterday—I can't remember—anyway, they're well. Pete's deal is going through and it looks now as if they won't be back till early spring."

"Come, Allen, let's go to bed."

He rose heavily. As they went down the hall he said, "I left word at the hospital they're to call me if anything happens. You'd better close your door so you won't be disturbed if the phone rings."

"I don't mind. You might need me in the night."

"Well, sleep well."

"You too." She hesitated.

He bent and for a moment laid his cheek against her hair. "Don't be frightened about Karen," he said, then he turned and went into his own room. She thought he moved like an old man.

They breakfasted together early, and when she asked his plans he said he had to spend a few hours in the office and would be going up to the Medical Center later. She would be busy all day at *Distaff* so they arranged to meet for dinner.

"We'll have a talk," he said. "Where do you want to go?"

"Why don't we eat here?" Seeing the look of uncertainty in his eyes she chided him gently, "I haven't been home in a long time. You have a cook who comes in, haven't you?" He acknowledged, reluctantly she felt, that this was so. "Does she know about me?"

"How do you mean?"

"She'll think you're a gay blade, won't she? One woman right after another?"

"Don't worry, she knows I'm married." She noticed that he did not deny Bierne's presence in the house and apparently her own troubled him. It was an odd feeling, this of being unwelcome in her own home, but presently he said, "If you're sure you want to dine here. I generally leave a little note telling her what to market for. Perhaps you'll do that?"

"I haven't forgotten how to run my house." On this slightly tart note they parted.

That evening, while she was freshening up, waiting for Allen to come home for dinner, Georgiana planned her strategy. With Bierne a paralytic the idea of his marrying her was now, of course out of the question, but what she had to verify, and as tactfully as possible, were his intentions regarding herself. With the tragedy uppermost in his mind he would be supersensitive, unreflectingly he might hold to the idea that the breach between them was so great that they should go ahead with the divorce anyhow. It was up to her to convince him that that wasn't necessary, but tact was of the essence.

291

Tact and sympathy. The sympathy wasn't too difficult. Secure in her own good health, relieved of her rival, she honestly regretted that the means of that relief should be so brutal. She would quite willingly have settled for Bierne's falling in love with another man, going to live in another country, anything that would have taken her out of Allen's life. Also, she was less frantic about Karen. The doctor had advised against alarming her, so, on the pretext that she had forgotten to tell her something in their phone conversation of the day before, she had called her again. Miss Goodyear's health was still blooming, so Georgiana made no mention of her leaving college.

When Allen got home his wife was looking her best. Her make-up was fresh and she wore one of her prettiest Paris frocks. She was very different from the girl in the hospital who lay motionless, flat on her back in an unironed hospital gown, her face gray from the ordeal she was going through, only her eyes moving, her blue eyes desperately searching his for the news that she would recover.

As he came in Georgiana was squatting in front of the fireplace rearranging the logs. She looked up quickly. "Well? How did you find things?"

"The same. The doctors say, though, that the fact that there's been no turn for the worse is encouraging. It's usually a few days before you can tell how these things are going to go. Tomorrow maybe we'll know more."

They had cocktails and dined, and after Mrs. McTavish had served them coffee in the drawing room and said good night, a very formal good night for Mrs. McTavish was sore troubled in spirit by the goings-on in the household, Georgiana turned to her husband.

"What do the doctors think about Bierne, Allen? Do they say she can be helped by those Warm Springs Foundation treatments? Anything of that sort?"

"It's still problematical. As I understand it the disease has to seek its level. Once the virus has stopped, once it's jelled, you might almost say, they can begin to work on it."

"What about Bierne herself? Is she conscious?"

"Oh yes, and, thank God, the pain has stopped, she no longer has those agonizing muscle cramps, and she can speak all right—her vocal cords aren't affected—but her whole body . . . She just lies there." He set his coffee cup down abruptly and got up and walked to the window, where he stood with his back to her staring out at the river.

When Georgiana spoke her voice was gentle. "Allen, look, I appreciate that you're heartsick over this, you couldn't not be, it's too immediate for you to have thought about anything else, but you will have to bring your mind to bear on other problems. You have to go on, dear. You have your work, and for Bierne's sake, too, as well as your family's, you have to think about it. You'll want to help her out financially, I suppose?"

"I'm taking care of her, of course."

"It's going to be expensive."

"I know that. I'll probably have to borrow on my insurance, but I think it can be arranged. I hope you'll agree to it, you and Karen, because she's involved too."

"Of course." The suggestion left Georgiana cold but she glossed over it. This was no time to bicker about money. "For Bierne's sake," she said, "I think you should put up as cheerful a front as you can. She's going through enough, poor child. The realization that she can never marry will only be bearable if she's convinced that you can accept it philosophically and can go on living a good, fruitful life as you did before you met."

He turned and stared at her. "Georgiana."

"Yes?"

"Do you think for one instant I'm *not* going to marry Bierne? Do you think for one instant I'm going to walk into that hospital room and say to a girl I love whose whole life has been destroyed, who lies there in despair, 'I'll always remember you, my dear, but you understand, of course, that this is the end'? What kind of a monster do you take me for?"

"Allen, don't be absurd. You're no monster at all, you're a fine, good human being, but at the moment you're under terrible pressure, you're emotionally overwrought. I think you should do everything you can for Bierne, I'm even willing to help you, but, my God, you can't throw away your whole life on a quixotic impulse! What you propose is grotesque."

"It's not a quixotic impulse. My love for her is deep and sustained and I'm going to marry her. Those are our plans and I see no reason to change them."

"Are you mad? Do you realize what that would mean? Married to a helpless invalid, a paralytic?"

"I could take care of her and it would work out for both of us very well."

"It would be hell."

He turned away.

"All right! If you think I'm unfeeling in this speak to Karen. She's fond of Bierne, she's rooting for her happiness, *I* know that, but this is a different story. Why, I remember over a year ago, I think it was the night you first met her, right here in this room, and you came in afterward and said she impressed you as being stanch. If she is stanch she won't *let* you marry her under these conditions."

"Won't—*let* me?"

"You claim she loves you. If that's true, do you think she wants to tie you to a hospital bed? To a wheel chair?"

"Why not? How many times must I tell you, this isn't some passing affair. I love Bierne. I'm over fifty, Georgiana, my life is more than half gone, why shouldn't I devote what's left of it to the person who's the dearest thing in life to me?"

"Well, for one thing, you still have a wife."

"No, I haven't. My wife went off and left me for another man. Oh, Karen never said anything to give you away, she didn't have to, it was common gossip. My God, you even lived in the same house with him. I don't reproach you for that, I don't give a damn. I did the same myself, but you only came back to me because your lover left you. Thinking it over you decided you had a pretty good thing in your home and in me. I suppose it's human, but it's too late. I told you that when you phoned me from Paris. I waited till you got here as I promised, but now I'm going ahead with it."

"Oh, Allen, *think*. How can you be so sure? Wait a little. See how things go. Don't hate me for saying this, but supposing there's a turn for the worse. Supposing Bierne should die? It's not impossible. Where would you be, what would you do? *Why* should you be all alone?" She saw that she had struck home.

In a voice that was barely a whisper he said, "That's horrible. Not that you say it but if I were to do it. Stick around, Georgie, if she recovers I want the divorce; if she doesn't, I'll hang on to you, either way I can't lose. I think it would be the most degrading act of my life."

294

"I don't see it that way. There was nothing degrading in our life together before. In many respects it was good. It was civilized, we often had fun. Why, all of a sudden, would it be so dreadful?"

"Because we would be doing it out of weakness, because we would be empty."

"That seems to me a pretty fine distinction. We would be doing what we have always done. We would be leading the kind of life that most people we know lead."

"No," he said, "no. Besides, you don't see this from Bierne's side. She asked me if you had arrived and I had to say yes. When we first knew you were coming over I told her I didn't think you'd changed your mind about the divorce but that if you had I would move out of this house, and I mean that, but she knows I haven't moved yet."

"My dear, that's a lot of damn nonsense. This is your own home, why should you leave it?"

"Because I want to."

"Are you sure? Are you sure it wouldn't simply be to impress Bierne?"

"The thought is characteristic of you, but that's not the reason although, since you bring it up, I do consider her. What must she be thinking? She who has nothing to do *but* think. Here we are sharing the apartment. That you and I have separate rooms, that our conversation revolves exclusively around divorce isn't important. *We* can walk, we're still married. What the hell do you think she thinks happens?"

Georgiana tried, not too hard, to suppress a smile. "Why, I had no idea that was on your mind." And then, like a darting bird, "And don't think it wouldn't be on your mind if you were married to a paralytic. Can she move at all? Can she move her hands or her head even?"

He looked at her with a cold, level look. "She can't hold a book, she can't turn a knob on the radio for herself. If the nurse holds the phone for her she can speak to me at my office, but once I'm home she doesn't dare to call me. I'm going to get out of here. I'm going tonight."

"No, Allen, no." That she must prevent at all costs. As long as he was still in the house she had a chance, however slim. "Allen, listen to me; let's try to talk without bitterness, without hysteria. Right now you're too tired to think clearly. Night before last you weren't in bed at all and last night you slept very little. I was awake myself and I could hear you. You must get some rest. This way you're of no service to Bierne nor to the office and I know you're swamped with work. Concentrate on it for a while and on what we're going to do about Karen. If you're spending hours a day with Bierne I certainly don't think Karen ought to be around. On the other hand, I don't care what Smith says, I'm worried about her and I don't think her being at college is fair to the other girls. Help me to decide what to do."

Appealed to in this way, Allen went to the phone and called the doctor, and they finally agreed that Karen should come home the following week end and stay for a few days. "I don't know what she's going to do," Allen said, "when she learns about Bierne. They used to laugh so much together. They used to laugh."

A week later Karen sat beside Bierne's hospital bed and the only laughter was remembered. "Oh, Bierne, darling Bierne."

"Don't mind, Karen, I'm getting better, truly I am. See, my right hand is quite good. I can't feed myself yet, but Dr. Smith said today he thinks there's a fifty-fifty chance. More, even." Propped against the pillows, she glanced down at her left arm. "This one, of course, is not so much, but it's wonderful that I can turn my head and my body even, down to the waist. See." She twisted herself laboriously and fell back with a little gasp, but in a moment she smiled unsteadily. "Need practice."

"How are your legs? Have they let you get up at all?"

Bierne shook her head. "I'm having all sorts of massage, though, and treatments. It's just fine what they're doing for me and everyone's so kind. Did you ever see so many flowers? Mrs. Barclay Hamilton sent that great big basket and Barclay sent me all the spring flowers. That was so sweet of him, I thought."

"He is sweet," Karen said; "he's wonderful."

"The carnations are from Monsieur and Madame Dauzat; I've lots of books, and—and——" The tears were streaming down her face. "Oh, Karen, make him understand that I can't marry him. I won't! I won't! I keep telling him, and he keeps insisting, but it would kill me to do it."

296

"Bierne, oh, darling. I know how you must feel, but I had a long talk with Dad last night, it was a very honest talk, to show you how much so I even asked him if your being ill changed things, if he and Mother felt differently about each other now, and he said he would love you until he died, and if you had to spend the rest of your life in an iron lung he still wanted to marry you. It's a big love, Bierne."

"But what about your mother? Doesn't she want to stay home, doesn't she want them to be back together again?"

Karen was silent. Allen had told her that Georgiana did want just that but it seemed too cruel to relay the information. Bierne's burden was heavy enough without the added weight of another woman's misery and desire, even her mother's.

But Bierne insisted. "She does want them to go back to their old life, doesn't she? To be together, the way it was before she left for Paris, doesn't she?" Under her probing Karen nodded reluctantly. "With me out of the way maybe he would," Bierne said.

"No, it isn't so; Daddy doesn't want to, he told Mother that. For him it's finished, completely. If you were dead, he said, he wouldn't go back to her."

Bierne looked at her, compassion written on her drawn young face. "You want to make it easier for me, I know that, Karen, but I wish he hadn't said those things, I wish you hadn't told me. If he truly feels that way, it makes it harder for me to put him off, yet I must, I must."

"But *why* if he wants you?"

"He wants me now because he pities me, because now he is in love with me, but it wouldn't last, and I haven't the courage to watch it die. Part of the reason he loves me, you see, is because in me he lives his life over again. When we used to go to theaters and restaurants and museums or to a ball game quite often I would become conscious that he was watching me instead of the pictures or the people who were doing the things. He enjoyed my enjoyment. It sounds conceited, but I think that's how it's been for him. Now it would be so terribly dull. Love grows on the memory of the things you do together. How can I be part of his life now? Oh, he'd be sweet and tender and wonderful to me at first, I know that, and even after he got tired of me and bored he'd pretend because he's so kind and dear, but as he gets older I'd be a terrible burden."

"No," Karen said, "that isn't true, and besides, how do you know you won't get better? Already you've improved a lot over the first few days. They're going to do everything in the world for you, darling, every treatment that's ever been thought of, I know that."

"That's another thing," Bierne said; "the expense. Allen can't afford it. It's frightening what every day costs here in the hospital. I must get out. At least if my hands would only get better I could be in one of those little wheel chairs and I could work. I think they'd let me keep my job down at Aid headquarters, so much is desk work anyhow."

She looked down at her hands. Slowly, slowly she could open and close the fingers of the right one. Karen watched, tense with the effort she, too, was thinking into the left. The index finger moved sideways a tiny bit.

The two girls looked at each other, and Karen turned away ashamed. Ashamed suddenly of her vitality and of the enormous news she had brought into the room with her. There was one marvelous thing about it in that it could help, but how to say to the ill girl on the bed who was her friend, and who was struggling desperately to give up the man she loved, how to say to her that she, Karen, stood crowned in glory, the gates of the world flung open to her happiness? At last she said, "Bierne, I have something to tell you. I don't know how to make you well, darling, but the doctors do and they will, and it doesn't matter what it costs because the most staggeringly magic thing has happened. Barky has asked me to marry him and I've said yes, and when he mentioned an engagement ring I told him I didn't want one, I just asked him right out for the money instead, and I can have it, and it's to be spent on you, on doing everything in the world to get you well. No! There's no use opening your mouth, there's no use saying a word, because it's decided. Barky wants it that way too."

"Oh, Karen, Karen, I never heard of anything so generous, and the terrible temptation is it would be a load off Allen, but I can't let Barky pay for me, why should he?"

"Because he's rich, because he loves me, and because I love you. Why, for heaven's sake, if the circumstances were reversed, wouldn't you do it for me?"

"Yes, of course, but . . ."

298

"Ah! Yes, of course, but . . . You know the trouble with you, miss? You're just conceited. You think you're the only one who can think of others. Well, we common people get these ideas, too, sometimes, and I will thank you to button your lip and not give the matter another thought."

"Oh, Karen, I don't know what to say, I can't . . ."

Throughout the pain and anguish of the last days Bierne had cried very little, but now her voice broke in sobs. Karen, too, had tears in her eyes. She moved from her chair to the high hospital bed close to Bierne and laid her head beside her on the pillow. "Sweetie," she said, "you're not to cry, there's nothing to cry about any more. We'll lick this monster thing; you'll be better than you ever were."

After a moment Bierne said, "Tell me about you and Barclay. When did it happen?"

"This morning. I never heard of being proposed to in the morning, did you? But it works out fine. You know when I was in France I realized what Barclay meant to me and I thought there was a time there when he had cared but I thought I'd lost him through my idiocy. And then I came home, and before I went back to college I saw him quite a bit, remember, and then those few times during the holidays, and each time it got more cozy and delightful and I hoped he was in love with me, and finally I decided he must be because whenever I saw Poppy she got meaner and meaner, for which you can't blame her if Bark had given her the impression he cared about her, and if he did, that was awful, and I must ask him about it some time, and then you remember right after Christmas Poppy gave up her job and flounced out to Hollywood to be with her father and I believe Dick Oppenheimer's out there, too, and I wouldn't be surprised if she got into the movies herself because she *is* terribly pretty, but, anyway, regardless of what hanky-panky might have been going on there Barclay explained that he'd been in love with me a long time and was all set to ask me to marry him before I went abroad, but then I opened my big mouth and it's only because there's a God and Mr. Hamilton is very dogged that I didn't gobble up my chance of heaven."

"But what has he been waiting for?" Bierne asked. "Why didn't he ask you the minute you got home from Europe?"

"He was a burnt child," Karen explained. "He said this time he wanted to be very sure which side of the ocean my heart was on as his couldn't stand any more nip-ups like the last time, and this morning coming out of McCutcheon's he suddenly felt sure."

"McCutcheon's?"

"That's where your bed jacket came from." She fingered the soft pink wool over Bierne's shoulders. "I got it there because they have good warm ones, not all that rayon gook. Bark came around to the house this morning because he knew how I'd be feeling after I heard about you. They only told me yesterday afternoon, you know, when I got home from school."

"I hope you weren't too frightened for yourself."

She had been for one terrible moment, but that, at least, she could spare Bierne. Aglow with health and with her new happiness, she could afford to laugh. "Darling, you forget you are talking to a horse. Oh, I was sick all right, but that was when they told me about you. Anyhow, Bark was driving me to the doctor's for the checkup Ma and Pa thought I should have—my God, the very core of my being is no secret from that man—and before we went to his office we went to get the bed jacket so I could bring it up here this afternoon, and then as we were driving uptown Barky said some very darling things to me, ending up with, 'And if you can see your way clear to doing it, it will mean quite a lot to me if you will become Mrs. Barclay Hamilton, Jr.; and I said, 'Dear Mr. Hamilton, I am the girl with the X-ray eyes,' and he stopped the car right at Fifth Avenue and Fifty-ninth Street and we kissed, and after a little while we seemed to be in a whole jam of cars, and in some mystic way one of the old horses in those victorias by the Plaza had got his head in the window and you should have *heard* the horns tooting. Honestly, I don't know what New York traffic's coming to. It's a strain on the cops, too; the one who came up to us was purple in the face."

Between tears and laughter Bierne had listened to her outpouring, now she said, "Does your family know about it yet?"

"There hasn't been time," Karen explained. "I'm telling them tonight."

Bierne was quiet, thinking of life in Fifty-second Street: the charming apartment; the mistress of the house at home in it with her husband and daughter, that daughter's approaching marriage in-

300

evitably drawing her parents closer together; the story breaking in the papers, the beautiful girl who was to marry one of the richest young men in the country; the congratulations; the round of parties; Allen and Georgiana Goodyear meeting the Hamilton seniors, entertaining them, being asked everywhere together; and she, Bierne, what was she? What was there to differentiate her from hundreds of thousands of other girls in New York who worked in offices, lived in obscure flats with an obscure family, and were in no way special, neither by birth nor brains nor achievement? That Allen should have loved her at all was a fluke, but at least she had been pretty. Now she wasn't even normal—a paralytic on a hospital bed. Six miles from Fifty-second Street, she might as well have been in China. But I can stand it, she thought, I can stand it all if only I don't have to live at home with Mother and Ben. Now that I've had Allen, now that I've known the fun and happiness that life can hold, I can't go back to those poky little rooms, to the dullness. She said as calmly as she could, trying to fight the hysteria that was mounting within her, "That place where they treat people with polio, Warm Springs, do you have to pay there, I wonder? They're always raising money for it with the March of Dimes, maybe if I could be there for a while, until I'm better. . . ."

"Bierne, you silly stoop, how many times do I have to tell you money is not your problem. Getting well is your chore. You've got to concentrate on two things: getting cured and making up your mind to marry Daddy because he's hell-bent he's going to have you."

"Karen, you don't realize, now that your mother's home, she'll never let him. Why should she? She wants him, and she's his wife. It isn't as though she'd find out about Allen and me and be outraged, she knows about us and she'll assume, or pretend to, that it's been a temporary affair, that he'll get over it, she'll overlook it, and their life will go on just the same."

"Your theory's fine, the only hitch is Daddy loves you, and don't forget, too, he knows what happened in Paris. All the overlooking wouldn't be on Mother's side. Oh, Bierne dearest, why are you so obstinate? How can I . . . Look, think of it this way. I love Mother, God knows I don't want her to be miserable and lonely, but a lot of things in the world interest her, her job and books and men and me. Mother can always make a life for herself. I don't say she wouldn't be unhappy for a while over the divorce but she'd get over it, whereas if there *is* no divorce you're wretched, Daddy I think will go screwy, and where the heck is Mother going to find any peace and contentment in a setup like that?"

"But what kind of wife could I make?"

"A darling wife." She looked up as the door opened and the nurse came in carrying a box of flowers and a vase.

"Another bouquet, Miss Honeywell," she said cheerfully; "you're beginning to set a record."

Karen jumped from the bed. "I'll take them," she said.

"Comfortable?" the nurse asked. Bierne nodded. Florence Nightingale gave her visitor a disciplinary look. "She's not to get tired and she's not to talk too much."

"No, I realize that," Karen murmured apologetically. "I'm going in a very few minutes, I'll just arrange these." The nurse gave a small disapproving grunt and departed.

"She's a dragon," Bierne said, "but she's nice."

Karen went to work on the flowers. "What I started to say was that you're a goose to worry about ever becoming a bore or a burden to Dad as he gets older because you're going to get well. The thing really is not to get too independent because he'll get a big kick looking after you. He's got a very strong paternal streak, Pop. I think secretly he'd have liked a large family. Now it'll be as if he had two daughters." She gave an admiring glance at her handiwork. "They're lovely, aren't they? Oh, and here's the card." She turned toward the bed and stopped in dismay, aware too late of what she had said. Bierne's head was turned away, her thin frame shook with sobs, her right hand was convulsively clasping and unclasping the bedclothes.

"Oh, God, what an idiot I am! Bierne, darling, I didn't mean it that way."

Bierne spoke when she could. "I love him so, it's always been so wonderful. That's why I couldn't bear to marry him, it would be torture all the time, it would be dreadful. For both of us. Your father's a man, Karen, he needs a woman. He's not some half-baked old maid who could be content with a paralyzed child bride—a daughter. He'd have to live a normal life, and if he couldn't do it with me he'd find somebody else. And he'd try to spare my feelings until it got too complicated and I'd try not to let him know what I

302

was feeling but I'd become jealous and embittered and all the heavenly beautiful thing that we've had together would be destroyed. I'd rather give him up now, I'd rather never see him again."

"That's no good," Karen said, "he'll never accept it, but will you agree to one thing, will you promise me one thing? It's something you can do for me."

"What is it?"

"Promise me that you won't hand out any ultimatums, that you won't make any decisions for six months. By that time, I should think, you'll be infinitely better or we'll know where we stand."

"Six months!"

"It'll go quickly, Bierne. Your time will be taken up with treatments, exercises, you'll be able to read, maybe they'll let you make things, work with your tools. Does the doctor know what a wonderful carpenter you are?"

Bierne smiled shakily. "I don't imagine so."

"You'll see, in six months it will be a different story. Promise?"

There was a little silence. "I promise."

"That's the girl. Face up to this mess. We'll fight it to a standstill."

But Bierne was thinking of a formidable enemy, Georgiana, who, given six months, might destroy Allen's love for her more effectively than poliomyelitis.

20

As soon as the doctor was convinced that she was in no danger Karen returned to college. Her parents and the Hamiltons persuaded her, not too much against her will, that, having got this far, it would be a pity not to graduate, so the wedding was set for late June.

She insisted that Bierne keep her promise, that she, too, would wait until then before deciding categorically that she would not marry Allen. Two or three weeks after Karen's visit to her in the hospital Bierne was pronounced well enough to travel and Allen took her to Warm Springs.

Georgiana did nothing to dissuade him from the trip; she had learned that when she was sympathetic Allen, out of gratitude, seemed almost to depend on her. If she was kind, if she was gentle, with Bierne away and the pressure of his work to distract his mind, imperceptibly she might win him back.

To Karen, Barclay, and Bierne June seemed far away, but it was not too far to please the Hamiltons. Having informed themselves on Mr. and Mrs. Goodyear they nurtured the hope that by early summer Barclay might experience a change of heart. Both Bierne and the Reams Asher episode they found disturbing. That his fiancée was so friendly with her father's mistress was not, as they did not fail to point out to Barclay, the attitude of a discreetly brought-up young woman. As Mr. Hamilton, Sr., put it, "We are not priggish son, but it's a remarkably irregular household. Both the father and mother have apparently lived openly with other people. It doesn't bode well for the emotional stability of this girl whom you think you love. It's not that she's not pleasant, I think she is, very warm and human, but marriage is something else again. Good stock counts. There appears to be a looseness in the family that is far from reassuring."

"I can't agree with you, Father," Barclay said. "I think to be pleasant and warm and human counts very much in marriage. I should say that both Karen and Mr. Goodyear have a sound sense of values. He's not a hypocrite, he wants to get a divorce so he can marry Miss Honeywell, and he wants to marry her even though she may be paralyzed for life. That seems to me admirable. Karen's devoted to her, and I like her myself; she has amazing courage."

"That may be, but I understand her family are a very humble sort."

"Well, I don't suppose you could call a day laborer on the railroad any too exalted." Barclay referred to his great-grandfather, who had founded the family fortune.

Feeling he was making little progress, Mr. Hamilton changed his tack. "What about the mother?"

"I don't think we know Mrs. Goodyear well enough to judge her." There was, Barclay feared, a shade of pomposity in his tone which he regretted, but how to explain to his father the curious attraction Georgiana Goodyear was capable of exerting when she chose, and over men of any age? Karen had told him about her mother and Reams, and to her surprise he hadn't been shocked at all. His com-

304

ment in fact had been, "I don't blame Asher. He was silly to leave her." Well, thought Karen, here are the Hamiltons so painfully conventional and proper with little Barclay turning out to be a darling black sheep. She had gone off to college much cheered by his reaction. It was Allen who first sensed that the young man might be finding the going difficult. Barclay himself came often to the apartment in Fifty-second Street, he got on well with his future in-laws, but though he said little about his family there always seemed to be some reason why the Hamiltons couldn't come to dine when Georgiana asked them and there was a notable lack of invitations issuing from their own camp. The situation, aside from being disquieting, had an element of the preposterous which Georgiana, though granting its comedy aspect, found hard to bear. Despite her arguments, tears, and persuasions and the difficulty of finding living space in postwar New York, Allen *had* moved out of the apartment, but in a desire to keep up appearances for Karen's sake he had agreed that when she was home from college and Georgiana wished to entertain he would be at the house and there would be no reason for casual acquaintances or the Hamiltons to assume he was not living there.

The difficulty was that neither of them had counted on the false alarms they would be subjected to because of the Hamiltons' reluctance to accept them as relations before the inescapable moment. If their son insisted on marrying the Goodyear daughter, they would swallow their morals, but they wished to bring home to Barclay their strong disapproval of his intentions.

Georgiana, however, ever hopeful that they would weaken, and indeed in order to see Allen, sometimes pretended to him that she had asked them when she hadn't, was constantly demanding his presence. He would arrive to find either that a few old friends were coming to dine whose attitude—they had invariably been primed by Georgiana—was "For-Pete's-sake-old-man-what's-this-nonsense-come-home," or else she would be alone and there would be a long evening of haranguing and pleading. After having been trapped about five times in a row he exploded one evening. "Damn it to hell, I feel like a girl in a house, always on call. The next time the entire Hamilton clan can come trooping in with olive branches in their mouths I'm not going to be here!"

At other times, however, weary and desperate when Bierne would reach a certain level of improvement and then appear to go no further Georgiana felt her chances freshening.

But one day, unexpectedly, the great news came for Allen. On a sunny afternoon in May his secretary appeared in the doorway of his office. "Warm Springs, Georgia, on the phone, Mr. Goodyear. Miss Honeywell, I imagine."

Allen felt his heart stop for a split second. Bierne's recent letters—she could write them herself now—had been reporting steady progress, but one never knew.

"Hello?" he said.

"Allen, darling, it's me. Do you know where I am, do you know what I'm doing?" She sounded tremendously excited.

"What is it, dear? Are you all right?"

"I'm in Dr. Carmichael's office; I'm standing up; I'm using the telephone on the wall, and I walked to it. It's only five steps, but I walked to it by myself. I walked, I–I——"

"Darling, oh, darling, I can't see anything, I must be crying too. Be careful you don't fall. Is the doctor with you?"

"Yes, he's here, he——"

The doctor's voice came over the phone. He was quite a young doctor and he sounded unscientific and happy. From his report Allen gathered there was little chance Bierne would ever compete in the Olympic Games, some of her muscles would always be affected, but in her arms and torso she was improving rapidly and daily gaining more control of her legs. "She's always going to have to take it easy," the doctor finished, "and she'll probably tire quickly for some time to come, but other than that she'll be able to lead a perfectly normal life in every respect."

Bierne was back at the mouthpiece. "He says I can come to Karen's wedding, Allen. I mean if—if it could be arranged. You'll tell her, won't you?"

"I'll call her at once," he said. "But you'd better begin to think about your own wedding, young lady. I shall tell Miss Goodyear she's not the only member of the family who's getting married."

"Oh, Allen, Georgiana has agreed? Absolutely?"

There was a fraction of a pause. "She is agreeing. I give you my solemn word."

306

"Darling, darling, are you sure you want to?"

"Certain sure, my dearest, with all my heart. I love you."

"I love you. God bless you." She hung up.

That evening Allen told Georgiana the news. It was, she supposed, the agent which finally brought their marriage to an end and yet looking back on it in later years Bierne's recovery seemed to her coincidental with the collapse of her life with Allen rather than being its primary cause. Too many other factors had been too long involved. The marriage crumbled as an old building might when the foundations are rotted through. For one thing, the Dauzats had offered her an excellent opportunity on *Distaff*. They themselves were going to be involved in founding a new magazine and Georgiana's responsibility and authority would be greatly increased but would necessitate her spending half her time in Paris and half in New York. She talked over the proposition with Allen in far more frankness than they had discussed her original job on the magazine. He advised her to take it.

"You'll be making good money, Georgiana. You'll have an excellent position, and, my dear, I should think you yourself would want to put an end to this way of living. You're being very patient, I acknowledge that, but if you'll forgive me I think it's calculated. It's no use, G, our marriage is through, and I respect us both too much, and I think in your heart you do, too, to go on this way. What do we have? Neither companionship, resignation, nor sex."

"We do have our child, however," she said dryly. "The Hamiltons don't think much of us, but I believe they go for family solidarity in a big way. Whatever we may feel I don't think we have any right to jeopardize Karen's marriage."

Allen apprehended dimly that were Georgiana wanting her freedom she would in some subtle manner be able to carry water on both shoulders: she would go ahead with the divorce and marry off Karen too. Her plea was more for her own ends than for her daughter's, but the argument of course was potent.

"You're right about the Hamiltons," he said, "but that doesn't include Barclay. Come hell or high water he and Karen will get together."

"And you and Bierne."

"And Bierne and I."

307

Suddenly Georgiana threw in her hand. "Pig-headed Allen. All right, you win. For what the victory's worth."

"Oh, Georgiana." After a little time he added hesitantly, "I don't suppose you have a very high opinion of men, I can see how experience with me would sour you, but you're a hell of an attractive woman. Should you be inclined to marry again I can't think you'll have any difficulty."

"Spare me the patronage," she said. "But if I should be so unfortunate as not to get a man, the be-all and end-all of any woman's life, naturally, perhaps I can hire an attractive pansy as a companion. They're usually very kind to older women—hope they'll leave them their money."

Allen threw back his head and laughed. "What nonsense. You'll always have warmth in your life. There's Karen and Barclay. I expect before too long there'll be the grandchildren."

"Yes, well, don't bother to relegate me to the fireside in my cap and slippers. I prefer to think of Karen's children coming to visit Granny in her chic little flat in Paris."

"I had something of the sort in mind."

"Perhaps accompanied by Grandpa's young wife while the old boy takes it easy at home. With his male nurse."

"Ouch."

"Serves you right, my lad. And don't think it can't happen."

"Uh, if it's not too delicate a question, how shall we go about this? I'm quite willing to go to Reno if it's easier for you, or would you prefer to get the divorce in Paris?"

"I prefer to wait until after Karen's wedding. We'll discuss it then."

"But you promised!"

"Don't be alarmed, I'll keep my word, but I think it means so much to a girl, don't you, to look at her parents on her wedding day and see in them the example of a happy marriage."